Adira's Assassin
Book One of the Chrym Chronicles

ILA REBER

ACKNOWLEDGMENTS

Thank you to everyone who reminded me to dream when I forgot how, and to everyone who fixed my wings along the way without my ever noticing.

PART I

CHAPTER 1

"Aja! What are you doing over there? Come help with Mother's water!"

It was a weary complaint, voiced by a dark-skinned man, thin and bent into early age by a hard life in a hard world. Aja lifted his eyes reluctantly from the dry soil that held his attention. For the life of him, he had no clue as to why he was so drawn to this patch of earth; it surely had no fertile qualities in this arid place. Aja and his family lived on the outskirts of a poor town, the poorest of a small cluster of towns that were themselves the furthest outliers of the Sik province. Provinces were named after the dragon queen or empress who ruled there, and Queen Sik was fierce in her domain. Every child learned early to watch the skies or suffer the price of the unwary. Aja's own mother bore the scars that served as a cautionary tale – do not be caught in the open when Sik flies.

Though Behar insisted she had been blessed to survive and paid an extra grain tithe every year to their local temple, Aja could not help but resent the food that did not stay on their table, most especially on behalf of his little brother, Qal, who seemed to grow sharper with hunger every passing season. Thanks to several years of poor crops, his brother was small for his age and unlikely to catch up to his older brother unless they experienced a prolonged bout of good fortune.

"Aja!" The summons was sharper and much closer. He ducked as he caught a shadow of movement from the corner of his eye, and the solid smack his father had intended was reduced to a whispering tickle against his ear.

"You'll end up as dessert to Sik one of these days," he warned, leaving Aja to understand that the blow had been for his own good. Merot was not a bad man and did his best to provide for his family in a place that did not yield food or resources easily.

Aja turned away from the rocks that bordered his newly found spot, trudging down the path to pick up two heavy buckets. Though the bar resting on his shoulders dug painfully into his flesh, it was a welcome weight. Twice this week they had come to the waterhole, only to turn away empty-handed. Seeing Qal go without water was even worse than watching him leave his parents' table still hungry. Reminded of his little brother, Aja surreptitiously patted the pocket of his worn trousers. He had found a small colony of flitters earlier that day, with eggs left unprotected while they raided farmers' fields for ripening grain. The birds were normally a minor nuisance, but the dry season had decimated their reserves, and every grain the flitters stole from dying crops would be felt over the course of the next year. Aja felt justified as he quickly pilfered several nests, wiping out a future generation of the little thieves. Qal would not go hungry tonight, and if he'd been careful enough in his thievery, the birds would continue to nest in the same small tree stand, guaranteeing a few more easy meals before they chose a safer spot to roost.

Aja's white teeth gleamed sharply against his dark skin as he spotted his little brother coming down the path. When Qal was close enough, he reached up to his older brother, grabbing for one of the buckets and unsettling Aja's balance. It was a familiar game between the brothers, and Aja was ready with a swift, light kick to Qal's rump. His little brother danced back, laughing with an infectious joy that made Aja's smile deepen. Though their height difference was marked, even accounting for the gap in their ages, the brothers had matching smiles, dimples flashing with good spirits as they bantered back and forth.

"Hey! I'm only trying to help, Aja!"

"Help! If you mean dump our drinking water onto the path to make the weeds grow, then that's help I can do without."

Qal flashed a brief pouting scowl, then raced ahead, hopping first on one foot then another. He paused and hunched down as a swift shadow passed overhead, but it was just a large bird of prey, coasting overhead on a thermal.

"Aja, will the priests take you away?"

The bird's shadow had brought dark thoughts to Qal's mind.

"No silly bird. You know the Gift doesn't run in our family," he assured his baby brother. "They only want Xarans with power. I've heard that they even reject Seekers sometimes if their Gift isn't strong enough."

Aja was aware that in some provinces the dragon queens flew out in search of Chrym Weavers, specially gifted Xaran who could somehow work the forbidden substance into any form. In those provinces, the queens would descend from the sky without warning, threatening to burn entire villages down if the children didn't come forward to be tested, but here in Sik, the Church had gained enough influence to force their followers to attend special quarterly ceremonies just prior to their seventeenth birthdays. Aja liked the local priest who visited several small villages along the border, though he knew from overheard conversations that not all the Church's servants were as kind. Adults spoke more freely when children were not around, and Aja was more skilled than most at slipping unnoticed into earshot. He recalled one of those conversations now.

"Imprana Jido's getting up there." The comment was not derogatory, just a practical observation from Tulomakpe, the baker's oldest son. Tulo had just wed a newly widowed mother of four from a neighboring village, a woman ten years his senior, so it was perhaps understandable that he was preoccupied with age. It was no secret that the bride had been his father's choice due to her family ties – the blushing bride was the only child of the wealthiest miller within a day's walk – and Tulo had yet to resign himself to the situation.

"Yeah, but have you seen how he gets around? He's more sprightly than most men half his age." Tulo's best friend Idrac slapped him on the shoulder before making a rude gesture at the third man who made up their small group that afternoon. The three young men, barely past boyhood, were tucked in a small glade just beyond the main village, within earshot if their elders called. Aja knew they were long past their lunch break, a fact that made him anxious as he kept small and quiet just out of sight, hoping his own absence would go unnoticed until the older boys, men now that they had passed the Choosing Ceremony, finished their conversation and returned to their chores.

"Still, I wonder what it will be like when they assign a new Imprana to our district."

Tulo seemed pensive this afternoon as he rubbed the fresh scar on his forearm. Like Idrac and Fespa, he had passed the Choosing Ceremony only a year earlier, and on this, the anniversary of the event, he seemed consumed with thoughts of the Church.

"Maybe we'll get lucky and they'll decide we finally rate an Imperal," Fespa finally chimed in.

"Pil and Hadra scorch you for wishing that on us!" Idrac turned on his friend angrily and Aja leaned forward, listening intently as the

conversation heated. He knew that Impranas were the lowest ranking priests in the Church, so it seemed to make sense that they would want a higher level priest serving their region. Why was Idrac so opposed to the idea?

"What?" Fespa protested loudly. "Mom and Pop both said it would be a sign that we're finally starting to prosper and the Church taking notice could be a good thing."

"Take a look around, Fes," Tulo said. "Does it look like we're prospering?"

Aja held his breath and curled even smaller as Fespa did just that.

"No, not really," came the disheartened response.

"And why by the two suns would we ever want the Church to take notice of us out here?" Idrac continued to berate his friend. "We're better off with some lowly Imprana who dutifully recites from the Book, takes a fair share of what we make, and is satisfied with a simple life. You think some Imperal's going to come here and not try to make a name for themself?"

Tulo picked up where Idrac left off.

"Yeah, and they'll make that name by taking more than we can afford to lose. I don't know what your parents are thinking sometimes, Fes." The baker's son shook his head in disgust.

Aja could see Fespa's wrinkled brow from where he crouched, tucked deep in the shadows of a thornberry bush.

"Whatever." Fespa was clearly growing angry as his friends continued to disparage his views. "Maybe you would feel differently if you had an uncle who'd made Impara rank."

Aja sucked a quiet breath of surprise. Impara was just one level below the highest ranking human on the planet, a position currently held by Imperion Cayl. Fespa was right to be proud of his uncle – even Aja knew that rising among the ranks of the priesthood was a difficult thing, especially coming from such lowly beginnings.

"Yeah, and you take advantage every year by only paying half the tithe the rest of us owe," Tulo retorted.

The argument devolved into long-standing resentments, and it wasn't long before the three men returned to their chores, surly for the moment, but sure to be back at their favorite spot again, all forgiven within a few days. It wasn't as though there were a great many social choices in their village, and Tulo needed every excuse to escape his new family.

Aja came back to the present and reassured Qal with what little he knew.

"You know that Sik only allows her Impara to have a little Chrym once a year to test all the seventeen-year-olds. Hardly anyone ever has the Gift, even in families with strong bloodlines, and no one in our family has ever tested positive, so there's no reason to think I'll be any different."

"Yeah, you're right." Qal didn't sound entirely convinced as he walked just ahead of his older brother, looking for all the world like a puppet whose strings have suddenly all been cut, and Aja wished he could shield the little boy from the world forever.

"We'll be fine." He forced a certainty he didn't feel, and grinned as Qal glanced back.

What Aja knew but didn't voice was that any child who tested positive was immediately removed from their family and often never seen again. He also saw no reason to mention that he knew of at least one boy several years ago who had not come home from the Choosing Ceremony, and not a hint of the Gift in that family. There was no reason to add to Qal's fears by telling him all the things that might not happen. Dealing with his own worries was difficult enough, for Aja had finally reached the age and season to take the test. He didn't know what to hope for – life as a Chrym worker under Sik's brutal yoke, or life in the farming village, watching his family court starvation year after year.

He rolled his shoulders under the weight of the water buckets, trying to cast off his thoughts as their home came into view. A modest structure, it was designed to allow as much air as possible to flow through the main rooms while the roof, wider than the house by at least half, blocked the two Sun Gods from reaching the interior during the heat of the day. In the evening, as the great Pil and his wife Hadra dropped in the sky, special screens were dropped from the overhangs to block the angling light. Aja hated the darkened interior, but it was the only way any home in Sik was tolerable during most of the year. The planet Ryxa had two seasons, one of which lasted only a few weeks and provided the only certain rainfall the Xarans could expect throughout the year. Before Empress Adira swallowed Ryxa's third sun, the planet had been like a furnace, only able to sustain life thanks to ingenious devices his ancestors built to access the water that hid deep below the surface. Thanks to the dragons those devices were all in ruins now, along with all the knowledge needed to rebuild them. For millennia, the Xarans fought extinction until Empress Adira created the rainy season. In true dragon fashion, she hadn't done it to benefit the Xarans, but he appreciated it just the same. The brief cold season was Aja's favorite time of year, spoiled only by the fact that the Choosing Ceremony was always held during the rains.

Once a year, a heavy band of icy rain made its way around the planet, touching every territory and washing it clean of the sand and dust that invaded every corner of every home before relinquishing the planet to its normal dry heat. Sik ruled one of the hottest provinces, an enticement to any dragon to be sure, but torture for the Xarans who served her. Aja scowled and kicked at a clump of dried grass on the path. Another mark against being chosen by the priests – it was rumored that Sik kept her home even warmer than the noonday suns.

Behar signaled the boys to come in, making a quick gesture of worship to Pil and Hadra as they crossed into the shadow of their home. It was rumored that long ago the Church promoted only worship of Pil, Hadra, and Halon, the sun gods, but with the arrival of the dragons and the destruction of ancient Xaran civilization, Xarans incorporated the dragon queens into their religion. The Book was now a confusing mix of sun and dragon religion, though one thing was made clear – worship the dragons above all else or be exterminated.

Aja's mother was painfully superstitious, though he supposed she had more reason than most. Her many acts of devotion throughout the days and nights were all that allowed her to master her fear of the open sky. The burns Sik inflicted upon her as a young bride had frozen the joints in her right arm and side into painful rigidity, and Behar needed copious amounts of special oils gathered from river reeds just to manage the small tasks she could. The oils could only be harvested after the rainy season, and he could tell from how stiffly she moved this afternoon that she had not used enough today. Their supplies were running low, and it looked as though the rainy season would be late again this year. The habitual clouds over the mountains hadn't formed yet in anticipation of relief, and no water flowed down the sharp-edged slopes towards them. The rainy season, and the flooding it inevitably brought, was dangerous but necessary, and Aja sent up his only prayer that year.

"Please let the rains come soon and keep us safe."

His mother looked up and smiled, still beautiful in spite of the scars that pulled tightly across her skin and caused such pain. "A good prayer to offer, Aja."

He nodded once and moved away, carrying the buckets to the kitchen where he covered them with a cloth to keep the flies and dust away. Behind him, Merot entered, carrying four heavy buckets. These buckets were for laundry, their two goats, and the barest of wipe-downs that constituted a bath during the dry season. Behar was unable to make the long trek to the last producing waterhole, let alone carry laundry such a distance. It was extra work for Merot, but he never complained. Aja caught an unguarded look between his parents. The expression in their

6

eyes made him swallow, a wistful longing rising in his throat. He had once overheard several matrons discussing the great love of Merot and Behar, how he had brought Behar back from death itself, thus saving his bride and their unborn child from the fate Sik had otherwise planned for them.

Aja knew that was part of why Imprana Jido watched him so closely now. Anyone fortunate enough to survive a dragon attack was of great interest to the Church and even more so if the dragon in question was a queen. He supposed the only thing that could have made them more of a novelty was if it had been Adira herself who attacked Behar. But of course, if that had happened, neither he nor Behar would be here now. No one had ever heard of anyone who had survived an attack by an empress, though by all accounts no such attacks had occurred in Aja's lifetime. Several thousand years ago Empress Adira had reached an age where dragon instinct and rages no longer ruled her behavior, and their world was far more settled with her maturity, though nothing ever fully dampened a dragon's violent nature. It was rumored that she lay in her caves, dulled by age and boredom and that the young queens ruled their provinces, waiting for the time when they could overthrow her.

There were many who wished for the dragons to war, hoping they would kill each other off, and Aja had once made the mistake of saying so to his father. Merot had made it clear to his young son that in a war so violent as to kill every dragon, there would be no survivors. Aja had looked at his mother and his young brother and stopped praying that night for war.

Merot sighed heavily as Behar motioned them all to dinner.

"The rains must come soon if we're going to salvage the fruit crop."

Behar hummed a soothing melody as she rubbed her husband's shoulder. "It will rain. I'd say before nightfall tomorrow."

She smiled with a knowing look in her eyes, and some of Aja's anxiety eased. His mother had a powerful weather sense, and every year she pinpointed the clouds' arrival with uncanny accuracy. If she said the rain was coming, it would be here, no matter how unlikely it seemed at the moment.

Dinner was a quiet affair of oats and rehydrated berries, brightened by the eggs Aja produced. His mother set some aside to make a rare, fruit pastry for breakfast, and quickly scrambled the rest with a bit of goat cheese and herbs. Qal inhaled his portion of their unexpected treat, and Aja quietly offered the rest of his eggs to his little brother.

Merot stopped Qal with a lifted finger.

"You need to eat all of your supper, Aja. It's important to keep your strength up."

Qal snatched his hand back from Aja's plate, a stricken expression on his face. Aja felt a burst of anger and assured his little brother, "It's ok, you didn't do anything wrong."

To his father, he insisted, "It's alright, Dad. The little bird can have the rest. There's just a few bites left, anyway."

Behar's expression held an odd tension, and her bright eyes were uncertain as she watched her husband.

"No, Aja. We have a special task for you tonight. Qal can have an extra pastry tomorrow."

Merot's tone was final, but Qal brightened immediately at his father's promise, sticking his tongue out briefly in Aja's direction.

"I'd rather have an extra pastry than plain old eggs any day."

"Not if I get up first," Aja retorted.

The good-natured teasing between the two brothers brought a slight lift to their father's lips, and some of the tension slipped from Behar's shoulders. Aja feinted for Qal's ears, then lightly pinched the boy's thin bicep. His little brother's skin stretched tightly over his bones and he wished not for the first time that they could afford a small flock of chickens, rather than rely on what they could forage from the untilled scrub beyond the farm. Such good fortune with the flitters could not be expected to hold, and Qal had hit a growth spurt. Aja hated watching him scrape his plate for every crumb but still leave the table hungry.

After dinner, Qal was sent to wash up before bed, and Aja sat at the table, waiting to hear what additional work his father had for him. Though it was not uncommon to spend many of their evenings inside, working to spin thread, weave canvass, and make oils, candles, and scented soaps to sell at market, Aja knew that they had used all their supplies up and were only waiting for the rains to spawn the next flurry of chores. That was their life – make the most of whatever was at hand, and hope to live off of what they'd gathered and stored until the next season brought new food.

After Qal was safely tucked away in bed for the night, his mother joined them at the table. Aja felt a tiny tremor flutter in his chest as their eyes came to rest on him with unusual intensity. Merot cleared his throat and Aja's gaze shot to his father's face.

"As you know, the Choosing Ceremony is barely a week away."

"There's nothing to worry about, Father. The gift doesn't run in our blood." This was not news to his parents, but perhaps they needed reassuring, much as Qal had earlier that day.

Merot and Behar exchanged a look. His father rubbed his ear as Behar cautiously answered.

"That's not entirely true, Aja."

Aja straightened in his chair, eyes widening as he glanced from one parent to the next.

Merot cleared his throat before elaborating on his wife's statement.

"Your mother had a sister."

Aja's lips parted slightly as he stared at his mother. Until this evening, he had known her to be an only child. He held his questions in, afraid to know the answers, and even more afraid that by asking, he would deter his mother's sudden wish to share what had been hidden. Behar smiled, a tiny lift and fall of her lips as she gazed past Aja's head into the shadows of the room.

"Nera was my older sister. She was smart and beautiful and kind, and when she reached the Choosing age, the priests came. I was just a year younger, and permitted to watch the ceremony. It didn't carry as much secrecy as it does now. The high priest carried a small box made of gold and silver, crusted with gems."

Behar's pale eyes darkened slightly, and she paused a moment to gather her thoughts as Aja silently willed her to continue. No adult had ever spoken so openly of the Choosing Ceremony in his presence before, and now that the story was begun, Aja was no longer quite so consigned to the idea that he must go to the Ceremony in ignorance of what to expect.

"The high priest went to the first child in the village and ordered him to hold out his dominant hand."

Behar's normally expressive eyes became as flat as her voice as she recounted the events of that day.

"His acolytes took the boy's arm while the Impara opened the box and placed a band of Chrym on his forearm. Then he used a small key to tighten the band. It had spikes which pierced the boy's skin, and though he wept and struggled, the priest tightened the band until the spikes were fully embedded, piercing flesh and bone."

Aja swallowed and glanced briefly at the scars on his parents' arms, their origins now appallingly clear. Merot caught his glance and gave a tiny affirmative nod, his fingers absently rubbing his forearm as though recalling the feel of the bracelet.

"One by one, they went to each of the children, and each one was forced to endure the pain of the bracelet, until Nera." Behar paused, and Aja saw the sheen of tears in his mother's eyes.

It was Merot who continued.

"I was the same age as Nera, the first boy to be tested."

Aja's gaze swept to his father's face.

"I watched as the priest came to Nera. I saw the look on his face when he saw her beauty. And then he put the bracelet on her arm and began to tighten it. Just as the Chrym would have pierced her skin, the metal spikes began to soften. As the bracelet continued to tighten, the spikes softened and became flat against the band. Try as he might, the priest was unable to injure Nera."

"That was when I saw true evil." Behar took up the story again. "The look on that priest's face made the hair on the back of my neck stand up. I wanted to turn and flee, but Nera stood her ground, refusing to show fear. He ordered her to be taken away, and I only saw her one time after that, the day she died."

"What happened?" The question slipped from his lips without intent.

"The Impara was a corrupt man, who kept Nera for himself. He was a cruel husband, and fearful of Sik's rage if she discovered that he had kept such a prize for himself, he imprisoned Nera in his temple rooms until she went mad from captivity and threw herself from a window to the temple floor below."

"Too broken to save, her husband allowed her to be carried home to us. She lived long enough to warn us of the fate that awaited me if I was Chosen as well. She gave us the gift of knowledge – the priests knew of an herb that could suppress the Gift for a short time. Before she passed, Nera was able to tell us where to find it, and how to prepare it."

Aja remained silent, watching emotions flit across his mother's face in response to the painful memories she recounted.

"When it was my turn to be chosen, the herbs so dulled my senses that I barely felt the Chrym when it tightened on my arm. I was completely unable to control the spikes, and safely passed the Choosing Ceremony."

Aja swallowed hard and Behar grabbed his right hand, his dominant hand.

"It's a small price to pay," she vowed. "A small price for us to be safe."

"Can you Weave Chrym?" Aja asked, not sure he wanted to know the answer.

"Enough," came the cryptic reply.

Aja cocked his head, his gaze flitting from Behar to Merot.

"The spot by the riverbed, Aja. What drew you there?"

He paled. "I don't know."

Behar gave him a rare crooked smile. "I think you do. It's forbidden for any but the priests and Chrym slaves to be in possession of Chrym, but for those of us who possess enough of the Gift, it is a small matter of will to bring a tiny bit to the surface for a child just coming into their powers to sense, or not."

Behar's eyes brightened with sudden intent. "Aja, I need you to bring me that speck of Chrym."

He started to rise from his chair, puzzled that she would ask such a thing but prepared to obey his mother.

"No, Aja. I want you to Call it here." She placed a particular emphasis on the word *call*, and Aja wondered if he'd understood her.

His lips parted as he stared silently at his mother.

"We need to know how strong your gift is so that we know how powerful the herbs need to be."

Aja had to swallow before he could force the next words out. "How do I Call it?"

"Think about how you felt when you first sensed it. Focus on that feeling, and think about how much you want to feel it again."

As his mother spoke, Aja closed his eyes and pictured the tiny patch of dry earth by the parched riverbed. He remembered the shiver that pierced him and settled in his belly as he stared at that spot. He brought the memory up and with a sudden sharp effort, he Pulled. He could feel something in the distance, could feel something within himself stretching out towards it, farther and farther, stretching so thin he was suddenly afraid, and then it was done. He was back in his body, sitting in the kitchen with his parents, looking in dazed wonder at their horrified faces.

"Wha-" he struggled to speak. "What's wrong? Did I do it?" He asked the question even though a cool weight in the palm of his hand told him what he needed to know.

His mother's lips tightened. "We're going to need more herbs, my love."

Merot simply nodded. "I'll take the eggs tomorrow to barter with the miller."

Aja bit back a protest. Qal would be so disappointed in the morning, but one look at his parents' expressions told him there would be no arguing.

"Will he tell?" Behar asked with sudden worry.

"No, love. I've been careful and only asked for small amounts here and there throughout the year. There's no reason to suspect Mir knows what use we've planned for it, and even less reason for him to inform Imprana Jido if he did. There's no love lost there," Merot assured her, and Aja thought back to snatches of overheard conversations and had to agree.

As his father turned away, Aja finally allowed his gaze to drop to his hand. For all his youth, it was a rough hand, already shaped by hard work. At the moment it lay open on the table, pressed down by a chunk of metal far larger than the speck his mother had brought to the surface for him to find. As his eyes fell at last to the death sentence in his hands, the candlelight caught the quicksilver surface of the Chrym he had Called, a large metal globe nearly the size of his closed fist. He stared in fascination. Forbidden to his people, he'd only ever caught a glimpse of the stuff as he'd hidden in terror with his family while Sik flew above their village in her terrible splendor.

He stroked the cold metal with unwilling fascination, watching as it reshaped to follow his finger, its behavior that of a living thing. Unbidden, the image of a koteeri came to mind. The smallest and most elusive of the desert cats, the dainty wild felines were barely larger than a flitter, yet for all their size, everyone knew not to tangle with one, especially one with kits. He had seen a domesticated one at the annual district market once and remembered how it rubbed lovingly against its master's hand. The Chrym reminded him of the koteeri, and just like that, he held a tiny metallic cat in his hand. It dissolved back into a solid lump at his mother's gasp of horror.

"A Swimmer," she said, her flat tone unable to mask her uneasiness as she watched her son cradle their death sentence in his hands.

Merot paled and pulled the last of their special scented candles from their shelf. Aja winced as they went into a second burlap sack beside the one that already housed the remaining flitter eggs.

"What's a Swimmer?" He asked the question as he stroked the metal with unwilling fascination. It continued to follow his movements, constantly shifting to meet his touch.

"The strongest Chrym wielders the Church publicly acknowledges can control it the way you just did, and you're barely old enough to have powers. The most powerful aspects of the Gift enable some people to – " his mother paused, gathering her thoughts, "merge, I guess, with the Chrym."

Aja gaped at her, disbelieving his ears. In all his life, he'd never heard anything so mad. Merge with metal? And why would the Church keep such a Gift a secret?

Behar smiled at his look.

"I'm not able, or at least I've never cared enough to try, but Nera told me that if she'd been strong enough, she could have accessed the vein of Chrym beneath the temple and Swum away from her sadistic husband."

He absorbed that astounding bit of news, aware of his mother's watchful eyes. "How did she know where she would end up if she could do it?"

"I don't think she cared. Anywhere would have been better than the temple. At any rate, she died before she could tell me more. I can only guess at how she knew about Swimming, seeing as how she knew she wasn't strong enough to do it. Now send the Chrym away before it's discovered here," Behar ordered briskly, and Aja understood that she was done speaking of the past, for now at least.

Aja sent the Chrym back to its resting place, and it felt easier to control this time, as though it had been tamed just like the koteeri in the marketplace. He stared at his empty hand while his mother busied herself preparing for bed, remembering the feel of the metal, the way the Chrym had pulled at him, even as he pulled it forward, and he resolved to try this "Swimming" the first chance he got. His first opportunity as it turns out was not until well after the Choosing Ceremony.

CHAPTER 2

Sik felt her brain rotting, cell by inevitable cell, as the *darkening* worked to claim her. The dream which awakened her was already fading, but she knew something important was hidden there, something she needed to remember. She had been searching for something, something she wanted desperately to destroy, and if she couldn't find it, it would take her instead. She shook her head, nearly mad with frustration. Dragons did not forget, could not forget, and yet she felt her life story slipping away. She was vulnerable, and she was dying. Fury rose up to sustain her, and she launched her massive black and scarlet body down the twisting corridors of her palace, but she couldn't outrun the illness she carried, a darkness that blurred the edges of her mind. She moved faster, nearly in flight despite the narrowness of the tunnels she claimed as her home. The Xaran slaves who were not quick enough to escape her path died beneath her talons, and in her frenzy, she cared little if they were talented Weavers or worthless drudges.

She burst into the open and caught a glimpse of Telek's handsome face, his green stripes Lacing bright with surprise at her sudden appearance. She surged upward without a word, aware that her First General took flight a half a wing beat behind her, ever loyal despite her increasingly erratic behavior. Once she'd gained enough altitude to extend her considerable wings and glide, she dropped back to allow Telek to slip into her wing-stream, and cast her great golden gaze toward him as they banked in a lazy circle above the colony, finally ready to acknowledge his presence.

"You are a pleasing ssspecimen, in ssspite of your ssstupidity." Though she was capable of human speech with perfect clarity, she stretched out the ssss in every word, spitting the words from her mouth to

14

watch with pleasure as they struck Telek's thick hide. She was in the mood to hurt something, and he would do for now.

"It is my deepest desire to please you," he replied, and the complete sincerity in his golden eyes lessened some of her terrible tension.

"As it should be," she responded in more normal tones. What might have been relief Laced across his heavily muscled body in a subtle pattern of color and light. She answered with an aggressive pattern that expressed renewed urgency. Human speech was a simple thing to master, but dragons spoke in other ways, far more complex than any human could dream.

All dragons were born with tooth and talon, tail and wings, horns and scales. While they did not technically breathe fire, every dragon possessed a unique organ called a *parra,* which regulated their core temperature. Humans found dragons hot to the touch even at resting temperature, but under stress, such as in battle or during mating flights, their *parra* enabled them to generate intense heat at will. This was known as Flaring and was a skill critical to a young dragon's survival in their first few millennia after hatching. Anything flammable within their range was reduced to ash when a dragon was in this state and a fully mature dragon could melt stone if they chose to Flare long enough, something Sik took pains to ensure her Xaran slaves did not forget.

These physical attributes were easy for the Xarans to recognize and label, but dragons possessed more subtle tools than tooth and claw, fire and air. They were also born with the ability to Lace. Every dragon, whether male or female, possessed thousands of tiny scales. While most of these scales were solid in color, always a lovely solid onyx for queens, and either blue or green for all the males, some of those scales had an additional function. These special scales formed a unique pattern of stripes on every dragon, male or female, which could fluoresce upon command. The males' stripes, or Laces, always matched the color of their scales, with the slightest of shade variations, but the queens displayed a more striking pattern and were considered the pinnacle of dragon beauty. Displayed in a variety of hues, some queens had Laces of palest pink, like washed out rubies, while some showcased a red so deep they were nearly lost against the velvety black matte of their scales. Without exception, every queen was gifted with solid black scales and brilliant red Laces. It had been so since the beginning of time, with one hideous exception.

"What do you think of Adira's beauty?"

Sik dropped the honorific Empress from her rival's name as she cast a coy glance at Telek. Her First General kept pace with an occasional smooth wing stroke, holding his position as her primary guard barely a wingtip away. His position made direct eye contact possible with the slightest head tilt, though a dragon's excellent peripheral vision made such a maneuver unnecessary.

Telek took careful note of Queen Sik's Laces to gauge her current mood. Tightly controlled, Sik revealed nothing of her thoughts to her First General. The question was not as casual as she wished it to appear.

"I find her pale, tiny and unattractive," he answered honestly. What he could have added with equal honesty was that although he was bound to his colony and his queen and could never leave Sik's side, he felt a reluctant fascination for the tiny empress. Though her smallness was displeasing, and her pale golden color absolutely revolting, she made the most of her size with incredible aerial acrobatics, performing maneuvers no other dragon could hope to match. If one could overlook the pale scales and the odd, rainbow-colored Laces, she was a beautifully formed dragon, long and slender, not heavy and solid like every other queen he'd ever seen. Yet for all her apparent daintiness, she possessed a power that astounded him, astounded them all. Telek was careful not to let any of this show in his own Lacing as he held himself tightly in formation with Sik.

"Do you not find her smaller form the least bit attractive?" she asked, and Telek wondered if he had Laced any signals in spite of his best efforts.

"You must know that you are the most beautiful dragon in existence," he protested.

She Laced, and a brilliant red warning splashed across the vibrant green of his own scales.

"I know I am *beautiful*," she spat. "Do you find *her* attractive?"

Telek held his Laces so tightly in control he nearly trembled with effort.

"She is tiny, but when you touch the ground, it trembles beneath you. She is pale enough to disappear in the sun, but when you take the sky, you take the light with you. She carries a thousand colors, but when you Lace, I see only you." Sik's pride in her brilliant coloring was well known, and her response to his passionate compliments assured him the crisis had been averted.

Any shade of red was considered beautiful, but Sik felt particularly fortunate to have taken after her mother, no more so in this moment as she flashed the brilliant crimson of her Laces at Telek, enjoying the stunned expression on his face as she teased him. A thousand roars blasted up at them as the rest of the colony observed her display and took flight. Telek hissed and Laced as well, a threat display to the males who raced to join them.

"It is my right to choose a mate," she reminded him, and for a moment his eyes flared as brightly as Pil, Hadra's husband sun. She wondered if he ever compared her eyes to Hadra, but the sight of her colony rising to greet her made her pulse with excitement. No longer interested in conversation, she watched as Telek controlled his Lacing masterfully, showing none of the frustration she knew he battled. Impressed in spite of herself, she slipped down and brushed against him, the slightest of touches before surging upward again.

He urged her to a higher, faster flight, but she would not be rushed, and the colony soon caught up. Most of the males remained safely out of Telek's reach, having spent centuries learning to respect his greater battle skills, but there were several males who might outfly him if Sik rose in a true mating flight.

She led them on through the night, taking note of who faltered and who kept pace, even when her own wings strained for air. There were several besides Telek who deserved consideration, and the flight was invigorating. She could only hope it triggered a true mating flight, and soon, or the *darkening* would take her. She had worked too hard to gain her place among the dragon queens and had too many unfulfilled goals to die now.

One of those goals lay just north of her territory, in the direction they now flew, and Sik Laced uncontrollably as hate speared through her. She ached to see the golden dragon, Adira, dead at her feet. That disgusting, tiny, *pale* dragon had risen from the filthy ground and taken possession of what was rightfully Sik's. She remembered how they had laughed and laughed when she challenged her first queen, but no one laughed over the next challenge, or the next. Impossibly strong for such a misformed creature, every majestic queen now bowed in fear when she took the sky, hoping it wasn't their territory she coveted next.

In all of dragon history, there were only three ways a dragon could die; in combat with another dragon, Chrym, or the *darkening*. Every queen strictly controlled access to Chrym in their territories in order to keep the Xarans from using it against their species, and death at the claws and fangs of another dragon was an honorable death, but the third possibility struck terror in every dragon. Sik ached at the thought of being brought down by something as lowly as disease. If only she could achieve the most coveted and rare state of dragonhood – a lifelong mate-bond – she could be saved from such a dishonorable fate. Sik ground her teeth together as she thought of Adira's reaction to her death, imagined her laughing as Sik succumbed to the *darkening*.

"I'll kill her first," the dark queen vowed, as the dozen or so males still struggling to stay with her Laced constantly through the night, signaling a thousand reassuring messages, all lost in their utter devotion to her. She dropped the tip of her tail to caress Telek's straining shoulder and allowed a smile to kiss her lips at the shower of light that rewarded her, sparking around them in a kaleidoscope of lust and yearning. He shivered again and cast a pleading glance at his queen, but her gaze was fixed north once more, all teasing forgotten as she planned for a future she might not have.

CHAPTER 3

Aja kept his head down, shoulders hunched as he placed one foot in front of the other. The wet soil physically resisted his presence with each step until his weight pressed him ankle deep. The mud demanded a price for each tiny victory, sucking greedily at his flesh as he raised each foot again. His lower back ached from the strain of maintaining his balance and his toes had long since gone numb. He had given up miles ago on his shoes, standing first on one foot, then the other as he fished the ruined footwear from its murky burial. Now tied together and looped around his neck, they were as clean as his feet were filthy, thanks to the torrential rains that had begun exactly when Behar promised.

Great, he thought. *My first trip to the city and I spend the entire trip cold and wet. Oh well, at least I'm sparkling clean – from the ankles up.*

He scowled as cold water ran down his forehead and into his eyes. At least the hard going kept him from minding the cold too much, though every rest they took had him anxious to continue on before sore muscles cooled and tightened, making the journey even more miserable.

We'll look like a litter of drowned koteeri when we finally get there. He smiled reluctantly at the image. Had he really been anxious for the wet season to start? A muffled moan penetrated the relentless drumming of the rain, and he turned carefully to look at his parents. If the muddy road to the temple was difficult for him, he could only imagine the struggle each step must be for his mother. Behar sensed his gaze and looked up, her amber eyes startlingly bright against her dark lashes, made thick and spiky by the rain. As he watched, a tiny bead of water slipped from her nose and was lost amongst hundreds of other drops. In spite of her pain, she continued forward, left foot raising easily and moving forward, right foot struggling to lift above the filth, making barely perceptible forward progress before sinking back into the mud. Merot was tireless by her side, supporting her weight as her left foot came forward again, leaving her awkwardly leaning against him for balance.

"Mother, let me help." It was an offer he had made countless times during the journey.

"We're almost there, love," came the same response he heard every time.

It was true; Aja could see the white spires of the temple quite clearly through the grey sheets of rain and realized they were very close now indeed. Knowing how soon they would reach the church didn't make watching his mother's suffering any easier. Though tall for his age, he was still no match for his father's strength. He wished not for the first time that he was a man grown, and that between the two of them, he and his father could carry her upon their shoulders. He'd seen a few wealthy women travel that way through the mud, perched on small cushioned seats that rested on the shoulders of servant men. If they had anything of value, he'd have traded it in an instant to see to her comfort.

The trip to the high temple would ordinarily take three full days under good conditions, but the rainy season made travel nearly impossible. If it wasn't for the Choosing Ceremony, Aja and his small family would spend the rainy season at home, alternating between gathering the special fruits, reeds, roots, and seeds that only grew in the rains, moving the goats back and forth to the few high grazing points to be found, and digging mud forts with Qal, the latter a particular specialty of the brothers.

Aja blinked more rain from his eyes, unsure if the haziness of his vision was from rain or the herbs his mother and father fed him several times a day throughout their journey. The mere thought recalled the peculiar and unrelentingly bitter taste of the pesa herb to his tongue. He cleared his throat against a sudden tightness as he considered and discarded a reminder to his parents for the next dose. Though the herbs had cost them dearly, he was in no hurry to shudder his way through another mouthful of the disgusting medicine.

Merot had returned home just before the rains with the additional herbs Behar needed. Aja had spent the entire day resisting the urge to call Chrym, and had felt oddly bereft the moment he took his first dose of the numbing potion. When the Chrym still answered his call, he had looked doubtfully at his mother.

"Perhaps a stronger dose?" Merot asked.

"No, I don't think so. If Nera was right, it will require several doses to take effect."

After an hour had passed, Behar had asked him to call Chrym. It came effortlessly to his hand. She pursed her lips, and without a word, brought him another dose of the bitter stuff. He dutifully swallowed it down and sent the Chrym back to the riverbed. She didn't ask him to call it again, but the next day, she gave him several doses throughout the morning and afternoon, and again after dinner when Qal was in bed, she asked him to call Chrym. Again, it answered, though it felt to Aja as though it slept, and only answered reluctantly. When he informed his mother she exhaled noisily and gave him another dose. He sent it away, not sure if it returned entirely to its resting place, feeling a slight numbness as it traveled further away. On the third night, he was unable to call Chrym. Their relief was short-lived as Merot had a sudden thought.

"What if he can't call it from so far? What if a closer source would still answer him?"

His mother's appalled look was answer enough. There was no way for her to reach the riverbed in the rains, and the Chrym was buried where his father could never reach. Behar spent the next several hours trying to pull the Chrym to her, and when at last she held a speck of the forbidden metal in her hand, she was flushed and sweaty, trembling with exertion. Aja finally began to understand just how extraordinary his Gift was.

Much to their dismay, the moment the Chrym touched his palm, it melted against his skin as though overjoyed to have found him. When Behar pulled more of the pesa herb from their tiny jar, Merot protested.

"We'll never have enough to make it through the Ceremony!"

"We'll have to find more along the way," came the answer, a hardness in Behar's voice that Aja had never heard before.

Aja swallowed the bitter morsel without complaint, steeling himself to show none of the disgust he felt. His family had sacrificed what little wealth they had to protect him, and he could do no less than accept their aid without shaming himself.

When he sent the Chrym away, he quickly lost his hold over it, and Behar had to push it towards the river, though she was so exhausted he doubted it returned fully. In the morning, when she called it back, it did not respond to Aja at all. They continued with his doses all day as they prepared to leave. Qal would stay with their nearest neighbor, an arrangement that had been planned for some time.

The next several days passed in a misery of cold rain, mud, and a peculiar numbness that seemed to dim everything in the world, much the same way that the clouds dimmed Pil and Hadra's glory.

And now here they were, just one day from the Choosing. If Aja passed without betraying his gift, they would return home where he would be safe, or at least as safe as possible under Sik's rule. Aja looked at all the fine homes that formed Sik's great city and briefly wondered what his life would be like in the presence of such abundant wealth. Since the temple had first come into view, they'd seen no signs of poverty. It was clear that no one in the shadow of the Church went hungry, and Aja almost regretted that he would pass the Choosing Ceremony and return home. Guilt spiked through him at the thought – his family needed him if they were to survive.

"Aja."

It was barely a murmur above the rain, but it was all the warning the boy needed. In spite of the herbs dulling his senses, he moved quickly enough to avoid being run down by a peculiar vehicle. Long and low, it looked like nothing more than a simple river skiff, though far larger than any they boasted in his village. How it moved through the muck, he couldn't fathom, though his mother's eyes grew so wide he could see the whites, putting him in mind of their barren old goat when she'd gotten trapped in a bog last winter and panicked before Aja could pull her out.

He looked again, blinking rain from his eyes as it slid past. Riding in the front were several men in black and red robes which matched queen Sik's brilliant hues perfectly, while sitting at the back of the conveyance were three men and two women. They were dressed simply but well, and all five shared the same focused expression. They looked neither right nor left, up nor down, staring straight ahead as though they could see through the backs of the passengers before them. Aja could still see no sign of how the boat moved through the mud.

"Chrym," his mother hissed, and shock lanced through him.

How could Chrym move a boat through mud? He looked with renewed interest at the boat, but it was moving rapidly away and he caught only a glimpse before the rain swallowed it from view. He would have asked his mother a question, but Behar shook her head sharply, a silent warning before continuing her slow, painful progress toward the temple.

The size of the temple made it seem deceptively close, and it was nightfall when they finally arrived, the grey sky slowly darkening to velvety black as the rains performed their nightly transformation into a heavy mist, shifting eerily with the passage of hundreds of people. Aja watched as the mist swirled about them, at times appearing to be heavy black smoke, then transforming into thousands of tiny diamonds sparkling through the air as the water molecules caught the lamp lights that were stationed at every street corner. The playful mix of water, air, and light consumed his attention for a time until he became aware of the heavy press of bodies, a growing, murmuring presence that offended first his nose and then his ears.

Aja pulled back towards his parents, trying not to grimace. Though the rains had washed them clean on their journey, from the smell of things, many others had arrived well before them and the city was clearly not prepared for so many visitors in such a small space. Without a doubt, the wealthier travelers had found accommodations elsewhere, but there were thousands of families like Aja's, who would spend an uncomfortable night on the filthy cobblestone courtyard before the temple, waiting for morning and the high priests of Sik to decide their fate.

"Let's set up here, Aja." He met his father's dark eyes and shared his unspoken relief that they would not continue to press through the crowd. Behar sighed with relief and leaned against a nearby building as Aja pulled the straps of his heavy backpack from his shoulders and began to help his father with her bed. An amazing contraption, his father had designed a sled-like frame, with large sections that broke apart and fit together again as needed, and legs that folded down on hinges to raise the whole device several inches from the floor. The end result was an easily portable, yet sturdy bed that saved Behar from the pain she would otherwise have suffered from sleeping on the hard ground, and the struggle to raise and lower herself with her damaged limbs.

They had the contraption set up in moments, and Merot carefully spread a nest of blankets for his wife. The whole process took no more than a minute thanks to the practice they had gained during their travels, but when Aja looked up, he saw that they had gained quite an audience.

"Where did you get that?" asked a lighter skinned man, his hand resting on a young girl's shoulder. The girl was lighter skinned like her father and blushed brightly as she met Aja's eyes. He felt an uncomfortable warmth stain his own nut-brown cheeks. The girls of his village had shown no interest in him, and certainly none of them were as pretty as this one. He wet his lips, afraid for a moment that his voice would fail him.

"My father made it," he managed, shoulders coming back as his chin came up. He didn't dare speak again, for fear his voice would break as it still sometimes did.

"Amazing," murmured another woman, leaning close to run a finger over the seam where two large pieces had come together.

Merot scowled as they crowded closer, suddenly anxious for Behar's safety, but she merely smiled and tucked in against his side as several people began asking questions at once.

"What kind of wood did you use?"

"How much does it weigh?"

"How long did it take to make?"

And finally, the question that silenced everyone. "How much will you take for it?"

All eyes were on Merot, who drew himself stiffly up. "My wife has need of this one, but if you've an interest, I could return here in three weeks' time with another just like it." His measured response made it clear there would be no arguing, and the fellow who had made the offer pursed his lips before nodding slowly.

"I've two more boys at home besides this big lug, and the wife to boot." Several men laughed as the wife in question gave her husband a warning look.

"The little 'uns can share two to a bed easy enough, but how well do they hold up, and could you make one large enough for the pair of us?" The crowd now laughed in earnest as his wife covered her mouth with both hands, her eyes growing large as she stared at her husband.

"Kervan!" came a muffled squeak. He shrugged and quirked an eyebrow at Merot, who quickly hid a grin as he considered the question.

"As to how well they hold up, I made this one for my wife four years ago."

Aja remembered helping his father painstakingly gather and form the water reeds that dried so tightly together they resembled a solid piece of wood. The trickiest part had been figuring out how to design the dried pieces so they would lock together, but Merot had persevered and eventually found a clever way to form grooves in one end that held dozens of narrow tongues from the other. The seams' joinings were then reinforced by Behar's weight, which locked each piece in place and pushed the bed down on its many legs until a sharp blow from the other side popped them loose again.

"As to how much weight they hold," Merot shrugged. "I've only made the one to come apart like this, but I've made solid pieces to hold summer grain, cherry brandy and such."

He considered Kervan's wife, measuring her dimensions against Behar. "My guess is a bed twice this size would hold you and maybe four of her, considering she's such a slip of a thing."

Kervan grinned. His wife's entire face was now hidden behind her hands, her shoulders shaking with laughter or sobs, it was hard to tell. Behar looked sympathetic to her plight and bumped Merot gently with her hip, who relented with his teasing.

"As to how much," Merot considered longer. "I've only the two sons, my wife, and some goats. We could use a good ewe in exchange for the big bed, and I wouldn't say no to five pounds of grain, a half-dozen young chickens, and a decent rooster for one like this." He indicated Behar's bed with his chin, squeezing her tightly against his side.

Aja's eyes widened as Kervan considered the offer. Assuming they could keep the hawks and other predators from the chickens, they would never have to worry about going hungry again. Chicks and eggs from future generations would feed them for years to come.

"I have a young sow and a half-dozen ducks I could bring for trade." Kervan countered with eager anticipation.

Merot considered. A ewe would have saved them having to barter for wool, but a sow to breed twice a year would produce enough piglets to feed their family and sell the extra on market days. Ducks would be trickier to keep than chickens, but at the very least, he could trade them for something else or eat them, though he hated to think they would serve such a short-sighted purpose.

"Done."

Both men promptly held out their hand to shake on the bargain.

Negotiating the timeframe was a bit trickier. The rainy season was a good time to gather reeds, but they were away from the farm and would miss most of the gathering time. Not to mention, the reeds took time to form and dry, and there were the complicated folding legs to build. The two beds would be difficult to complete unless Aja and Qal worked all day to help. That meant other tasks such as fruit and seed gathering would have to wait, but Merot weighed their needs and decided it was well worth the loss of prime gathering time. In the end, the two men agreed that Merot and his family would wait at the temple for four days after the Choosing Ceremony. Kervan would return with the sow as partial payment. In three weeks' time, they would meet here again to exchange the beds and the ducks as final payment. In this way, if the beds weren't finished, Merot would have gained nothing but a sow to feed and possibly breed, at which point, Kervan would take possession of a sow and soon-to-be piglets. Aja would have preferred the ducks as down payment – eggs could be layed and eaten every day – but he could hardly complain about the sudden wealth they anticipated.

Another couple spoke up. "We'd only need two beds." This from a quiet, smooth-skinned man. He looked down at his wife and continued. "We've got six children, but they only need to come one at a time, and they've their own beds at home. Could you make another for the pair of us and a smaller one? I've got that ewe you were angling for from Kervan, and a stripling peach tree I started this spring."

Aja closed his mouth, working hard to hide his astonishment. Wool, eggs, bacon and ham, peaches for jam – all of this for some water reeds?

His chest swelled with pride as his father appeared to consider the offer.

"Well my wife is partial to peaches, and as I've said, the ewe would come in handy." He looked around the crowd. "If you could see to it that she's carrying before exchange, I think I could have your two beds ready when I bring Kervan's to the temple."

Aja winced inwardly, flexing his fingers as he thought of the hard work ahead of them. The reeds were supple but tough, and cutting was hard work. Nearly as hard was the weaving process, when the fibers scored hundreds of tiny cuts, striking the same points of contact again and again. By day's end, both Merot and Aja's fingers had been swollen and sore, so much so that on the first several days of weaving, Aja had chosen to go to bed without eating his dinner, too sore to hold a spoon. That had been the price of making one bed. He kept his face still as another couple stepped forward and made an offer. This time they wanted just one bed, but Merot hesitated.

"It's not that I don't want to," he promised. "I'm just not sure there's enough of the rainy season left to gather what I need."

Behar murmured in his ear and he brightened. "You're right love. We can use the water barrels!"

Aja realized what his mother intended. If they could gather enough reeds to make all the beds, they could be kept alive and pliable in the large water barrels that Merot had built and positioned at the corners of the house, giving Aja and Merot one, possibly even two more weeks of weaving after the rains ended. Those barrels were meant to hold rainwater for laundry and farming, but for the opportunity at such wealth, Aja was willing to carry a few extra buckets of water from the river, and from Merot's expression, he could guess his father felt the same.

A final deal was made, and Merot got his precious chickens at last, as well as a half dozen more bags of grain, which would help feed the sudden influx of livestock until they could earn their own keep. Aja began to wonder how they were going to get all of their new residents home. He had a sudden image of chasing chickens and ducks from the back of a bleating ewe as they scattered across the road before him. Some of what he was thinking must have shown on his face when his father glanced his way.

"We'll figure it out, son." Merot chuckled, and Aja's dimples made a brief appearance in response to his father's laughter.

The crowd's attention gradually shifted from Aja's small family, though a few men and their wives remained to discuss the possibility of buying a bed, if not for this year, perhaps the next. Behar settled down in her bed at last, her eyes shining as she watched her husband discussing terms and timeframes. She smiled as Aja settled next to her on his own bed of blankets, spread over the stones of the courtyard. It was a bright, open smile that dimmed only slightly as she reached into the bag she had placed at the head of the bed and handed Aja another dose of pesa.

He swallowed it quickly, glad that he would soon see an end to the bitter stuff, one way or another. He dropped his head to his blanket and looked up at the white steeple that lifted high above them, clearly visible thanks to the many windows in every level, each shining brightly with torches to light the way. The overall effect had most likely been intended to make the temple seem welcoming, but to Aja, it seemed cold and menacing. Far from eliciting feelings of warmth and security, the stone edifice was a hard white presence that speared like a wound across the night sky, the huge dark doors on the ground level a hungry, open mouth, ready to consume the unwary.

When he closed his eyes, the temple was superimposed against the darkness of his eyelids for a moment longer, and from the top window, he saw the silhouette of a woman appear and then fall. He shivered and pulled his blankets closer, feeling Behar's fingers trail through his short hair. He wondered for the first time what his mother felt, seeing the temple again, the place where her sister had suffered such a grievous fate, and it seemed as though it was hours later when he finally fell asleep to the feel of her fingers rubbing his scalp and the sound of the soft melody she hummed to Qal when he was ill and needed comforting.

Aja awoke the next morning to hard, driving rain. It was a familiar and unpleasant morning wake up call, and he pulled his blankets up over his head, grateful for the citrus-scented outer layer that kept him from getting a thorough soaking. It was yet another time consuming and difficult task to process the oils they used to soak his lightweight rain cloak, but the waterproof canvas was extremely versatile and worth its weight in Chrym in times like these.

He listened to the sound of the crowd, a few soft exclamations here and there that grew in number until the volume became a din so loud it was impossible to distinguish a single voice. People were rising, choosing to stand in the rain, rather than lay in damp or soaked bedding, letting the heavy rains sluice away the filth brought in by a few thousand travelers. A few families had enough extra materials to construct small lean-tos, and Aja created a tiny gap in his own bedding to peer out at the gathering, breathing in the cooler, but unpleasantly perfumed air as he watched families ready themselves for the ceremony.

The girl he had noticed the night before was brushing her hair, long wavy locks of dark honey brown, heavy and darkened by rain. The girls of his village all had dark hair like Aja, some as curly and tangled as the thornberry bushes that grew among the rocks, some as straight and smooth as a young water reed, but all nearly the same shade of rich dark brown. In the city, with Xarans arriving from all over the province, there were many skin tones throughout the courtyard, and Aja found himself fascinated by their differences. Here and there were small clusters of three that stood out from the rest. Here a family with hair so light it appeared nearly white, there a family with skin and eyes so dark they looked as though the night sky had touched them and refused to let go, but overall, most families were somewhere between the dark honey brown he'd admired last night, and a rich walnut brown. His own family he realized was somewhere in between the two, and he raised his hand to the dim grey light to judge its shade, watching as his skin was immediately beaded with rain. Moments later the bell in the temple began to ring, deep solemn tolls that vibrated through Aja's bones.

"Aja! Last time," came an anxious hiss, and he reached back, fumbling for his last dose of bitter medicine. As he swallowed it down, he caught the eyes of an ebony skinned girl. She smiled, a flash of bright white teeth and shining almond-shaped eyes, and he smiled back. He imagined her swimming in the river with the village girls all sleek and beautiful, a glistening ebony gem amongst a school of almond fish. He thought of the figure he'd seen, falling from the top of the church tower. Perhaps, like Nera, she would never swim in a village river again. He felt a slight tremor pass through his body and lowered his eyes, straightening his clothes to hide his unease. When he looked back up, he saw she still watched him. As their eyes made contact she flashed him another quick grin before looking forward, her parents stepping to either side of her as they faced the now open temple doors. A soft chuckle nearby made him flush. For a moment, he'd forgotten the crowd, and he realized that as he'd been busy observing the gathering, others might well have been watching their interaction, amused by the small flirtation.

Families shuffled forward slowly as trios entered the temple and the crowd outside slowly thinned. From time to time as they moved closer to the open mouth of the temple, Aja heard muffled wails, and once it sounded as though a scuffle began and just as abruptly ended. He suddenly understood that the guards flanking the priests were not there for purely ceremonial purposes. Their spears and swords were elaborate works of art, heavily crusted with precious jewels and clearly not meant for every day use, but up close, Aja could see their well-honed edges, and the stares of the men who carried them were nearly as hard and sharp. He suddenly felt smaller and wished he were still a baby like Qal, to reach for the comfort of his mother's hand. He forced himself to straighten and step forward as one of those fierce men stared directly in his eyes, and with that single step, he passed from the open sky of the courtyard into the shadow of the temple. The guard stared at him a moment longer, and Aja felt like a fish on a hook, being examined before being tossed in a basket or perhaps let go. Then the moment passed and the man's hard gaze went to the next trio in line.

His eyes took a moment to adjust, and he blinked, instinctively looking down to shield his vision from the blazing torches that ringed the priests' pedestal. He frowned when the shadows refused to dissipate, and then blanched as realization dawned. Not a shadow, but an ever widening pool of blood which spread across the floor to greet him. Aja felt his stomach lurch as the guard pushed him forward that last step.

Thank Pil and Hadra I remembered to put my shoes on this morning, he thought as his foot slipped slightly. He thought of the girl with the bright smile and skin black as dragon scales. Her blood was somewhere on this floor. He felt nausea burn hotly in his throat and nose at the thought. Or perhaps she was already in the towers above, under guard before the short trip to Sik's court, or worse, being taken away by a man like Nera's husband. He was glad for the numbing effect of the herbs as he watched a young girl whimper and then shriek when the Chrym bracelet tightened. *If I could, I would Call the Chrym and use it to gouge their eyes out*, he thought fiercely, tightening his hands into fists.

"Steady, boy." A low warning from his father brought him back to himself, and he breathed out through his nose, unable to loosen his clenched jaw. He nodded and exhaled again, and then it was his turn. If he'd thought it was bad to watch the others go through the Ceremony, it was a thousand times worse to experience. He could only wonder at the stoicism of the ones who'd gone before.

The Chrym tightened and he felt a thousand sharp needles, felt the tear of each spike send screaming pain through every nerve in his body. Nothing he'd ever felt prepared him for the pain. If he hadn't been numbed to the Chrym, he would never have been able to withstand it without commanding the metal to shift. The spikes drove deeper and he realized he was whimpering deep in his throat, teeth clenched to hold back the howl that threatened to erupt at any moment. Deeper still, and he understood that there was no mercy in the men holding his arm, in the priest turning the key. He felt their sick pleasure, their twisted joy as the band tightened so completely he thought it might cut off all circulation to his arm. The priest looked deeply into his eyes, searching for something, and Aja found the will to stand tall on his own, a deep tremor wracking his body as blood spattered from his fingertips to the once white marble floor. He swallowed and stared back defiantly, glad that he'd managed to hold back all but a whimper from his torturer. Then the priest's eyes reached behind him, and Aja saw a slow, terrible smile transform his face. It was a mocking, knowing smile that made his blood run cold.

"You!" It was a whisper, barely formed, but the priest heard it. If anything, his smile widened as he met Behar's eyes, then slid his gaze back to Aja.

"Those lovely eyes are unmistakable. It's a pity that's the only thing Nera shared with you, boy. It appears your mother has passed her bad blood on to you instead."

Aja felt rage swell within his chest, and for the briefest moment, he touched the Chrym cutting into his arm, but the herbs were too potent and the metal passed out of his awareness. Something of his intent must have shown in his eyes, for the man before him actually took a half step back, causing the guards beside him to reach for their swords before the priest collected himself and gestured to the others.

"He has failed to show any signs of the Gift. Release him and take down their names. They'll pay the extra tithe this year for not offering a Gifted child, and keep their worthless son."

The pain had begun to lessen; perhaps he was numb from shock or the tightness of the band, but as soon as the bracelet was removed, unwelcome sensation returned with it. His fingertips throbbed in time to his heartbeat, and he struggled against a surge of dizziness as Behar wrapped a white cloth provided by the temple around his forearm. They crossed the huge room to another set of open doors and were met on the other side by thousands of voices, most lifted in relief, punctuated by sobs of grief as husbands and wives consoled each other over the loss of a child. Aja looked around and saw the same solemnity staring back at him from thousands of pairs of young eyes. No one wept now for what they'd suffered – it seemed a minor injury compared to the mothers and fathers who would never see their child again.

"We'll sleep outside the city tonight," Merot announced. "I'll come back in alone in four days to meet up with Kervan." The thought that he might well have lost a child today went unsaid.

Behar's lips tightened and she blinked back unshed tears.

"I'll only come to this city one more time," she vowed, and the thought of Qal experiencing the Choosing Ceremony was another blow to Aja. He had a new respect for his parents and what they had suffered, what they must still suffer, knowing they could not protect their children from the Choosing. He wondered why they'd even chosen to have children, knowing the life in front of them, but it was an idle thought, without bitterness. His parents had taught him to observe and respect the natural world, and he'd come to understand years ago that life begat life. He'd observed various plants and animals that were willing to die, just to bring the next generation into the world. There was no getting around it, and though there was certain pain to come with it, Aja knew that when the time came, he would choose a girl to marry, and they would have children, and they would come to the city where he would suffer with them, wishing to carry their pain and allow them to remain children a bit longer.

He looked up at his father, who had been watching him as he gathered his thoughts. Merot nodded once, and Aja knew that although he would not see seventeen years until tomorrow, he'd left his childhood behind today.

CHAPTER 4

I laughed with my head back and mouth open, easy and free in the summer sun. Chubby little arms clung to my neck and my laughter subsided into helpless giggles over the way Maggie tried to copy my laughter. Too young to know the source of my amusement, my precocious little girl still tried to join in on the fun. I felt solid warmth at my back, and two strong arms circled my waist.

"You enjoyed the show, did you?" He squeezed in mock threat and I tipped my head back to rest against the notch between his neck and shoulder. I could feel the scrub of his five o'clock shadow catch in my hair.

"The best seat in the house." I giggled helplessly again, reliving his awkward stumble and save.

"I've never seen ones that big before."

I snorted, and then howled as he finished with, "Especially not on a boy."

Mike settled down on the blanket, pulling us with him to nestle in, our amazing family. I'd given up hope of ever finding him, my perfect man, but now here he was. Here we were, with our beautiful, perfect little girl, sitting on a blanket on the capitol lawn, lounging in the sun. It was a holiday, and I wanted to share this beautiful moment, build family memories for Maggie to cherish in the years to come. A concert and fireworks, and time spent with Mommy and Daddy. Mike had laughed when I suggested the picnic.

"She's too young to remember," he'd said. But I remembered riding on my Daddy's shoulders, the pride and joy I felt to be so high, to be so loved, holding two bright carnival balloons. I knew that no matter what Mike said, it was never too early to start building those memories.

Maggie hit the edge of the blanket, like greased lightning since finding her legs six months earlier. Mike caught her wrist and tumbled her back towards us, turning an impending temper tantrum into a tickle game. The sun passed behind clouds and a breeze picked up.

"It's not supposed to storm today," I said with a frown. A strong chill arced up my spine, and I knew something terrible was coming. I wanted to hug Maggie close and keep her safe, but as I looked back, Mike and my daughter suddenly seemed impossibly far away, the blanket having stretched by several feet, and then farther and farther until they were barely visible. I reached desperately to bring them back, and then the world dropped away and I was falling, falling and screaming, and I knew with terrifying certainty that I was dying again.

Empress Adira launched from her bed, eliciting several startled screams from her servants. She barely restrained a wild swipe with wings and tail, holding herself in check with an agitated hiss. Eyes blazing, she swept the room for the source of her agitation. Finding nothing but the young servants who kept her chambers heated in the winter chill, she settled her spikes, shaking like a dog to relieve the last of the prickles that made her scales rise up. Though she would not have admitted it to anyone but herself, she took care not to shake too hard, not wishing to fling molten gold where it might strike and injure one of the Xaran slaves in her bedchamber. They saw it as an honor to serve her, and she would not return their devotion to her with a careless act.

A second, more restrained shiver settled the last of her scales, and her *parra* slowed to a more relaxed state. It was an uncomfortable feeling, those raised scales, not unlike the gooseflesh she had observed on the humans on a particularly cold day, though in her case, such a physiological reaction indicated strong emotion – rage, arousal, very rarely fear. Unlike the Xarans, all of whom had been born to this hot planet, cold was merely an irritant which could cause her no lasting harm. Thankfully, there were not many cold days on Ryxa, the world she currently resided on. It was a pleasing planet, full of sun and heat, save for a brief two to three week period of torrential rain and heavy flooding. Adira admitted to herself that it would be warmer if she hadn't destroyed one of the suns the silly humans worshipped. At least she had chosen the smallest sun, the one they called Halon. She had been young and more primal then, and there was no use crying over lost daylight. It wasn't as though the destruction of Halon had been without its benefits, so if the price for its destruction were an occasional disrupted night's sleep during the cold season, Adira supposed she could live with that. It was just as well, seeing as how she couldn't very well bring Halon back, and with the energy she'd gained by absorbing the tiny star, she was now nearly certain that nothing was capable of killing her except the loss of a bonded mate or the *darkening*. She barely restrained a new shiver. *Near certain madness and death for power. A poor bargain, indeed.*, she thought. She almost hoped for the vulnerability of a mate-bond to save her from disease, assuming she could keep her mate safe. Neither option was without its flaws, though the loneliness of millennia weighed heavy on her. She knew what she would choose if she could, but a mate-bond was extremely rare, and not something any dragon could control.

Adira sighed, and the sound echoed through her sleeping chamber, returning from every direction as though a hundred Adiras sighed back, each more melancholy than the last. It was unlike her to dwell on what couldn't be undone. She felt a sudden urge for open skies and picked her way through the sleeping chamber to the warren of corridors beyond. A shower of tiny gold flakes marked her passage as she left the room, but she gave it no thought. Her servants would sweep the gold back into her bed as soon as she was gone. A large shape detached from the wall just beyond her room, and she needed no greeting to recognize the handsome form of her First General, Oryd.

Doesn't he ever sleep, she wondered, suppressing a snap of irritation in his direction, though she did little to control her Laces, leaving him well aware of her feelings.

"Greetings, Empress Adira." He coupled the words with an impressive bowing of his chest, and his next words were just as predictable, "Our night patrols have just reported in and I have important news."

You always have important news. Adira suppressed her retort with effort.

"Queen Sik has once again tested your borders in the south on what appears to be a preliminary mating flight. I fear she will soon issue a more direct challenge if you continue to ignore her."

Sik was a frequent point of contention between the two, with Oryd arguing hotly for a direct confrontation, while Adira preferred to ignore Sik's small transgressions in exchange for the buffer she offered against some of Ryxa's younger, more impetuous queens. Adira knew he believed her to be too lax, too complacent in her rule, and he never missed an opportunity to point out another's trespass, but most especially Sik's, who he considered the only potential threat to his own queen. Her seeming indifference to each trespass bewildered him, and he could not graciously accept her refusal to act. As a result, he made a point of documenting every tiny transgression in the hopes that one day he might finally push Adira into putting Sik in her place. It was normally quite a bore, but this morning she feared he might get more than he bargained for.

"If a mating flight is truly in her future, I have no doubt she hopes to steal a few First Sons." Oryd pushed harder for a response, and Adira's teeth came together in an audible click, a clear sign he'd struck a nerve over the suggestion she might lose any of her sons, when she had so few compared to the other queens. He knew she was sensitive about her failure to rise and mate as frequently as the other queens, having only completed two mating flights throughout her unending existence. He couldn't quite hide the tiny smile that lifted the edges of his lips when she failed to suppress her reaction to the jibe.

A dragon's smile was a fearsome thing, sharp-edged and dangerous, and under normal circumstances she would have taken the time to admire his display, but at the moment, sleep deprived, harassed by her oldest rival, and challenged by this *hatchling* who thought he knew better, all she wanted to do was rip his throat out. It was definitely time to remind Oryd that he served her, not the other way around. She was no bond mate to the First General, however much he might wish otherwise.

She looked up, and then further up, silently cursing her diminutive stature. Every dragon queen she had ever seen in her immeasurable lifespan had been massive, nearly half a wingspan larger than the biggest male, while Adira herself was barely larger than a year old hatchling, only a little more than half Oryd's size, and not even half the wingspan of her largest rival, much to her disgust. Adding to each queen's impressive stature was the coloring that was distinctive to every female but Adira. Only queens possessed bands of red phosphorescence that covered their black, scaled bodies like the stripes of the great jungle cats in the south. Their bands were unique, as was the intensity of their coloring, with some queens possessing wide bands of red, so dark they nearly disappeared into the black edges of their stripes, while others were a rich, ruby red, and still others a deep, hot pink. Adira's own scales were brightly shining gold, and her phosphorescent stripes were any color of her choosing, save for one – red. Try as she might, she had never come close to the shade, her best attempt a brilliant ultraviolet hue that put her in mind of a lightning bolt.

Each dragon used these phosphorescent bands as signals; mood and so much more communicated through the brightness, color, and flashing pattern of their stripes. Some Lacing was instinctive and nearly beyond control, but most was deliberate and served as a complex form of art and communication that surpassed anything the humans could ever achieve with their limited vocal skills. Adira had mastered the art of Lacing at an early age when every difference between herself and the mature queens who ruled this planet could prove deadly. She had survived to adulthood only by turning her weaknesses into strengths, testing her limits, and pushing herself to learn skills the other dragons wouldn't even consider. While she could never match their beauty, she took pride that no other could match her skill in that regard.

As she finally met Oryd's great golden eye, she Laced a brilliant multi-colored pattern of unspeakable threats and opened her mouth in a deliberate yawn. Wider and wider, she unhinged her massive jaw and let him see down her throat, into the furnace of her very being.

That's right, hatchling, she thought as he shifted subtly away, his wings lowered slightly in submission, teeth now fully hidden behind tightly sealed lips. *Never forget that I am the only living dragon to have swallowed a sun, and while it doesn't burn as brightly within me as it did in the sky, it would still gladly destroy a lesser dragon such as you.*

Though tiny, the empress was shockingly strong, and Oryd was abruptly aware of his peril. Adira was exceptionally tolerant, but every male understood that his very existence within the colony was determined by his queen's will. More than one queen had dined on a dragon who displeased her. He dropped the very tip of his tail in a tight loop and Laced contrition, admiration, lust, hope, awe, love, fear, submission, mate-bonds, loyalty, determination, First Sons, and more. A thousand messages, all sent and processed at lightning speed.

Adira's Lacing slowed as she allowed herself to be appeased by his submission, but she resolved to show less tolerance for his behavior in the future. It wouldn't do to let Oryd become impertinent. He challenged her more and more every day, most especially over Sik.

"I get the distinct impression that you would very much like me to do something about her, Oryd." She returned to their spoken conversation as though the threat and submission displays had never happened.

"If you so desire, my most impressive and beauteous Empress." He responded with the perfect amount of humility and admiration. "It is ever my intent to perpetuate your great and shining glory."

He had reverted to more formal court speech as a further sign of atonement, and her Lacing responded instinctively this time, a subtle pulsing which triggered an answering brilliance from Oryd's own blue stripes.

"I will consider what is to be done," she murmured noncommittedly as he moved closer, his clawed feet striking the floor in ringing tandem with her daintier, but just as wickedly adorned toes. They were still in sync as they stepped into the great courtyard where her highest ranking males gathered, and Adira knew what they all saw - their empress, emerging from her sleeping chambers in lockstep with First General Oryd. She wouldn't have put it past him to have planned the whole thing. Oryd was young and impetuous, but he hadn't reached the rank of First General at his tender age through strength alone. He had passion and charisma, but more than that, he showed a clear talent for strategy and leadership.

Nearly three hundred years earlier, she had watched him play a brilliant game of intrigue to earn his current position. Barely more than a hatchling, Oryd had brought down her then First General Petra and managed to snare the highest possible male rank for himself, a nearly impossible feat for a fully mature male, and unheard of for one so young. She had watched the byplay, impressed by the innuendo and misdirection that eventually led to a direct challenge, and could have stepped in to stop it all if she had been so inclined, but despite siring her second clutch of sons, Petra had been no favorite of hers and she had not lifted a claw to save him. She wondered darkly if Oryd suspected that in spite of his solicitous behavior, she was much the same inclined towards him. In all her long life, there was only one First General who had managed to generate any true feelings of longing in her solitary dragon heart. Since then she had been at best indifferent to the dragons who had held and subsequently lost the highest rank a male could hope to achieve.

"Empress," he inclined his head and launched himself skyward in a surge of powerful muscles and spread wings. It was another calculated display, and Adira looked more closely at the hundreds of dragons gathered in the enormous courtyard that opened to the sky just beyond her throne room, carefully analyzing the intricate Lacing that had begun with her appearance and continued after Oryd's sudden flight. It was all too clear to her that Oryd's aggression was not the only sign of unrest within her colony. Several males hissed and bowed up in threat displays as her gaze touched them, and she was forced to acknowledge that every dragon had become unsettled by her recent changes in behavior. Many times, such a change could herald a queen's readiness to mate, and males were always attentive to such an opportunity. Even if a mate-bond did not occur, siring a queen's next clutch would result in an incredible rise in status.

The period leading up to a mating flight was a dangerous time for any male, for to attract a queen's attention during her breeding cycle, he had to be bold and aggressive. Not too bold, of course, or risk being killed and eaten, but a queen would have no interest in a weak male when it came time to select a mate. Adira knew her pheromones were gradually increasing in potency, a sure sign that she was readying for a mating flight, though it could be years or even decades before she reached a critical point in her cycle.

Some queens rose to mate as frequently as every five or six thousand years, though most mated far less frequently. Sik was a "breeder", as Adira had dubbed queens with short breeding cycles, and in fact, Oryd was one of her last clutch. Adira herself had only risen for one mating flight in her long lifespan. Disappointingly, it had not resulted in a mate-bond, though she'd gained nearly a thousand strong young sons to fill her ranks. Many of the blue Lacings she saw in the courtyard were offspring from that flight. The legendary First General Mar had sired them, and she still mourned his loss, as well as their failure to bond. As first generation offspring, her sons would not join her mating flight. Though they could not help but be aware of her growing readiness to fly, as part of the species' resistance to inbreeding her sons were immune to any mating pheromones she might produce, an intoxicating concoction of scent and chemicals that would drive the rest of her colony mad.

In spite of their inability to participate in a mating flight while part of her colony, her sons would remain with her forever, or until they were enthralled by a rival queen, if she was able to attract them during a mating flight. Such a move was risky, for each queen guarded her territory fiercely and saw the theft of First Sons as a tremendous insult, so Adira had little fear that Sik would actually attempt what Oryd suggested. Unable to enthrall her own sons, they remained solely because of the social structure dragons instinctively formed, and here they would remain unless she was foolish or unwary enough to allow them to fly border patrols when Sik tested her boundaries.

She felt pride in her children, even as she wondered if they preferred freedom to find a mate of their own. Did they think such things, she wondered, or was she alone in that regard, as she was in so many others.

No, she decided. Her sons seemed to accept their fate, as all male dragons did. It was imprinted in their genetic code that they would remain with their mother's colony unless a rival queen rose in a mating flight and was close enough to affect them with her pheromones. Once enthralled by a breeding queen, a dragon would remain with her until death. On the rare occasion when a queen succumbed to the *darkening,* her colony would fall into disarray and eventually bond with a new queen. Her territory would remain unclaimed until a new colony bond was formed. A male might also serve a new queen on the rare occasions when a newly born daughter was powerful enough to challenge and defeat her mother, or more commonly, when an older queen returned from the banishment imposed on her at birth. If the ruling queen was killed in battle, her colony would form a temporary bond with the victorious queen, which could only become a permanent bond after a mating flight. Until that time, they were known as Second Mates, or more simply as seconds, and were vulnerable to poaching during another queen's mating flight. That was just one of the many reasons challenges between queens were so carefully timed around mating flights – it wouldn't do to win a new territory and promptly lose the entire colony to another queen.

Fortunately for Adira, her second mating flight from several millennia ago had finally secured a permanent bond with all the seconds in her colony, which left only the loss of First Sons to concern herself with. Sik frequently flew Adira's borders in search of unbonded males during her mating cycle, so First Sons were kept from border patrols at the first sign of such activity. It was a common tactic, but there were other ways to discourage poaching. Due to the finality of dragon disputes, queens frequently avoided direct contact with each other, so if an impending mating flight was suspected, neighboring queens sometimes flew patrols with their soldiers, forcing their rival to risk a direct conflict or raid another territory. Another tactic was to reside in the most central portion of each territory. Adira's territory was massive, which made it easy for her to stay well out of others' range, but Sik was not so fortunate.

Oryd took his frustration out on the sky above her as Adira considered her options. Perhaps her First General was right and it was time to teach Sik another lesson. A unexpected flight along her southern borders at her current pheromone levels could bring a massive influx of males, increasing her choices for an actual mating flight and decimating Sik's ranks. The blatant daylight theft would be a huge insult, which of course was an added bonus. Even though her actual mating cycle wouldn't peak for months, or even years based on her previous flight, she would easily attract several thousand males, certainly any within leagues of the border. Sik had many sons – she could afford to lose a few thousand.

It doesn't hurt that so many of them take after Mar, she thought, feeling another unusual pang for things lost. First General Mar was long gone, though Oryd and so many of Sik's sons had much the same look, with their deep blue scales and broad Laces, long curved horns and heavily muscled bodies. *Sik makes handsome sons, I'll give her that at least.*

Decided, Adira launched skyward into the driving rain in a flash of gold and quicksilver Chrym. A few of her higher ranking would-be suitors immediately took wing behind her, but she made it clear in no uncertain terms that she had no wish to be accompanied.

Let's see how Oryd handles some competition, she thought grimly as she winged her way south, keeping low on the horizon in case he looked back and thought to join her. An influx of new dragons to sort out and rank would do nicely to keep him occupied and give her some breathing room, and if a handsome young dragon caught her eye, so much the better for it.

CHAPTER 5

"How dare she!" The scream reverberated through the massive chamber where Sik held court. Slaves flinched and Telek clamped his ears closed in a vain attempt to block the sound of her rage. Fortunately, his queen seemed in no need of a response as she stormed across the receiving chamber. She was a glorious sight as she glowed with outrage and heat, both *parra* and Laces fully engaged. It would soon be too hot for the Xarans to remain in her presence, and he watched with narrowed eyes as they scurried toward tiny, human-sized passages, momentarily distracted from his lustful thoughts.

Smart of the filthy little beasts to avoid the main passageways, he thought dispassionately. Most of the dragons in Telek's command paid no attention to the humans other than to command their service, but the First General remained vigilant. It was easy to overlook these wingless abominations, but sometimes, like now, he was reminded that these uneducated animals possessed a cunning that had once nearly wiped his kind from existence. Born so long ago he remembered mountain ranges where dry riverbeds now languished, Telek was old enough to believe the stories he'd heard as a hatchling. The younger dragons believed them to be no more than the dragons' version of the boogeyman, but then the youngest among them doubted the history of the failed rebellion that Telek and Sik had both lived through. Telek had more faith in the history of his ancestors than most. It tempered his contempt for the humans with a healthy dose of caution, an uncomfortable combination for any dragon, and he frequently encouraged Sik's cruelty towards their slaves. It kept them in line, too worn out and afraid to plan a new rebellion.

"That hideous bitch," Sik continued, pulling him out of reflection.

41

"She took some of my very first sons!"

A terrible sound emanated from the queen's breastplate, and Telek wondered if dragons could moan. He kept his thoughts to himself, his Lacing so tightly controlled that he was nearly a shadow in the great room.

"Something must be done. Something *will* be done," she vowed. Telek was fascinated by the options she considered and discarded, and wondered not for the first time at how openly Sik displayed her inner thoughts. Sik had always been more volatile than most, but until recently, she had not cared to share so much with him. He hoped her sudden lack of inhibition was due to an upcoming breeding cycle, and not something less pleasant. Perhaps the oldest queen in existence, Sik was the fifth queen he had served, and he did not wish to suffer such a loss again. Telek watched as she continued to fantasize and abandon one scenario after another.

If it comes to it, he thought, *I'll find a way to die with my queen.*

Resolved to end his existence with Sik, he determined to keep a close eye on her behavior. If the *darkening* had truly begun, she could deteriorate over several decades or be gone within months. One way or another, he would see to it that he went with her.

CHAPTER 6

Aja repositioned the weight of his heavy load, anxious to get home. The rainy season continued, and they had sacrificed their oil lined canvasses to build a sled of sorts that Merot pulled behind him. Half of the chickens and grain were perched precariously on top, the grain wrapped in Merot's poncho to keep it dry. Aja carried the young peach tree on his back, an unwieldy burden that seemed determined to poke holes in him at every turn. Wrapped in canvas and soaking wet, it seemed to Aja as though the large root ball were deliberately trying to pull him backward, forcing him to lean farther forward with every hour. The past two days had been a never-ending battle, the roots reaching for the ground as Aja strained to hold the sapling up to the sky in an effort to retain ownership. With every step, the small tree seemed to gain weight, mocking his efforts. Merot fared little better for, in addition to his own pack and the sled he pulled, he held the leash of a small grey and pink spotted sow, who was none too pleased to be dragged along through the muck. It was not the mud so much which displeased her, Aja thought, as Merot's refusal to allow her to wallow.

They were nearing the end of their second day of travel and Behar was exhausted. Aja met Merot's eyes and made a tiny gesture. His father nodded, and without a word, the two men turned off the main road to seek a camping spot. Behar followed silently, collapsing into her bed as soon as it was set up.

"We can't keep going at this pace," Aja murmured, watching his mother struggle to find a comfortable position among her blankets. At least the rain had lessened to its typical nighttime mist. They had kept Behar's poncho aside so that she would have protection as she slept, and both men settled down against some nearby rocks, neither bothering with

43

their sodden sleeping blankets. They would take turns keeping watch, as they had the night before. With livestock and grain to manage on the return trip, they had sudden wealth to protect or lose.

"Perhaps I should go on ahead tomorrow with the sled," Aja suggested. "I can start the reed gathering and have the first barrels prepared before you arrive."

Merot scowled. "I don't like us separating. Not with you so young and with such a burden to carry. There are far too many along the way who would seek to lighten your load, Aja."

"I'm a man now," he claimed with more confidence than he felt. He subtly flexed his forearm, drawing Merot's attention to the stained badge he'd earned just days ago in the temple, proof of his new status. "Let me prove it."

The silence stretched out and he knew his father would say no.

"Then what do we return?" He asked the question without heat, matching his father's earnest gaze as long as he could before looking away with an uncomfortable shrug. His mother listened from her bed, and her strained face compelled him to continue after a long silence from Merot.

"We need to get started or all of this will be for nothing," he insisted quietly, certain his plan to go ahead was their best course of action.

"Aja's right, Merot."

His father pursed his lips when Behar joined the conversation, and Aja could see his resolve begin to crumble.

"I'll be careful, I'll keep moving when I reach each village, and I'll make sure I move from the road whenever I take a break." He spoke quickly, then held his breath as he waited for his father's response.

His words, along with Behar's obvious approval swayed Merot at last, and his father nodded reluctantly. "All right. You'll take first watch so you're more rested in the morning. At first light, you head out with the chickens and grain."

Aja started to protest, but Merot cut him off.

"I can strap the tree to the sow, which we should have done from the beginning. Then it's just a matter of convincing her to keep moving along. We'll make slow progress, but progress it will be."

A reluctant laugh passed Aja's lips.

"Fools, the lot of us, for not thinking of it sooner." This from Behar, and Aja was forced to agree.

His father shrugged. "Better late than never," and Aja was forced to agree again.

At first light, or more accurately, at first downpour, Aja rose on aching feet and pulled the sled's makeshift harness over his head. One chicken made a baleful noise, then tucked her head back down, hiding from the misery of the day as best she could. Aja wished briefly that he could do the same as he settled himself grimly to the task at hand.

"Be safe," came a soft plea from his mother and he flashed a brief smile in her direction, white teeth gleaming in the semi-darkness. Merot gripped his hand, squeezing tightly before letting go, and Aja knew he hadn't slept at all through the night, imagining the worst for his newly independent son.

Aja set off without a backward glance, slogging carefully through the mud. As soon as he was out of view, he picked up his pace as much as he dared in the treacherous footing, finding that the sled moved much more fluidly through the muck if he stayed at a slow but steady trot. By mid-morning, he was steaming from his exertions and forgot to check his surroundings before taking a break. Luck was with him though, and after a meal he barely tasted, he pushed himself to continue.

Anxious to prove himself the man his father expected him to be, he made record time, passing the next to last village before his own just before nightfall. The darkness made it impossible to safely continue, and Aja settled down to another uncomfortable night's rest. He worried about his mother and father on the trail behind him, but knew with unswerving certainty that he would be most helpful to his family by leaving them behind and completing the simple but exhausting work of gathering reeds before his father arrived to help with the tasks that required more skill. He slept lightly that night, his first night alone, and woke at every rustling feather, certain that thieves had found his resting place, but luck continued to favor him, and he awoke to pouring rain once again with all the chickens and grain still in his care.

He was home before mid-morning, legs and back burning with the effort. He took no time for himself, only making sure the chickens and grain were safely tucked away under the shelter of the porch before grabbing a scythe and heading to the river. He'd sensed the Chrym there last night, but had half convinced himself he was imagining it. In the morning, as he moved closer, he'd known the feeling was real. Chrym had become a tantalizing presence in his life, and he felt a frightening compulsion, even after seeing what the priests were capable of, to Call the Chrym up, to touch and shape it.

Forcing himself to focus on the job before him, Aja took a deep breath and stepped ankle-deep into the rushing water. He gathered as many reeds as he could manage, pulling them tightly together. Ignoring the pain in his forearm, he neatly severed the reeds, twisted to place his bundle on the sled and repeated the process. Twist, gather, cut, twist, gather, cut. The world receded as Aja cut reeds until he wasn't sure he'd ever stand straight again. He piled as many reed bundles as he could before making the trip back to the house. Four trips later, he had all the barrels filled to the brim, nearly two-thirds of the reeds within reach of the river shallows were cut, and it was nightfall again. There was no sign of his parents, and Aja belatedly wondered if he should have retrieved Qal from the neighbor's when he arrived home. No, he decided. It was too dangerous to leave Qal unattended by the river as he worked, and he could only imagine the trouble his little brother could have created home alone. Too tired to bathe or eat, Aja stood in the rain and let it wash him clean of mud before stumbling to his bed.

In the morning he walked to Talima's house to retrieve Qal.

"Hey little bird," he called as he stepped into the covered porch of his neighbor's home.

"Aja!" His brother exploded through the front door and hit him so hard he was knocked back a step into the pouring rain.

"Oomph! Not so little anymore," Aja teased. "You gained a few pounds, no doubt eating all Talima's cookies when she wasn't looking."

Talima supplemented her family's income by baking cookies for Mir. It was a secret family recipe she refused to share, and everyone loved them more than anything Mir could offer. Eventually the baker had given up and made Talima an offer – provide Mir with her specialty cookies for market days, and he would give her enough fresh bread every week to feed her growing family. It was a trade that seemed to work well for them, though Aja worried that Qal had indeed eaten all of this week's cookies.

"Nah, the girls weren't feeling good, so Qal ate their share of bread at every meal," Talima laughed.

His little brother had the grace to look shamefaced before joy over Aja's homecoming resurfaced. "I knew you'd come back," he shouted as he danced around Aja, spinning circles until Talima reached out to stop him.

"You're making me dizzy just watching you, Qal."

"Sorry Tally." Qal grinned without an ounce of remorse in his expression.

"Mmm hmm," Talima observed his antics with her arms folded over her chest. "Go get your things. Your brother's a young man now, and I'm sure he has more important things to do than stand around and watch you fall all over yourself."

For the first time since he arrived that morning, Talima looked directly at Aja, expressing a warmth and relief that surprised him. "We're all glad you're back, Aja. The girls would be here hanging off you if they felt up to it."

Aja smiled wryly and held out his still bandaged forearm. "Probably just as well they aren't."

Talima's eyes slid over the bandage and she rubbed absent-mindedly at the bracelet of old scars on her own arm. "I'm sure you're right. Still, we're glad just the same."

As Qal passed her with his bedroll, Talima asked them to wait a moment longer, returning with a small wrapped package. At Aja's inquiring glance she shrugged uncomfortably.

"It's just this week's leftovers."

When he would have protested, she raised a hand to quiet him. "I'm sure there's not much in your house right now, what with you and your parents being gone so long. And before you think I'm being too kind, I should warn you it's gone hard as a rock, so you'll want to soak it in some goat's milk before you break a tooth trying to chew it."

She reached out her hand to take his, and Aja paused. It was the first time an adult outside his own family had offered to shake his hand as an equal. He took a moment to absorb the feeling before meeting Talima's gaze and firmly grasping her hand.

"Thanks for watching Qal, Tally. We'll be back with something for your troubles."

She smiled and nodded. "No worries, Aja. That's what neighbors are for."

When Aja and Qal returned home, his little brother could barely contain himself over the chickens.

"What're their names, Aja? Are they all girls? Do we get to keep them all?" The questions rolled so quickly Aja had no chance to answer.

"I'm gonna call this one Pinky Teapot, and this one Spike! This one looks like Chomper, this one is Dusty Derval, this one is Fuffle and this one is Plucky."

"You'd better rethink that last one, or Mother might think you mean her for the dinner pot."

"No! I'll run away with them first," Qal burst out, already fierce in defense of his new pets.

"It may not be up to her," Aja warned. "We've got some work to do if we're going to earn them, little bird."

"What? I'll do anything," Qal rashly promised.

"See those barrels over there? We're going to fill them with reeds from the river."

"All of them?"

"Every single one. If we can do it before Mother and Father return, they might let you name the ducks, too."

Qal lit up like the horizon at morning, and grabbed his small sled where it rested against the house, dragging the large sled Aja had used the day before as best he could. "Let's go!"

The men from the village had already cleared most of the reeds within easy reach, so Aja and Qal had to travel further along the riverbed to find a good harvest. Aja bent quickly to his work, and Qal impressed him with his determination to keep up, grabbing handfuls of cut reeds as Aja passed them along and piling them up on the sleds. They quickly established a routine, with Qal dragging his sled back to the house as soon as it was loaded while Aja continued to cut until his sled was full, and it didn't take long before every rain barrel was packed with reeds. Each sled was piled high from their last trip before the two brothers stopped for lunch. Poor little Qal was so tired he could barely keep his eyes open at the table.

"Take a break, Qal. I'll start weaving reeds while you nap."

"No! I want to help!"

Aja guessed Qal feared losing one or more of his precious birds, and quickly reassured him. "I promise, you've done enough already. More than enough," he added. "Mother and Father will be so impressed with you."

"Well maybe a short nap," Qal agreed, "but then I'm helping to weave reeds."

Aja silently hoped his little brother would sleep through the afternoon – weaving was tedious and painful, and he wasn't sure how much help Qal would be.

Merot and Behar returned home at nightfall the next day to find Aja and Qal silently weaving reeds. Though Qal had whined at first over the sting of the reeds, Aja had been impressed by his baby brother's determination once he'd explained the bargain their father had made and what it could mean for their family. Qal had already named each and every animal and was not going to give up his pets without a fight.

"You've done well, boys," his father approved, and Qal swelled with pride.

"Mamma!" Qal's little face lit up as he spotted Behar. Though she winced with pain, Behar returned his embrace, stroking his dark wavy hair.

"Oh how I missed you, little one," she said, and Qal turned his face into her skirts.

"I missed you too, Mamma," came his muffled voice. "Talima don't make my favorite breakfast like you."

"Doesn't," corrected Behar, with a smile and a final tousle of his hair. "Come along now, I have a special treat for you."

"You do?" Qal looked wonderingly at his parents, and then at Aja, who shrugged in feigned bewilderment.

"News to me, little bird. Don't know why they'd bring you a present, when all you do is eat and make a mess."

Qal made a face and stuck out his tongue, and Aja dramatically grabbed at his chest, feigning a mortal wound. Gifts were opened, and Aja was surprised to find that his mother had carried something home for him as well. Somehow she had found the time to slip away and purchase a tiny wooden koteeri. It was not made of Chrym as his had been, but the rare farfi wood was a perfect match for the koteeri's pale golden coat. He gaped in awe at the delicate carving, tracing the fine grains that mimicked the cat's striking markings.

"It's beautiful, Mother."

Behar exhaled the breath she'd been holding.

"Good. I know it can't compare – "

Aja cut her off with a gentle hug. "It's the best gift ever," he promised.

Qal opened a pouch filled with glass marbles, and another filled with fat round, brightly colored sticks. The marbles brought a shout of glee, the sticks a puzzled look. Aja grinned and pulled one from the bag.

"Look," he said, walking over to the stone floor of the patio. Bending over, he pressed the stick against the smooth dry surface and began to draw. It was all the demonstration Qal needed, and hours later Behar had to cajole and eventually threaten him with the permanent loss of his coloring sticks to get them out of his hands and cleaned up for bed.

The rains continued for an unprecedented two more weeks, and Aja and his father made several more trips to the river for reeds, keeping them far too busy to worry overly much about the sudden dragon activity spotted along the border. In the end, they gathered and wove enough reeds to form all the beds that had been ordered, plus four more. As the clouds cleared, the sun gods Pil and Hadra did their part to dry the large pieces, and Merot was able to test each leaf to ensure it fit properly against its mate while Aja finished attaching the last of the folding legs. The road had dried considerably, with only a few treacherous spots along the way, and Aja and Merot made excellent time returning to the city. They each dragged a canvas sled with their belongings, having learned from their recent experience.

Kervan and the others were all waiting solemnly at the very edge of the temple courtyard, and the exchange was made quickly and quietly in the shadow of that malicious presence. From there Aja and Merot made their way to the city market. Though Aja worked hard to appear unaffected, he found the market overwhelming, a massive, boisterous affair for which their own small market had ill-prepared him. Merot displayed the remaining beds to several disinterested vendors before finding a broad-faced woman with a great many knives on display who was willing to barter for them. After much haggling, they agreed to three of the four beds in exchange for two new scythes, a whetting stone, a flint, and a thin gold bracelet, made of three woven threads with a yellow topaz trapped within a wide opening in the weave.

"It's not worth much around here," the shopkeeper said dismissively, and Aja blinked in surprise.

"Three strands and the topaz," said the vendor next to her, noting his surprise. "That's for Adira, the three-tailed devil who swallowed Halon and consigned us to the rains."

He quickly genuflected in atonement for his sacrilege, his head almost touching the ground as Aja frowned. He had, of course, heard of Adira – no child grew up without being taught the history of the great Pil and Hadra, who had lost their wayward child Halon to the fierce appetite of the Golden Empress. The story went that Halon had always been a stubborn, rebellious child who refused to stay safely with his parents. One day as he trailed far behind, the unwary god-child was overcome by the voracious Adira. Since that time, Pil and Hadra wept great tears on the anniversary of his passing and punished Adira with their chilly absence. Nowhere in the stories was there a word of Adira having three tails. Aja traced the strands of gold, his touch so light he barely felt the metal beneath his finger pads. The topaz sparked in the sunlight but he felt strangely cold.

"It's all nonsense of course," proclaimed the first vendor, drawing a gasp of protest from her counterpart.

"Cela, how can you say that?"

"Oh Filat, you'd better let your shirts out if you can't relax. One day you're going to puff right up and pop a few buttons off. You know the Empress doesn't have three tails," Cela responded scornfully.

Aja hid his amusement. The entire story was ridiculous, but Cela took offense to Filat's claim that Adira had three tails? The ensuing squabble made it clear that the two had a long-standing debate running, which ended when the chubby Filat turned his back in a huff, refusing to engage further with the "heathen" next door.

"Where might we find another generous vendor such as you who would be interested in this final bed?" Merot gazed solemnly at Cela as she smiled after her departing neighbor.

"I do love to get the old goat's goat, you know," she confided with a chortle. "Another vendor, you say? Hmmm, I suspect Gazial or Ditro would be interested in your merchandise. They're both on the southern side of the great fountain." She waved vaguely and shooed them away to make room for paying customers.

Aja barely contained his surprise at her offhand comment about merchandise. *Who would have thought my father would become a businessman with actual merchandise to trade or sell*, he wondered with pride. As they moved away, Aja heard Filat muttering angrily.

"One day you'll go too far in your sacrilege, Cela, and someone will use one of your own knives to silence that wicked tongue."

Cela hefted one of those knives threateningly at Filat, and they quickened their pace in order to leave the feuding pair behind. In the center of the market, Merot sold their last piece to Ditro, a giant of a man who clearly had feelings for Cela, asking after her before offering a large quantity of fragrant herbs, some dried and some live, as well as several small barrels of dried petals in exchange for the bed. It was an excellent deal, and Aja wondered if Ditro's generosity wasn't in part for any news they might provide of the lovely widow.

"Your mother will have the house smelling of flowers for days," Merot warned Aja, grinning from ear to ear, and Ditro laughed.

"A small bit of oil added to the distilling process will make for more potent perfume," he suggested slyly. "More product for the product, so to speak."

Merot considered, and in the end traded back some of the larger potted herbs for two vials of oil, and a few of the smallest live herbs.

Even with the potted plants, their load was far lighter this time, and with dry roads, they easily made the trip in three days. Behar exclaimed over the herbs and flower petals, and when Merot showed her the bracelet, she grew teary-eyed with emotion. Aja looked to his father with alarm, but Merot simply smiled and folded Behar in his arms.

"I love you," one murmured.

"To the great suns and back," the other replied.

This was a daily confirmation of their bond, and Aja rolled his eyes, though it secretly pleased him to see such open devotion between his parents.

He went to bed that night brimming with anticipation and a full belly, thanks to their new livestock. The rainy season had ended, his mother had put up all the fruits and seeds they could gather between weaving, and though there was still the perfume to make, his mother preferred to handle that delicate task on her own. That left Aja with most of his days free for a while, which usually meant fishing or hunting for flitter eggs, but not tomorrow. He toyed with the Chrym by the riverbed, his reach expanding with ease. He could now feel the vein of metal beyond the small pocket his mother had created, reaching deeply below the surface, and he idly stirred the metal, the feeling not unlike running his fingers through water, which was quite strange, considering his fingers were firmly clasped upon his chest. The Chrym sang a welcoming song, and Aja knew that tomorrow, come what may, he was ready to take his first Swim.

CHAPTER 7

I swiveled my hips, twisting and turning in time to the raucous music blasting away in the kitchen. The artist was belting out a truly horrible holiday song that always made me think of my mother. Though the singer had a spectacular voice, as a child I'd gritted my teeth through this particular piece, a fact my mom seemed to take a perverse pleasure in. Now I smiled in fond remembrance, and yodeled away with the music, cheerfully off tune and not caring a bit when Mike entered the kitchen, rubbing an ear as he stared at me.

"I can hear dogs howling through the neighborhood," he complained with an overblown wince.

I promptly turned up the volume and wailed off tune, going for loud and obnoxious over finesse any day.

He charged me and I folded over his shoulder, a perfect fit as he spun me around and around until I was too dizzy and out of breath to continue my torture. When he put me down, I leaned forward and up to meet his lips. I love kissing this man, *I thought.* I love everything with this man.

He pulled slightly away. "I really can hear dogs howling," he said with a slight frown. "Wait, is that Maggie?"

I cocked my head in confusion. Why was Mike worried about Maggie? Maggie didn't belong in this moment – she hadn't even been born yet.

"Jenna, you need to get Maggie, she's crying." There was an urgency in Mike's voice now that frightened me, and just like that, I was on a blanket that was expanding, stretching further and further away. Mike and Maggie were out of reach, and the sun passed behind clouds.

"It's not supposed to storm today."

53

And then I was falling, falling and screaming, screaming and falling. I was dying again.

Adira woke to the echoes of a shriek.

"Empress!" Oryd's voice boomed through her bedchamber, and the servants cowered.

Adira was standing on all fours, spikes raised, wings spread and tail lashing as her neck snaked rapidly back and forth, searching for an unseen enemy. Her Laces formed a dizzying kaleidoscope of colors that strobed under her beating wings.

"I'm fine," Adira snarled, though she felt far from fine. Every night this week her sleep had been disrupted, and each time Adira had awakened, it had been to that most hated and despised emotion – fear. There was never any cause for her alarm, and Adira was beginning to suspect that one of the servants was causing her unrest. Why or how that could be she was uncertain, but she was nearing the point where they should be banned for their own safety, and if it would give her a good night's rest, she was prepared to do just that.

"Leave me." The command was sharper than she'd intended and the servants blanched and fled the room. She held back a sigh and turned to Oryd, who had used her distraction to step farther into the room. Her eyes blazed brighter with irritation – there was clearly no need for his presence, why would he think to trespass?

"Did you think I meant only them?" This time she meant to be sharp and followed the question with an equally sharp smile. Oryd flinched and stepped back, though not before his glance fell upon her rapidly cooling cocoon of gold. The longing in his eyes irritated her.

"Ever looking for what isn't there, Oryd. Even Mar didn't share my chambers with me. Do you think to step above one such as him?" She was deliberately hurtful, but Oryd drew himself up stiffly and answered with rare directness.

"I am no more or less than any First General before me, Adira. I have no doubts that we have all desired the same thing from you. The mating bond is our greatest hope, and it can occur only with you. That makes *you* our greatest hope. I have seen you grieve for a failed bond with Mar, so I know you wish for it, or at least you did once."

She had the grace to acknowledge his point with a gentle Lace of color and light.

"Why should I not also wish for the bond, a partner with whom to honor and share the skies? And I would honor you as no other, Golden One," he vowed with conviction. His eyes glowed with strong emotion, though he controlled his Lacing to a slow, steady pattern. Adira nodded curtly.

"I do not disparage hope, only warn that First Generals can expect no preferential treatment when the time comes."

It was the best she could do considering her ever-growing animosity towards Oryd. The young dragon had done nothing to earn her recent displeasure. She was well aware she could not afford a rift with her First General, not if a mating flight was truly in her future, and especially not with Sik hounding her borders. There was no question of his loyalty, but if left without hope or even the least little encouragement, Oryd's discontent could easily lead her ranks to disorder. She suddenly wondered how he would respond if her mating flight resulted in a mate-bond with another dragon. *If that happens, I might have to kill him.* She realized the thought caused more discomfort than she expected, and resolved to start anew with the young male tomorrow.

"I wish to fly the southern borders in the morning with my First General." It was both offer and order, couched in a dismissal, and Oryd took it as such.

"It is always my pleasure to serve you." He backed gracefully from the room, no stranger to tactical retreats, though his next words nearly ruined her current reconciliatory mood.

"I have been anxious to show you the strength of our borders and offer suggestions as to how we might stifle Sik's aggression," he added as he bowed from the doorway of her chamber.

"We," she snorted. "There's no we when it comes to fighting Sik."

Unbonded males did not fight queens for any reason, not even to save their own queen from death. If Oryd genuinely desired Sik's current passive-aggressive behavior to escalate into something more open, any direct checks to Sik would have to come from Adira.

"Still," he responded in measured tones, "there are many ways we could make it more difficult for her to continue her recent behavior. I have some new ideas for your approval, in the morning, of course."

Of that, she had no doubt as he left her to her solitude. Oryd was a gifted strategist and had been instrumental in designing a new flight pattern that addressed a few glaring flaws in their border patrols. Mar had been beautiful and compelling, and other than the Empress herself, none could have bested him in flight, but even Adira had to admit that Oryd was thermals above her former lover when it came to military strategy. Petra, Oryd's immediate predecessor, had been a disaster at strategizing, defeating the First General before him through brute strength alone, so she would have had no complaints with Oryd's performance in that regard, even if he'd only been half decent. But her current First General was exceptional in all regards. For Hadra's sake, it had been a mere three weeks ago that she had flown south and lured a few thousand of Sik's offspring to her own colony, and already Oryd had them well under control, though many of them were potentially a thousand times his senior. Perhaps that had more to do with Sik's own discipline of her dragons than Oryd, but Adira rather suspected it was all Oryd's doing. She simply could not find a flaw in his performance as First General.

I wonder if that's the problem, she mused. *Even Mar had his faults, and I loved him for them, as much as I could.*

Did she resent his latest replacement? Perhaps if Mar had been as perfect as Oryd, they might have formed the coveted mate-bond those long years ago. She sighed, glaring at her cooled bed. The cold season in the south was ending, but her more northern territory had a few more weeks of chilly rains in their future. She hated the dampness that pervaded everything and felt as though it was trying to smother her with cold clammy fingers.

Well, there was a way to take care of that, she resolved, even if it wouldn't last. Closing her eyes, she took several deep breaths into her lungs. In. Out. In. Out. With each inhalation, she took more air, expanding her diaphragm as she stoked the great furnace that smoldered within every living dragon. Her head tipped back and her mouth opened slightly as the warmth from her core began to spread, her *parra* vibrating rapidly to accommodate her call for more heat. The joining of wings and body began to glow with a white hot heat, which rapidly spread through the membranes of her wings, reaching the very tips, and still she wasn't done. She breathed in again, an exhalation so deep she felt it to her curled toes, the talons scraping and digging into the stone beneath her as if to hold her down as she expanded even more.

When she opened her eyes again, heat curled off every surface in lazy waves, and there wasn't an iota of pesky moisture anywhere. From the corridor beyond her chamber, she could see a wild light show of blue phosphorescence reflecting on the stone walls. Oryd had felt the intensity of her Flare and reacted instinctively. Dragons found the heat of their queens to be incredibly arousing which was a good thing, considering that mating flights often left a queen's chosen partner slightly singed. Even a dragon could be killed by a fire that burned hot enough, and Adira burned hotter than any dragon on the planet, even before absorbing Halon's energy.

She leaped a few feet into the air and slowed her descent with a gentle downdraft of her wings, landing softly in her bed. The gold was warm and liquid again, a luxurious caress that made her shiver with delight. The draft from her wings made the hot air around her swirl over her scales, and Adira nearly growled from the pleasure of all that heat. Oh yes, she was going to burn hot tonight, rid herself of this miserable chill and start tomorrow anew with her First General.

CHAPTER 8

Aja stared at the dust that coated his bare toes as he tried to steady his breathing. He was far upriver from the usual bathing spots, and well away from the shallow beds where the villagers gathered for laundry. Since coming home from the Choosing Ceremony he'd had his fair share of attention from several of the older girls which had brought about an unpleasant realization – he was now safe to consider as a suitor. It had never occurred to him, but with hindsight, it was blazingly obvious. Why waste time mooning over or courting a boy or girl who may be gone forever at their seventeenth year? Having passed the Ceremony and returned home, he was now a marriageable candidate, and where before he had come and gone without any notice, it seemed that every unmarried girl in the village was on his periphery, no matter where he went. He'd never before realized there were so many of them, and wondered if the Gift was more common among boys, for otherwise their village was uncommonly gifted with female offspring, almost all of whom seemed obsessed with his comings and goings.

It had required all his considerable skill, and a faked drowning by Qal, to slip away unnoticed. At last he was alone, a bundle of nerves and anticipation. He took another deep breath to steady the trembling in his limbs, and tipped his head back, eyes closed against the glare of the suns.

"Concentrate," he said fiercely. "The Chrym is your friend."

He recalled the koteeri he'd formed just weeks ago and felt the Chrym beneath him respond. It seemed aware of his presence, and almost eager to see him. The metal's vaguely sentient nature panicked him, and he pulled back, not ready to commit yet.

"Picture your destination," he reminded himself. Without any guidelines to follow, he thought it best to try a short Swim first and to

58

know beforehand where he wanted to end up. He had not forgotten his mother's tale about her sister, Nera. Unlike his aunt, he was not desperate, nor willing to die. In fact, he would consider the entire experiment a complete success if he merely survived.

"I'm just hoping to survive intact," he muttered, then blanched as he pictured returning home to Behar minus an appendage or two. He hoped that particular outcome was just a wild imagining, and wished for just a moment that he was not alone out here on the edge of wilderness, about to Swim for the first time.

"Picture your destination. Picture your destination." It was his mantra, a shaky chant he panted as he clasped rough hands around his bare elbows. Aja had stripped down for the attempt, unsure whether the Chrym would carry anything beyond his person. It wouldn't do to have to explain to his mother how he had lost his clothes. Although their sudden influx of wealth had allowed them the luxury of new garments, Behar would not welcome such waste, so Aja had carefully removed and folded his new shirt and trousers, placing his shoes facing soles up upon the clean, plain fabric. His garments were now tucked safely away from the river bed, and Aja stood partially crouched, hidden among the dried and dying reeds that stubbled the receding river's edge in order to shield his nudity from any unlikely passersby.

Another shaky breath and it was time. Aja imagined the Chrym as another river, flowing just below the one that stretched in front of him. He Dove, and much to his astonishment, the Chrym parted like water to receive him, flowing in the direction he wished to travel. Aja panicked briefly at one point, wondering how he would breathe, but once he thought about it, there was no burning in his lungs, warning him of a need for air. It seemed as though his Chrym Swimming abilities precluded the need to surface – a useful skill, he acknowledged. He kicked hard to accelerate forward and caught a glimpse of his hands, fingers cupped to pull him through the vein. He ceased his efforts and lay, buoyed by the Chrym around him as he stared in wonder. His hands, his entire body in fact, were no longer the sun-warmed brown he was so familiar with. He had merged so completely with the Chrym that he had become Chrym. There was another panicked moment as he tried to reconcile his oneness with the Chrym, and his fear of losing himself, but he was reassured by the very fact that he seemed to be controlling his environment, and while he was very much a part of the vein, his own edges, his Self, as it were, was clearly defined. That realization helped him to stay calm, along with the reminder that Swimming was a known talent, documented in secret Church writings. Obviously others had successfully merged with, and more importantly, had successfully unmerged with the Chrym. He would do the same.

Aja continued on through the vein, picturing his destination as the Chrym moved him along. He had not gone very far when he felt a tingle through his body, as though the metal were aware of his goal and set off a thousand tiny bells, reverberating in a clear signal: Surface. He felt a rush of adrenaline as he wondered exactly how he was supposed to surface, but once again the Chrym seemed to know exactly what he needed and surged upward, forcing a way back to the surface of the planet for him to follow, and in the next moment, he was standing ankle deep in water, blinded once again by Pil and Hadra.

There was a shriek and a splash, and Aja quickly cupped himself. Though still partially blinded by the suns' bright glare upon the water, he recognized a feminine shriek of surprise and outrage when he heard one.

"Sorry," he called, looking frantically about for cover. Once he was safely behind some river scrub, and his eyesight had returned to normal, he looked up and realized the extent of his error. He had surfaced exactly where he'd planned, nearly two miles north of their village, on the border of Queen Sik and Empress Adira's territories. It should have been a safe place, given that Adira's nearest village would also be a minimum of two miles from the border. Unfortunately, it appeared as though he was not the only one to have had that thought.

Awkwardly submerged in water up to his grey stubbled neck, the local baker was treading water with precarious dignity. Trying desperately to hide behind him was the miller's wife. Aja's eyes widened in dismay.

Mir decided to bluff his way out of their situation.

"What are you doing here? The borders are forbidden!"

Aja bit back the retort that formed and cast about for an excuse.

"Yes sir, but we lost a pair of our ducks, and I was sent to find them."

"Without your clothes?"

Aja flushed, unable to think of a quick response.

The miller's wife laughed suddenly.

"He's probably here to meet a girl, Mir."

That statement brought a new sharpness to the baker's expression.

"Is that true, Aja?"

Aja nodded his head and mumbled a bit of nonsense under his breath, striving to look guilty.

"I can't say I approve, but I'll say nothing to your parents if you keep quiet about what you saw here today," Mir finished.

Aja looked up with relief. "Yes, sir. I understand."

Although he was now considered an adult and thus safe from

parental discipline, Aja didn't relish facing their dismay if they learned he was meeting a girl in secret. He still lived under their roof and was expected to follow proper behavior with the young women of the village. Naked, unchaperoned cavorting was definitely off limits, and it wasn't as though he could admit the truth. He felt guilty enough practicing his Gift in secret – he could just imagine their response if he was found out.

Aja backed away towards deeper brush, and as soon as he was reasonably well covered, he ducked down, ostensibly to gather his clothes. As he made loud rustling noises to simulate his dressing, Ylfa's voice carried across the water to catch his attention.

"I swear he appeared out of thin air, Mir."

"Nonsense, Ylfa. Pil and Hadra's reflection off the water is near to blinding this time of day and we just didn't see him until it was too late."

"No, I'm telling you, I was looking right at that spot. One moment there was no one there, and the next moment, there he was."

"Ylfa, you're imagining things. The boy was just crouching down amongst the reeds until he could jump in."

The couple grew quiet, and Aja hoped that Mir had managed to convince his lover of a more reasonable explanation for his sudden appearance. He wished now that he knew whether his first Dive had made any noise, and paused there uncertainly, hesitant to submerge once again for fear of alarming Ylfa further. New sounds began to drift across the water to his ears, and he realized abruptly that the couple had moved on to their original purpose. Apparently, Mir had soothed Ylfa after all. Taking advantage of their distraction, he Dove once again, this time heading back toward the village.

He surfaced further north of his initial entrance, afraid of a repeat performance. His caution was well rewarded, for a few hundred yards downstream a group of girls had found his swimming hole and abandoned clothing. They were searching the area, full of mischievous laughter.

"Aja, you can't hide forever. I have your trousers."

"I have your shirt," another called, while his name echoed along the river bank.

Aja rubbed his nose and considered his options. While he would have been pleased to have caught a pretty girl's eye a few months or even weeks ago, he found it disconcerting to be at the center of attention of so many. He supposed there was nothing for it, and he would have to brazen his way out. He moved from his hiding place into the deeper, faster currents of the river, letting it carry him downstream towards the watering hole.

One of the girls called his name gaily as he came into view.

"Aja!" she smiled happily, and he saw one of his shoes dangling from her hand as she waved to the other girls.

"Wicked boy, to disrobe in mid-day in the open," one of the older girls said slyly, reaching for the hem of her own shirt.

"Tam!" gasped another in outraged disbelief while the first girl giggled nervously, still holding his shoe.

Tam paused with her shirt lifted, boldly displaying a smooth taut belly, with just a hint of her small, rounded breasts visible in the shadow of her raised hem. Aja swallowed and licked suddenly dry lips. *Sweet Hadra,* he thought, *she's actually going to do it!*

"What! He did it first," Tam said defiantly, pulling the shirt off with a scornful glare at the other girls. Once bare, she seemed to lose her confidence, brown hands covering her pretty, plump breasts as she bit her lip, considering her next move.

"Tam, what would your father say?"

At that, the girl's eyes hardened and her features set in mulish lines. It was no secret that Tam's father struggled with the recent loss of his wife, and the village gossips suspected he'd been beating his children. Whether it was true or not, it was the wrong thing to say at that moment. Suddenly brave again, Tam strode out into the river until she was hip deep. There, she crouched down to remove her skirt. Tossing it in a sodden heap on the bank, she looked at the other girls in clear challenge.

"Come and join us, or go home," she called defiantly. "And if anyone says anything to my father, they'll wish they hadn't."

Tam's friends gazed uncertainly between the two of them before drifting slowly from the water's edge. Teasing was one thing, but clearly they had lost their nerve at the idea of joining him in the water. All but Tam that is, who was now observing him closely, her head tilted slightly to one side, dark eyes bright against her smooth skin. Aja's own eyes were nearly a match for his mother's pale amber eyes, though right now they were squinted nearly closed against the suns' light. His heart beat as fast as a flitter's wings as he remained frozen in place.

Tam tossed her hair back over her shoulders, the long ends already wet and clinging. Several strands clung stubbornly to the bare skin just below her collarbone, and she smiled as she noted where his attention wandered. Aja couldn't tear his gaze away as she moved closer, and from just a few feet away, he could make out several droplets of water that clung to the upper slopes of her breasts, each dainty drop clearly outlined against her flesh. Her skin was paler there, and up close, he could make out the faint outline of several light blue veins that traced across her tender skin. He watched a bead of water slip from her body like a shooting star and followed its path into the river. Tam looked as soft as velvet as she smiled, but he was frozen in place, treading water as she watched him.

You're an idiot, he thought as she faced him expectantly. *Do something, or for Pil's sake, at least* say *something!*

Tam suddenly ducked under the water, resurfacing with slicked hair and face, lips glistening and parted. He could see small, even white teeth as she smiled again, but he was still frozen.

At least I haven't forgotten how to swim. He imagined what the town gossips would say.

"Did you hear about Aja? That poor boy, struck dumb by a pretty girl."

"Yes, I heard he was struck so dumb he forgot how to swim and drowned in the river."

"Oh no, I heard he wasn't too bright to begin with. After all, he never even got to kiss her for his troubles."

He stifled a snort of laughter - Tam wouldn't understand or appreciate his sudden humor.

"Aren't you going to kiss me, Aja?" She'd grown tired of waiting for him to make the first move.

His eyes darted to hers. It was likely Tam knew he'd never kissed a girl before – in a small village like theirs, it hardly seemed possible to keep secrets, though Mir and Ylfa had certainly been a surprise. Another unwelcome thought surfaced. An afternoon dalliance such as this could easily end with marriage vows. He liked Tam just fine, more than fine, judging by his reaction to her brazen disrobing, but seventeen was young to settle down.

As though she read his mind, Tam moved closer, and her legs brushed against his as they tread water just inches apart. "It's just a kiss, Aja, nothing more." She smiled coyly, but Aja could see a hint of uncertainty and hurt forming in her eyes, and that was all he needed to spur him to action.

He used his hands in a light skimming motion, barely enough to bring him forward the few inches now required, and made contact. A light, fleeting touch was all he allowed himself, but in that moment he was struck by several things. Her lips were every bit as soft as velvet, with a pleasing resilience that made him long to press harder against them, while the sweet scent of flowery soap she'd used on her hair felt intoxicating to his senses. He could now make out the darker outline of her nipples through the water, slightly engorged by cold or something else, and in that moment he suddenly recognized the scent of her shampoo as one of his mother's favorite recipes. Tam frowned as he pulled away.

"Wait," she murmured. "Don't you want to kiss me again?"

"I think that's the problem," Aja said as he propelled himself a few feet away from her tempting form. "I want to just a little too much."

Not giving either of them a chance to do more, he turned and made his way to shore with strong strokes. Once there, he had no option but to step naked from the water and retrieve each article of clothing from where the girls had left them. Deciding to brazen it out, he did just that, pretending that Tam wasn't still in the water, staring after him with longing in those large dark eyes, a smile still on her lips from his admission.

Neither of them noticed the young boy hidden in the reeds on the opposite side of the river, his eyes burning like coals as he stared at Tam. Two years younger than Aja, Rikor already had big plans of joining the priesthood and rising through the ranks to wealth and power. When he left this dusty pit behind, Tam was coming with him.

He had watched her disrobe and entice Aja with outrage burning a hole in his heart. He knew it was unfair to blame her; after all, Aja had just become a major catch, passing the Choosing Ceremony, with sudden wealth to boot. All the girls were interested. But not Tam – Tam was *his*, even if she didn't know it yet.

Rikor watched her swim around the waterhole for a while before coming back to shore. He took note of her long slender limbs, the dark shadow at the juncture of her thighs, and the pale, full globes of her breasts. His skin felt tight as he watched her dress, his breaths shallow as though he'd just run the whole way there. He was only fifteen, and by the laws of their people she was already a woman, but he wouldn't let that stop him. He recalled the look in her eyes as she gazed after Aja and knew he would never convince her to wait for him. More certain than ever that she was meant for him, he settled back to consider the problem, remaining hidden by the swimming hole as long as he could before his own father might notice his absence. As the afternoon shadows lengthened he hurried home to make sure his younger brothers had finished his chores while he was gone. If their father returned from the bakery and discovered his truancy, the punishment would be swift and severe. For a man who worked with dough for a living, Mir had fists of stone and no hesitation in applying them to his wife and children. The thought triggered an idea and he smiled at Tam's house as he passed. His was not the only household ruled by an angry man. All he had to do was make some information available to the right people and her father would see to it that Tam engaged in no more flirtations with Aja. If he was clever enough, and he was, she'd never know he was behind her punishment.

CHAPTER 9

Aja made several more Swims before his world changed again. Each time he submerged in the Chrym, it felt more familiar, more right, and each time he returned home, he felt the Chrym pulling, urging him to head north instead, as the metal sang a nearly irresistible song. There was something strong, something pure to the far north, something he needed to find. *Come find it, come see,* the Chrym implored.

Finally, he could resist the summons no more. He had experimented with numerous short Swims and now knew that he could successfully carry small objects with him on his travels, though he was deeply affected by his burdens. Lightweight material was easiest, as he had discovered that materials with greater density were lost in the Chrym, left behind during the Swim. For instance, clothes held up fairly well, but he had a tendency to lose shoes and now looped them around his neck with a piece of twine or went barefoot. After losing a second pair to the river, a necessary lie for his mother's sake, she had threatened to do just that.

On the morning he made his longest Swim, he wore a simple pair of trousers with a plain linen shirt. His shoes were tied together and looped over one shoulder, and he had a small pack which contained a few dried bars of seeds, grain, nuts, and honey. He'd found that the conversion to Chrym and back again left an odd taste to the food, but it remained edible, and if merging with the metal was possible without lasting side effects, a little residual Chrym in his food certainly couldn't hurt, he hoped. Swimming was a tremendous exertion, so much so that within an hour of returning home from his first trip, he'd stumbled to his bed before dinner, leaving his mother to worry about an impending summer fever. The next day he had been back to normal, perhaps a bit tired, but ready to try again. He figured that as with anything else, it took regular exercise to improve his new skill, and so he had practiced for several weeks leading up to this latest attempt, carefully gauging his growing strength.

In an effort to further strengthen his abilities, he arranged to have access to the vein closer to home. As he completed chores throughout each day, he continuously Called the Chrym in a whisper. He found this was easy, requiring little or no effort as long as he kept the pace slow and steady. It was no more than a gentle hum in the back of his mind, but after several weeks, he had managed to divert a small channel of the metal to a better hiding spot, one far less likely to be uncovered. It was close enough to be reached in minutes, but far and deep enough that Behar would not sense it unless she deliberately searched for it. After careful consideration, he'd chosen a small tree stand as his entryway, not far from the new chicken coop he had built with his father and Qal. He had also discovered that if he sent a small stream of Chrym to the surface ahead of him, he could get a vague sense of whether he was in an isolated area, a skill he wished he'd known about before his first Dive.

With a final quick glance over his shoulder, Aja Dove, moving swiftly into the main stream and pushing north immediately. The Chrym sang gleefully, *north, we go north*, and Aja was again struck by a sense that the Chrym was a living entity. It was extremely responsive to his will, often responding before he'd fully realized what he wanted, and Aja reassured himself that it was just a reflection of his own thoughts and desires he was picking up from the Chrym, as he kicked eagerly forward.

He had Swum far farther than he ever had before when he became aware of two very important facts. One, he was suddenly and completely exhausted; two, the Chrym vein narrowed immediately ahead and then split in a maze of tiny streams, none of which was a clear path forward. Aja attempted to surface, only to find his strength exhausted. His second and third attempt failed, and though he had no need to breathe, his lungs burned with panic. Holding his terror at bay, he centered himself and with a final desperate effort, forced a few flecks of Chrym to the planet's surface. He pictured the pale blue sky, imagined the heat of the suns on his skin, and pushed as hard as he could. There was a peculiar leaping sensation, and then he lay gasping on the hard, wet surface, feeling the chill of rain rapidly sink through his hair and clothes. He lay there until his breath no longer steamed, then longer still. He blinked up at the sky until his heart no longer raced and the trembling in his hands had ceased. *That was too close,* he thought, and yet the Chrym still called, *Come see, come see.*

Sobered by the alarming speed with which his strength had waned, he spent the better part of an hour resting, one eye constantly on the sky

for Adira or her soldiers as he consumed the first of the sweet honey bars
he'd brought for energy. He was far beyond the no-man's land between
territories, well into Adira's territory, and although he knew little of her
ways, one thing was certain; all dragons were best avoided, and that went
doubly so for any dragon that Sik feared. With tensions escalating
between the two queens, it wouldn't do for Aja to be caught in the open
during a skirmish. Adira's slaves might only capture him and hand him
over to the Church as a spy, but the dragons wouldn't be bothered with
such niceties.

Males from both sides flew the borders almost non-stop these days,
watching for encroachment. They Flared constantly as they flew,
resulting in a wide path of barren rock along their route. It was for
exactly this reason that no village was ever established within two miles
of a border. Even hardy thornberry bushes couldn't survive the constant
exposure to such temperatures, and they were far tougher than Xaran
flesh and bone. The bare landscape of Aja's desert surroundings made
hiding from sharp dragon eyes nearly impossible, and as soon as he was
able to move, he tucked himself amongst an outcropping of rocks,
hoping to mask his presence.

When he was ready to move on, he took a few moments to reach out
with his senses, trying to find the clearest path through the fractured
Chrym ahead. Once he was satisfied that he had mapped his course, he
glanced down at the ground and was transfixed by a tiny metal fleck
staring back at him. If not for this tiny piece of metal, no larger than a
grain of sand, he might never have reached the surface. Awed anew by
his Gifts, Aja reached down and pocketed the tiny grain.

Let them sentence me for possessing Chrym, he thought defiantly.
Just try and take me into custody.

He had a sudden image of dissolving into the ground beneath their
feet, leaving the priests raging in impotent fury. Just as suddenly, he
imagined the fate they would mete out to his parents and little Qal in his
place. Perhaps it would be better to leave the Chrym where it lay instead,
but Aja kept it in his pocket a bit longer. There was plenty of time to
discard it before returning home.

The rest of the trip passed more slowly, perhaps because Aja was
forced to remain more aware of himself and his energy levels. He sensed
the source of the signal getting closer, and then suddenly he was directly
underneath, racing to the surface. He tried to slow down and take stock
of his surroundings, but for the first time since the Choosing Ceremony,
he had no control over the Chrym, and it spat him out, depositing him
unceremoniously on a marble floor, cracked and filthy with age and
disuse. He leaped up, prepared to flee if he had just materialized in front

of witnesses, and froze in awe. Just in front of him, on a jewel-encrusted pedestal, sat a node of Chrym so pure, so perfect, it was almost blinding. Shaped like a cut diamond, the Chrym's reflective surfaces gleamed a thousand tiny Ajas at him as he leaned closer. Had he passed through this gem, he wondered wildly, feeling vaguely sacrilegious to even think such a thing. But there was no Chrym anywhere else in the chamber other than the tiny fleck he had picked up that morning. This had to have been his entry point.

His feet made tiny scuffing sounds on what looked like a few centuries or more of dirt on the floor, and he tore his gaze from the node to stare about the chamber. Large enough for perhaps a dozen men, it appeared to have been designed with the node at the center, a focal point of sorts. There were four doorless entries to the chamber, and from the dimness without, Aja was hard pressed to say what direction he was facing. Choosing a doorway at random, Aja left the chamber. He had no fear of becoming lost, for the Chrym node was far too powerful a beacon to his senses, a bright and shining song that called, *here I am*, no matter how far he went. He spent most of the afternoon exploring, finding empty room after empty room. It was nearing late afternoon when he found the library.

Easily five stories high, the massive room had shelves that reached from floor to ceiling along the walls, with dozens of additional shelves marching in formation down the length and width of the room. Most astonishing of all, every single shelf was filled with books. Some were thin tomes, as slim as a water reed, while others were massive, with spines wider than his forearm. He touched the spines on the first shelf reverently, eyebrows raised over the uniform lettering. He whispered tunelessly as he read some of the titles. There was not a single religious or agricultural reference.

All Xarans were taught basic letters so they could read the scriptures, and Aja and Qal were no exception. Poverty was not an impediment to learning, but idle reading was considered almost sinful. Here was a mouthwatering array of never before encountered literature, and Aja regretted that he had not stumbled upon this room first during his exploration. It was time to head home, or Behar would surely worry. They might already be looking for him, though he had taken pains to complete as many chores as possible that morning before leaving.

He grabbed a thin, brightly colored book from the shelf and tucked it into his belt, allowing it to settle against his belly. He gobbled the rest of his fruit bars and made his way back to the node room. The Chrym node drew him in effortlessly as he thought, *Home*. The node seemed to give him an extra measure of strength, and he completed the Swim home in a tenth of the time it had taken him to travel there, which was truly fortunate. He barely had time to tuck his new treasure above the door jamb to the chicken coop where Qal would never see it when his brother came looking for him.

"Mother needs more water," he announced, chest puffed with importance as he fed his feathered friends. He was only just old enough to handle chores out of sight of the house and on his own, and the novelty had not worn off yet.

Aja grinned and ruffled his hair on his way to the river. "I bet I can beat you back," he called.

"Not likely!"

Qal promptly dumped the entire bucket of grain on the floor of the hen house rather than spreading it around, and was immediately swarmed by hungry birds. Aja laughed as the boy shouted with indignation and milled his arms in an attempt to keep his balance.

"Not funny," his brother called, but Aja was already jogging for the river. He would have to remember to return the water bucket to the chicken coop tomorrow, or Qal would waste a trip. Maybe he would forget, just for the fun of it. He grinned as he pictured his little brother's outrage in the morning.

The next several weeks settled into a similar pattern, with Aja rushing to complete his chores and racing off to explore his abandoned city. His guilt grew with every trip, but the lure of the library was too great to resist. He consumed book after book, learning the ancient history of his planet, which he now knew was one of many in something called a solar system. His planet, called Ryxa, was sixth from Hadra and Pil. There had indeed been a third, rare sun, the lamented Halon. These three celestial bodies had created a strange, wobbly path for all their planets to follow. So many suns meant that planets closest to their heat were uninhabitable, but the Xarans had been star travelers once, and settled on Ryxa after discovering a new metal. Harder than any known substance, his ancestors had been excited about its potential for improving space travel, increasing their speeds beyond anything they'd safely managed before.

From there, Aja discovered newer tomes, describing the horror of the dragons' arrival, the carnage, the violence that ensued as the dragons took over and gradually destroyed Xaran civilizations. He realized that he was standing in what might be the last of the great cities the books spoke of. Somehow this library had survived, as had many scholars who continued to document the invasion and their new masters.

He read volume after volume about the dragons, their physiology, their social structure, breeding cycles, and the rarely observed mating bond. There was nothing about golden dragons in the literature, and Aja was unsure if Empress Adira was an aberration, or simply unknown to the scholars at the time of their documentation.

The weeks passed, and before Aja knew it, they were nearing their next rainy season. He had read less than a fraction of the books in the great library and struggled to balance his heavier workload against his absences. It was a dangerous time to be away, for Adira was always more fractious and argumentative during the brief cold spell that gripped their planet, but the city and its knowledge proved a powerful lure for Aja. He continued to slip away every chance he got, and on one such occasion he learned that there were classes, or power levels, for Xaran who could sense or control Chrym.

There were Xaran who could only sense Chrym. They were known as Seekers, and had varying degrees of strength: some barely able to feel a great vein directly beneath them, and others able to sense the tiniest fleck, like the grain Aja still carried. He blanched and carefully removed the Chrym from the pouch he carried around his neck. From now on, it would remain in the library, safely away from his family.

There were Xarans who could bring Chrym to the surface, and they were the Callers or sometimes known as Miners. Miners performed the bulk of the Chrym work for each dragon queen. By the time a Xaran Miner came fully into his or her power, they were bringing their weight in Chrym to the surface several times a day.

Weavers were even rarer, and if Miners were worth their weight in Chrym, a good Weaver was worth a dragon's weight. One witness swore two queens had done battle to the death over a particularly skilled Weaver. While the Miners could bring Chrym to them from anywhere they could sense it, they lacked the necessary finesse to do anything more than form the most basic shapes. Weavers could create anything from Chrym, limited only by their own imagination and powers. Among the Weavers were some Xaran who could build entire cities from Chrym, and Aja's jaw dropped as he viewed incredible pictures showing some of their creations.

The very last, and rarest class of Chrym gifts were the Swimmers. Men and women like Aja, who could merge with the Chrym and travel through veins to anywhere they desired, so long as enough Chrym existed to carry them. One Swimmer had proved powerful enough to rest within a single tiny speck of Chrym, which was carried into the sleeping chamber of a dragon queen. There he remained until she slept, at which point he emerged and used her own Chrym jewelry to assassinate her. Although they were able to kill several other queens in this manner, the dragons were no fools. One queen might die peacefully of the *darkening* in her bedchamber, but to lose so many in such a short period of time was no coincidence. The humans, with their Gifts, were behind the murders. The remaining queens began to wipe out entire villages, systematically destroying the resistance. Eventually, the Xaran rebels realized that the dragons would destroy the entire planet unless they surrendered. Once the rebellion was quelled, the dragons created new laws, forbidding books, limiting access to Chrym, and requiring Xarans to be tested for powers. The Church once solar-centric, evolved into something more complex, with dragons held more sacred than even the suns that made life possible. As their religion evolved, so did the structure of the Church, led by a group of Xarans made fanatical by the war, and promised power and safety by the dragons they served. Many of them lacked any Gifts at all, but they moved swiftly to enslave those who did, identifying bloodlines and relocating entire families to benefit their queens. Xaran scientists were rooted out and executed, and their knowledge was erased from the world as the new Church worked systematically to eradicate the old ways.

It was all quite fascinating, but what intrigued Aja the most were the chapters that described each Gift and the abilities associated with every level. It was clear that the text had been written by someone with personal knowledge of each skill, and written in such a way that Aja was able to follow the instructions and successfully complete each task on his first attempt. He wished once again he'd had access to such knowledge when his powers first blossomed.

The next volume in the set went on to warn of Swimmers who had become exhausted and perished, trapped within the Chrym for eternity, and Aja shivered, wondering if that was the strange sentience he glimpsed sometimes as he traveled through the veins. Were the souls of lost Swimmers truly lost, or did they live on still, sparked to awareness by a passing brother or sister?

Aja also discovered that after several generations of Xarans were imprisoned, the dragons became greedy and impatient as they burned through Gifted humans. After one queen nearly lost all of her Weavers to summer fever, she implemented a planetary-wide Xaran breeding program, risking outright war with the other queens in order to strengthen her bloodlines. It became appallingly clear to Aja why the Church controlled village populations so rigorously, allowing intermarriages only under special circumstances, and he wondered if the priests of today enforced marriage regulations out of ignorance, or if they knew how deeply they betrayed their own people. He recalled Nera's husband and felt certain that at least some of the priests deliberately chose power over their own people. He continued reading until his tired eyes made him aware of the passing time.

"Suns curse me," he exclaimed as he marked his spot and placed the book on the table in front of him. He raced from the library, comforting himself with the knowledge that he would be back within a day, two at most, to finish the text, but when he arrived home, all his plans for the future were ended.

Before surfacing, he sent his awareness tunneling up through the Chrym, a habit he'd taken pains to establish after that first Swim. He sensed nothing, not even the chickens, and surfaced warily. It was possible they had moved far enough afield that he couldn't sense them, but unlikely. They didn't like the cold rainy season any more than his mother did, and were far more likely to stay in their little shed all day while it rained rather than venture out. What he saw as he emerged from the earth chilled him to the bone. Shattered pieces of blackened wood splintered outward in a wide circle. Feathers lay in damp clumps here and there, clearly no longer attached to anything living. Beyond the chicken coop, the field before him was ash and smoke, rising weakly against the rain. A small scrub tree nearby was still smoldering, and Aja recognized the source of the damage. Without bothering to check for feathered survivors, he ran for home.

"Please let them be ok, please let them be ok," he chanted over and over as he ran, but when he topped the last hill, his worst fears were realized. The entire village was gone, homes flattened and fired, some still smoldering angrily but most already cold and dark. His own small home, set further away than the rest had fared no better.

Aja lost count of how many times he lost his footing and sprang back up from his knees on the race home. He made up for every missed prayer to Pil and Hadra along the way, but the great sun gods showed no mercy. When he reached his destination, he discovered his parents' bodies, together in death as he had always known them in life. From their position, it was clear that his father had died while trying to shield Behar, but there was no sign of little Qal. He found his brother at last, or what remained of him, tucked in behind the southeast corner of their home, next to what had once been a water barrel. Aja's baby brother had tried to find refuge from the intense heat that accompanied a dragon attack, hoping the water barrel would shield him, but nothing could withstand the heat of a dragon bent on destruction. Aja dropped to his knees and howled with grief, fingers gripping his skull in abject misery.

He was still there hours later when Swimmer Davi arrived under orders to search for survivors. Davi hated this part of the recruitment process, but they had found some of their best, most committed soldiers this way. The stench of burned bodies, the sounds of despair when he did find a survivor, stuck with him for days and weeks afterward. It didn't matter how many times he bathed after a trip such as this, he would wake up with the smell of smoke and ash and more terrible things, so strong sometimes he swore he could almost taste it. He'd once rolled his wife out of bed, slapping at imaginary flames before she'd awakened him with her startled cries. Vasia would never ask him not to go when a village was destroyed, but he knew that she dreaded the haunted look in his eyes when he returned, all too often with news of no survivors. Sometimes it was worse when he brought someone back. Exhausted by grief and a long, frightening journey, many of the so-called lucky ones were blank and unresponsive, only to experience violent episodes of rage and grief at the strangest times. The rebellion nursed these survivors back to health and gave them something to focus on, namely their hatred of dragons.

The village he'd been sent to today was so small the rebels had only given it a number on a map, but like countless others he'd seen over the years, it was decimated. While dragons did not generate actual fire, the heat from their furnace-like bodies was so intense that anything flammable in their vicinity during a battle, or simply a wild, unprovoked rage, as Sik was known to experience, went up like an inferno.

Davi searched through the village as ordered, telling himself that the small childlike shapes he found along the way were bundles of gathered wool, the larger shapes, sometimes in pairs or trios, were livestock. For such a small village, there had been a great many livestock, and no small amount of wool.

He didn't know whether to be relieved or horrified when he came upon the only survivor. By the low animal sounds of pain he heard as he approached the last farm, Davi knew something had survived. He didn't know whether that something was Xaran or actual livestock until he caught a slight movement next to the remains of a wall. As he drew closer, he saw that the only portion of the wall which remained upright was the low stone foundation common in this region.

The young man kneeling before him was rocking slightly, hands pulling at his dark wavy hair. Davi reached to touch his shoulder, then hesitated. The tiny charred bones nestled against the blackened stones told their own story.

Davi backed up a step and crouched down, taking care to cough gently as he did so. A slight stiffening of his shoulders was the only sign the mourner gave to indicate he'd heard. Davi waited for the young man to compose himself.

"Your son?" he asked when it became clear he would not be acknowledged.

"Brother," came a whisper of sound, hoarse and broken. "He was seven. Just a little bird of a thing, and she killed him. They both killed him with their incessant warring."

He looked up then, and there was the fire Davi had been sent to find. A morass of pain and rage, and already it was focused in the right direction. Davi nodded.

"Yes, those warmongering dragons kill for the simple pleasure of it," he agreed.

"No," the young man disagreed, rising at last from his brother's ashes. "I don't think they cared at all. We matter so little, they don't even see us, not really," and Davi thought, here it is, the moment where he either accepts what has happened and moves on, or I stoke the fire and gain another soldier for our cause. His gentle wife would have helped this poor fellow move on, but Davi was a soldier, and more importantly, he believed in his cause.

"It doesn't have to be that way," he said, holding out his arm in solemn greeting. "I am Davi, and I came here by way of the Chrym, looking for survivors. If you'll let me, I can show you how to make them pay."

"You Swam here?"

Davi's eyebrows shot towards his hairline at the question, but he recovered quickly.

"What would you know of Swimmers?" For reasons unknown to them, the Church had chosen to keep the existence of their most powerful Gifts a secret from their masters. General Tal had his suspicions regarding their motives, but in spite of their best efforts to infiltrate the Church, they had no certain answers. If the boy knew about this highly coveted skill it was possible others outside the rebellion and the Church knew of it too. That knowledge could prove costly.

The young man shrugged, eyes fixed on the ash at his feet. "We had to know before the Choosing Ceremony."

Davi glanced at his forearm and the fresh scar that shone like pale starlight against his almond-colored skin. "A good thing you passed."

A pity was more like it. They desperately needed more recruits with Gifts, particularly Swimmers, for the few they had were dangerously overworked. Davi himself was nearly done in from the unscheduled journey and had only made this trip because the previously scheduled Swimmer had succumbed to a summer fever, brought on by overexertion.

"We had to *know* before the Choosing Ceremony." There was an odd emphasis to the young man's repeated words, and then Davi felt it. He was Calling Chrym from the vein Davi had Swum to get here, and he wasn't just pulling a trickle. He was diverting nearly the entire stream in a show of raw power that was unmistakable to anyone with the Gift. Davi gaped wordlessly as the boy met his eyes at last, his own amber gaze darkened with grief and defiance.

"I'm Aja. I'm a Swimmer, and I have nothing left here. Use me as you will."

And with that, Aja clasped hands with Davi and pledged himself to the Xaran rebellion.

PART II

CHAPTER 10

Aja forced himself to continue, exhaustion dulling his senses to the joyful song of the Chrym. He was still miles away from the rebel stronghold he needed to reach, and rest was a luxury he could not afford. Without the information he carried, their forces in this region could be wiped out within the week. The priests were finding new ways to identify Xaran rebels, and word had come just this morning that they had captured and broken a young spy, one of Aja's most promising protégées. He promised himself he would rescue Teera, or what was left of her, on his own if he had to, as soon as he had gotten word to the dozens of good men and women who were now in danger because he'd misjudged her readiness.

The thought of one of his students in the hands of the priests drove him on, past good sense and even fear. He'd seen what they could do first hand, would carry their scars forever, and feel it every year during the cold season, deep down in bones that had healed but never forgotten. Even if he couldn't pull Teera out alive, he could at least prevent more assets from falling into enemy hands. In the years since joining the rebels and making his place among them as master spy and assassin, he'd come to hate the priests even more than their masters. The dragons were just being true to their nature, but at the highest level within the Church, the priests were wicked and corrupt, preying on their own people with avarice and cruelty in their hearts. They were traitors and cowards, and as far as Aja was concerned, there was no punishment severe enough for their crimes.

The Chrym node he sensed in the distance was pulling him now, giving him the added boost he needed to reach his destination. He caught a glimpse of shocked faces as he surfaced through the node and collapsed on the floor at the captain's feet.

"Pil and Hadra's heat," she swore as she helped him to a sitting position, back against the solid stone of the chamber wall. "I will never get used to that."

"Water! Now!" she barked, her head thankfully turned away from Aja's overly sensitive ears. Within moments, rapid footsteps approached, and a cup was pressed into hands too numb to hold anything. For a moment, Aja wondered if he'd failed to surface after all, then realized it was only water slipping down his chest. The captain cursed again, this time at the incompetent soldier.

"Haven't you ever seen a burnt out Swimmer, Jacca? He can't hold a damned thing right now."

The unfortunate Jacca grabbed for the cup and missed, leaving the captain to rescue the last bit of water. She was surprisingly gentle as she brought it to Aja's parched mouth, steady and patient as he choked the liquid down.

"Bring some more, and make sure it's not too cold."

In spite of her discomfort over the manner of his arrival, it was clear the captain was familiar with the needs of overextended Swimmers. He would have liked to commend the woman for her efforts, but he was running out of time.

"We've lost another operative," he rasped painfully and the captain stilled. Papers rustled briefly and were furiously silenced.

"How much time do we have?"

Aja appreciated soldiers who could grasp the obvious. What was obvious at this moment was that a Swimmer would not have been dispatched to this location if it couldn't be compromised. What was equally obvious was that the location *would* be compromised, the only question was when.

"Taken during the night," he managed brokenly as a second cup of lukewarm water was raised to his mouth. The liquid pearled through him, giving him just enough strength to give them the worst news. "Maybe tomorrow, but they've brought in their best, so more likely sometime today."

He stopped and looked up at the captain's suddenly grey face.

"The entire region could be compromised within hours. Get everyone out. Get everyone out now."

The captain's grey face turned to mist and disappeared. Aja passed out.

CHAPTER 11

Aja rested within the Chrym bracelet, sensing vibrations from the pain it had caused over the years, the normally joyful song of the Chrym dulled by unhappiness over its purpose in the hands of the priests. He remembered his early experiments with Chrym and his suspicions, even as a boy, that the metal was aware of his presence. He was now certain that Chrym did indeed have sentience, though it was quite different than Xaran or dragon intelligence. The metal seemed more instinctive and without an ounce of guile, but it was most definitely aware of the world around it. He knew that Chrym recognized many Gifted Xaran by their touch, reacted differently to each of them, and the Chrym he resided in currently was deeply miserable. He could feel an unformed question within the sentience and promised, "When I'm done here, you'll never hurt another soul."

The resulting vibrations of joy nearly knocked him out of his rapport with the metal, which would have been unfortunate since the Impara he'd come to kill was still surrounded by guards. Aja was fairly certain he could take them all, but it wasn't worth the risk when there were quieter, easier ways. He had arrived earlier that day, completing the nearly impossible leap from the Chrym vein he traveled to a separate source within the temple and settled in to wait. He knew he was too late for Teera, but he could still take his revenge and send a message at the same time. Though his young protegee had broken early, his sources told him that this particular Impara had continued with his play, not even asking for information at the end. When it finally came, death had been a mercy for the young woman. The priest wouldn't find mercy with Aja, though by necessity his death would be quick. As he waited for the opportunity to strike, he recalled the events that had brought him here.

Just two days ago, he awoke to a skull-splitting headache and opened his eyes to find himself upside down, rocking against a horse's side, tied securely to its saddle. The pain and disorientation proved too much, and he retched, sending waves of pain rolling through his head until he felt certain it would truly burst.

"Whoa!" The horse mercifully stopped. He felt rough hands work the straps that secured him, then grab his ankles to pull him up and over the beast's back. As his head came even with the saddle horn, he regained his equilibrium and gripped the saddle tightly, controlling his descent. Once somewhat upright, he felt immediately better and stepped back, though he kept one hand on the horse's back as a security measure.

"Where are we?" It was barely a croak, his voice dry from thirst and sickness. He took the canteen of water that was thrust at him and rinsed his mouth, spitting away from the booted feet of his companion.

"A full day's ride from camp," came the response, and he looked up shocked. "Yep, you've been out a good twenty-four hours. Captain didn't even bother with a bed, just told us to strap you on and haul ass."

While Aja appreciated the concern and haste shown to remove him from their compromised location, he was furious that no one had tried to wake him during that time. When he voiced that opinion, the guard laughed. "I tried every three hours or so at first, then every two. Since lunch, I've tried every hour with no luck. My guess is you just needed to wake up when you were good and ready." He shrugged nonchalantly, seeming neither offended nor concerned by Aja's irritation.

Everyone knew that a Swimmer who'd exhausted their resources needed commensurate rest to replace the energy they'd expended.

"At least your Captain had the sense to send me along a Chrym vein," he commented after taking a deep swig of water. This new opinion was greeted by another shrug from his companion, who held out his hand in greeting.

"Name's Pel."

Aja reluctantly remembered his own manners.

"Aja," He offered his hand along with the name.

"Holy suns!" the grizzled soldier crowed, face splitting into a wide smile that took years off his appearance. "I figured you were someone special the way they told me to hightail it out of there with you, but I never figured you for the Choosing Assassin! Wait 'til the boys hear about this. Nursemaid, my ass." He snorted and moved away to his own horse which stood patiently nearby.

Aja scowled at the nickname Pel spoke so gleefully. Gained years ago when he'd been under orders to cause as much havoc within the high priests' ranks as possible, he had taken to killing Impara in their chambers on the eve of the Choosing Ceremony. Even though the pattern was clear, his unprecedented powers and virtually unlimited ability to travel through Chrym had made it impossible for any Impara in possession of a Choosing Bracelet to block his assassination, and had forced the Church to spread the ceremonies out, traveling from village to village in the hope of avoiding detection. As a result, they were unable to reach some villages more than once a year, which gave the rebellion a chance to find Gifted youths before the Church could mark them for slavery, either to the dragons or within their own temples.

His first kill had been the Impara who stole his Aunt Nera from her family. He remembered the sick feeling in the pit of his stomach as he'd waited for his chance, the fear that he might fail, and the fear that he wouldn't. He'd used the man's Choosing bracelet to end his miserable life, and when it was over, the act hadn't brought peace or satisfaction. He'd felt a weight settle on him like a stone, and realized that the act of violence, though warranted, would never leave him. With each kill, the weight had grown, a stone for every death. For each failure, he carried a similar burden. He remembered the faces of the men and women he'd sent to their deaths, each and every one of them proud to serve the Choosing Assassin's purpose. Every time he gave an order, it was with the knowledge that they might become another stone in his heart.

I have enough stones to ground a dragon, he thought darkly, *and I'm nowhere near done gathering them. I won't be until the Church is done, or I am.* In his darkest dreams, he wondered if he'd be nothing but stone before his life was done.

Pel returned with a small package, which he handed to Aja.

"Figured you'd want this as soon as you were up and about."

Aja peeled back the top layer to find a welcome sight – several small pouches filled with Chrym paste nestled together within a cushion of fabric. Far more effective than the honey bars Aja had used in his youth, the rebels had come up with a recipe that consisted mostly of nuts and fruit ground into a thick paste, which was then sweetened with a bit of honey. Sealed in specially treated cloth bags, the paste lasted for weeks at a time, and was easily transported through nearly any conditions. He made an appreciative sound and opened the first pouch, squeezing some of the paste directly into his mouth. It would go a long way to restoring his strength, and he would need it if he was to rescue Teera.

"Is it true you once killed three different Impara in one night, in three different cities?"

Aja swallowed his first mouthful and looked up, measuring Pel's expression. No hero worship, just interest, one soldier to another.

"True enough, and an ugly night's work," he replied, and Pel grinned, realizing he was about to hear the story right from the source.

"The priests were starting to be suspicious of how the rebels were always able to access their sleeping chambers, passing dozens of guards to reach them. Some clever bastard figured out the only thing in common was the Chrym."

Priests were the only Xarans lawfully permitted to carry Chrym other than Gifted slaves, who were overseen every hour of the day to ensure they never had the opportunity to use their Gifts against their masters. Families were often kept separate as insurance against rebellion. Since Chrym was such a regulated substance, it was always kept with the Impara for the Choosing Ceremony, held as closely as possible. In other words, once they took possession of it the day before the ceremony, that bracelet never left their presence until it was returned to the queen's treasury.

The Church had been so certain that their ceremonies had fully culled the adult population of Gifted Xaran that it had been months before Imperion Cayl was willing to entertain the possibility of a Gifted assassin from outside their ranks.

"Their first step was to put as many locked rooms between them and the outside world as possible, figuring that if they could put enough distance between them and the Swimmer killing them, the Chrym couldn't be called. But they stayed on the ground floor, thinking the walls would protect them."

"When that failed, they tested the guards again, figuring someone had faked their way through the Choosing."

Pel snorted.

"Everyone always blames the guards," he complained good-naturedly.

Aja grinned in sardonic agreement.

"Next they started sleeping in the top chamber of the church, locking every level down." That had made things a lot harder. The Chrym bracelets were very pure metal, but so high in the temple, it had been agonizing to reach that far, pulling himself through the structure, contained within a tiny grain of Chrym until he was close enough to make the leap.

"I still got through, but it wasn't easy. By that point, we'd broken up the ceremonies enough that they couldn't have regularly scheduled gatherings in every city, but we had to make the Church question our resources, so General Tal decided to go for broke."

Pel nodded his understanding but didn't interrupt again as he leaned forward to hear the rest of the story.

"I hit the first Impara early before he'd even gone to bed. The second was done by midnight."

Aja paused, gathering his thoughts, feeling the weight of this next stone more keenly as he recalled the memory of how it had been earned. He steeled himself against it – a soldier did what they had to do.

"The last Impara was a real piece of work."

"Aren't they all?" Pel rejoined bitterly, and Aja allowed his own bitter smile to surface briefly, reflecting the hardness in his eyes.

"This bastard had a young girl with him, a Gifted Weaver. Son of a bitch figured he'd fight fire with fire. It was just before dawn, and he was already awake. He'd raped the girl of course and had a knife at her throat. Scared the crap out of him when I materialized, but not enough to drop the knife. He alerted the guards, but Chrym makes a damn fine sound barrier when you need it to."

The only problem had been that with the Chrym of the Choosing bracelet stretched thin over the door, all that had been left was the tiny piece he'd traveled with. He'd already formed a hair-thin needle with it and was prepared to make the kill when the girl intervened. Bleeding and terrified, she'd used all her strength to thwart his efforts, the priest cutting her throat with a dozen shallow cuts every time the Chrym moved closer. Under normal circumstances, she wouldn't have slowed him even a second, but he'd been exhausted by several Swims and was now forced to hold a Chrym barrier *and* fight the girl.

"After a brief struggle, I was able to subdue the Weaver and kill the priest."

Exhausted by their battle, he and the girl had simply stared at each other for nearly a minute before the growing warmth of the temple caught his attention. There was at least one dragon here to protect the priest, and if it couldn't force its way past the barrier, it could still roast them alive or eventually tear through the temple walls and devour him. As though reading his mind, the temple shook and plaster rained down from the ceiling. The dragon was bypassing the door and creating its own way in.

"I barely escaped that night. It was the last time we attempted three assassinations in one night, but we got our point across."

"The girl?"

Aja contemplated the stone in his heart again. "She wasn't a Swimmer, and we couldn't afford witnesses."

Pel was silent for a moment.

"Hadra carry her home."

It was a common soldier's remembrance for a fallen comrade, and his casual acceptance of Aja's actions was both salve and fresh wound.

They were fighting this war to free the innocent, not slay them, and of all the deaths on Aja's hands, this one weighed most heavily. He was sure that he could have saved her if he'd just been strong enough to carry her, if she'd been brave enough to try. He had begged her to Swim, but she'd been unable or unwilling to even make the effort, and there was no way past a hundred or more guards and at least one furious dragon. Though she swore not to tell anyone what she'd seen that night, Aja had already learned that everyone could be broken. He'd tried one last time, but her strength was expended, and if she'd ever been able to Swim, she was past the effort now. When he realized it was no use and accepted her death as the only solution, she read the intent in his expression and turned her tear stained face away at the last moment, sparing him that much at least, not that he deserved it.

The two men remained in silence a few moments more, then Aja wrapped the rest of the Chrym paste for later use.

"Leaving already?" the other man asked, not sounding surprised.

"I have a spy to retrieve, one way or another," Aja replied.

"May Pil light your way." It was another common expression, an offering for good luck, and Aja was grateful for it today, even though he'd left his praying days far behind.

Now here he was, biding his time, waiting for the kill. The Choosing Assassin was well and truly in his element. He let his thoughts settle and slow, steadying himself. The guards were leaving, and Aja did a final sweep, using the Chrym to heighten his senses and determine the location of every living thing within the priest's bedchamber and the rooms without.

He was almost satisfied with his surroundings when he sensed it. Nearly out of his range, a dragon guard coiled patiently, seeking to outwait the would-be assassin. Aja considered his options and leaped, Weaving Chrym the moment he cleared its essence. He regretted that he couldn't take his time and make the man pay more dearly for the pain he'd caused Teera, but at least he would never break another good soldier. Aja smiled as the Chrym pierced the priest's skin, burrowing through muscle and bone to clench around his heart, bringing the priest to his toes in a spasm of pure agony. Aja moved so quickly the priest never called an alarm before dropping to the floor, but somehow the dragon sensed him, for he could hear the beast closing in, barreling through closed doors and walls with jarring power. One door, two at most separated them, and Aja took precious moments to gather his thoughts and energy and gave the Chrym one final command before Diving. He was not a second too soon – the dragon burst through the door mere seconds after he was completely absorbed by the Chrym. A moment sooner and he would have been trapped, forbidden on pain of death to reveal the only secret the Xarans had ever been able to keep from the dragons. The need to keep this one great Gift a secret from their masters was the only thing the rebellion and the Church seemed to agree on. Aja might have been tempted to reveal his Gift just to see the Church brought low if he hadn't seen a dragon's rage first hand. It was true that they might wipe the Church and all its clergy from existence for their betrayal, but they would likely destroy the entire planet in the process, and that wasn't a risk worth taking.

CHAPTER 12

When Aja returned to headquarters he was met with somber looks. The rebellion had lost a promising asset in Teera, along with their first significant foothold in Zim's province. He knew the general would have already informed her family of their loss, but he always made it a point to speak with the families personally. Each death notice was a personal failure that others paid the price for" a miscalculation, an overestimation of someone's skills, or underestimation of the enemy. Experiencing their grief first-hand fanned the fires of his rage and strengthened his resolve, forced him to become a better, smarter leader, but it also weighed him down: a stone for every lost soldier. He knew that if his heart were harder the weight of his responsibilities would seem far lighter, but he also knew he'd be a poorer leader for it. He'd seen too many commanders sacrifice men and women without thought because they didn't care. There were better, smarter, and yes, more compassionate ways to achieve their objectives, even in war. War was a difficult thing, but the tenderness that made Teera's death such a burden to his heart was exactly what they fought for. He would suffer the guilt of his choices a thousand times over if it meant that others would have the privilege of living and loving freely one day.

The sound of children playing nearby eased him a bit, though even that carried a hint of bittersweet for him. It was no easy thing to see a child grow up in war, knowing that one day they would take up arms next to parents, brothers, sisters. The more Gifted children were brought to schools where they could be taught to fully utilize their talents. Unlike the dragons and the Church which served them, the rebels permitted these children to visit their families, to show off their progress, though even among the rebels, Swimming was not a widely advertised talent.

There had been only a handful of recruits since Aja to possess the skill, and each had been forbidden to tell their family the true extent of their Gift. Weaver was the highest level officially recognized by the rebellion. General Tal believed it was dangerous to broadcast their Gifts, even within the rebellion, and was particularly worried about labeling their Swimmers publicly, fearing the target that might be painted on their backs if the wrong person were compromised. Given his own experiences at the hands of the clergy, Aja was inclined to agree with him.

"Aja!" The summons came from a man who expected to be obeyed.

"General." He acknowledged his leader with a respectful nod of his head. Though General Tal was one of Aja's closest friends, he was not off duty yet, and a soldier gave respect where it was due.

"What news, Master Spy?"

"Our foothold to the west is lost for now, all soldiers safely evacuated. Teera is lost to us as well," he confirmed woodenly.

"Avenged, I expect." The last was hardly a question, as Tal knew Aja's hatred of the priests rivaled his own.

"It's done, and quicker than he deserved."

"That's usually the way of it."

Aja inclined his head in agreement.

"Take some time to recharge, Aja. You look terrible."

As Aja turned in the direction that would take him to Teera's parents, Tal reinforced his last statement.

"I mean it, Aja. We can't afford to lose you. We have a strategy session planned for this evening but I'm going to push it back to tomorrow. You need some downtime."

He half raised a hand in acknowledgment of the general's concern.

"Understood, sir."

They parted company, Aja headed resolutely to break a family's heart, while the general went off to plan more skirmishes against the Church.

The next night General Tal's highest ranking officers joined him in the war room. It was a modest space compared to the many buildings that remained standing in the ruined and partially submerged city Aja had discovered nearly two decades earlier, but it suited their needs perfectly, as though another general had once needed a quiet place to plan his battles. The walls and ceiling had an odd slope to them that muffled sound, making it impossible to pick up anything less than a shout from just beyond the door.

When he had first brought them here, one of their young engineers had exclaimed over the room's acoustics. Ever curious, Aja had retreated to the library to do some private research. Several books later, he admitted defeat. Clearly, engineering and the mechanics of sound were not for him. No matter, for he had other skills that were of use to the rebellion.

Those skills were in use this evening as the General conferred with his advisors. The question for debate was Empress Adira. Thanks to Tal's growing network of spies in Adira's territory, the rebellion had learned several alarming facts.

Firstly, Adira generated tremendous awe among the Xarans who populated her territory, so much so that her priests were virtually powerless, mere figureheads compared to a living Goddess. Xarans chose to bring themselves before the Empress herself, not hiding their Gifts. It was considered an honor to serve, and the Choosing Ceremonies were held in her court, rather than the church temples. Her priests were there merely to oversee the process, a simple test that left parents and their young crestfallen to fail.

This made things more difficult for Aja's operatives, though not impossible. If they wanted to travel freely in Adira's court, they would have to use Gifted soldiers who had never undergone the barbaric tests used in other provinces, or disguise the scars that marked Aja and a handful of others. He'd been surprised that the pesa herb was so well known for its numbing properties; when he first arrived with Davi eighteen years earlier, there had been a surprising number of "Giftless" Weavers within the rebellion. Temporary tattoos could be used to cover scars, and since many northern territories embraced the elaborate skin art, he would not raise any eyebrows as a tattooed refugee. Properly applied ink would stay fresh for nearly a year unless washed away with a special solution, and even slightly faded ink would pass inspection, which was not true of his bracelet of scars. Nothing would arouse the Church's suspicion more than a Chrym slave from another territory who had passed the Choosing Ceremony but possessed a Gift, and these priests would know of the Choosing Ceremony, even if they didn't participate in the ritual under Adira's watchful eye. There had been rumors of a faction within the priesthood who argued against the barbaric Choosing, but Aja had been hard pressed to believe it. The power hungry priests would never have tolerated such blasphemy from within their ranks. If those proposing a new way were from Adira's territory, it lent credence to the talk. Even top-ranking church officials would be reluctant to court the Empress' wrath if they started wiping her people out.

Their second concern was a rumor regarding the true extent of the Empress' power. Her people swore by a legend that she had once melted

Chrym. It was a story rarely told, and only by the older generation, but an older version of the legend involving the destruction of Halon started with the true reason for Adira's wrath.

Several thousand years ago, another rebellion had formed. A powerful Weaver had constructed an elaborate Chrym trap, believing that if they could lure Adira to a place of their choosing and trap her, they would be able to kill the empress and throw the rest of the dragon empire into disarray. The trap had worked, to a certain extent, but before the Weaver could strike his death blow, Adira's First General Mar had intervened, sacrificing himself to save her. In her resulting fury, Adira had burned so hot that she had melted the Chrym holding her in place, consuming everything around her, including her would-be assassin. She had then launched into the sky and consumed Halon, warning the rebels that she would leave the planet in total darkness if they did not surrender immediately. Fully aware that she could and most likely would act on her threat, the rebel leaders surrendered and were summarily executed. From that point on, it was said that Adira burned more hotly than any other dragon, and could melt Chrym with a mere thought.

The third, far more alarming concern was that by all accounts, Adira had entered the first phase of her mating cycle.

"Are you certain?" pressed General Tal. He pursed his lips in a habitual expression of concern, exaggerating an absurdly narrow face with dark, intelligent eyes perched precariously above sharp cheekbones. His dark skull shone in the bright lamplight of the war room as he stared his captain down, skewering the unfortunate soul with his penetrating gaze.

"Yes, General," came the fervent response. "There's no mistaking it. She's taken to flying every day now, always with scores of dragons in her wake, and it's been said that First General Oryd fears to leave her side, even to sleep."

Aja's eyebrows went up, as did General Tal's. She would be close indeed if her pheromones were disrupting her First General's sleeping patterns.

"Her colors are brighter, more intense, and the only Weaver I was able to get within a hundred feet of her chambers tells me her Lacing is almost nonstop through the night. She's erratic and moody – I swear to you sir, she's ready to fly, perhaps within the month!"

That was bad news, and from General Tal's expression, it was clear he understood the ramifications. They all knew from the dragon histories in the library that when a dragon queen rose to mate, there was a chance that it would result in a mating bond. Though the Xaran scientists who had lived here when the dragons first took control of Ryxa had been unable to closely study the phenomenon, it was believed that on very rare occasions, a queen and her chosen mate synced their pheromones so closely that they formed a life-long bond. Upon completing the bond, her mate's scales would darken in hue, remaining their original color, but shifting to a deeper shade, nearly the black of his queen. He would also become stronger, much stronger, all of which seemed to depend on the strength of his queen. In Adira's case, her bonded mate would be virtually unstoppable.

The pair would develop an incredibly strong bond and some texts went so far as to suggest they would become telepathic, seeming to know each other's will without the need for words, but there was much disagreement on that subject. Aja rather thought it was just that they were so in tune with each other that made them seem capable of reading each other's minds, but who was he to say that telepathy was impossible? Twenty years ago, he would have said that merging with metal was impossible. Just a few years ago, he would have argued that leaping from one entirely separate Chrym source to another was impossible. He and the other Swimmers were lessons in impossibility. Why then, could a mate-bonded dragon pair not achieve such a level of union as to allow telepathy? Who was he to say otherwise?

Once the mate-bond occurred, one thing was clear – a dragon queen was exponentially both more powerful and vulnerable. Queens were nearly un-killable as their histories proved. Other than the *darkening,* or battle with another queen, the only recorded deaths of a queen dragon came with the death of their bonded male, and in one notable case, a Xaran Chrym Weaver, which was why the substance was strictly regulated by the dragons. If a queen was able to kill the bonded male of a rival, she was assured of the enemy queen's death. Their dragon histories told of one queen who lived as long as a week without her mate, but almost every account before the histories ended told of queens who died within days, some within hours of losing their mate. As a result, bonded queens were extremely solicitous of their mates, seldom separating, even after a mating flight, when a queen would habitually spend days alone in the laying chamber, after which thousands of eggs were carefully tended by previous offspring.

Of the eight queens who currently ruled Ryxa under Empress Adira, only two had bonded, and of the un-bonded females, Adira and Sik were greatest in power and influence. The rebels would not be the only ones watching the skies over the next few weeks. Sik would be observing closely as well, looking for any chance to take advantage if Adira bonded.

The other fear if a bonding occurred was the possibility of a new queen. The histories the rebels had access to had no information about whether golden dragons were different from black and red queens, but they suspected she was similar to other dragons when it came to reproduction. That meant the possibility of a few thousand more dragons, or worse, a new-born queen.

"It's more important than any of you know," Severn, General Tal's senior advisor announced, tossing a rolled parchment on the table.

Tal's lips puckered again as he picked it up and quickly scanned the manuscript.

"This came from the south, just above the dead zone?" he asked.

Exclamations burst around the room like falling meteors, and he hushed them impatiently before handing the parchment to Aja. The men listened as he read the legend that had been copied onto the cracked paper out loud, struggling to control his surprise.

Though their recorded histories were far older than the religions that had sprung up around the Xaran conquerors, many of the newer myths and legends had come directly from the dragons themselves, some of whom had survived the deaths of stars in far distant solar systems. He thought he'd heard them all through his travels, but here was a new tale, one that told of another great empress, known as Oryxa. The similarity between her name and that of their planet was lost on no one in the room. There were suggestions that she was not like the other dragon queens in color or stature. She, like Adira, was god-like in her powers, yet benevolent with her rule. According to the legend, she saw the birth and death of solar systems before finally arriving on Ryxa, where at last she formed a mate-bond. Some claimed the bond was formed with her own First General, others insisted she somehow managed to steal a rival queen's First General, but all agreed on one thing. The bonding had resulted in one offspring, a daughter who was powerful beyond description. The only time a queen produced a live birthing, rather than an egg-laying, was for female offspring. It was this new queen, Therrah, who ended her mother's reign. Of Therrah's end, none could say, but if the legend could be believed, it was possible there had been a Golden Empress before Adira, which meant that just like Oryxa, her reign could be ended.

"Young dragons are so much more violent than the older ones," a captain pointed out when Aja was done reading. It took a moment for the man's name to come to him. Igre, he suddenly recalled as he watched the torchlight catch frown lines that no longer faded from his face at rest. Along with the name came a list of qualities. Igre had a reputation as a good commander, fair and thoughtful, and men and women frequently requested to serve under him. "I don't think we can afford to wait this out and see if she births a queen that might or might not kill her."

"There have been several new queens that have killed their mother and taken their territory," argued another man.

"Not to mention the half dozen or so that left and returned to claim a territory," said another.

"Yes," Igre agreed. "But the histories all tell us that the older the queen, the more settled and the less violent she is towards *us* once she takes control. We can't let her fly and risk losing her to a more violent youngster."

"I think we absolutely have to let her fly. Then if the mating flight results in a bond, we kill the male and let her die," suggested Severn.

This suggestion was met with a loud eruption of agreement and naysayers. The only time in their recorded history that a Xaran had killed a bonded male, his queen had erupted in such fury before her passing that nearly all Gifted Xaran had been culled from the planet. No, far better to kill the empress herself than her mate, and there were those who argued against even that.

"Adira hasn't shown herself to be a threat, doesn't even seem to be interested in what happens most of the time," mused Davi during a lull in the argument. "She's pulled the teeth from the Church in her territory and keeps the other queens' aggression in check. I say that doing anything to take her out of play would be ill-advised."

Aja found himself agreeing.

Severn responded angrily. "You're forgetting the danger she poses should she decide to act, Davi. We have one less sun because of her!"

Davi shrugged, spreading his hands wide. "I'm not saying she's without her flaws. Many of our own rulers have been less than popular."

A pointed look recalled to everyone the history of one Xaran King, Detrime, who had called for the sacrifice of every firstborn son and daughter to commemorate the death of his own firstborn. The tradition had lasted throughout his reign, a long and bloody period in their own history thousands of years before the dragons' arrival ended the Xaran monarchy.

"But she could prove to be," here he paused, head cocked to one side as he considered how best to finish his thought, "approachable."

Aja gaped at his friend.

"Approachable?" Severn exploded with fury. "What do you suggest, that we march in there as she's preparing for a mating flight and suggest an alliance with the dragon Empress herself? She's The Destroyer of Worlds, The Devourer of Suns, for Pil and Hadra's sake!" he finished, nearly purple with rage.

General Tal held up his hand, motioning for silence.

"Do you have any intelligence suggesting that she might be responsive to an overture?"

Severn stiffened in renewed outrage. The rebellion had harried and killed dozens of priests, and even a dragon scout party, so it was impossible that Sik was unaware of the rising resistance, though it was highly unlikely that she had informed the other queens, not wishing to appear weak. Imperion Cayl had kept their activities from public knowledge for much the same reasons, though his refusal to acknowledge their existence worked against the Church more times than not. Although they had a presence in almost every territory on the planet, the rebellion had carefully chosen to be visible only in Sik's territory for now, not wishing to give the queens cause to band together against a common enemy, so it was highly likely Adira was currently unaware of their existence.

"You suggest marching in there and revealing ourselves to her?" Severn asked caustically.

"I suggest," General Tal paused for pointed emphasis, "we consider all of our options."

"Adira's power is vast," he continued, "and an ally, or even an assurance of neutrality could mean the difference for us. The real question is whether our intelligence has, or can, gather enough information to support the possibility."

All eyes went to Aja and his second in command. Davi rubbed the bridge of his nose.

"I'm not saying we have proof of anything, just observing her behavior throughout my lifetime, listening to the legends."

Severn snorted.

"We all know that nine-tenths of every legend is wild supposition," Davi continued, ignoring Severn's dismissive behavior. "But most every legend I've ever learned has a grain of truth, I swear on Halon's honor."

The oath was a well-placed jibe at Severn's incredulity. To a man, they had read the records, which proved the existence of a third sun. There was no denying Halon was now gone. Whether the legend of Adira consuming the child-sun was true or not, the evidence could not be ignored. Legends, however wild and improbable, always started with a kernel of truth, regardless of how much remained as the story was told by generation after generation of superstitious Xarans.

"The few Xarans to voluntarily leave Adira's territory all tell us the same thing. Since the death of First General Mar, and the destruction of Halon, Adira has become complacent. She defends her borders but makes no effort to expand into other territories. The only conflict she's currently engaged in is with Sik, who we all know is mad for power."

"If an alliance could be made, it would need to center around Sik, and her never-ending harassment of Adira's borders," Aja interjected the statement as he considered the possibilities. They were now certain that the *darkening* had begun for Sik. It was a dangerous situation, and not just for the Xarans.

"She might be more open to an alliance if she's about to fly," suggested a new voice. It was a young captain, the same one who had distinguished herself with quick action to close their compromised station and remove an unconscious Aja from danger just days earlier.

Aja dipped his chin at the woman, a nearly imperceptible acknowledgment.

Severn threw his hands up. "Are we really considering this?"

A hard glance from the general tempered his protest, and he continued with slightly less heat. "By all means, let's court the enemy, people!"

"Go on," General Tal ignored the muttered protest, well used to Severn's outspoken ways.

"If she's about to fly, possibly to bond, she's got to be thinking what we're all thinking."

General Tal nodded encouragement to continue.

"She has a dangerous enemy in Sik. If we could offer an advantage, a way to preempt an assassination attempt on her mate..." The young captain trailed off, leaving another to pick up on the plan.

Davi continued. "It might be our best chance to form an alliance, General. We actually have something she might need."

General Tal nodded, considering the plan Davi and the young captain were offering.

Severn laughed. "And what happens after we kill Sik? Hmmm?"

He sneered at the general's advisors when no one answered. "Have you thought about the destruction her colony will wreak on all of us, all those unsuspecting civilians? Haven't they suffered enough?"

Davi squared his shoulders and faced Severn's contempt. "It's why we'd need the Empress to work with us. If we can get her close enough to Sik's court when we kill the queen, her dragons will respond to the first queen they see."

The histories were very clear on that point; every queen who died left behind a colony in chaos until another queen claimed them.

"If Adira's there when it happens, they'll be too distracted by her pheromones to go after the Xarans in Sik's province."

"If Adira's there when it happens, what's to stop her from issuing the challenge and killing Sik herself?"

"If she wanted that, she'd have done it already!"

The planning session had devolved into chaos again, and General Tal issued a shrill whistle for silence.

"If," he paused for emphasis, "we explore an alliance with Empress Adira and the assassination of Sik, what kind of resources are we talking about?"

Aja answered steadily. "It would require two high-level Weavers at the very least, one in each court."

Severn scowled, then joined the conversation, unable to resist the opportunity to display his brilliance.

"More than one Weaver, possibly a Weaver and Swimmer combination, especially in Sik's court. She's got Chrym slaves who are so broken they'd kill or die for her, or at least for the families she's got imprisoned. I'm not sure even our best Weaver could kill that bitch on her own if they intervened."

Aja nodded. "If we make this attempt, we need to go to Adira with people already in place in Sik's court, people who can either kill her or get the hell out of there quickly if she decides to alert Sik to our plans instead of ally with us."

Davi swallowed as Aja voiced the worst possible outcome. "Yes, we should be prepared for that. There's nothing in their history that suggests they've ever truly turned on their own species in conflict with another, but Adira's mating flight could give us the leverage we need. I volunteer to lead the team to Sik's court," he finished, refusing to meet Aja's eyes.

"No!" The younger man exploded. "If anyone goes to Sik's court, it will be me."

Everyone knew Aja's history with Sik, his lost family, a mother, father, and little brother, gone in a fit of wild rage over a lost border skirmish. His loss had earned him the right to end her life if the order came. Davi stared at General Tal as he made his argument.

"I'm a good Swimmer, but no match for Aja. If you team me up with Mardra and Fet," he named a married pair of strong Weavers, "we should be welcomed in Sik's court as refugees from Zim's territory."

He named the dragon queen to the west of Sik, whose cruelty toward her Chrym slaves was rumored to be even worse than Sik.

"And their scars?" Aja asked angrily, though he knew the objection was pointless.

Davi shrugged again, seemingly unbothered by his superior's opposition.

"A temporary tattoo like the ones Xarans to the north and west of Sik wear should do nicely to cover them."

Aja clenched his jaw as Davi's gaze passed over his own scars in a pointed but silent rebuke before returning to the General. It was true, many of the refugees who crossed forbidden borders were tattooed on their dominant forearms and more than a few refugees had passed their way through Sik, hoping to cross her vast province to reach the relative safety of Adira. In almost all cases, the ink covered the wearer's forearm in a heavy solid band, which descended at various stages into stripes very similar to dragon Laces. Some tattoos were more extensive than others, with the stripes extending down to their very fingertips. Aja had even seen a young woman with stripes extending up over her shoulder, ending on her throat, just below her jawline. Temporary ink had served quite well to disguise the faded scars that adorned Aja's right forearm on more than one occasion, and his objection to Mardra and Fet on that basis was ungrounded. A sympathetic glance from Davi didn't help.

"It could make anyone with a tattoo an unfair target if this doesn't work." It was a weak argument at best; the rebellion had placed more than one spy in Sik's court with temporary tattoos, though their preference was to use Gifted Xarans they'd found before the Choosing Ceremony rather than the rare Xarans like Aja, who'd known how to disguise their Gifts long enough to pass the test.

"We would need a strong Swimmer in Adira's court, one who could handle himself, both in diplomacy and in a jam." The General's eyes flicked to Aja as he made the comment, and the corners of his mouth lifted briefly.

"I'm not sure Weavers would be useful there. If she were to refuse and can melt Chrym, there won't be a battle." It was true – Aja knew that failure to gain her compliance would mean flight or death, and almost certainly the latter.

The conversation continued well into the night, and when they left the war room in somber silence, all men were in agreement. Davi would lead a small team to Sik's court, insinuating themselves among her servants, getting as close as possible. As soon as they were in place, Aja would travel alone to Adira's court with much the same plan. The only difference was the expected outcome – alliance for Aja, assassination for Davi and his Weavers.

CHAPTER 13

"Davi!" The Swimmer's head came up as he heard Aja's call.

"Aja, I'm glad you made it." His smile was warm and genuine. Another man might have resented Aja's climb through the ranks, but Davi knew the price the younger man paid for each success. He counted his own success in different tender, his wife's loving embrace and their five beautiful children, two of whom were well on their way to becoming powerful Weavers. He and Aja were both closely watching the youngest, who had yet to reach an age where the Gift would fully materialize. She already showed signs of sensitivity, and Davi knew that Aja hoped for another Swimmer to join their ranks in a few years. Two out of five children with the Gift was extraordinary; three would be unheard of. Aja had joked that if a third child proved to be Gifted, Davi would be put out to stud in his retirement. Vasia had threatened Aja with a gelding if he ever tried to carry through with that particular assignment, and he had thrown his hands up in surrender, the Choosing Assassin yielding with only somewhat mocking fear to Davi's wife. Of course, she had been holding a kitchen knife in one hand, the other fisted on her hip at the time, but with or without the weapon he had secretly been in awe of her fierceness and not a little envious of the great love his friend had found for himself.

Davi himself was conflicted in his hopes for his youngest daughter – he was committed to the rebel cause, but that was a choice he'd made for himself, many years ago. Finding love and building a family had shown him another way, and while he would never turn his back on the war, in his heart of hearts, he had hoped his children would find a more peaceful path through life. But each so far had found their own niche within the army, his two Weaver sons were already part of Aja's elite unit, placed together in Zim's city, watching the temple and its priests, sneaking information to the rebellion and occasionally taking action when called

97

for. His third son was in training as an engineer, and his oldest daughter was already working her way up the ranks of General Tal's army.

Vasia had hoped that at least one of their children would choose a quiet family life within the rebel community, and there were certainly others who had, but given the strong will and passionate nature of each of their children, Davi guessed that the Gift wasn't the only thing that ran strongly through his blood, passed down to the next generation. At any rate, it would be another year before Kit's Gifts would become fully known, and Davi had an assignment to complete.

The two men clasped hands, and Davi took care to avoid the newly inked skin on Aja's forearm. The design was fairly small compared to most tattoos coming out of the west but seemed very complex. As he looked closer, he realized that his friend's tattoo consisted of an incredibly delicate striping, as fine as Vasia's best lacework. Just below the solid band that covered his scars, the stripes descended in a regular pattern except for one small section, and Davi raised Aja's hand, looking more closely. There amongst the stripes, were three that stood out just a bit from the rest, each one subsequently shorter and more slender than the first. Instead of solid ink, these three stripes were actually words: Merot, Behar, Qal. Davi blinked moisture away from his eyes.

"Well done, Aja," he murmured.

Aja's lips twisted in the half-smile Davi knew so well.

"Though as distinguishing features go, I think you've taken top prize. Didn't you once tell me that a spy's best talent was to be so unnoticeable as to be unnoticed?"

The half-smile turned into an open grin, and Aja's white teeth sparkled in a rare display of true mirth.

"One more story," he rejoined. The quip recalled a long-ago conversation held between the two men after listening to a campfire story of a well-known hero. One of the younger men in their group had commented that it was his greatest hope to one day be the hero of such a story and Aja had scoffed. When Davi reproached him for embarrassing the boy, he'd said only, "They tell stories about fools. Wise men are forgotten in history."

Davi thought there was a certain truth to that, though he personally believed that even wise men picked their battles and Aja didn't give himself enough credit.

Aja sobered quickly, still grasping Davi's hand.

"Be safe, old friend."

"Yeah, yeah." Davi was always uncomfortable with send offs. "You can't afford to lose any more friends."

"I can't afford Vasia as an enemy," Aja returned, and both men laughed. Mardra and Fet arrived, trailed by a veteran soldier, dressed in plainclothes. It would be a long slow journey; since only Davi was capable of Swimming, they were forced to travel by foot, or more precisely, by horseback to their destination. With Adira nearing her mating flight, Sik's patrols would be quite active, making their travels far more dangerous.

One soldier wasn't much, but three grown men and one woman traveling together should be a large enough party to deter any but the most determined thieves of the human variety. A larger party might draw too much attention, especially the winged kind.

"If the word comes, make it quick. Don't give her a chance to sound the alarm, and get out of there as soon as it's done." The warning was unnecessary, Aja knew, but he still felt compelled to utter the words.

"I'll keep him safe or die trying." It was the guard, assigned to their unit. Aja stared at him, trying to place the grizzled face, and his name wouldn't come to him until the fellow smiled.

"Pel," he said with a tone of discovery.

"Yes sir, and I owe you big time."

Aja raised his brow, inviting clarification.

"When the boys heard who I carried out of that stronghold, I got extra rations all week. Gonna burn them off soon enough though." He finished somewhat mournfully with a fond pat of his slightly rounded gut.

"I think we can help with that," Aja grinned and motioned to the two men who had followed him to the stables. They picked up the packs they had carried along and handed them off to Pel and Davi, who grunted in surprise at the weight.

"These are for all four of you."

"Won't get very far carrying this kind of weight. We meant to travel light, live off the land." Pel frowned.

"Go ahead and open it," Aja invited. "I think you'll find it's worth the bother."

The old soldier's face split into another wide grin and he whooped with delight when he saw the contents of his pack, causing his mount to fling its head back in surprise.

"These are usually reserved for Gifted! Are you sure, sir?"

Inside the packs, carefully wrapped and packed tightly together, were dozens of pouches filled with Chrym paste. Each pouch could easily restore an overextended Swimmer's strength or sustain a grown man for a day, making it unnecessary to hunt for food along the way, and while they were mostly used by the Gifted in the city, they were not restricted from the general population. Aja frowned at Pel's surprise.

"Of course they're for everyone. It's more weight to carry, but should save you plenty of time in the long run, especially through the border regions where provisions are scarce."

Mardra and Fet had already mounted, and Mardra was looking to the southwest, the direction of their travels. Sharp and focused, Aja sometimes wondered what had drawn her to the perpetually unkempt Fet, who never failed to appear in public looking for all the world as though he'd just woken from a nap. Even on horseback, his sleepy expression didn't waver, and Aja wondered how long it would be before he fell off, sound asleep and left behind, his horse continuing on without him. No doubt Mardra wondered the very same thing as she glanced back at the dawdlers in her group.

"I'll take rear guard," she announced with a pointed look at her husband, and Fet nodded amicably, quite used to following his wife's direction.

"That's our signal," Davi said, pulling Aja in for a brief shoulder slap before mounting up. Once seated, he looked down and gave his own blessing. "May you have many new stories left to share."

Davi laughed and kicked his horse forward, ending their goodbyes. Aja watched a moment longer, then turned away. Although his journey to Adira's court would be much safer, neither man would rest easy until this mission was completed, one way or another.

CHAPTER 14

A scream ripped from my throat, followed by another, and another. I could feel my larynx shredding as air raced past me. I was falling at a mind-numbing, terror-inducing pace. Impossibly far from earth, I watched helplessly as I approached the nearest clouds, unable to affect my trajectory or momentum in any way. I'd always thought I would be stoic about impending death, but no scenario I'd ever imagined involved a flight like this. The sudden warmth I felt as my bladder released was barely a blip when the first flimsy cloud slapped my face in cold wet affront, wrapping around me and releasing just as quickly, mocking my reflexive grab at anything even remotely solid.

I was still screaming, still falling, my next rasping exhalation interrupted by a sharp grunt as an incredible impact threw me sideways and briefly upward before releasing me to my freefall again. I felt more warmth but didn't mistake it for a bladder malfunction this time. I'd been bitten. Again.

Unlike the first time, this bite was brief, and the creature didn't bother to carry me skyward, thus delaying the inevitable. In spite of the burning pain caused by the first and now the second attack, I found myself wondering why they couldn't have the good grace to carry me safely back to earth so they could finish me off.

Another cloud, a sudden tangle of massive bodies and teeth. Snarling, snapping, shrieking – I had dropped between two savage creatures who immediately challenged each other for their prize. Some prize I was, still screaming, plummeting toward the ground, covered in rapidly cooling blood and urine. Still, each snapped at me, one grazing ribs, the other tearing at my tail – my tail! – as the ground rose up, closer, closer. I had no more breath to scream, my momentum sending air past me in a scream of its own, and then there was no more sky in my view.

I hit a tree first, bones snapping on impact. My teeth clicked together, hard, and I realized that I'd just swallowed a piece of my own tongue, but what did it matter as I pulverized one tree limb after another in my agonizing journey down. Some small part of my mind marveled at my ability to process anything that was happening by this point. And then, just as the ground was about to meet my face, I had a moment of clarity that finally released me from my terror. The truth had been revealed. From the moment the first dragon had appeared in the sky, my mind had stopped processing anything at all. None of this was real. I was crazy. Stark raving mad, because dragons didn't exist, and there was no way I'd just fallen from one's mouth.

Empress Adira woke with a violent shudder, the echoes of a dream still rippling through her muscles, her large golden eyes opening with the moment of her waking. Narrow cat-like pupils flared wide in the darkness, her sight expanding as though both suns had risen on the horizon.

Aja watched as the Empress launched from her bed. Fortunately for her servants, the moment was not unexpected. Although he had only been elevated to his recent status a few days ago, he would have recognized the signs even without the warning issued by the other servants. Adira had begun to twitch mere minutes earlier, her wings rustling against her back, at least the portions that were above the melted gold. Her extraordinary Lacing, a stunning combination of colors which distinguished her from any other dragon, flashed a nonstop warning. If the cause of her distress had been external, Aja had no doubt the warning would have worked. As he watched the wavelike pattern wash over her body in ever brighter and faster pulses, he felt both compelled and repelled, and dizziness forced him to look away just moments before she awakened with a scream that sounded all too Xaran, save for its sheer volume and pitch. It was the pain in her voice – Aja would never have dreamed a dragon could feel such anguish and fear.

He moved with the other servants, hastily stoking the fire as she glared about the room, the activity undertaken as much to appease the moody Empress as to escape any chance of injury from the melted gold that dripped fat and heavy from her large body. She fanned her wings slowly now that the initial disturbance had ended, Lacing already settled into a gentler pattern as she continued her examination of the room. This too was a predictable behavior, but she would find nothing here. The only danger in her bedchamber was one she had placed there herself, and having witnessed an impressive display of Flaring within days of his arrival, Aja had serious doubts as to how much of a threat he would truly prove to be if it came to it.

Flaring and Lacing became much more prominent in a queen about to mate, and Adira seemed to burn hotter than the noonday suns these days, lending credence to the reports that she was nearing a flight. It was one reason she wanted her chambers so warm – Aja guessed the cool air was an irritant of sorts and she was already on edge.

Her First General, Oryd, was on edge as well, having entered her chamber with a hiss of rage as she erupted from her bed. Though this occurred every night, his instinct was such that he could not ignore his queen's distress. And as she had on every previous evening, Adira turned her anger outward, lashing Oryd with a tongue as sharp as her impressive teeth.

"Always the faithful lackey," she grated, her voice dripping with scorn.

Oryd froze in the process of taking another stealthy step into the room. From the histories Aja had read, he knew that a dragon had a far greater chance of success in the mating flight if his pheromones were more widely distributed around the queen beforehand. He wondered if Oryd was aware of what drove him forward another step, or if it was pure instinct.

"I seek only to ensure your safety and comfort, Great Golden One," he replied smoothly.

Over the past decade, they had come to an understanding, he and his queen. It had taken far more patience than Oryd had ever thought to possess, but he had finally won Adira over, or at least won her grudging respect. She was angry over her disturbed sleep, frustrated by the hormones that were building up in her system, and aggressive towards her colony, all clear signs of a mating flight.

It was the first mating flight Oryd would participate in, but by all accounts, it was a difficult time for any queen, and possibly more so for Adira, who had mated only one other time since her first flight to solidify her throne on Ryxa. Though he anticipated the flight with every fiber of his being, he suspected that Adira did not appreciate being a slave to her nature.

"My safety is my own concern," she spat, "and my comfort is clearly beyond you."

It was an unfair jibe and she Laced a quick apology across her lithe form. Oryd steadied his breathing with effort as lust spiked through his body. The empress might be tiny, but none could compare to her swiftness in flight, her power, her skill.

"You have but to ask, and it shall be yours," he replied, taking another step forward, risking much. A queen who was nearing her flight but not yet receptive was dangerous, unpredictable, and deadly. She Laced warning and his own Lacing began a compelling pattern, both soothing and seductive.

Her eyes widened as she perceived the pattern.

"I'm not yours yet, Oryd," she grated with muted fury.

He nodded in acknowledgment.

"I may never be yours," she added, wings shivering with agitation.

He bowed his head lower. "I only hope, as do all."

He hid a smile, knowing the jibe found its mark as it was intended to do.

"Just leave, Oryd," she answered wearily. "I would seek a few hours of sleep tonight."

Oryd had hoped for a longer exchange, knowing every hour spent in her presence at this point could only help his chances, but he obeyed readily, backing from the room with bowed head.

"Until morning then." His voice carried an intimacy which did not exist between them yet, and his last glimpse of the empress burned in his heart. Oh, how he longed to share her quarters, to possess such a fierce, strong mate to share his long years with. There could be no finer queen than Adira, and he had answered her lure thousands of years ago as a mere hatchling with little hope of ever gaining her attentions. Now here he was, with every right to expect a successful mating flight within the next few months. It would be successful, even if he had to kill every dragon who had the slightest chance of taking his queen. Oryd's eyes narrowed. Tomorrow there would be blood spilled on the practice grounds, and if he had his way, at least one challenger would be out of the way for good.

Aja observed the interaction and wondered how the open tension between the empress and her First General could be used to his advantage. An offer to remove Sik from the field would create a vacuum, in which tens of thousands of dragons might suddenly become available to join the colony of any nearby queen. Such an influx might greatly increase her chances to form a mate-bond, which she could do in relative safety once Sik was out of play.

On the other hand, several servants were of the opinion that the current tension between Oryd and Adira was only because of the mating hormones that made every queen irritable. A few of the Chrym Weavers who had been with the empress the longest believed that Oryd had every chance to win Adira during her flight, having seen him work hard to impress her with both skill and intellect. They had an uneasy relationship, but Adira was no longer openly antagonistic toward the young general as she had been in years past, in fact seemed to seek his counsel from time to time, and was not opposed to flying her borders with him, though such was not the case at the moment.

As Aja stoked the fire he was tending with another of Adira's favorites, he toyed absently with the unworked Chrym in the next chamber. He had to find a way to be alone with Adira long enough to approach her with their offer, in a place where he had at least a slight chance of escaping her sight long enough to Dive if she took offense. His best chance at that lay with the Chrym. If he could create a large enough sculpture that required more of the substance, he might convince the golden dragon to seek a new vein. It seemed the Empress liked to fly out herself to investigate new sources of Chrym, and would actually carry a Gifted Xaran on her travels, flying them great distances above the ground so they could search out the precious metal and map the veins that ran through her territory.

He'd seen the maps, painstakingly drawn in the Miners' quarters, and was relieved to see that the large vein which bisected Adira's border with Sik had not been discovered. It was dangerous to draw Adira's attention to that vein, given that it led to the ruined city and the rebel headquarters, but with a little effort, Aja should be able to divert a portion of the stream, breaking it off from the rest. If he moved it far enough away, the Miners wouldn't sense the rest, unless they had someone as Gifted as Aja, and if that were the case, Adira would already know about Swimmers. To their knowledge that particular Gift was still their secret advantage, but it was only a matter of time before one of the Gifted who served Adira so willingly possessed the highest rank of Swimmer. If they had not managed to either destroy her or form an alliance before then, the rebellion could well be lost.

An idea formed, and he began to work the Chrym, spinning effortlessly from three rooms away, through solid stone walls. Hours later, the sweat pouring from his brow was not solely from the miserable heat of the room and he was nearly spent, but completely satisfied, even though he had not laid eyes on his creation. He Saw with other senses, and the Chrym had formed as he wished, intricately, delicately intertwined in an exercise of empty space. He only hoped the empress would be impressed enough with his creation to wish for its completion. As he used the last of his reserves along with the last of the Chrym, he became aware of an odd sound emanating from the empress' bed. The noise, which at first he mistook for snoring, was a song. The empress was humming in her sleep, a simple melody she repeated again and again. Dragons were capable of speech, but nonverbal communication was typically relegated to snaps, snarls, growls, shrieks, and clicks. No one had ever spoken of, or even guessed that dragons were interested in, or even capable of song. Aja glanced at the Chrym slave next to him, wondering if his ears deceived him, but Zamir shrugged in response, as baffled as he. It was a pleasant sound, the melody unknown to him, and he drifted off to sleep, dreaming of his mother and little Qal.

In the morning, Adira woke to excited murmurs and exclamations from the Weaving room. On her way to investigate, Oryd fell into step beside her, her nighttime irritation forgotten or forgiven. She was glad he never seemed to hold a grudge – it would have made their relationship quite awkward indeed.

"It seems that one of your pets has created quite a stir." Oryd referred to her cherished Weavers as pets, a reference to her kind treatment of what others among their kind considered slaves, barely more than insects.

She glanced coyly up at the general. "One day you may yet concede their value, Oryd."

He did a double take, almost comical in his surprise at her good mood.

"Perhaps that day is today," he acknowledged, if only to see her smile. A dragon's smile was a terrible thing to behold, for anything but another dragon, that was. And there, for a brief moment, was his reward. His empress was feeling quite pleasant indeed this morning.

Upon entering the Weaving room, Oryd received his second surprise of the morning. There, in the center of the room, was a hollow, life-sized sculpture of Adira. Roughly one-third of the golden dragon's form had been recreated in glorious, shining Chrym, but what was truly breathtaking about the piece was the fact that the sculpture had shaped the Empress' form based solely on her phosphorescent stripes, in shockingly accurate detail. There were places where the laces were so widespread that a full-grown Xaran male could step through them and stand in the empty space within the sculpture, and indeed, one Xaran had done just that, standing approximately where Adira's heart would be. Oryd felt his teeth bare at the uncomfortable thought.

Adira gasped, circling the sculpture, carefully holding her wings and tails tightly against her body to avoid damaging the piece. If the piece had been solid, there would never have been enough Chrym in the Weavers' supply room to manage more than a small fraction of her form, but open as it was, the unfinished piece had enough structure to be unmistakably Adira, and was visually stunning. She felt a wave of heat wash through her in response to the Chrym masterpiece.

"Who Wove this?" she asked in a reverent voice, and Oryd

experienced his third, far less pleasant surprise of the day. There was a glow to Adira that he had never seen before, and he was suddenly, shockingly jealous of a Xaran slave, disgusting flightless vermin, for giving his Empress something he could never offer.

"Aja Wove it last night as he attended you in your chamber."

Adira's Lacing evidenced her surprise, though only Oryd read her emotions. Xarans had never shown any aptitude for learning the finer nuances of dragon body language.

"My newest servant?" Her voice held a strange note, almost purring with delight. "He Wove while attending me, from several rooms away?"

"It was the only way I could hope to match your glory, Shining and Beautiful One."

This came from the Xaran who had silently watched Adira circle the sculpture from within the cavity, turning to follow her form, all the while holding his place in the heart of the dragon. Humans might be limited in their communication skills, but this one had certainly mastered their courtly speech. Oryd took his measure swiftly; a tall, lean man, a stranger still to Oryd, though Adira had welcomed him to her colony and swiftly raised him to a personal attendant. He was pleased to note the wary glance Aja shot his way as he approached the sculpture, his Lacing as aggressive as his posture.

"I hope my humble effort pleases my Empress in even the smallest way."

Unctuous barbarian, thought Oryd, as Adira preened.

"It is beautiful, but you look tired, Weaver Aja." The concern in her tone appalled Oryd, and he drew himself up stiffly, not daring to say a word for fear of losing her good will.

"I would see this sculpture completed, but not at the expense of your health." She glanced about the room, and Aja suddenly feared she would leave the sculpture to the many other Weavers at her disposal. It was true that none of them had his power or skill, but if they worked together, they might be able to continue with his efforts, now that he had provided the template for them to build upon.

"Not so tired that I could not continue, if only there were more Chrym to work."

It was a calculated risk, for he was indeed tired. He would need to convince the empress to fly with him, alone, and work the Chrym stream along the border from a great distance, separating enough to be worth further mining efforts and making sure it was far enough away that the larger vein leading to the city would remain undetected. The effort would leave him exhausted, unable to escape Adira if his offer were rejected, but Davi and his team were in place and suffering greatly in Sik's court.

He had to move quickly, both to remove Davi from harm's way and to take advantage of Adira's upcoming flight.

Adira stared at him, considering the offer, and Aja prayed that his exhaustion wasn't as evident as it felt.

"Very well. You will breakfast, and meet me just beyond the training grounds. I wish to leave within the hour."

"Adira!" Oryd hissed, too outraged to follow protocol. He paid for it instantly, sharp teeth scoring the scales on his neck. He leaped back, away from Adira, who stood between him and her precious sculpture, and of course the filthy Weaver who had created it last night, *from her bedchamber, while she slept.* It infuriated the general that another male, even one so insignificant as a Xaran slave had observed his empress in her sleep, had so lovingly and faithfully recreated her essence in Chrym over several hours, while Oryd, all unknowing, had stood guard by her door.

"You forget your place, First General." All good humor was forgotten, but Oryd was too incensed to listen to reason.

"You near your mating flight, yet you would stoop to carry Xaran filth like a beast of burden?" he protested. "It's beneath one of your power, Great Empress."

"Shouldn't I be the one to choose who is beneath me?" It was a less than veiled reference to their mating rituals, and he Laced wildly, enraged that she would even suggest such an aberrant act with a Xaran.

She Flared dangerously, causing her pets to scramble for the exits, even her precious favorite, he noted with small satisfaction. *Focus on me,* he thought, *forget the sculpture, forget the slave. Focus on me, and fly, damn you.* But she didn't, and after a tense stand down, he capitulated.

"I will carry your pet." It was a compromise, and one he despised with every fiber of his being, but it would allow him full access to her in case the flight should begin while she was absent from the colony.

"No." The answer was firm, resolute, final.

His golden eyes narrowed, and he Flared slightly himself, nearly beyond control. The other dragons would be in a frenzy over her absence, and it would be all he could do to prevent all-out carnage among her ranks.

"Think of what you're doing," he argued one last time, risking more than a warning snap from his queen. "So close to the mating flight, you would leave your colony for Chrym? It will be there waiting, let it lie for just a little longer." For a moment, he thought he might have reached her, but she turned her head aside and became transfixed again by the sculpture.

Oryd gnashed his teeth and barely restrained the impulse to smash the thing to bits. Only the knowledge that the effort would do little more than blunt his own teeth and claws just before her mating flight, as well as the likelihood that Adira herself would kill him, restrained him from acting on the violent desire.

"I see you will not be swayed," he grated, and she turned those great golden eyes on him. He almost wished he could hate her, but still he felt the compulsion that had gripped him centuries ago when he'd first caught her entrancing scent. He would never leave her, and he knew it. Even if the unthinkable happened, and she bonded with another male, there was no other for him.

"Go then. Take your precious pet, find your Chrym, and let his sculpture be my gift to you, an offering for a strong, successful flight." He could have sworn then that he saw relief in her eyes, and realized that finishing the sculpture was perhaps a compulsion tied to the mating ritual. He recalled now that other queens sent their dragons in endless quests for Chrym in the weeks leading up to their flights, the only difference was that Adira preferred to go herself. While it galled him to be separated from her at such a vulnerable time, Oryd realized he had no other option, and risked their tenuous bond by protesting further.

Less than an hour later, Oryd stood on the training ground, watching his heart disappear in the sky in the form of a golden arrow streaking rapidly from view. Adira never failed to both awe and arouse in flight, and today, even with his throat still burning from her sharp teeth, was no exception. The scales he'd lost from her reprimand changed today's strategy and ended the hope that he might eliminate at least one hungry competitor – he would not risk personal contact during training sessions when he was vulnerable. There was no way to hide the injury from his sharp-eyed challengers, but there was also no reason to give them any inkling as to how much it might impede him in battle or during flight. He was reasonably sure he could still take any challenger, and also somewhat comforted by the dim remembrance of conversations that had passed between newly lured dragons from other colonies, who spoke with longing of a queen's mating flight. If the stories were true, he worried unduly that a mating flight would begin while the empress was away.

Oryd had barely paid attention, preferring instead to plot his rise to his own queen's side, but he recalled now that every story had begun with the same lines, with hardly any variation. "The Queen had finished building her Chrym treasury, and after several days in near seclusion, with only her Weavers to keep her company, she launched from her chambers in a sudden rush to the sky." At this point, every dragon would be Flaring eagerly, reliving the tale with the storyteller, all of them young dragons who had likely never participated in a flight of their own. Oryd would usually stalk away before the maudlin tale could continue, dreaming his own dreams, plotting his own path, every successful campaign leading him to one outcome, the Golden Empress, the shining pinnacle of his desire.

"Let her fly off with her Xaran Weaver," he thought, reassuring himself with the reminder of all he'd accomplished. Oryd would use this time to his advantage, doing what he did best, shoring up his position and weakening his greatest threats.

His shrill whistle was a call to attention, and without further delay, he assigned practice drills, selecting the senior-most dragons to go against each other in head-to-head battle. The youngsters stayed out of it, for the most part not mature enough to take part in the mating flight, but watching with tremendous curiosity as their elders sorted out their place. This was a time when opportunity was most prevalent, opportunity to rise, and to fall, and the dragons held nothing back. Oryd was sure that even though he would not participate in today's drills, more than one dragon would fall for good. If he had chosen his pairings well, he would have far fewer serious contenders to watch over his shoulder as they pursued their empress across the sky. Let Adira gather her Chrym – he would trim the flock's wings a bit in her absence. There was a reason the sands of the training ground were stained forever black, and he intended to soak the ground before this day was done. His thin lips curled in a faint smile as a particularly brutal blow landed against a competitor, causing a shower of bright blue scales to scatter on the ground, settling like iridescent petals upon crimson rivers of blood below the battling contestants. Today might turn out to be a good day after all.

CHAPTER 15

Hundreds of miles to the south of the training grounds, Adira carried her Xaran Weaver in search of other rivers of another kind. The allure of Chrym called to her, helped distance her from the fright that woke her every night now. Far worse than the sleepless nights were the memories of the dreams that now stayed with her during her waking hours. She felt as though she were fragmenting in two; one entity was the Golden Empress Adira, everything she was and knew, the other some nameless female, impossibly frail of form, yet somehow gaining power over Adira's mind. She remembered the feel of a man's hands on her body, his lips on her mouth. How could that be, when her earliest memories were of endless dark skies and a flight she had feared would be the end of her? She had been new then, a tiny golden speck among thousands of bright green and blue bodies, monstrous of form though dwarfed by the terrifying beast that led them. She'd hidden among the jewel-toned bodies of her companions to avoid the attention of the black and scarlet queen, instinctively knowing that the older female would challenge and kill her if she were aware of her presence.

Though newly born, Adira had found comfort in following her instincts. They had told her to fly close to the sun, and though some part of her had screamed in terror, she had obeyed. And oh, how the sun had greeted her, tongues of fire caressing her, giving her the strength she needed for the long migration home. Home, because young Sik, tired of her endless travels from planet to planet, had decided to challenge her aging mother. Sik's power had grown in tandem with her savagery, and she was equal parts beautiful and terrible to behold. The tiny golden queen both feared and admired the other's dark form, watching, learning how to be a queen, modeling her own flight patterns and Lacings after the massive creature that she instinctively recognized as her mortal foe. Unlike every dragon before her, she had no memory of birth, just the sun and their travels from star to star, hiding from Sik even as she desperately followed, her instinct screaming, *don't stray, don't stray, or you will be lost and alone forever.*

How then, did she possess these memories of another life, a life with a husband, a child, a love and happiness that felt so real, she woke aching with grief over her loss? It was not the pain of dying over and over in her dreams that stuck with Adira during her waking hours, it was the pain of a heart, breaking over and over again. She thought she might soon go mad if this torture didn't cease, and when she'd laid eyes on her favorite new Weaver's sculpture, for the first time in months, Adira had felt something beyond the constant fear, grief, and perpetual ache of hormone-driven instinct. She had felt loved, a sensation she'd thought long behind her, if indeed she'd ever felt it. The tiny creature she clutched daintily in her claws had given her an incredible gift, and she would move heaven and earth to provide him with whatever he needed, at any cost. She needed something to hold on to, something that anchored her amongst her shifting realities, and in the space of a few hours' time, Aja had done just that.

CHAPTER 16

Aja grimly clenched his jaw, holding nausea at bay through sheer will. Adira's skyward launch, her tremendous power and accelerating velocity had been bad enough, but the never-ending vertigo combined with the slight up and down motion that rocked him in time with the beat of her wings were nearly beyond bearing. His weeks of planning had all led up to this, but every time he'd thought of getting Adira alone, searching for Chrym, his mind had curiously blanked on the mechanics of how they would arrive. His stomach heaved, and Aja acknowledged that perhaps his mind had already known what his stomach had now learned – he and flying were not compatible.

A shiver worked its way up his spine as the empress's talons shifted slightly, maintaining a firm, cage-like grip on his torso. Although tiny in comparison to the rest of her kind, smaller even than the males, who were typically two thirds the size of a queen, the empress was still several hands taller than his own six-foot frame, even on all fours. Long bodied and slender, if she rose to her hind legs in the most impressive threat pose of her kind, she would be easily five times his height. Even as small as she was, his extra weight seemed negligible, and she soared ever higher, catching a thermal, and suddenly flying wasn't so bad after all, if he could just block out the sight of the ground below. He had never imagined the ground could look like this from above, a patchwork of white and red, with occasional bands of green and even thinner slivers of silver. He knew if they were closer to the ground, those silver threads would resolve themselves into rivers and streams, but what he knew and what he felt were two very different things. Better to focus on other things, Aja decided and closed his eyes.

Instantly his discomfort increased as the irrational fear that Adira would open her claws and let him drop arrowed through his heart. Without thinking, he grabbed for her claws, anything to hold onto, and touched the Empress's scaled foot instead. He should have let go immediately – it was one thing for a dragon to choose to carry a Xaran, another thing entirely for a Xaran to lay hands upon a dragon, even in accidental contact. But Aja found that he simply could not unclench his hand, and after a moment, he ceased trying. The empress was astonishingly warm, even at her extremities, and as soft as a woman's lips. Admittedly, this was his first contact with a living dragon, but he would never have imagined her scales to be so pliant, having seen and touched his fair share of dead dragons over the years. While violent encounters between the rebels and dragons were few, General Tal did authorize the occasional attack on small dragon parties, in part to keep up morale and train newly Gifted Weavers, but mainly to remind his soldiers what they were truly capable of. Those dead dragons had been covered in scales, large and raised, sharp, hardened spikes that could draw blood if pressed upon too forcefully. Those scales remained hard and sharp, long after their bodies cooled, and more than one soldier had dulled his blade, trying to carve a scale from a dragon's carcass as proof of a kill.

He wondered if a queen's scales differed in density from a male's, in much the same way that they differed in size and coloring, though it seemed unlikely. He'd seen Adira lash out at Oryd, seen her own scales rise in response to her disturbed slumber. It was far more likely that her scales were naturally as they were now, soft and supple, slightly raised against the warm skin underneath, and only responded to physical danger, or strong emotion, he amended. A strange vibration passed through Adira's claws, pulsing rhythmically through his diaphragm in a not unpleasant sensation. He realized she was humming as she flew, the same strange melody he had heard the night before. He risked a glance through eyes slitted against the velocity of their flight, carefully looking up, rather than down, and saw that the empress' own eyes were half-lidded, head slightly lowered on her long graceful neck. Could dragons fall asleep while flying? Would she wake if they slipped from the thermal they rode and fell earthward? Aja decided not to find out. He would rather face a hormonal queen's irritation than a terrifying freefall toward earth any day. He tried a discreet throat clearing first, followed by a gentle tap, tap, tap on one golden talon.

"Most Glorious One?" he tried, going for a casual tone and barely managing a squeak. Good thing she was half asleep, he thought, then admonished himself for the moment of embarrassment. She was neither a soldier nor a lover to impress. The thought steadied him, and he rapped more solidly on her thumb talon.

"Most Glorious One!" More commanding, closer to his usual baritone, and at last a response, though not the one he had hoped for.

"Hmmm?" She shifted, arching her spine, stretching luxuriously like a koteeri, then slipped abruptly out of the thermal, into the freefall he had feared.

He lost the battle with his stomach and she shifted suddenly, apparently quite experienced with Xaran Weavers and their delicate sensibilities. He felt rather than heard her chuckle, and with a snap of her wings, their descent suddenly slowed into a graceful downward glide. He spat, courteously aiming down and away from her large form, as he tried to clear the taste of terror from his mouth.

"You sensed Chrym?" she asked eagerly, and he realized his error in pulling her from the thermal so soon. They were far from the colony, and he could actually sense a thin stream of the metal now that they were closer to the planet's surface, but he would prefer to bring her south, along Sik's border where the southern queen's threat would feel more imminent.

He decided to go with a partial truth, fearing she would sense deception and grow uneasy with him.

"I did not sense Chrym, Great One. That is the problem. Perhaps we fly too high for me to feel its presence," he suggested, gripping her warm skin once again without intent. If they stayed out of the fast-moving thermals, it would be a more uncomfortable flight for him, but would give him much needed time to rest. The vein he sought would need to be diverted, and that would take a lot of power.

She dropped her head on that long neck, bending, bending, until he had the peculiar experience of being eye to eye with an upside down dragon. At least that was how his mind interpreted what his eyes saw, and his stomach lurched again. Between the flying and the sensation that he was both right-side up, and upside down, Aja wasn't sure he could trust himself to speak at the moment.

Apparently sensing his discomfort, she swiveled her head, impossibly flexible, and was suddenly right-side up again. With this more normal perspective, he was struck by several thoughts. The first impression was that up close, every part of her was much larger than she first appeared. For instance, each of her golden eyes were nearly the size of his head. Then there was the sharp intelligence of those eyes; the empress was no fool to be toyed with, and though she was a creature driven by instinct, she had proven time and again to be mistress of her domain. Case in point, the way she had relegated the growing power of the Church to a benevolent figurehead within her territory, or the way she treated her servants. While they were truly servants to her, she was intelligent enough to treat them as individuals, to place value upon each and every Xaran in her care. He had seen her quietly take an orphaned Xaran girl aside, too young to display any Gift, and sing her to sleep, ignoring her First General's obvious disgust. It gave him hope for the delicate negotiations he must soon attempt.

Finally, there was the sheer beauty of those golden orbs. From a distance they appeared bright and metallic, but up close, he could see a thousand variations in their surface, creating a sense of depth, as though he could reach forward and immerse himself in shimmering gold.

"It's a good thing I don't work in gold," he murmured. "I could never do those eyes justice."

She blinked, self-same eyes widening in surprise, as her Lacing exploded like lightning along her torso. Aja regretted the words the moment they came from his mouth. How was she to take the compliment, when he wasn't sure how he meant it himself? Certainly, flattery from a Xaran could be only that and nothing more. He only knew that in spite of everything he'd been told, and decades of hatred, this creature continued to impress him.

"I like Chrym," she responded simply, and the moment passed. She had side-slipped the comment and its possible meanings as easily as she had earlier avoided his motion sickness, and again, he had to appreciate how perfectly she handled each interaction, whether with a crying child, an aggressive general, or a moon-eyed Weaver. His hand did not leave the flesh of her taloned foot as she untwisted and raised her neck, facing forward again.

"We fly low then, though it will slow our travels."

He nodded, though she could no longer see him. "Yes, I think that will work best."

He closed his eyes again and expanded his senses, reaching for and finding Chrym periodically as they flew south, a pocket here, a pocket there, occasionally small streams that intersected with larger ones, and then finally, at the edge of his senses, the stream he was searching for. He had read of the great super-highways of his ancestors, and if the Chrym resembled their roads, the term super-highway was a fitting description for this particular stream. This was the vein that had carried him to the ruined city that now housed the rebels, and he strained with all his Gift to divert a large portion, separating it out in small wide arc, forcing the separation to go wider, wider, until only a Swimmer of his level, or perhaps Davi's would sense the second larger stream from such a distance. It was a difficult maneuver that sapped his remaining strength to dangerous levels, but a necessary precaution for what was to come.

Necessary, because if the Empress refused the rebellion's offer and he was unable to escape and warn them, she would return with her Chrym Miners and follow the vein to its eventual end right under the rebel headquarters.

He was nearly done, but they were closing fast and he was still recovering from his extraordinary Weave of the night before. In an effort to buy time, he gently squeezed her flesh, feeling the scales beneath his hand raise slightly in response even as she dipped her head to him again, courteously twisting as she did so. She was a fascinating study in strength and softness, casual cruelty and thoughtful courtesy, and he wished for the time and familiarity to study her more closely. No dragon had ever held his attention so fully before, though truthfully, no dragon had ever been a potential ally before either.

"Perhaps my Empress might consider a break for lunch?" he asked hopefully.

"Perhaps my Weaver might promise to keep this meal in his stomach where it belongs?" she returned with a chuckle, taking the sting out of her words.

She felt easy with the Weaver, unlike her interactions with Oryd, which were fraught with tension these days. They had come a long way since Oryd's early years as First General, and could almost be considered friends, but the mating hormones were hard on all dragons, driving them to extremes of behavior, bringing aggression to the forefront of every interaction. She had not been kind to poor Oryd, she thought remorsefully, remembering her parting words and his rejoinder. Perhaps they might form a mating bond yet, though something in her heart said it was not meant to be.

Ah well, daughters are the death of every mother, she mused, unaware that she'd spoken the words aloud until a startled, "Excuse me?" sounded from below.

"Just remembering my mother's words to me," she lied easily, not wishing to explain herself further. It was true for the most part; Sik was the first queen she remembered, and as such held a significant place in her life. Upon their return to Ryxa she had observed Sik's battle against her mother, had heard Sik's last words to the great queen she had just defeated and knew without a doubt that she couldn't be Sik's daughter; Sik would never have suffered her to live. Unbidden came the memory of warm, chubby arms wrapped around her neck, and she felt a now familiar ache squeeze her heart.

As a result, their landing was perhaps a bit too hard, and her ego suffered for it. Moving nonchalantly away as her Weaver steadied himself on his feet, she pretended an interest she didn't feel in their surroundings. Perhaps he was unaware of how sensitive a queen's skin and even scales became in the days and weeks preceding a mating flight, but she had been acutely aware of his touch during their flight. As she had stared into this human's amber eyes, she'd felt a tugging at her heart that was all too absent in the presence of the ever devoted Oryd.

"Your sculpture," she began suddenly. "Where did the idea come from?"

Aja shrugged, uncomfortable with the answer. The Empress waited quietly while he gathered his thoughts, golden eyes unwavering.

"It was your vulnerability as you slept." He winced over his word choice – dragons, and particularly queens, did not think of themselves as vulnerable. But Adira simply cocked her head to the side, for all the world like a quizzical puppy, and he cautiously continued.

"Perhaps not vulnerability as such, but just a sense that while you lay dreaming, part of you was absent."

From her sudden stillness, he sensed he had touched a nerve.

"Yes," she said slowly, the word drawing out into a sibilant hiss. "That is as good a description as any. Perhaps it is why I feel so drawn to the piece, wish so desperately for its completion. Perhaps in completing the sculpture, I will find my own missing half."

Aja sensed she would not have spoken so openly in the presence of others, and remained silent, not wishing to risk an end to this extraordinary encounter.

"Do you ever dream of other worlds, Weaver Aja?" she asked abruptly. "Worlds where dragons do not fly the skies, and metal is just metal. Worlds with one sun, and one moon, and music and… fireworks." She spoke the last word carefully, feeling the syllables roll off her tongue. It felt right, felt real, though she could tell that her Weaver was at a loss as to how to respond.

"No," he finally answered carefully. "I dream of only one world."

Aja could not believe that she had just given him such a perfect opening for his negotiations to begin, questioned whether she had been playing him all along, but he was here to make the attempt, regardless of the cost to himself.

"I dream of only one world," he continued, "where Xarans and dragons live side by side, not as master and slave, but as companions." It would not have been true mere months ago, but as he spoke the words now, Aja realized he could indeed envision such a world. For most of his life, he had wanted the dragons gone, but having come to know Adira, he realized that much could be gained by an alliance of species, and if any dragon could accomplish such a thing, it would be the Golden Empress.

"An interesting dream," Adira mused, shifting closer.

Aja forced his muscles to remain loose, appearing casual and unconcerned over the dangerous topic he was circling. They were only speaking of dreams after all, so he had uttered no blasphemy, no treason. She had no reason for concern.

"Tell me more. How does this dream of yours begin?"

Again, Aja could scarcely believe how readily she invited his confidences. She shifted closer still, and without his volition, he reached out to stroke her scales again, feeling compelled to follow the iridescent scales that formed her stripes, the source of her Lacing, the pattern he had followed in his sculpture. He stood inches from impending death, yet felt only enthralled, enchanted by his discovery of her softness, the heat radiating gently from her skin.

She tolerated his touch, more than tolerated as she leaned into his hand like a tamed koteeri, only pulling back as he approached the joining of wing and body. He pulled his hand back, and her eyes opened instantly.

"I only seek to avoid injury to you," she said softly and extended her closest wing so that he could examine the joint more closely. He had never been so close to a living dragon in his life, and he found himself fascinated, studying the delicate Lacing pattern she exhibited, even at rest, the way her scales flashed iridescence as her wing lifted. From the underside of her wing, heat curled out as though from a furnace, and he was impressed by how well the wing had shielded him. It was most intense as he followed her wing back to her strong shoulder muscles, and his hand became distorted by waves of heat so intense he could only come within a foot of her frame. If the Empress burned this hotly at rest, he could well imagine a Flare hot enough to melt Chrym.

"You would not know," she continued, "without warning. Steer clear of a dragon's wings. Even at rest, in the deepest of slumbers, we burn hottest there."

Aja had a sudden image of the dragons in her colony, resting in the noonday suns, wings extended as though the blazing rays Pil and Hadra were a welcome caress. Was it possible their love of the suns' warmth was more than mere physical pleasure? Was it more deeply rooted in their physiology? Unbidden came many other questions he knew she would not welcome. The forbidden history books told him that his ancestors had arrived in great spaceships, traveling immeasurable and unforgiving darkness between the stars, but by all accounts, the dragons had simply come from the stars themselves. How had they survived the great expanse? How had Adira swallowed a sun? Why did the dragons become so agitated during the cold season, and why were nearly all mating flights since the destruction of Halon flown immediately after the cold season ended? He kept those questions and a thousand others firmly locked behind his teeth, returning his light touch to her sleek side as she folded her wing tightly against her body once again.

"Your dream," she said, returning to their original subject. "How does it begin, this world with Xaran and dragons as equals?"

Aja began his cautious tale.

"It begins with a secret rebellion, an unusual dragon, and a daring plan."

"The beginnings of a good tale," the Empress commented, allowing Aja the freedom to safely continue with his "dream."

"The rebellion had been formed many generations ago, quietly growing in power, seeking to reclaim their rights from their cruel overlords."

A sharp exhalation from Adira was the only warning he required and Aja paused, his hand light as a feather against her scales until her breathing resumed a normal pattern.

"Even worse were the priests, who claimed to serve their dragon masters, but used their position for personal gain and cruelty towards their own people." Another quick glance at Adira showed her eyelids at half-mast, but Aja was intensely certain that he had her full attention.

"It was the end of the cold season, and the unusual dragon, a queen of extraordinary beauty and wit showed alarming signs of an impending mating flight." A brief explosion of Lacing arced under his fingertips, and he was shocked to discover he could actually feel the colors shift, as though the muscles and scales flexed to produce the phosphorescence.

"The rebellion saw similar signs of flight from a southern challenger, a fierce black and crimson queen renowned for her cruelty." Another snort erupted from Adira, probably over his audacity in calling Sik a challenger.

"They understood that with a mating flight came the possibility of a mating bond, a singular and much-desired communion between a queen and her mate, which results in a life-long pairing that cannot be broken, save by death itself."

Adira had gone dangerously still – Aja revealed much of what the Xaran rebellion had learned from their forbidden histories, and she might well decide that the humans were a greater threat than Sik, but he forged ahead, trusting that a dragon who sang children to sleep might hear him out.

"The rebellion hoped to strike a new peace with the dragons, one based on the idea of equality, forged by an act of incredible value to their chosen ally. They placed a small team within the enemy queen's court, a trio of talented assassins, and offered their services to their new friend.

They could remove the rival queen and allow the Empress to fly safely, perhaps forming the mate-bond, without fear of losing her mate."

Adira's body temperature rose sharply as he referred to her directly, so much so that Aja was at last forced to raise his hands from her scales and step back. As he did so, her head snaked around and he was transfixed by her great golden gaze again. This time the feeling did not engender the same admiration he'd felt earlier. She no longer resembled a tamed koteeri, and he was painfully aware that he stood within prime striking distance, a position she had maneuvered him into as she allowed his shocking advances. The Choosing Assassin was forced to admit that perhaps he had been manipulated even as he sought to manipulate Adira.

"And in this dream of yours, did the rebellion also send an assassin to the Empress, thinking she might yield to threats if reason did not prevail?" she hissed, uncoiling her long sleek body from its resting place upon the sand. Adira was clearly incensed, scales raised in a profusion of flashing colors.

"They did, though he was under orders to do no harm to the Empress, would not have done so, even if he could." The second truth surprised him as it passed his lips. It seemed to mollify her somewhat, though the heat from her body continued to radiate in rapidly undulating waves, heating the sand beneath his feet to an uncomfortable level. He stepped back again seeking some relief, and she tracked the movement closely. He was sharply aware of her predatory nature and forced himself to stillness.

"The assassin found reason to be hopeful in the Empress' presence. Here was a creature he had not expected to find, one possessed of great strength and beauty, but also reason, compassion." He stared directly into her eyes, willing her to remember the little orphaned girl. After a moment, Adira blinked and lowered her wings a tiny fraction.

"He went to her court with a stone in his heart, and found instead a dream."

She stared at him, weighing his words, the sincerity on his face, in his eyes. Aja stood before her, all pretense gone, completely open and vulnerable. He was no diplomat in spite of General Tal's hopes - she would accept the truth or not, he had done his best. At last, she settled back upon the sand and lowered her head to eye level.

"Your rebellion wishes to do me a service." She said it flatly, all pretense of the dream gone. "Tell me, what makes you think I have need of such a service?"

It was a cold question, challenging, and Aja sensed that although she seemed calm and relaxed, she was ready to snap him up in her terrible jaws and rend him in two. A painful but quick end, perhaps no more than the Choosing Assassin deserved for such a clumsy attempt.

"Need? No." He responded carefully to the trap he sensed within her question.

"The rebellion believes the Empress is perfectly capable of dealing with her enemy. However, the mating flight is a time of great," he paused delicately, "distraction, for a queen and her colony. A rival queen might take advantage of such a moment to strike a terrible mortal blow at a weaker, more vulnerable target than yourself, and if that rival were suffering from the *darkening* she might not care if she succeeds or fails. We seek to eliminate such an opportunity." Left unsaid was the knowledge that a mortal blow to a mate-bonded dragon was a mortal blow to his queen.

"In return for what?" she asked scornfully, but she had bothered to ask, and Aja allowed himself to relax the tiniest bit.

He shrugged, keeping his hands held loosely at his sides, to appear as harmless as possible. He hoped he would have no need to prove otherwise.

"For starters, a willingness to consider Xarans as more than slaves, something you seem to do already to some extent. How much greater an effort would it be to elevate honored servants to the level of ally, trusted resource?" he questioned.

"We could be your eyes and ears in other courts –" He'd gone too far, farther than he'd planned, and her raised wings indicated as much.

"You suggest a scheme far greater than the elimination of one queen, assassin." The title assassin was an epithet she spat from between razor-sharp teeth.

He winced – she was truly a clever creature to have grasped the implications of a barely uttered offer. Already he'd begun looking ahead to an alliance with the Great Empress, and perhaps a time when all other queens and their vicious clergymen were nothing but a dark remembrance of a dark time.

"Perhaps there will be no need," he conceded with a calmness he didn't feel. He wondered suddenly if Adira could hear how rapidly his heart beat in his chest, and a droplet of sweat gathered on his brow suddenly slid down his temple, compelled by gravity at last in a swift race to an ignominious end. He hoped it wasn't an omen for how his negotiations would end, but moved forward despite his misgivings. He had committed himself to this mission, and there was no going back.

"But as Empress, you must be well aware that the death of a queen, even one as hated and feared as Sik, is not without … implications. Especially if the manner of her death is unclear."

He deliberately avoided the use of any words that suggested murder and did not directly suggest the use of Gifted assassins since he was not permitted to reveal the true power a Swimmer such as Davi or himself possessed, but she clearly understood exactly what he offered. Her golden eyes widened slightly as the implication hit home.

"You would use Chrym? The rebellion truly thinks to wield Chrym against a queen!?" Astonishment caused the level of her voice to rise, and he restrained a pained wince. She would not take kindly to a request to lower her voice, but the urge was there, all the same.

She stared off in the distance, cool intellect battling outrage over his suggestion. As the sands beneath his feet cooled, he dared a small step forward, then another and another, until he was once again within arm's length. A fool he might have been, but his fascination with the Golden Empress had grown nearly as strong as her obsession with Chrym. His hand once again found her warm scales, and perhaps he was growing accustomed to her warmth, but she didn't seem nearly as hot as he'd first found her to be.

At his touch, her skin rippled, then settled into stillness. She dipped her head on her long neck, looming above him. It should have seemed threatening, but he was coming to know his Empress rather well.

"I will think on your offer, Weaver Assassin." She combined the two titles, a distance still in those great golden eyes, though she readily accepted his touch.

He nodded acceptance. It was a tremendous decision and unfair to expect an immediate response, though he had hoped for such, if only for Davi, Mardra and Fet, who suffered deeply under Sik's watchful eye. Davi had escaped only twice since they had been brought before her, once to inform them they were in position, the second time to warn that they were dangerously overworked, and would have to move quickly if they hoped to have the necessary reserves to kill the queen. Aja had loaded him down with Chrym paste for the return trip both times – Adira did not stint on her Chrym workers and there was always plenty to eat in her court, even for the non-Gifted born amongst the dragons, who often chose to stay and serve with their families in other ways.

"Shall we continue in our search for Chrym?" he asked quietly. He could have called the precious metal to him, had recovered enough strength to do so, but hoped for a longer flight, if only to give her time to consider his offer without other distractions. He delicately traced a stripe along her forearm, subtly reminding her of the partially finished sculpture.

"Our trip should not be wasted. Find me Chrym, Weaver Aja." Her narrowed eyes told him she knew what he was doing, but as he had suspected, her compulsion to gather more Chrym was too strong to ignore.

Their second flight of the day was mercifully short, and as soon as Aja was within what he thought might be considered a reasonable range for him to have sensed the Chrym offshoot, he indicated that they should descend. Adira was excited by the quality of the Chrym he Called to the surface and prepared for an immediate return flight. In the morning, she would send a full wing of dragons, each carrying a precious Gifted Xaran to begin the mining process.

Though their third flight was against strong winds, Adira felt something deep within her untwist and relax. Flying with Aja, Weaver or assassin, or something in between, felt right. Though he kept his eyes tightly closed for most of the return journey, his hand remained ever present on her taloned foot, and she felt not alone, for the first time in centuries.

CHAPTER 17

I tipped my head back, letting my eyes unfocus until the thousands of tiny lights strung above us resembled the night stars, humming along to the classic, somewhat sappy song Mike had insisted should be our first dance.

The artist's voice was lost on me as my new husband crooned in my ear, his deep voice sending chills down my spine.

I closed my eyes and let myself go, in the moment at last, the stress of planning, and seating arrangements and rehearsals all spinning away even as I spun in Mike's arms. Now there was only anticipation of the wedding night that awaited us and I shivered as his warm breath touched passed over my skin.

"I love you."

"I love you most."

He dipped me, raising one leg high on his hip to the catcalls of our gathered friends and family, and I let him see everything I was feeling in my eyes.

The musicians kept playing, but Mike was satisfactorily silenced, keeping me upright now, all fancy dance moves forgotten as he used his strong arms to hold me tight against his chest. I pressed closer, nuzzling in against his chin, settling my forehead against the side of his neck, my cheek against his lightly starched shirt so that my mouth and nose rested just above the vee of his loosened formal wear, just breathing him in.

This was our moment, and I was never letting go, never ever letting go, but suddenly Mike was pulling away and I couldn't hold on.

"Is Maggie crying?" he asked, and I stared at him, panicked. Mike wasn't Mike anymore, heavy muscles melting away to whipcord leanness, tanned skin darkening, hair lengthening and becoming wavier,

125

and now he was Aja, and he was slipping away on a blanket that stretched impossibly far. It was our special picnic day, with music and fireworks, but Maggie was crying, and Aja was moving away. I had to reach him, had to reach them both, keep them safe, was nearly weeping with the effort when the sun slid behind clouds. Distracted, I looked up.

"It's not supposed to storm today," I said, and then I was falling. Falling and screaming, screaming and falling. I was dying again.

Adira kept herself from launching skyward through sheer willpower, the sensation of falling still buzzing along her nerves. She remembered her wedding ceremony, the music and laughter of the guests, the feel of Mike in her arms. Though the dream hadn't carried her there, she remembered their wedding night, the whole affair, their whispered vows, repeated after eager lovemaking, in the tender quietness afterward. There was no way she could remember these things, but she did.

Adira felt eyes upon her and turned toward the fire pits. There was no need to keep them burning tonight now that the cold season was truly ending, but she had wanted them lit, unwilling to admit even to herself, exactly why she'd wanted it. There, standing in the front, shielding a young boy from the melted gold she had flung perilously close, stood the reason for the fires.

Her eyes slid over him, not wanting the others to see or guess at her thoughts, the impossible things she felt as she gazed on his small frame. Her waking must have been silent this time, for Oryd did not intrude for once.

"Empress, is everything all right?" The timid question was voiced by one of her newest Weavers, a young girl who had beamed from ear to ear just last week when her Gift first manifested. Adira didn't trust herself to speak yet, only inclined her head towards the girl.

"Is it too cold? What can we do to ease your discomfort?" the girl pleaded, and Adira realized that it bothered them, truly bothered them to see her agitation, the sleepless nights she suffered.

"No," she said at last. "Perhaps I am overly warm."

The girl looked stricken, having just placed more fuel on the fire and Adira sighed, putting herself out to reassure the poor child. When all the servants would have left, Adira called one back to her. Keeping well clear of her molten bed, Aja stepped further into her chambers.

"Tell me a story," she commanded, and it sounded like a plea. Past caring, she let the sound of his voice carry her back into slumber, dark and at last undisturbed.

In the morning, she awakened refreshed and alone. Aja had sought his own rest at some point, and though piqued by his abandonment, she could not in all fairness blame him. She herself had released the servants, Xarans, she silently corrected herself, from tending the fire pits, and one could only speak so long to a sleeping companion.

Her intensifying attraction for the rebel assassin was a problem to be solved, and not solely because of the alliance he offered. As she luxuriated in the warmth of her melted gold, the inkling of a plan sprang to mind. It required the relearning of an old skill, one she had not utilized since her very first days on Ryxa, when newly born and too weak to withstand a direct challenge from another queen, she had relied on stealth and camouflage. If her plan worked, it might yield more than one answer to the growing puzzle of her rebel assassin. It was time to revisit those talents.

CHAPTER 18

It was mid-morning, and although Aja continually sensed eyes watching him, he was reasonably certain by this time that it was only his imagination. Word had come early that morning that Adira had released him to come and go as he pleased, and at the moment, he pleased very much to visit the small village that housed the families of many of Adira's Gifted servants. Like many Xaran villages of any size, they had a marketplace, and as luck would have it, today was market day. The Empress was generous to her servants, and wealth abounded, but even if she were not, Aja swiftly discovered that the Gifted were treated reverently here. Any object that caught his attention was swiftly offered, free of charge, to the Weaver who had so caught the Golden Empress' attention. He deferred, uncomfortable with the near hero worship on their faces, aware that he would never learn anything of value as Weaver Aja.

At last, he had resorted to stealth, sneaking into shadows, creeping under wagons and stands, snagging a baggy tunic here, a pair of trousers there, a long sleeved overcoat to hide his tattoo. A few more touches and he was no longer recognizable as Weaver Aja, most likely just one of the many refugees who had fled to Adira's territory, seeking safe haven from more violent rulers. There was no denying that a safe haven was exactly what they had found here, and Aja found himself desperately hoping for the alliance he had been so unsure of to begin with.

Circling the marketplace, he at last found what he was looking for in the shortening shadows cast by Pil and Hadra. Leaning against the thatched side of a small lean-to, a young dark-skinned man was making quick work of a handful of fresh fruit. A bright, easy smile creased his face as Aja spotted him, and he straightened from his post, tossing aside a peach pit before clasping Aja's forearm with sticky fingers.

128

He sighed and returned the gesture. Sefti was perpetually sticky with fruit juices, his love for them widely known among the rebels, but he was so infectiously happy to see his superior that Aja found it hard to remain irritated with the young man. That lightness of spirit was one of the reasons Aja had rejected him when he requested assignment among the assassins Aja trained and led, choosing to spare the young Sefti from the guilt of difficult decisions and the weight of lives lost and taken. The other main reason the young man found a different role in Aja's service was explained by his presence today. Though the power of his Gift was technically at Swimmer level, Sefti was barely capable of remaining within a stream for an hour, which made him an unreliable spy or assassin. As a courier for less than critical information however, he was ideal. After Davi's second Swim to warn the rebellion of Sik's brutal overuse of her Chrym workers, they had needed to find another way to pass information without further taxing Davi or Aja, who would have been forced to make the Swim from one territory to the other and back in a single night to avoid detection. The resulting exhaustion gave the appearance of sun fever and left the Swimmer utterly spent and unable to work Chrym for several days, regardless of their strength. Sik would not have tolerated such an illness in Davi a third time. Sefti had been the perfect solution.

"Any news for the reb- um, father, I mean?" Sefti finished, shamefaced with his near miss.

Aja barely restrained a second sigh. It was yet another reason Sefti had not joined the ranks of the master spy. Subterfuge was a difficult thing for one so lighthearted and open as Sefti. Aja rather thought that had he lived, Qal might have grown to adulthood with the same sweet spirit.

"The offer has been made, the target is considering." Sefti's eyes widened and he choked on a mouthful of berries.

"Holy suns!" he exclaimed. "Everyone else was sure she'd eat you alive, but I knew you could do it."

The reverence that shone in the boy's eyes made Aja's stomach squirm.

"I haven't done it yet," he reprimanded sharply, "so don't get everyone's hopes up."

Crestfallen, the boy nodded quickly. "Sure, sure, I understand, A-brother," he amended swiftly. It was likely unnecessary, but Aja had insisted that no names were to be used in their conversations. The market was a noisy place, with many conversations happening around them, and the Choosing Assassin's eyes were everywhere, taking stock of those around him, noticing tiny details. It was for this very reason that a certain amber-skinned man repeatedly drew his attention. Aja frowned, looking more closely without ever seeming to notice the fellow. Something was definitely off.

"Go now, tell Father the news and then off to our brother in the south, as quickly as you can. I'll want you back here for the next market when I should have an answer for you."

Sefti grimaced – it would be a hard Swim for him to reach so many in the allotted time, but he drew himself up proudly, and Aja knew the boy would put everything he had into the effort. He was fairly confident Sefti was capable of the journey, but just in case, "Take some extra Chrym paste when you leave Father's home," he advised, and Sefti nodded, turning away with a determined light in his eyes.

Aja was already moving away as well, following a winding path that would take him ever closer to his own target. The lighter-skinned man continued wandering through the market, and now Aja could see that he was deliberate in his direction, targeting specific people. Some seemed taken aback when the man spoke to them, others looked furtively about, then pulled him closer for whispered conversations. It was the fervent gleam in a heavy-set shopkeeper's eyes that brought an unwelcome realization – a priest was wandering the marketplace. This was not just any priest, for Adira's priests moved openly, benevolently among her people, demanding nothing and offering blessings. This priest moved cautiously, in disguise, and he would not have Adira's or the rebellion's best interests at heart. It appeared that even as the rebels sensed opportunity within the Empress' court, the Church was also making its move, and Aja felt the fool for not having considered that possibility. Regardless of whether it should have been anticipated, he had identified the threat, and it would be dealt with.

Though cautious, the priest did not have Aja's particular skill set, and in the end, it was painfully simple to separate the man from the market crowd, and eliminate this particular threat in a swift, silent altercation in a deserted side street. The struggle began and ended before anyone even noticed that something was amiss. Aja moved with the crowd, taking care not to move directly from the scene as another stone earned in service to the rebellion settled on his heart. When the body was discovered, no one gave a thought to the slightly scruffy southern refugee browsing for nearby pastries, except a slender, golden-eyed young woman, with long chestnut-colored hair and skin nearly the same pale amber as the dead priest, who spoke to no one and passed through the crowd with the animal grace of a predator.

CHAPTER 19

When Aja returned to the colony, he found First General Oryd in a rage. The Empress, it appeared, had gone missing without a word to anyone. The cold season was ending, the Empress was building her Chrym nest and had now gone into hiding. Aja felt a curious empathy for the fierce dragon – it could not be an easy thing, having only one opportunity in several thousand years to win a mate. He thought back to Tam, the first girl he'd ever kissed, and how he'd thought after her death that an early marriage would not have been such a bad thing. He remembered the many casual encounters he'd had since joining the rebellion, and somehow every memory included golden eyes and glowing skin. Yes, Aja acknowledged, he could certainly understand the general's agitation. It seemed that a queen's pheromones were powerful indeed if she could affect other species.

When Adira finally reappeared, she seemed out of sorts, and proceeded to spend a great deal of time with First General Oryd throughout the week, discussing border patrols and the steadily growing stream of refugees. Aja remained close, ostensibly to study the empress's form in order to finish his sculpture, but using the time to learn as much as he could about the inner workings of Adira's court. Adira was certainly aware of his dual purpose but seemed unconcerned by his presence, which was either a good sign or a terrible blow to his ego, not being considered enough of a threat to remove from their strategic planning sessions.

Aja wished he could warn her that those refugees coming from other territories were not all innocent victims, fleeing for their lives. He now suspected that a fair number were sent by Imperion Cayl, seeking a new foothold in Adira's territory. Perhaps not all were priests, but they were certainly believers, sent to spread the word – worship the Church, not Adira. Unfortunately, there was a new tension between Aja and the golden queen, caused no doubt by their nightly conversations about what his new world would look like. His version of the world had Xarans and dragons living side by side as equals, both having certain skill sets that complemented each other, but Adira would not, or could not, see it as such.

"You would have us become nothing more than beasts of burden," she erupted furiously at one point during one of those late night conversations.

He glanced at the entrance to her chamber anxiously, concerned that Oryd may have overheard her exclamation. She caught the look and settled herself, speaking more quietly.

"We would become slaves to your people."

"No," he tried to explain. "We would work together, build a better world."

"Better for Xarans," she returned bitterly, unmoved by his bright and shining vision of the world, and her new place within it.

He began to despair that she would ever accept the rebellion's offer and feared what that refusal might mean. By week's end, the only commitment she would agree to was to take no action against the rebels. She insisted that she cared naught whether Sik lived or died, but as she uttered the words, he caught a tell-tale flutter of her wings and knew that she was lying. Whether she would admit it to herself or not, the empress was growing nervous. How he knew, he could not have said, he knew only that he was coming to understand her mannerisms, the cadence of her speech, the rhythms of her Lacing, the nuances of her Flares, the rustling of her wings. All of it culminated in the eloquent language of Adira, both common to her kind, yet utterly unique to her alone, and over the course of his time in her court, he had become well-versed indeed.

But now his week was up, and a nameless southern refugee with Aja's amber eyes roamed the marketplace. The atmosphere at the market was tense, almost angry, and when he found Sefti, tucked against his usual hiding spot, the youth seemed haunted and spent. Aja felt alarm spike through his gut.

"Is everything well with our brother to the south?" he asked urgently.

Sefti looked up with tortured eyes.

"We have to get them out of there, Aja," he whispered intensely, and Aja gripped his arm to pull him down a narrow alley, away from the crowd.

"Settle yourself, little brother. Deliver your report." At the words,

Sefti seemed to gather himself, remembering his duty.

"Father asks for an answer. Our brother to the south cannot last beyond the week." Sefti faltered again before continuing.

"Brother, it's bad. The things Sik- the- the things- ," he stuttered, unable to finish, and Aja cursed quietly. Sik was ancient, by all accounts as old as Adira herself, perhaps even older. The forbidden texts indicated that it was not age which ended a queen's reign, but rather the weight of time. Their legends told of dragon queens who gradually went mad, declining into a vicious insanity that was only ended by another queen. These declines typically occurred earlier in more violent queens, and it was surely no surprise that Sik would eventually succumb, but if this was indeed happening now, on the cusp of Adira's flight, with the Church making its move, the timing could not be worse. Unfortunately, when a queen succumbed to madness, she often decimated her own territory before being challenged and killed by a neighboring ruler ready to take advantage of her weakness. He truly should have been the one to take Davi's assignment, he thought, worried for his friend. Davi was strong, but older than Aja by nearly three decades. He should have been considering retirement, not his first assassination attempt of a queen, and certainly not under such terrible conditions.

"Tell Father that negotiations have stalled. I need another week that I'm not sure we have."

Sefti paled and swallowed. "If you knew, brother," he was almost pleading, and Aja felt his face harden in response. Too much depended on the outcome of his negotiations to allow sentiment to interfere, no matter how badly he wished to spare his friend.

"I cannot force her decision, little brother. She has ruled for thousands of years, and a change like this does not come lightly. We may need to consider bringing our brother home and sending another in his place when the time comes."

Aja refused to consider that the time might never come when Adira would speak the necessary words, did not want to think of what might follow, but a maddening queen was an immediate danger, and whether her death signified the beginning of an alliance between two species, or simply the elimination of a planet-wide threat, Sik required immediate attention. He quickly outlined a variation of the existing plan for Sefti to relay to the General and Davi. His new suggestion was far riskier than the plan they'd chosen, but if they pulled Davi and his team back now, Aja might be able to pull off a long Swim and the assassination of Sik. Even with his daily Chrym Weaving, he felt stronger and more rested than he had in years. The young courier nodded, then hesitated, reluctance showing clearly in his posture. At Aja's prompt, he delivered his own report.

"Father feared a delay, and believes we may have no choice but to eliminate both threats."

Aja stifled his initial protest and returned calmly, "We cannot be sure that method will have an effect on this target."

"True," Sefti nodded miserably and continued. By his studied cadence, it was clear that he was repeating General Tal's orders, word for word, "but the target must be awake and aware of the danger in order to deflect an attack. It is agreed that a Flare of enough intensity to melt Chrym must be voluntary. If the order is issued, the attempt will occur in the target's sleeping chambers, where an asset currently resides."

Sefti's gaze shifted to Aja's face as he finished. "Father wants a test to be carried out before the next market day. We must know all of our options before we proceed."

Having given his report, Sefti clasped Aja's forearm, gripping firmly. "Be safe, brother," he murmured fervently, before releasing his grip and turning away.

"Here again next week," Aja called to his thin shoulders, and Sefti raised one hand without turning around, index and middle finger extending in a gesture of acknowledgment.

"May the Great Pil and Hadra light your way," he called back as he disappeared from view.

Aja lingered in the marketplace after they parted, for once unwilling to return to Adira's side immediately. He regretted the tension between them, the gulf created by their differing views, but saw no way to bridge the growing divide. He struggled with his orders and the sense that their plan was spinning out of control. Wandering aimlessly, he passed from vendor to vendor, creating no stir in his refugee guise, until a jeweler's display caught his eye. The woman's stones were not overly large, but very high quality, and the glimmer of an idea came to him. Several minutes later, he was assured the jeweler could obtain what he desired, and he turned towards Adira's court with a lighter heart.

He'd not crossed more than half the market when he realized that tensions had risen higher and voices were rising to a near shout. A large number of market-goers had gathered; some were refugees, but the vast majority were established citizens. At the center of their agitation stood a young woman. Dressed simply but well, she wore no jewelry and bore no distinguishing features, save her coloring, which was more in keeping with the far northern territories, who rarely crossed the borders to other cities. Skin like sun-kissed honey, dark chestnut hair waving slightly in the breeze, she stood silently, watching the crowd gather. If she sensed the danger she was in, her face gave no sign. Trailing from her right hand were several small charms on dainty silver bracelets, though she had no coin purse.

Aja suddenly recalled the charms he'd seen dangling from the arms of the beggar children, many of whom were the starving offspring of desperate refugees. He'd watched earlier as one bartered his charm for a loaf of bread and some roasted pig. Carefully rationed, such a purchase was likely to feed the child until the next market day, and Aja realized the woman had been handing them out throughout the marketplace. With the thought came understanding. Any act of kindness that lessened the desperation of these refugees was a threat to the Church and their attempt to gain influence. Happy people had little interest in conversion and no need for change, but Adira's city was overrun by nearly thousands of people fleeing Sik's lands with every passing day, dozens and then hundreds of temporary camps cropping up around the city itself as people gathered near for protection from a queen who was slowly going mad.

So far the mass evacuations had not led to outright hostilities between the two queens, but the Church was taking full advantage of the chaos and building more confusion and panic than the situation warranted.

"She's a spy!" One thin man pointed, eyes blazing with conviction. "A heretic spy!"

There had been recent rumors that Sik's madness was caused by Adira herself, working through human intermediaries to undermine her adversary through poison or some other unsavory means. Aja made a mental note to get a complete update from Davi's oldest boys, who were finally making some progress in their efforts to infiltrate the Church. If Imperion Cayl intended to use Sik's madness and Adira's mating flight to further his standing, it was a bold move, and not one the rebellion had seen coming. Up until now the Church had steadfastly served dragons first, perhaps helping themselves to a bit more than they deserved, but never openly disloyal to their rulers. If that had changed, Aja would bet everything that someone with ambition was pulling strings behind the Imperion to manipulate the outcome of these next weeks and months.

The political and social structure of Ryxa had been stable for thousands of years, but a major shift in power was coming, and it looked as though the Church was looking to capitalize. Imperion Cayl was power-hungry, but not given to open conflict, something the rebellion relied upon when making their own plans. If the Church was making aggressive in-roads into Adira's territory, he would bet it wasn't undertaken lightly. No, this plan had taken time to develop, to reach its current boiling point, and it was time to find out if the Church had any new faces. Someone with a lot of resources and a very clever mind had set all of this in motion, and Aja feared he was about to witness the unpleasant consequences in the very heart of Adira's city.

He moved casually towards a vendor's cart as the northerner turned to face her accuser, his hands moving quickly and unobtrusively in a small task before he turned away to join the crowd again.

"For whom do I spy?" she asked, her voice loud and clear.

"Adira! She works for Adira!" came another voice from the back of the crowd, one of the priests, no doubt, keeping a low profile as they stirred things up.

"How do I spy – Why do I spy for Adira, in her own marketplace?" the question was scornful, mocking.

Aja hid a quick smile, enjoying her fiery challenge in the face of danger, impressed against his will of her understanding of dragon psyche. To need a spy in her own city implied that Adira felt threatened, and anyone who knew the Empress knew that she had no fear whatsoever of the Xarans and their intrigues. Disapproval and anger, yes, but fear? The idea was laughable, and this woman knew it.

He spotted an older woman, stooping to the ground and then straightening. Scattered throughout the crowd, he saw other faces slowly rise and realized what was coming. He glanced to the unattended cart that had recently received his attention, silently urging the small flame to catch and spread. A stoning was an ugly affair.

He began to press through the crowd, moving people aside with a carefully placed hand or knee, startled exclamations following his path as he steadied one suddenly unbalanced person after another. Several people marked his progress, and he was certain he saw recognition flare in one man's dark eyes as their gazes met. He gritted his teeth. It could not be helped. This was one time he would not sit idly by.

As he neared the center of the crowd, he could see the wide circle of cobblestones that separated the woman from her accusers. Only a few people remained between himself and his target when her gaze met his. He stumbled to a halt, disbelieving his eyes. There was no way it could be, but he'd looked into the Empress' eyes on many occasions, been mere inches from those great golden orbs, and there was no mistaking that it was Adira herself, staring back at him through the Xaran northerner's eyes.

The first rock flew – with little force behind it, it bounced away harmlessly as it struck Adira's skirts. Another rock, and she turned sharply towards its source. He could see startlement on her face, and a sharp tear in her forearm where the rock had struck. Blood formed, dark and red, unfurling slowly toward the pale stones at her unshod feet. The blow had stung, and he realized two things: In her current form, she was not invulnerable, and with that knowledge came the second realization. He felt real fear, fear for her, fear he had not felt since seeing the smoke rise above his village the day Sik had destroyed his family.

"Fire!" Came an alarmed yelp, and the next stone flew wide of its mark. Heads began to turn, the circle began to break apart, and Aja seized the opportunity he'd made, stepping across the open space to grab her uninjured arm.

"Fire!"

"The market's on fire!"

"Open the tower!"

On every block, some long-ago, clever architect had designed a small water tower. Living amongst dragons made the threat of fire a daily reality, and the Xarans who populated these great cities were well versed in fire prevention. As children, their responses were drilled into each and every one of them, and Aja counted on that behavior now.

"Come with me." He tugged sharply on her arm, and she moved without protest or resistance, following him across the tide of people surging forward to grab buckets and form lines against the blaze. He pushed hard through the throng at times, his mind racing furiously. She would not welcome a direct approach or reprimand for putting herself in harm's way, so how to handle this? There was opportunity here, if only he could slow his heart and mind enough to grab it.

They reached a deserted side street, empty save for the occasional city dweller, running to assist with the blaze, and Aja continued, turning the corner onto another street. They were well over a block away and he slowed now, though he kept moving forward with the certainty of a man who knows his destination. He ducked into a side street, then another and another in quick succession.

Adira moved silently at his side, tethered by his hand on her arm, puzzlement furrowing her smooth brow. When she would have questioned his behavior, he shushed her sharply, something he would never have done in her true form, and her mouth formed a dainty circle of surprise before snapping closed. At last she set her feet and pulled against him, rather like a recalcitrant horse, and Aja was surprised by her strength. He might possibly have held her against her will, but they had lost their last pursuer several turns ago, and he had no further cause to force her compliance. Releasing her arm, he swung around to face her, and was struck once again by her appearance, somehow so completely Adira, and yet so different.

"Who are you?" he asked sharply, not giving her time to go on the offensive. Pretending ignorance of her true identity seemed the safest move, allowing her the security of anonymity until he decided what to do with this new knowledge. Nothing in any of their forbidden texts had ever even hinted at shapeshifting as a skill that dragons possessed, and Aja found himself wondering what else their ancestors had gotten wrong.

She flinched, unused to such sharpness from him. This was not the Aja she knew, this was the Choosing Assassin. She had spent hours roaming the city in this form since first taking it last week, listening to the tales people told, mostly from the refugees. Aja and his rebellion were not nearly so secretive as he supposed, any more than the Church was.

She had thought to introduce herself to him at some point, had prepared a story, but now shocked by the violence of the crowd and the strange hardness Aja had shown, she struggled to remember the plan.

"Your name?" he prompted, reaching for her injured arm, thumb stroking gently over the paler skin towards her wrist. "I'm Aja," he said, encouraging a response.

"Jenna," she whispered, then froze in shock. Of all the names she had considered as she imagined contriving a meeting with her Weaver Assassin, that one had not come to mind.

"Jenna." He rolled the unfamiliar syllables on his tongue and smiled. The expression changed his face completely, and suddenly he was the Aja she knew again.

The sound of that name coming from his lips was not as discomforting as she had feared, and there was no waking shift between Aja and that other memory that had begun to occur nightly in her dreams. The name did not summon memories, only pleasure as he tasted it on his tongue, much as he tested the softness of her form, the smoothness of her skin. She felt breathless, nerves zinging as his hands traced her arm.

"Ouch!" She twitched away from him to examine her wound with dismay. "That hurt."

The pain itself was unnerving – there was little that could cause actual injury to a queen, and her cut was throbbing again in response to his careful, probing touch.

"We'll need to clean it to prevent infection," he said, and she was shocked again.

Was it possible for her to suffer an infection from an injury in this form, perhaps to carry it during the transformation? How would she explain an injury of this nature to First General Oryd, who watched her so closely it was nearly impossible to shift without discovery?

She pulled back, a flurry of dismaying possibilities tumbling around in her mind. She felt off balance, all her plans to discover more of Aja's rebellion, more about the man himself, and perhaps do something about the feelings he engendered in her, were slipping sideways into chaos.

"I must go," she said, and if he seemed bothered by her seeming indifference, he hid it well.

"Please stay and let me treat your wound." He held his hand out to her and she was tempted, so tempted to move closer and let this man soothe her wounds, and perhaps her heart, but the urgency of her fear was too strong. She could not be discovered in this form, could not be compromised. She had to know if the transformation back to her true form would obliterate the injury.

She had taken three steps away when she suddenly whirled in a swish of skirts and hair. Aja looked up in surprise as she moved closer, closer still, until she was lost in his amber eyes, just a few shades darker than her own. She rose on tiptoe and pressed soft lips to his, eyes sliding closed as she pressed gently closer. He held still, allowing her the freedom to end the caress as he angled his head slightly in invitation. Stay, his lips said, explore.

Her lips parted beneath his, and for one breathtaking moment he thought she might yield to the enticement, then he felt her whisper-soft breath, the words meant for his ears alone.

"Thank you for saving me, Aja." And with another swish of her skirts, she was gone, running lightly on the balls of her feet, childlike and free for all the sensuality she had just displayed, and he was lost. He knew it, felt the exact moment Adira defeated him. Whatever the rebellion asked of him he would do, save one thing. Adira's life was sacrosanct, and he would sacrifice anything to keep her safe.

CHAPTER 20

The week passed quickly, and Aja spent much of his time by Empress Adira's side, nearly rubbing elbows at times with First General Oryd, who seemed ever less inclined to like the Empress' pet Weaver. As her Chrym portrait neared completion, so did his dislike of the Xaran, with whom his queen seemed inordinately fascinated. It was unbecoming and disconcerting, and no amount of maneuvering and displays of skill on the practice grounds seemed to hold her attention for long. Oryd feared the time to impress Adira had come and gone, and his opportunity to gain any further advantage during her mating flight was slipping away.

If he could only force himself to show more of an interest in her obsession, he thought, but his teeth clenched in the presence of the Weaver, and all he could picture was spitting him from his mouth in a broken bloody heap. The Weaver took to keeping the Empress between them while in his presence, and Oryd felt a grim satisfaction over his intimidation of the man.

When he realized he'd been reduced to intimidating Xarans to impress his queen, Oryd fled in disgust, taking his frustrations out on the dragons under his command. Trim the flocks' wings, he reminded himself every day. Trim their wings and wait for her flight.

In the meantime, Aja made several excuses to leave Adira's side during the week, hoping she might take the opportunity to shift and find him. On the fourth day, she found him sitting by a water fountain in one of the many smaller courtyards within the city. The noonday suns touched his dark skin, and she stood in shadow, simply admiring him. *Such a strong man,* she thought, *fierce yet gentle, a killer, but capable of creating such beauty it makes my heart ache.* She wondered what his life might have been like if he'd been born to a world without dragons, what

140

great heights of creativity he might have achieved if he hadn't been shaped by war and greedy queens.

She watched as he touched a simple leather pouch at his side again, her curiosity piqued by his repetitive gesture. Whatever was in the pouch, it clearly had value to him. She found that she wanted to know everything that mattered to him, she wanted to know what sort of things he cared about beyond the rebellion, hoped that she was perhaps at least a little on his mind. She was holding her breath as she crossed the courtyard, stopping just before her shadow fell upon his form. Afraid to catch his eye, she watched shadow Aja look up and reach for shadow Adira.

"Jenna, you came." The name brought her eyes to his at last – she'd forgotten he would not know her as Adira. A tiny frown creased her forehead. It felt wrong not to share that with him and she wondered if he'd felt the same way as he played his role for the rebellion, wooing her, preparing her for their pitch. It was what his initial flatteries had been, she was no fool. But somewhere along the way, she had to believe his feelings had changed, just as hers had.

His hand touched her wrist, the very tips of his fingers sliding down her hand, slipping between her own fingers as he pulled her down next to him. She allowed it, wanting that closeness, and needing some sense of stability. Her Xaran legs seemed far too weak and she folded against the stone wall of the fountain, watching as their joined hands rested between them, lightly touching Aja's leg. She could feel his warmth through the cloth he wore, and to distract herself she asked, "Were you waiting for me?"

She expected a courtier's words and was surprised by the simple sincerity of his response.

"Of course."

And her heart was glad. He was a rebel, possibly sent to kill her, certainly prepared to kill another of her kind, to plunge her world into chaos, and with two simple words he disarmed her.

"Is that for me?"

She indicated the pouch at his waist and he smiled.

"Yes, but not for here and now, where other eyes might see."

She thought he might rise then and lead her away, but he stayed where he was, fingers laced with hers as they listened to the music of the water.

"I wish life were simpler," he finally said, and she squeezed his hand lightly.

"I do, too."

When he rose, she followed, willing to go wherever he would take her. A tiny part of her was afraid at the thought of revealing herself to him – he'd discovered her vulnerability in this form earlier in the week. Would he use it against her? She would not agree to the rebellion's alliance, knew it was the wrong choice for her species. That left him with few choices. Was life without her the simplest choice? She raised her chin and walked on.

At the edge of the town square, mere paces from her near stoning, Aja came to a halt. They were still in shadow, and the marketplace was deserted under the heat of the noonday suns. He removed his hand from hers and placed the pouch there in its stead.

"Open it."

He held his breath, she noticed, as she loosened the ties and tipped the contents carefully into the palm of her hand. With a heavy clink, a large piece of yellow and gold fell against her skin and settled into several individual pieces. Aja gently lifted each piece, separating them further for her dazzled eyes. The heavy jumble of metal resolved itself into a pair of bracelets, two bands for her ankles, and several small rings to adorn her fingers. Each was the same delicate design, incorporating three strands of thin gold, wrapping around each other in an intricately repeating pattern until they widened to reveal a brilliant yellow topaz. Each topaz was a perfect match in color and clarity, and Adira gently traced the stone in one of the bracelets Aja held.

"For me? Really?" she asked, breathless.

"Yes," he answered, unsmiling.

She watched as he placed the first bracelet on her arm.

"You know, don't you." She stated the question as a fact, flatly and with certainty.

His hands stilled briefly, then continued with the second bracelet, then the rings. His fingers were light as a feather against her flesh as he knelt to place an anklet on first one leg, then the other. When the last piece adorned her body, he stayed at her feet and looked up.

"I knew the moment I saw you."

She blushed and bit her lip, eyes downcast, looking for all the world like a simple Xaran girl with her beau. It was hard to believe she was something else, something ancient and powerful, capable of destroying him in the blink of an eye if she were in her true form. That thought brought him to his feet, and he took her hand again, leading her through the empty marketplace.

"Where are we going now?"

He gave her a mischievous grin, the smile forming deep grooves on either side of his mouth, and she felt an answering smile bloom across her face.

"Away from here."

Confused, she followed silently where he led, further and further from the town square until there were no solid buildings, only tents and shabby lean-tos, and then not even that. They walked into the brush, and then the scrubby grasses that led to the desert wasteland north of the city. It was a desolate, deserted place more than private enough for any tryst Aja might have planned, but he continued onward toward a small outcropping of rock. They had walked for more than half an hour before Adira realized that the small clump of stone was much larger than she'd first imagined.

"I wish I'd known we were going to hike to Melio," she said crossly, naming a city to the far north as she bent to remove a sharp piece of grass that had become wedged under her shoe. He winced as he looked at her small feet. At least she'd learned from earlier events to find footwear, though unlike the dress, they did not fit well.

"Here," he said, crouching down in front of her with his hands reaching over his shoulders.

"What are we doing?" she asked suspiciously, backing away slowly.

"We're rescuing your poor feet," he responded, waggling his fingers. "Come on, take my hands," he encouraged.

When she finally did so, he pulled her against his back and leaned forward until she was draped against him. As her feet left the ground, he pulled her arms around his neck and reached back to tuck his forearms under each thigh, hefting her higher until her legs circled his waist.

"Oh," she said as he began to move forward. Her slender arms clutched his shoulders and she leaned towards his ear. "Who's the beast of burden now?" she whispered mischievously and he bounced her hard on his back.

"What was that?" He challenged her to repeat the words.

"Nothing," she replied, settling against his back and letting the side of her face rest against his shoulder. He felt her lips curve into a smile as her cheek made tiny, nearly imperceptible passes over his skin that could have been nothing more than the slight jarring of their passage.

The rest of their journey passed swiftly, and when they arrived, Adira saw that Aja had planned ahead. A basket with bread and fruits nestled against a small divet in the rocks. A few feet beyond was a tiny ground spring, which Aja used to quench his thirst. The little picnic spot was completely isolated, hidden from view of the city by the rocks.

Their lunch started off quietly, each consumed by the issues they would need to confront soon, neither eager to begin. As Aja reached for a small clump of dark berries, Adira reached out to touch his tattoo.

"There's something there," she said. "Nestled among the stripes."

Her fingertips traced the outline of each stripe, a delicate questing touch that pressed against the three names engraved upon his skin.

"Merot." He said as her finger passed over the largest stripe.

"Behar," as her finger passed over the middle stripe.

"Qal."

She glanced up questioningly and Aja decided it was as good a place to start as any. He told her about his family, how he'd come to join the rebellion, the lost city and the treasure trove of books that taught him what he knew of dragons. He shared with her the history of how the Xarans had come to Ryxa.

"So strange," she mused, "to think that neither dragon nor Xaran truly belongs here. I wonder if the animals that called this place home before our arrival long to throw off the yoke of Xaran rule as desperately as your rebels wish us gone."

It was an uncomfortable thought, but passed quickly as Aja pointed out, "There are no other sentient species besides us here."

Strictly speaking, that was true. Chrym was not a species, as far as Aja could tell. Furthermore, the somewhat sentient metal seemed pleased with its role among the dragons and Xaran, happily forming and reforming in whatever shape was required of it. He doubted there were secret Chrym armies plotting a rebellion, though the thought gave him a slightly queasy feeling. Perhaps he would think twice before his next Swim, after all.

To take his mind from the disturbing image of Chrym rebels, Aja asked, "How did the dragons come to Ryxa?"

"Ryxa," she responded pensively. "Who knows what name this planet answered to before it was tamed by man and dragon."

Aja waited quietly, not distracted by her musings.

"I cannot say how all dragons came to be here." She shrugged. "Understand that dragons were here long before I arrived."

Aja struggled to remain relaxed on the blanket, a casual pose that belied his fascination. Here, at last, might be a clue to the golden dragon's origin, a mystery that had intrigued him and many others for years.

"I came across the stars, between the endless black ocean that separates them." She tipped her head back to look at the bright sky, seeming for all the world to see them still, though they were well hidden from Aja's sight by Pil and Hadra's bright light.

"They look so small and close together from down here. Perhaps it would surprise you to know that they are immense, some easily a thousand times the size of this tiny planet, some so hot that even I could not survive their burning core." She sounded small and lost, sad as she spoke of the world beyond Ryxa. "Would it also surprise you to know that the journey here nearly ended me?"

He frowned, no longer willing to consider a world without Adira in it, and said as much. She shrugged, as though it was no matter, and perhaps to her it wasn't.

"I wouldn't have felt sorry to die. No one would have mourned me." She paused again as she traced the veins in his hand where it lay against the blanket by her hip. "But I was more animal then, all instinct and tooth, too stubborn to die."

"I made it here, and rested on the planet's surface for days, too weak to do anything but breathe. It was hotter then," she smiled wryly, "and the warmth gave me strength, melted the ice that seemed to reach my very core."

Her words offered another clue to some of the mysteries the ancients had been unable to solve. Aja and others had speculated that the dragons literally fed off the suns' light. Though they were certainly carnivorous, they seemed to feed infrequently, and many of their behaviors were linked directly to the seasons and how much sunlight the planet received, such as Adira's impending mating flight, for instance.

"All I've ever known of life was the interminable flight across the stars, that and Ryxa." She was still staring at the blue sky above when she murmured in a tone of loathing, "And Sik, always Sik. I sometimes think I was born among the stars to follow her home."

"What?" Aja stiffened. Had the rebellion offered to assassinate Adira's own mother? "Is Sik," he paused, afraid to say it. "Did Sik- "

She shrugged, not forcing him to say the words aloud. "I don't think so. But who can say? I only know that I followed her colony here, hiding amongst her thousands of dragons. It was not a comfortable journey, so it's no wonder I do not think of it often."

She smiled then and reached for a branch of grapes, the movement pressing her hip against his hand. It seemed natural then, to allow his fingers to follow the curve of her flesh, to press and pull her closer. She toppled forward, stiffened arms catching her fall. Leaning over him, her hair formed a curtain around their faces, blocking the angling sunlight. An errant ray of light struck the topaz on her arm and fractured into dozens of tiny spotlights that patterned their skin.

"Our own little universe," he pointed out.

"You are my universe." She seemed shocked to have said it, her expression arrested, eyes somewhat distant as she weighed the words she had just uttered. Aja's breath caught in his throat and finally released in a quiet confession of his own. "I feel the same way."

He was rewarded with a slow smile, one that reached those golden eyes, and the heat he felt next had nothing to do with the sun or dragon queens.

Afterward they lay coiled together, hands clasped as they stared up at the darkening skies.

"Will this interfere with the mating flight?" Aja asked, not sure what he wanted the answer to be.

She placed her small hand on his chest.

"Listen."

He frowned and listened, hearing nothing but the occasional bird or insect, the rustle of a light breeze through the brush growing by the oasis.

"I don't hear anything."

She lifted onto her elbows, then her knees, and reached forward, cupping those delicate hands over his ears, unconcerned with her nudity.

"Listen," she repeated, her voice muffled now.

He heard a soft rhythmic noise, a rushing in his ears and realized it was his heartbeat. She pulled him up to face her and lay back, pulling him down to her, pressing his ear to her chest.

"Now listen."

He listened to the sound of her heart, not understanding what she tried to tell him.

"Our hearts beat together."

He frowned again, still confused.

"The mating flight has come and gone with none the wiser. I've found my bonded mate right here on the ground."

Aja stiffened and paled.

"No!" He rejected the idea violently and Adira drew back. "A dragon and a Xaran can't bond!"

He was on his feet pacing, and Adira rose to a sitting position, legs curled under her with her hands resting on her thighs. Her dark chestnut hair lifted gently in the breeze, and he'd never seen anything lovelier, never in his life wanted so much for something to be his. But there was terror in his heart now. What had she done? Her fate was bound to his now, a weak mortal Xaran.

"There's a way to undo it, right?" he pleaded.

The hurt look on her face faded to cold anger. "If there were, you'd be well on your way," she retorted, rising to her feet and casting about for her clothing.

He relented, reaching for her as she lifted her skirt and shook the fabric out, removing any creatures that might have found a hiding place during their tryst. "Adira," he began, and she knocked his hand away, hard enough to sting.

"Adira," he tried again, hand still extended but wisely not touching her as she yanked her clothing on one piece at a time, angrily jerking at the sleeve of her blouse until the fabric tore. She stood looking down at the rent fabric, lost again, and Aja realized she was silently crying.

He came to her and wrapped his arms around her waist, risking rejection again, but this time she allowed the embrace. "Shhhh, shhh, my love," he murmured, one hand coming up to stroke her hair. "I didn't mean it, of course I want you, want you more than anything."

He felt her soften against him, arms slowly coming up to wrap around him. "You're my universe, remember?"

"Then why?" It was a pained question, full of hurt and accusation, and he pressed his lips together.

"I regret that I did not handle the news better, my love, but Adira, you've tied yourself to a Xaran."

"No," she responded stubbornly, "I've tied myself to my universe."

He shook his head in frustration as her eyes met his.

"You've killed yourself," he exploded, and he saw understanding dawn in those golden eyes.

"Your histories," she breathed. "You know what the mate-bond is."

"Yes, and I won't be the cause of your death," he vowed.

"Even if it means you're the cause of my life?" she asked softly, warm and pliant again as she at last understood his objections.

He stood silent, gazing into her eyes, too conflicted to express his thoughts.

"You are, you know." She reached up and pushed his hair back from his face, tucking it behind his ears as the breeze threatened to pull it forward again. "I've lived so many thousands of years I've lost track, but until you, I never lived."

She placed one hand on his chest, the other on her own and pressed. "This, Aja. This is what life is all about. This is my reward for surviving my mean and meager life so long. This all any dragon ever asks for, the chance to find the only creature in the world meant just for them, to never be alone again."

Tears spilled out from her eyes, tracking down her lovely face, and Aja felt his heart clench. "Don't leave me alone, Aja."

He lowered his head, and she raised her lips to meet his – soft and sweet and gently clinging, they parted with the slightest encouragement, and they sank to the blanket and back into bliss once again.

The sky had darkened completely, lit only by stars when Adira requested, "Tell me of your dream again?"

Aja made a noise of deferral, not wishing to ruin the contentment he felt with another argument, but she would not be denied.

"Is there room perhaps for an empress who rules all her subjects as equals, both dragon and Xaran? An empress who would be willing to consider maintaining a permanent Xaran advisor in her court?"

Aja smiled sadly. "We won't be ruled, Adira."

"But your own histories are full of kings and queens," she protested. "Many of them did terrible things to their subjects, but others used their position to improve the lives of the people who depended upon them. How would my rule be different?"

He shrugged helplessly and she scowled.

"How do you undo millennia of hatred caused by unending slavery?"

"Forcing us to step down and accept menial labor will never work," she warned.

Aja stroked her long hair back from her face. "What if it wasn't menial labor?"

She snorted.

"No," he said becoming animated. "You said yourself that some rulers are benevolent and kind, seeking to improve the lives of their subjects. You yourself have set your dragons to building levees to hold back floodwaters, to repair building structures damaged by storm or old age. Was that done out of servitutde?"

"No," she said slowly.

"Then why? If we don't matter, why would you put yourself out, ordering your dragons to help us?"

"Because you needed it," she replied simply, as though he were daft.

"If you would do these things for your subjects, why not your equals, your partners?"

"It's different," she stubbornly insisted, and he supposed to her it was.

The return home was silent, though at one point, Adira pointed to the sky and Aja could make out great dark shapes passing beneath the stars. First General Oryd had sent out a search party, impatient for Adira to return. They were still out of sight from the city when she stopped, pulling her hand from his.

He would have protested, but she said simply, "I must return as the Empress."

He stepped back as she commanded, and watched as she simply vanished into mist, a mist that resisted the light evening breeze, grew, reformed into something much larger, and suddenly she was solid again. Her Lacing glowed dimly in the darkness, outlining her shape clearly as she moved toward him.

"We'll fly the rest of the way back," she said, and so they did.

It wasn't long before the dragons discovered their queen and formed in ranks behind her. Even without their wild Lacings and Flares, Aja would have sensed their agitation. He wondered how they would take their queen's bonding, and fear for Adira curled within his gut. Dragons followed their queen without question, their loyalty absolute once they joined a colony in response to a female's call, but to his knowledge, no queen had ever before refused a mating flight, let alone formed a mate-bond with a lowly Xaran. How the dragons would react to that news was beyond him, but every outcome he pictured was worse than the one before.

CHAPTER 21

Aja scowled and squinted against the early morning suns. The cool season was well and truly over, and the early morning heat was enough to make him irritable, though he admitted to himself that his true issue was with his queen. Her failure to admit their bond to the colony both relieved and rankled him. Taking his cue from her, he had resumed his role of favored Weaver, troubled by the easy way she relegated him to servant, to slave, though he said nothing. These were her people, she would handle the news as she thought best. He had his own concerns, like how exactly, he was going to tell the General what had transpired.

"Oh, by the way sir, the asset you sent me to acquire or kill? I've fallen in love with her. We've bonded, and when her people find out, they may just kill us both. I guess it goes without saying, but I won't be carrying out that assassination attempt, just in case you were thinking of ordering it."

Aja snorted. Yes, that would be well received indeed. He was on his way to meet up with Sefti at the marketplace, still undecided on exactly what he was going to report. So much depended on how badly things progressed with Sik, and when he met up with Sefti at last, his worst fears were realized.

"Father has ordered the southern target to be eliminated," Sefti reported solemnly. "Our brother in the south is too weak to make the attempt."

Aja's heart sank. Things were far worse for Davi and the others than he had imagined.

"Father asks that you see this task done for him, and then report directly back for further orders."

Something in the younger man's eyes warned Aja that he wouldn't like those orders.

"He doesn't wish to know of my progress with our asset?"

There was a flicker of some unnamed emotion in Sefti's eyes, but he said simply, "Father wishes to see his son again, and will wait to hear his news in person."

Something didn't feel right.

"And our brother?"

"Returns the long way home."

"Good."

Davi and the others were out of harm's way at least. Sefti's eyes shifted again, and Aja wondered what the boy knew but was not saying.

"Do I act tonight?" Aja asked.

"No. Father wishes it to take place in one week's time."

Aja frowned. There should have been urgency over Adira's mating flight if they hoped to use the assassination to cement their alliance. There was no way for the General to know that no mating flight would now occur.

"What of our alliance?" Aja asked.

"Father wishes to speak of it in person," Sefti repeated.

"Very well. Report back to Father that it will be as he wishes."

Sefti appeared relieved, and nodded, breaking into his characteristic grin. "Oh, and if you're able, Father asks that you return to report in person the same day the deed is done."

Aja frowned, considering the possibilities. It was a long Swim from Adira's territory to Sik's court, though not quite as far back to the ruined city after the assassination, assuming he survived. He stilled – assuming he survived. He couldn't afford to think like that anymore. Failure wasn't just the end for him, now that Adira had bonded with him, his death was hers.

"It is difficult to say what will be possible," he finally said. "The task may require more than expected."

Sefti nodded in understanding. "Father asks only that you try," he returned before disappearing back into the market crowd. Aja watched him go, unsurprised when the young Swimmer deviated from his path to purchase a small bag of plums.

He would have to impress the seriousness of their situation on Adira somehow if they had any chance of salvaging an alliance with General Tal. He headed back to court, showing no interest in the vendors' wares. There was nothing for sale here that would help them out of their predicament.

CHAPTER 22

They were alone again, further afield than their usual picnic spot, flown to a new spot by Adira's swift wings. As expected, First General Oryd had protested their leaving, though it seemed as though he yielded easily these days, having discovered that Adira's will was unbending when it came to her Chrym searches. No matter how many veins her little pet uncovered, she still searched daily for more. He resigned himself to waiting, and if he wondered why her absence did not disturb him as greatly as it had just a week ago, he did not let himself think on it too much.

"General Tal is done waiting for an alliance, Adira." It was a somber warning, but Adira seemed unconcerned, smiling a tad mysteriously as she patted the empty spot next to her. Several rock walls loomed haphazardly around them, and Aja braced his arm against one as he leaned forward, staring morosely back in the direction they had come from. She was unwilling to understand their danger.

"Adira." He tried again, willing himself to patience, to find the right way to express his concerns. "They've ordered the assassination of Sik, with or without your approval."

"Sik is a danger to all of us. If the rebels don't take of her, I will." There was dismissal in her tone.

"You're missing the point, and the opportunity to ally with us."

Warm hands reached around his torso, dipping lower, lower still, toying with the top button of his trousers.

"And here I thought we were already allies." She nipped playfully at his earlobe, and he turned his head towards her against his better judgment, giving her access to his jawline, which she proceeded to shower with little nips and kisses. They needed to discuss their situation. Before the bond, he could have understood her lack of concern, but with the mate-bond firmly cemented between the two of them, she was incredibly vulnerable.

"You know we're more than that," he responded. "But I still serve the rebellion, and our situation is perilous. General Tal has decided to move without you. That makes you expendable in his eyes."

Her hands dipped lower still. Goaded by her lack of concern, he gripped her wrists tightly and shook her slightly. At last he had her attention.

"Two weeks ago, he ordered a test."

Tiny flames seemed to dance in Adira's eyes. "Not that," he said, exacerbated.

"Oh," she said, the fires banked for now.

"He wanted to know whether Chrym could injure you."

She stepped back now of her own accord, and he released her, allowing the distance.

"And did you find out?" she asked coldly.

Aja felt his lips curl as anger simmered in his gut. "You would know if I had. But you should also know that I would never do so."

Her hands found her hips in an age-old stance of opposition. "How would I know that? You declare that I am your universe, our hearts beat in unison, yet you still claim to ally with the rebels." There was hurt in her tone, a distance widening between them that had nothing to do with their physical placement. "You tell me in one breath that you still follow their orders, and in the next that you defy them for me."

"Only for your safety," he gritted, frustrated nearly beyond measure. "I will never betray a secret that could lead to your death."

"No! Just my enslavement!" she burst out, turning from him in a swirl of fabric. She'd chosen a bright cheery yellow dress today which matched the topaz jewelry he'd given her, though when they first arrived she'd teased there was little point to getting dressed after the shift. She knew now why he'd insisted and was oddly grateful for it. Being clothed as they argued gave her some protection, as though the thin fabric was armor against words, made her somehow less vulnerable. In spite of being unclothed for thousands of years, it had not taken her long to adopt Xaran modesty, she thought bitterly.

He shifted to press his back against the wall, hands pressed to his skull as he tipped his head back and groaned in frustration.

"I've been ordered to kill Sik."

Her jaw dropped briefly, and he thought he saw a glimmer of fear in her beautiful eyes. "You? When?"

"A week from today."

She stared thoughtfully at him. "That is a very long distance to cover in such a short time," she said, and something in her tone held him quiet, a tiny seed of hope uncurling. "How will you get there?" she asked, head tilting as she held his gaze.

She couldn't know the full measure of his Gift; though he had resolved to tell her about it against orders, the opportunity had not presented itself yet. No, he corrected himself, he'd had opportunities since the mate-bond. It was the thought of what such information might mean in Adira's stubborn hands that had kept him from revealing his last secret.

"I'll find a way," he finally answered. He was disappointed by her response – it took a few moments to understand why. Given their bond, he had more than half expected her to protest his dangerous assignment, but the empress was an astute judge of character, his at least, and had simply turned her mind to the logistics of the task.

"A swift horse might get you there if you left this morning, but you're not concerned, which tells me you have other transportation in mind," she added, her golden gaze still holding him pinned against the wall. "So how do you plan to do this thing, the murder of a queen?"

She paced towards him, and he was reminded uncomfortably of the great desert cats. No little koteeri this time, but one of the lions that roamed the wastelands far from humans and dragons alike. Full of stealth and power, just like Adira in her current form, they seemed too beautiful to house such destructive force, though the kills they left behind proved otherwise. He reminded himself of their bond and held steady as she reached one hand out to his chest, long slender index finger making contact, lightly at first, then harder, until he felt the sting of her fingernail through his shirt.

"Have you always thought to make the journey by wing?" she asked almost pleasantly, and he knew she'd gleaned at least part of their plan.

"I had not thought to involve you in the assassination itself," he answered indirectly. "Sik's death is all I wanted for so long, and I never planned to have any help accomplishing it. I only wanted you to know that things progress beyond our control."

He reached up to take her hand in his, relieving the stinging pressure over his heart as he stared into her eyes. "Please reconsider, Adira. Give me something to give the general when I report to him."

Another flicker of flames danced in those golden depths and his heart sank before she opened her mouth. "My mate should not report to anyone!" she spat.

"How would anyone know what I am to you," he retorted, trying to sound reasonable, not wanting her to know the hurt her silence on the matter had caused.

"You know why I haven't told!"

He sighed and moved away from the wall, following her as she paced away. There were many good reasons for her silence, not the least of which was the fear that one or both of them might be branded as traitors. If the dragons discovered that she had bonded with a Xaran slave it might drive them to madness. At the very worst, it would be a death sentence when the other queens learned of it. If word of their mate-bond got back to the rebellion before he could report it himself, he might well be handed his own death sentence. As it was, he would have his hands full spinning this into something the rebellion might find favorable.

He reached out and folded his arms around her, pulling her close and shifting his weight lightly from side to side. She allowed him to pull her back, leaning into him as he rocked her back and forth. "Aja, what are we going to do?" she whispered, and for the first time, the empress seemed unsure of herself.

"The answer lies with the rebellion," he answered, more certain than ever. "Let me deal with Sik, and report to General Tal. I'll explain that we're working on a plan," she snorted at his description of their stalemate, "and you're willing to meet with him," he continued stubbornly.

"I am?" She sounded astonished.

"Please, my love. Give me something to work with here," he pleaded.

She scowled and he barely contained a grin. He knew her well enough, whether in dragon or Xaran form to know that this was a petulant, I've lost and I know it, scowl. Moments later, she confirmed it.

"Very well." A sharp glance warned him not to celebrate too soon. "But I will be flying you to Sik, and I will join you when you give your rebel report." She spoke with finality, and unlike First General Oryd, Aja had learned when to hold his peace. Adira could only be moved so far with each attempt. He had pushed as hard as he could on the subject for now.

His hands had begun to wander, seeking to turn her thoughts to more pleasurable pursuits, when she pulled away, turning suddenly to face him. "I had a reason for bringing you to this spot," she announced, a strange excitement lighting her face.

"Oh?" he answered, busy shedding his shirt, his own intentions clear on his face.

"A gift, for you."

He paused and looked around.

"Yes," he said slowly. "I see that. What lovely leaning stones these are." He smirked as he reached for the trouser buttons she had been so eager to undo moments earlier.

"No, you idiot," she said without rancor. "Look!" and pulling away the dead vines and dust of centuries, she directed his attention to the stones' surface.

At his exclamation of disbelief, she gave a little pirouette of glee. "You like it! I knew you would!" Sometimes Adira could be so childlike in spite of her years, and it made his heart glad to see her joy. He looked up to watch her dance, momentarily distracted from the amazing discovery she'd offered. Adira in dragon form was a thing of beauty to be sure, but she was equally terrible to behold, a creature made for death and destruction. Adira in Xaran form was pure beauty, lithe and slender, perfect in all her glory. He could never choose one over the other, but as he watched her spontaneous dance of joy turn into something more sensual and beckoning, he knew which he preferred at the moment.

Stumbling to his feet, he followed her summons, the engraving on the stones forgotten. He was quite confused when moments later, she dropped to her knees and began digging in the dirt, an exclamation of discovery springing from her lips.

"Aha! I knew it was here. I remembered, Aja," she looked up and faltered at the expression on his face, "from my early years." Her voice trailed off as Aja stepped around her and forward, descending slowing down the stone path she'd uncovered.

"Aja?" she called uncertainly. "What if there are sicari down there?" Large biting insects, they were highly toxic, their bite causing excruciating pain to their victims, sometimes even resulting in death. They preferred to gather in dark, moist places, and the structure Adira had uncovered was exactly the kind of place they might dwell. Already Aja could feel moisture in the air – there must be a living source of water nearby. He felt the Chrym as well, had felt it all afternoon but chosen to ignore it in favor of other concerns. Now, however, he felt the pull, felt it as strongly as he ever had, and was suddenly quite certain that there was a node somewhere down there.

"It's all right, Adira," he called back. "I've been stung before."

Earlier that week one of Adira's Gifted slaves had been badly stung by a single sicari and quickly died from an extreme reaction. Adira had been distraught and ordered a burning of the entire area to remove any remaining creatures before allowing any of the Xarans back to their work.

"Stay there," he ordered sharply when she would have followed, an unpleasant thought suddenly occurring. "We don't know if you're immune to their poison."

The words froze her in place, and at any other time he might have been amused to see the Great Empress Adira discomfited by a few insects, but for the first time since his childhood, he feared for the safety of another over his own. Although her first shift back to dragon form had completely healed her injury from the marketplace stoning, sicari venom acted quickly, and the transformation required concentration. It was hard to concentrate on a shift of that magnitude when your veins felt on fire. Aja knew from experience the particular agony of the bite, and that was without the sensitivity that could prove fatal. He would not risk her, and continued down the stairs alone.

"Aja," she called plaintively, and despite his warning, she took another step down. Her refusal to be separated forced him to reconsider.

"All right," he relented, emerging back into the dry desert air. "Can you turn and Flare, hot enough to roast any of those little devils to a crisp?"

It was a huge risk, he knew. The heat she generated might also destroy any artifacts that still remained, but he felt reasonably sure that if she avoided any flammable surfaces and simply raised the temperature of the stone structure, she would create an oven effect without causing a fire, consigning any sicari within to a certain death.

She cast him an exasperated look. "Step back."

He moved away to gather their belongings before stepping well outside the ring of stones.

"Further," she called as she tossed her dress in his direction, and he raised his eyebrows. It appeared that Adira was taking no chances, and intended to well and truly roast the entire site. He watched as she shifted into her natural state, just as intrigued as the countless other times. Her slender shape seemed to lose focus, like a sculpture made of sand that was sliding to the floor, but instead of falling, the tiny particles that formed her shape began to swirl and expand, spinning rapidly outward to fill the space her dragon form would take. It took only seconds, and then the great golden dragon Adira stood where a beautiful Xaran woman had been just a breath ago.

"Back!" she insisted, and he could already see waves of heat curling off her form. He hastily stepped back farther, and farther still as the heat surged toward him like a storm blast. Even that wasn't enough and he was forced to hold her dress over his face to shield his skin from the heat.

"Adira!" he choked, knowing he didn't have to speak loudly for her excellent dragon hearing. "I'm pretty sure you've roasted anything with a quarter mile of the ruins."

"All right," she called as she stepped from behind a stone, already in Xaran form. He shook his head as he tested the temperature of the sand.

"I don't think so. It's going to be a while before I can get anywhere near those stones. No matter what your appearance, you're clearly still a dragon."

He grinned as she picked up a handful of sand to luxuriate in the heat she'd created.

"I, on the other hand, am exactly what I look like – a weak human who would shrivel to a crisp on those sands."

"But that means we might have to wait for hours before exploring the ruins together," she realized. Aja hastily dropped their belongings to catch her as she jumped into his arms with childlike abandon. "On the other hand, I'm sure we can find something else to do."

It was late afternoon before they entered the stone stairwell again and made their way quickly into the wide hallways beyond. The building they discovered was laid out in a similar fashion to many in the rebel city, with a wide main corridor, bisected by two shorter corridors. Each corridor had dozens of rooms, and each of the shorter corridors had a stairwell, leading to other floors. The rooms were empty, and the pair gazed at each other, disappointed by their failure to find anything of interest.

"Another floor?" Aja suggested.

Adira frowned at the small torches they each carried.

"I didn't plan very well for your surprise, did I?"

"I'm not complaining. I love an adventure."

"Well I don't, not when it could get us both killed."

"I don't think anything could have survived that Flare, Adira."

She shook her torch at him for emphasis. "These aren't going to last much longer, and a fall down stone steps could easily kill me in this form, not to mention if something were to happen to you."

Aja wondered if she regretted the mate-bond every time his physical limitations held her back, but kept the thought to himself. It wouldn't be fair to put his insecurity on her. It wasn't her fault they were from different species, though perhaps it could benefit them in this instance.

He looked at her more closely, scanning her exposed skin, and she glanced wildly about.

"What, is there a sicari on me? Aja!" she practically yelped when he failed to answer right away.

"I wonder," he responded and moved closer. She watched quizzically as he lifted her hand in his, holding it up to the light. As they both stared, the flicker of the torch caught a lighter, almost silvery section of skin on her forearm, then another, and another. Adira gasped in surprise, examining her skin more closely. Patterned across her body, visible only when the light caught them just so, were dozens of thin, subtle stripes, continuing up her arm, and she supposed, her entire body.

"I thought so," Aja said.

She stared at him, astonished he had noticed the faint striping that remained in her Xaran form when she herself had not.

"You could say I am slightly obsessed with your form, regardless of which shape you choose." He shrugged as if to say, what can you expect, and she shook her head.

"See if you can Lace," he suggested.

"I've never tried in this form," she protested.

He leaned toward her and kissed her breathless. "I have faith in my Empress," he encouraged, and she closed her eyes and tried. Nothing. She scowled angrily at the stripes and focused harder. Still no Lacing. Throwing her hands up in exasperation, she exclaimed, "It's not working."

Aja shrugged again, then grabbed her arm. "Look!"

Her Laces, while not as brilliant as in dragon form, were clearly visible now. "Try again," he demanded, and though she took exception to his tone, she was too determined to control her abilities to take him to task. Several minutes later, she had achieved a faint phosphorescence over her entire body. Since she was still fully dressed the resultant effect was rather eerie, giving her the appearance of a glowing head, shoulders and arms floating above a dimly lit gown. It was far from perfect, but more than sufficient to keep them from complete blindness if the torches went, a far greater likelihood given the time they'd taken.

"Downward?" he asked again, and she nodded emphatically.

They went back to the stairs, but this time Aja did not diverge on the first floor they reached. He continued ever downwards as though he had a destination in mind, and Adira followed, one hand extended to rest lightly on his shoulder. When they reached the bottom floor, it did not match the pattern of the upper floors. Though it had several small rooms nestled against the wall they stood closest to, much of what would have been the main corridor was a massive, open room, easily three stories high. Their footsteps echoed through the cavernous space as Aja led them towards a giant marble table that predominated over the room.

Adira felt a flicker of unease, as memories of another life threatened to surface. For a brief moment, another room appeared in ghostly overlay to the room she now stood in. This room was well lit, a series of massive crystal chandeliers dominating the high ceilings, rich, sumptuous pieces of furniture strategically placed to break the space apart into multiple seating areas. A heavily muscled man in a nice suit looked up and spotted her. A smile creased his face as he gestured her towards him. Adira took one hesitant step in his direction before the spell was broken by an exclamation of delight.

"I knew it!" crowed Aja. "We're in the municipal building of an old Xaran city. If it follows the same pattern as the rebel headquarters, the library should be directly in front of the main doors, just across the street." He turned away from the desk, trying to get his bearings against the stairwell they'd entered, establishing the direction to look in when they returned to the surface. Turning back to the desk, he ran his hands lovingly over the seal that proclaimed the building's purpose.

"It's fortunate our ancestors weren't very creative when they named municipal buildings," he murmured. "Hopefully they were just as predictable in their design."

Adira glanced at Aja where he crouched before the desk, hands caressing a large seal embossed on the front of the marble surface, then glanced up, half expecting to see a darkened chandelier above her, but if there had ever been a chandelier there, no trace remained; not even a fragment of broken glass on the dust-coated floor. Perhaps the Xarans had had other ways of lighting their buildings, she thought, and wanted to say as much to him, but the eerie feeling of being in two places at once was nearly overwhelming. She wanted to stay here with Aja, but the memories were so strong in this place she wasn't sure she could control them if they surfaced again.

"What is it?" Alerted by her silence, Aja moved away from the desk, coming to stand before her as he scanned her for injuries.

"I want to leave this place." Her tone was just shy of panic, and Aja moved immediately toward the stairwell with her. He could return on his own if need be, but was fairly certain where to find the library now that they had uncovered the first of what he was sure were many buildings buried beneath the desert. He could feel the Chrym node calling and was fairly certain he could leap to it from here, though he didn't dare until he knew what he might be leaping to.

When they returned to the surface, Aja left Adira standing next to the stone wall that marked the entrance to the municipal building and paced off the distance he thought would be necessary to reach the library, assuming the cities shared the same design. He marked the spot with several heavy stones, then returned to his mate, who stood with her arms crossed at her waist, silently observing him.

She tipped her head back to meet his gaze as he came to stand before her. "What happened down there?" Silence coupled with an angry shrug was the only answer he received.

"Adira." He drew the name out, reaching for one hand. She tucked her arms tighter against her body, refusing to be drawn out. "Come little koteeri, tell me what has you so upset."

At the endearment, her eyes flashed to his, and he could tell she wasn't sure if she liked the endearment. Seeing only sincerity in his dark gaze, she let the term pass without comment. As he cajoled further, she finally allowed herself to be drawn from the stone wall to their blankets. It was nearing dusk, soon time to return or risk First General Oryd's patrols finding her in mid-turn as they searched for their empress, but Aja wanted answers and she could tell he was not going to allow her self-imposed silence to last.

"Tell me what happened down there," he insisted, and she began to explain, or least try to.

"It was not one thing, so much as many, I think." She began slowly. "Their buildings are alike, yet different, and," she stopped, searching for the words to continue. "It's like the dreams. I never know what I'm going to see, but I always know how it will end. When we were down there, on that bottom level, I experienced a waking dream, like a memory surfacing through time. It was so strong, Aja, and I felt like I was losing this place, you. I wasn't sure I was strong enough to stay with you." She shivered as she recalled those moments in the bottom level of the ruin.

"A dream?" Of course he would key in on that word, she thought, having been privy to her disrupted nights. "Tell me more about this dream."

So she went back to the beginning, telling him all about the dreams that had begun nearly two decades earlier, beginning with the start of each cold season and lasting sometimes weeks beyond.

"At first, it was just a string of restless nights. I would wake up tired, with no memory of why I was awake, why I was so restless, frightened even." It wasn't entirely true, but she wasn't ready to admit a fear of falling, not even to her bonded mate.

"Eventually I decided that occasional restless nights were part of a building breeding cycle and figured I'd just have to put up with it until the flight." She grimaced and shrugged, as matter-of-fact about the downside of fertility as any Xaran woman.

"But then a few years ago I started remembering bits and pieces of the dreams. I was human, I was married, I had a little girl. And then one day I lost it all. It felt so real, like a story, but *my* story, Aja." She became more animated as she tried to convince him. "They're not just dreams, Aja. They're memories of another life before this one."

"That's not possible," Aja argued. The thought of Adira with another man, in another life, building a family with someone she loved didn't sit well, though the pain he saw in her eyes as she spoke of losing

161

them seemed real enough.

"Isn't it?" she gestured bitterly to her current form. "Why can't I remember my birth, when every dragon on the planet remembers the exact moment of their hatching?"

"Those are hatchings, not live births. Maybe you're not supposed to remember your birth. Couldn't Oryd or one of the others tell you?"

"How?" she asked irritably. "They're all males, remember? How would they know the first thing about what a queen remembers when she first draws breath?"

"What about the other queens? Couldn't they tell you anything?" he pressed, and she scowled.

"I was far more violent than most in my youth, Aja. After killing all those other queens, do you really think the rest were eager to tell me any stories of their early days? We are not exactly friends in the best of times, you know."

He ignored the sharpness of her tone. "Aren't there any queens who might be approachable?"

"None," she responded morosely. "Even Klis and Rana," she named the two youngest queens, "are wary of me, and they were born tens of thousands of years after I became an empress. They do not even remember Halon, yet they are still wary."

Rightfully so, Aja thought, though he wisely did not voice the words. Adira seemed so normal, so Xaran in her present guise, that it was easy to forget what a fearsome creature she truly was. When she spoke offhandedly of devouring a sun, he felt nearly as discomposed as he had when he'd first discovered her secret. The great Devourer of Suns, the most powerful creature on the planet, sat before him in a simple yellow dress, hands folded demurely in her lap. She was stubborn and arrogant, thoughtful and loving, and most importantly of all, this sun-devouring, Chrym-melting, glorious creature was his.

It disturbed him to see the fear in her eyes, fear of a past that was finding its way back to her through dreams, and he realized that it was perhaps the loss of control that bothered her most. Dreams could not be fought, could not be escaped, nor killed. Adira, for all her might, was powerless against them.

"Perhaps there is an answer." He suggested carefully.

"I've tried everything," Adira responded.

"Have you tried choosing what you see in your dreams?" Aja asked. "Directing your thoughts where you'd like to travel before you sleep?"

Her golden eyes widened, and he surmised the answer for himself.

"What should I seek to find?" she asked, excited by the possibilities. She had told him already of the family her earlier self had possessed, a husband and little girl, and while Aja did not care for the thought of sending her back to them, he felt that these memories, with their strong emotional component were what she struggled with the most.

"You should focus on what causes you the most emotion," he said, forcing himself to say the words. "The loss of a family is just about the greatest pain I can imagine. If you want answers to these dreams, that's where I'd start."

She frowned, but he knew her well enough by now to know she was frightened, not angry. "I think it far more likely that dying every night is what disturbs my slumber," she suggested, not wanting to confront the emotional pain of that loss, imaginary or otherwise.

"Let's assume for a moment that your dreams really are past memories. You said in every dream you were normal, human," he worded his thoughts carefully, in an effort not to offend or alarm her. "You called your attackers dragons as though you already knew the name for them, but you believed they didn't really exist, except as a myth."

She frowned, nodding in puzzled agreement, not seeing the direction his mind went.

"They didn't exist in your world," he said again with emphasis, and at last she understood the point he was trying to make.

"If my dreams are true memories, I couldn't have been born a dragon," she exclaimed, astonished by the possibility.

"They attacked, and you didn't turn to defend yourself or your family, not because you wouldn't, but because you couldn't!"

"But I don't understand," she frowned. "Dragons don't convert their prey, they just kill or maim."

Aja tried not to picture his tiny village, his family's charred remains.

"How would an attack on my home planet," she said those last words with a sense of incredulity, "turn me into a dragon?"

"Not just any dragon," he reminded her. "A golden dragon. We recently stumbled across an ancient myth that mentions another queen who was different from all the others. It can't be proved of course, but if she was real, she could have been the first shape-shifter. You could be some distant descendent, born on some other world. Maybe this is the answer to your origins, why you're so different, how you could bond with a Xaran."

A ghost of some nameless expression flitted across her face. "I wouldn't be so sure her story can't be proven."

Aja worked hard to contain his excitement. In all their research of Adira, they had never come across a definite reference to another golden dragon.

"When I was young, I lived by instinct. It made me wary when I was weak, and aggressive, very aggressive when I was strong." She offered the explanation as an excuse and an apology for behavior she couldn't undo.

"The first queen I killed was old, the most ancient of our kind still alive. As she lay dying, and her eyesight dimmed, she gazed upon me and called me by another name. I thought perhaps she mistook me for a daughter, but her First General swore she had no daughter by that name."

Adira was looking up at the darkening sky as she retold the story, as though she couldn't bear to look at Aja. She truly seemed repentant for those long-ago actions, and Aja realized for the first time what a burden long life could be, especially when ruled by nearly uncontrollable instincts, all while retaining the capacity for compassion, for empathy. Adira had once told him that every dragon was born violent, which was the primary reason they were kept contained in the hatching caverns for so long. It was only once they reached an age of at least one hundred years that they could be trusted not to devour everything in sight. Aja had been shocked to learn of it, one of the many things their ancient scientists had been unable to discover. He'd been more horrified to learn that for every dragon to emerge from the caverns, a hundred more had likely perished there, torn apart by stronger brothers. Adira had smiled wryly as she called it population control and he had wondered if she considered her own early aggression toward the other queens in the same vein.

"You only did what you were born to do," he comforted. "You did what you needed to do to survive." He was suddenly, overwhelmingly grateful that this amazing creature had overcome such odds in order to be here now, with him.

"Oryxa," she murmured to her starry audience, and Aja stiffened in disbelief.

"What did you say?"

"That was the name, the name the old queen called me as she lay dying. She looked up at me and said, 'I always knew it would be you who would end me. Daughters are born to kill their mothers, why should you be so different, my bright and shining one?'" As Adira finished the old queen's dying words, her gaze met his. "Bright and shining! Could Oryxa have been a golden dragon?"

Aja was almost certain of it, based on the old legends the rebels had discovered from the southern territories. While she was never referred to as golden, the name Oryxa had passed almost reverently from the lips of the few refugees who came from the far south, hushed and quiet. It had taken tremendous patience to get even that much from them, confirming the rebellions earliest assessment that southern-most province would require significant effort to infiltrate. What he knew of the great queen was that she had lived, thousands of generations before Adira by all accounts, and she had been greater than any dragon known to their kind. Lured by stories of the Chrym, she had arrived from another world long after the Xarans were overcome, which might explain why the ancients hadn't written of her. Back then apparently the dragons had been more nomadic, always seeking new worlds to conquer and devour. She had arrived, and through audacity and will, had taken over the entire planet, ruling the other queens, uniting all dragons until her death, at the teeth and claws of her daughter, Therrah. Aja had taken the tale for wishful thinking, but he'd forgotten his own counsel – every legend starts with a grain of truth. Of greater interest to him at the moment were the parts of the legend which stated Oryxa had come from another world, and a strange choice of wording by the dying queen.

"Why should you be so different," he repeated. "Are you sure that's exactly what she said?"

Adira flashed him a cross look. If there was one thing he'd learned, it was that dragons hated having their memory questioned. Renowned for their memory, confusion over small details was the first sign that a dragon was succumbing to the ravages of time. It put a new light on Adira's discomfort over her own inability to recall her origins.

"Why would she say that? Why say, 'Why should you be so different?' Why expect Oryxa to be different from any other daughter- "

"-unless she wasn't born, but made!" Adira finished excitedly.

They stared at each other, electrified by their possible discovery.

"Some of the refugees we've brought in from the sourthern territories pass along stories of Oryxa," Aja reluctantly revealed, and Adira leaped to her feet to pace between the standing stones.

"We could go there. We could go there and speak to them, find out what they know." The hem of her dress swirled with her rapid movements.

"They're incredibly suspicious of outsiders, Adira. It took years just to get a handful of our people into a few of their border communities, and after years of living side by side with these people, they're still barely tolerated. No one's going to speak to us if we just show up, and if one of my contacts welcomes a pair of strangers into their home, they'll become true outcasts from that point forward."

"They won't speak to anyone?" Her disappointment was obvious and he reached for her hand as she sank to the blanket beside him.

"We'll find a way, love. It just won't be right this moment. Give me a chance to figure something out." What he knew but didn't say was that the fastest way to gain entrance to this insulated community was to engineer some kind of disaster where he or Adira could step in as heroes.

"You could put more thought into it if Sik were no longer a problem," Adira suggested, and he sighed.

Sik's death had been his only goal for so long, but his longing for revenge was overshadowed by his fear of what would have to come first. In truth, the longer he'd hidden the true extent of his Gift from Adira, the more he dreaded revealing it. And he would have to reveal it, because if Adira carried him within sight of Sik's palace, she would never stop there, and while he had full confidence she could defeat Sik in battle, being certain of the outcome and watching his mate fight to the death were two very different things. He also knew that if he couldn't stand and wait while she faced Sik alone, it would be doubly hard for Adira to remain at home and behave as though nothing was amiss while he slipped through Sik's palace to assassinate a queen. No, his fiery mate would insist on coming, or at least being close, and frankly it was necessary. Once Sik died, the pheromone bond that held her colony in place would dissolve rapidly, leading to chaos among her males until another queen claimed them. The sooner that happened, the fewer human casualties there would be. That meant flying with Adira most of the way to Sik and Swimming in alone. There were other advantages to the approach, not the least of which was the energy flight would conserve while in enemy territory. He only wished Adira had formed an official alliance with General Tal before offering to help him complete his mission. Without that agreement, the rebel camp he had called home for nearly twenty years might all too soon become enemy territory, for he knew now that he would never choose the rebellion over Adira if it came to that.

CHAPTER 23

It was late the next night when Adira and Aja slipped from the palace to make the flight to Sik. Adira had risked discovery to shift into Xaran form in order to escape Oryd's ever watchful eye. As far as the First General knew, his Empress still slept soundly in her chamber, the disturbances that awakened her during the cold season well and truly over. Aja knew they were not over, just better managed, more focused throughout the week, thanks to his suggestion to visualize what Adira would experience, what she wanted to see.

"We're far enough away," Adira whispered, eager to fly.

"No," he argued. "All the way to the rocks."

They had chosen their first picnic spot as their take-off point earlier that week. Not too far to travel by foot, but far enough away from a permanent water source or anything else of interest that might attract casual travelers, the location's true value lay in the rocks themselves. Large and closely clumped together, they formed a natural feature in the landscape, capable of hiding a dragon's significant size. Even as tiny as she was in comparison to other dragons, Adira was hard to miss on the flat desert plains.

They picked up their pace, and he was thankful he'd been able to provide her with sensible, well-fitting shoes for this leg of their journey. Though the transformation would heal any minor wounds, it bothered him more than he cared to think to see her injured in any way. She kept pace easily, a remnant of her dragon strength, which though greatly reduced in Xaran form, was noticeably different from a true Xaran.

At last they reached the rocks, and Adira undressed by the simple expediency of pulling her dress over her head, tossing it aside for Aja to gather while she kicked off her sandals. He grabbed them quickly as she

167

moved away.

"Wait!"

She paused, a dim glimmer in the darkness. He could see the faint outline of her face by the phosphorescence she called easily now in this form, the golden eyes that glowed dimly, eerily, like a desert hunting cat.

"Aja, we must hurry. Even by wing, it will take most of the night to reach Sik's chambers." Adira was eager to fly south, seeking answers regarding her extraordinary existence. She had seized upon the hope of finding more details about the dragon she now believed to be her mother, and perhaps in the process, discover some clues leading to still living relatives. She still believed they would be free to head to the far south and confirm her origins as soon as Aja had completed his task and reported to his superiors. He had his doubts that any of it would be so simple, and he was not wrong.

Their troubles began with his admission regarding the true extent of his Gift. Another reason for choosing the rock cluster for the transformation was the Chrym. It had an affinity for water, and a small amount of the precious metal nestled here, far beneath the stones that collected small pools of water during the rainy season. It was enough for the task at hand.

"I need to show you something first," he said.

"We don't have time," she responded, impatient now.

"Adira." He said her name calmly, quietly, and at last she gave him her full attention, moving towards him in the dark, her features becoming clearer as she came closer, finally halting within touching distance.

"What," she said, enunciating each word with precise clarity, "is so important that it cannot wait?"

He winced. They were not off to a good start.

"Watch," he said, pointing to the ground as he began Calling the Chrym. He had pulled it closer earlier that week, and with very little effort it now surfaced. It was too dark for him to see when it reached the surface, he only knew by his Gift, but Adira's exceptional night vision allowed her to spot the metal immediately. Her glowing face turned towards him again. It was a measure of her impatience to be gone that her only response was, "Lovely, Aja. Now let's be gone."

"Not done yet, my love." She watched with head cocked as he formed a long, thin ribbon of the stuff, then compelled a small amount to break off and move several feet away.

"Is this another sculpture of me?" she asked suspiciously. "It looks rather like a beheaded speckle." She referred to an extremely poisonous snake which lived near granaries, feeding off the rodents that fed and reproduced in the surrounding fields, and the manner in which Xarans typically dealt with the creatures.

Vaguely surprised she knew of the snake, he chuckled and tilted his head, Seeing the Chrym with his Gift. "It rather does at that. But that's not what I wanted to show you," he finished quickly at her huff of impatience.

He led her to the disembodied "head" of the snake, then stepped several feet away to the body, holding her gaze in the darkness, and Dove. He entered the stream as slowly as possible, aware of the small 'oh' of surprise she made as he disappeared into the metal. Swimming swiftly along the stream he'd created, he knew she was unable to follow his progress. The Chrym sang happy thoughts and feelings at him, and he reached the end of the short path within moments.

"*Leap?*" the Chrym asked happily, and he was shocked at how clearly the metal communicated with him now. His astonishment nearly threw him from the Chrym, but he caught himself just in time and managed an answer.

The Chrym seemed to throw him forward, the separated piece was ready to catch him as he crossed the small distance between them, and Aja was again reminded of legends of telepathic dragons and lost Swimmers, Xaran conquerors and Chrym rebels. But if the Chrym wished to rebel, he felt fairly certain this happy vein was not party to their plans. Controlling his unease, he waited a moment, then gathered himself and emerged from the little puddle of Chrym near Adira's feet.

She shrieked with surprise and leaped back, arms windmilling for balance, then recovered quickly and punched him in the arm, hard.

"What was that for?" he asked, rubbing the injured limb in surprise.

She shrugged and responded, "It made me feel better."

The petulant tone made him laugh, which had the direct result of making her even angrier.

"It's not funny Aja! You scared me!" then, "How did you do that?"

He sobered quickly. Here was the hard part. The explanation was swift now that he'd shown her the Gift – he wanted this over. Her silence was painful.

"Understand Adira, I was sworn – am still sworn – to secrecy on this. It is the one secret Gift that all Xaran, commoner and priest alike, have kept hidden from the dragons."

He could practically feel her seething beside him, and when he reached for her and pulled her close, she was as unbending as a tree.

"The rebellion would order my death if they knew I'd told you of this," he ignored her wordless protest, "but I couldn't continue to keep it from you, not only because it affects our plans for tonight, but also because I couldn't bear to keep any secrets from you any longer."

She had melted slightly against him at the thought of the rebellion taking action against him, and melted further at his confession that the secret had weighed on him.

He knew he'd passed the first hurdle to forgiveness when she asked, "How does this change our plan?"

This was the next difficult part of the plan – convincing Adira to let him finish the journey to Sik alone. It was best to get it over with quickly he decided.

"You're not going beyond Sik's border."

She pulled away and Laced so brightly he could see every detail of her widened eyes, flared nostrils and thinned lips. Perhaps blunt had not been the best way to go. The silence that followed felt dangerous and he hesitated to speak again. Could a mate-bond be broken by a particularly block-headed male, he wondered, and realized he was sweating.

"Tell me truthfully you could resist the urge to challenge if you came any further." He held his breath and waited, but no answer was forthcoming.

"She killed my parents, Adira. She killed my baby brother. He was seven years old, and she killed him. I wasn't there and I could have been. I wasn't there, and I might have stopped her. I wasn't there because I was selfish and secretive and looking for answers I didn't deserve. I need to do this. I need to do this for them, and I need to do it for me."

He was shocked by the rage and grief that swelled through him as he finally voiced the guilt he'd carried all of these years. Adira's form dimmed slowly as he spoke, until only a faint glow from her eyes remained.

"Yes, you do."

He closed his eyes as a wave of relief swept through his body. Her arms slipped around his waist and she pressed her head against him.

"It's not your fault, what happened to them. You were a child. You were a child," she repeated as he would have protested, "No matter what our laws say. How can a seventeen-year-old be blamed for wanting answers? How can a seventeen-year-old be responsible for a stopping a centuries-old queen in her prime, with skills he only barely comprehends. It wasn't your fault," she repeated, simply and with conviction, now raining kisses over his face.

"I'll let you do this alone. Not because I'm ok with it, believe me, I'm not. I'll let you do this because it's what you need, and that makes it something I need, Aja. Do you understand how this works yet? It's not about you, it's not about me, it's about us. Sometimes that's not easy or comfortable, and I'm sure as the suns not happy about it, but I'll give you what you need because we won't be alright if I don't."

His arms wrapped around her as the words sank in. He'd expected fury and maybe even contempt, but her response humbled him. She didn't condemn him for failing to protect his family all those years ago, and she didn't condemn him for needing revenge on his terms. They held each other a while longer, quietly taking comfort in the rapport of their bond, before the passing of time forced them to take action.

Adira might have accepted his need to continue alone once they reached Sik's borders, but she wasn't happy about it, and worked her anger out in rapid wing strokes that took them high above the planet, higher than he'd ever gone before. The air was thin and cold, and he thought at first she'd done it to punish him. Then they caught their first super thermal. If he'd thought dragon flight was fast before, this was like nothing he could have imagined. He finally understood why Adira was so sure she could travel such a great distance before dawn.

Unlike all the other thermals they'd ridden since their first flight together, Adira didn't glide passively on the stream of air, but powered forward, speeding their flight until Aja was forced to bring his shirt up over his face to protect his skin from the burning kiss of the wind and help bring some air into his lungs. Adira would have slowed then, but he indicated for her to keep moving.

When they finally landed near the Chrym vein that bisected Adira and Sik's territory, Aja told himself that it was choice that kept him prostrate on the ground for several minutes. Adira remained in dragon form and stood silently by the river, just feet away from him. The silence stretched for several minutes as he concentrated on breathing and the solid feel of the earth beneath him. At least in the darkness he had not had to watch the shifting horizon during the flight, though he wasn't sure if that made things better or worse.

"This is where you grew up?" she asked quietly, and he looked up to see her indicate a small fishing raft, nearly grounded now that the cold season had ended and the river was drying up. It was in fairly good shape, evidence that the village had been revived in the years since his absence and presumed death.

"It's where a lot of us grew up, and many didn't," he answered simply.

"Merot. Behar. Qal."

He looked up in surprise as she spoke the words with solemnity, acknowledging the family that had lived and died here at another queen's hands.

"Is this vengeance, or service to a cause?" she asked then.

"Why can't it be both?" he countered, and she gave no answer, only sighed and moved away.

"When you return," she refused to entertain the other possibility, "how do we reach the rebel city?"

She was already fairly certain she knew the answer, that Aja believed he would relegate her to waiting in the shadows again. She would have protested if she believed her presence would aid him in explaining his new circumstances to his general, but feared she might make things worse. Though she literally could not live without Aja, she was not yet willing to accept a life of servitude amongst those she had once mastered, however gently.

"I'll need to go alone, at least at first."

His answer was not unexpected, and she caught naked relief in his eyes as she agreed.

"I will wait, but on one condition."

A wariness entered his expression.

"I need to know the rebel's location," her voice rose as he opened his mouth to protest, "and a promise that you will return to me by noon tomorrow."

"It is non-negotiable," she added as his mouth remained open. Left unspoken was the thought that she would raze what was left of the ruined city to the ground if they did not return her beloved in the prescribed amount of time.

"We'll discuss it when I return."

She would have snapped a response, but he Dove, irritating man, managing the last word at last, leaving her to stew and worry in the dark.

The ensuing hours gave her far too much time to think, and she did not dare sleep, and perhaps dream of her past, in this open place. This village had already suffered one terrible burning – with all these dead and drying grasses that spread between the river and the village, if she panicked because of the dream or her concern over Aja and Flared in her sleep, she could easily bring the whole place down again.

CHAPTER 24

Aja finished his Swim in record time, buoyed by a new connection with the Chrym, which seemed more sentient than ever. He wondered briefly if the change had anything to do with his bond to Adira – all the ancient texts were clear – a queen's mate grew in strength after the bond, though never as strong as his queen. Aja was not a dragon, and could not therefore expect to gain any strength from the bond, yet there was no denying that he Swam more strongly and easily than ever before.

Even with his increased strength, there was no way to Leap directly from the vein to Sik's court – she had mined every tiny scrap of Chrym within miles of her colony. He was fortunate enough to catch a small transport of Chrym just leaving the vein he had traveled, and made a wild Leap, barely catching the new source. As before, both sources seemed aware of his presence and intent, facilitating the transition from one to the other.

Once settled within the mined Chrym, he rested quietly, gathering his strength. There was no way for him to know where freshly transported Chrym went when it arrived at Sik's colony, though if it was anything like Adira's court, the Chrym would be sent first to the younger, less skilled Weavers who would sift through the metal for impurities before handing it to the more skilled Weavers, who would work in much closer proximity to the queen. If he could manage to reach that point, a Leap to any Chrym adorning Sik's chambers might be possible, and then it would be quick work to finish his task, or so he hoped. He'd once dreamed of making Sik's death as slow and painful as possible, but now he just wanted it over and done so he could return to Adira.

With that thought in mind, he began to Weave the Chrym, a truly odd experience while residing within the substance. Pulling, asking, he separated the metal from the heavy rock the unskilled Miners had brought to the surface with the Chrym, then safely nestled within the pure metal, he broke it off from the larger piece it had bonded with.

"*Goodbye, goodbye,*" a few tiny flecks of Chrym sang from the culled stone as Aja's piece clanked and rolled away, rattling around in the bottom of the wagon for what seemed an eternity. His head ached from the vibrations long before the wagon stopped, and it didn't take long before he decided to Weave the metal into a depression in the floor to minimize his suffering. Under other circumstances he might have found it interesting that the Chrym itself seemed unaffected by the constant jarring, but he could feel himself settling into the space he needed to be the Choosing Assassin, and welcomed the calm quiet that allowed him to do what needed doing.

Rough hands picked him up and tossed him out – another jarring blow that nearly broke his rapport with the metal. Softer hands passed whisper light, then returned with a firmer touch. A Weaver had felt the purity of his vessel. He had a sensation of being examined, once, twice, again. Alarmed, he tried to align his thoughts with the Chrym. He had never held rapport with Chrym while another Gifted Weaver examined the metal. He had no idea if the Weaver could sense him, but his vessel had certainly caught their attention. Another probing touch pierced through him, and he turned himself inward, hiding all but one thought – *happy, happy.*

Eventually the examination passed, and his vessel moved onward, into the hands of another, stronger Gift. Fortunately this Weaver was not interested in examining the Chrym they held, and he moved swiftly through Sik's court. At last he was in the main Weaving room, and from a distance, he sensed a great deal of very pure Chrym. It had to be Sik's private chambers.

Hiding from the young Weaver had taken a great deal of energy, and he rested again, vaguely aware of the passage of time, but experienced enough to pace himself. He didn't need privacy to Leap from one source to another, but he did need the strength to finish the job once he was in her chambers, and the best time to take Sik, when she was most likely to sleep deeply, was just before dawn. So Aja waited, and hoped he would not be pulled for Weaving in the meantime. Sik worked her Weavers day and night, forcing long shifts on her slaves to keep production high.

While he waited, he became aware of another useful enhancement to his skill. Before the mate-bond, he had only been able to sense the proximity of other people, but now as he concentrated, he found he was able to listen to the conversations taking place around him. He discovered the skill none too soon, as two Weavers approached the table he rested on.

"Young Typetras tells me there's at least one uncommonly pure piece in the latest shipment from the Layrak vein."

"That's a good sign. Maybe we if we start pulling better quality, our people can get a bit more rest. Do we know if it's the quality of the vein or maybe a Miner with a strong Gift?" asked the second Weaver as she picked up the piece Aja rested in.

"I don't have a clue, but I'll start asking around to see if there's anyone who stands out, or if anyone has noticed an increase in purity at that location."

"Hmmm," the woman was focused on Aja, and for one alarming moment he felt sure she'd discovered him, but she replaced the Chrym on the table, setting the metal down so lightly he barely felt the impact, and moved on.

"Yes, I think it would be wise to focus our attention on the Layrak team. If we can shift some of the culling burden to earlier stages, we might not see so much burnout here."

Aja couldn't hear the response as the pair moved away, but from the many reports he'd received over the years, he was well aware of the punishment Sik's Weavers suffered for failing to perform, or rather the punishment their loved ones suffered. He moved from the pure Chrym nodule that had carried him to Sik's palace to a larger piece with more impurities just to be safe. The tiny node he'd created was much easier to hold rapport with, but called far too much attention for his purposes, and once he made the move the rest of the night was uneventful.

Just before dawn, Aja gathered himself for the enormous Leap to Sik's quarters. Again, the sentient metal assisted, seeming eager to help with his goal. Perhaps the Chrym wished to be free of such a malevolent creature. From everything he was able to gather, Chrym did not like cruelty or violence, in as much as it was capable of disliking anything. With hindsight Aja realized it was one of the things he'd enjoyed most about Weaving at Adira's court. The metal had sung with joy, lighting up in her presence, happy in the hands of her Gifted.

He gathered his strength again and extended his senses outward. The massive shape of Sik's crimson and black scaled body rose above her bed, a deep circular pit built into the floor that was filled with gold. Unlike Adira, Sik kept no fire pits, not trusting her servants to tend faithfully to her in her sleep, and Aja faced his first true challenge. Sik did not maintain fire pits in her bedchamber, but that did not mean the queen suffered any chills. Heat curled off her body in massive waves as she Flared through the night, the kinetic energy distorting the shape of the stone walls around her. Even nestled within the Chrym, he could feel the heat of her massive body, and Chrym was the most heat-resistant substance known to the dragons. He knew instantly that he wouldn't survive his first breath if he took his physical form within the queen's chamber.

The long ride and multiple Leaps had exhausted him, but Aja was determined to complete his task. Sik twitched and moaned occasionally in her sleep as he considered several alternatives, but all seemed risky at best, doomed to failure at worst. As he pondered the situation, he became aware of a growing sense of urgency. The Chrym was trying to get his attention.

Kill?, it asked. *Kill?*

For a brief moment, an alien sentience pushed into his mind, showing him the sleeping form of Sik, and he recoiled from the connection. The Chrym pulled back immediately, and Aja felt as though it attempted an apology for the trespass.

Kill?, it asked again. And then finally, *Free?*, in a hopeful tone.

The last question decided him, as he recalled his conversation with Adira and her suggestion that perhaps the Xarans had taken Ryxa by force upon their arrival and that dragons were not so different after all. He had been so certain from the history books that no sentient beings had existed before the Xarans discovered Ryxa, that they had settled peacefully here. How could he remain so certain of his ancestors' pure motives with this new knowledge?

The Chrym knew it served a terrible master, and it wished to be free. With that certainty came a new course of action, and for the first time in his life, he asked the Chrym a question of his own.

How?

For a brief moment, the Chrym was completely silent, the constant humming that was such a part of the merge so totally absent that Aja was afraid that he'd somehow lost the bond. Then, in a flurry of images nearly too swift to process, the Chrym showed him exactly what to do to end Sik's terrible reign.

Sik's massive collection of jewelry began to dissolve and run down the wall where it hung in all its cold glory, streaming across the floor in a silent race toward the large doorway that led to the corridor beyond where her First General kept watch over his ailing queen. It rose slowly, quietly building a thin, impenetrable barrier between the queen and her colony under Aja's careful control. He hoped her death would be silent, but couldn't afford to alert Telek with even a whisper of sound. The First General might be sleeping, but he wouldn't miss the sound of a struggle or a Lace of warning, however faint, coming from his queen's chambers.

Once the doorway was sealed, Aja pulled away from the remaining metal, maintaining his bond with the Chrym so the heat of Sik's Flare was bearable. He moved swiftly but without his normal grace, unused to actually being the physical form of the metal instead of simply existing within it. Something must have alerted Sik, for he was only halfway across the room when her massive head rose from the lip of the pool and huge, lantern-like eyes opened to illuminate his shiny form.

"You dare, little human?" she rasped, heaving her solid body from the molten gold. Her wings rose and fell in a powerful downdraft that would have covered him in molten gold and slammed him against the wall if he wasn't still bonded with the Chrym. She reared back when her wings cleared the room and she realized he was still standing in front of her.

"No!" she raged. "I'm not afraid of you!"

She lunged from her bed, shockingly fast for something that size, and Aja felt the vibration of her teeth grinding against him, felt pressure as one large fang caught on the crook of his arm. He allowed the metal to harden against her so that as she thrashed and slammed him against the wall, the force she'd intended to kill him worked against her. She shrieked in pain as two teeth broke away, and he allowed the metal to soften again so he could slip easily from her mouth. She lashed at him with her tail and bellowed for Telek, but the barrier held, and no sound alerted her guard.

She tracked his movements across the room, wings slightly extended from her body in preparation for another attack. He had to lure her back to the bed before he could kill her – there was no way he could move such a massive form once she was dead, and it was imperative that Telek believe she died in her sleep.

Aja braced himself as she lunged forward again, dissolving in a puddle of metal at her feet just before her teeth closed on him. Sik screamed with rage and scraped at him with her talons, but he hardened again and felt bone-deep satisfaction as her claws dulled against him.

"How?" she bellowed. "How are you doing this?"

He formed again, this time in front of her massive bed, and when she lunged for him a third time, he struck. His weapon of choice, a needle-thin, foot-long sliver of Chrym, pierced Sik's eye and passed into her brain. She collapsed forward into the bed, thrashing as she died. He could feel the heat of her Flare cool, and the brilliant red of her Laces was almost completely gone when she suddenly turned her ruined eye toward him.

"I feared it would be the *darkening* that took me, that or Adira," she spat his lover's name. "I thought that was the worst fate I could ever imagine, but to be brought low by a human, a slave! I'd rather have died a thousand deaths at her teeth." The revulsion in her voice filled him with rage.

"You've earned a thousand deaths," he replied, his voice like a bell as it passed through metal vocal chords. "But you only get one, and I offer it to you for the lives you stole from me."

There was no response, and he realized that Sik was gone.

CHAPTER 25

I held Maggie in my arms, my darling little girl, and felt such a wealth of love rise up within me that I was nearly choking on it. Tears stung my eyes and I looked up at Mike in time to see a drop of liquid spill over his own eyelids and roll down his cheek.

"We did it, Jenna."

His smile was jubilant, and the nurses were distant forms, moving with some unknown but certain purpose.

Here she was, our perfect little daughter, strangely quiet though the nurses had assured us she was breathing well and healthy in every way. I cradled her against my skin, holding her so gently, afraid to believe she was finally with us.

"Ten fingers, ten toes," I said in a sing-song voice.

"No tail," Aja said, sounding almost disappointed.

"Of course not," I replied, and then to our precious girl, "Silly Daddy, he was sure you'd have a tail."

Maggie blinked and looked around the room, and I was suddenly certain she could see us, really see us, which shouldn't be possible – babies couldn't focus on anything further than ten to twelve inches away for several days. Yet Maggie tracked a nurse's progress across the room with unerring precision, her blue-eyed gaze coming back to me. She reached up to me, trying to sit up, and I gaped in horror as tiny scales began to form on her still wet form.

"No, no," I was sobbing, and Aja was telling me it was all okay, we knew this could happen, it's ok, Jenna, it's ok. I was trying to hold Maggie, but she slipped from my arms, and she and Aja were beyond my reach, the blanket was stretching, stretching, and the sun disappeared behind clouds.

"It's not supposed to storm today," I said, and then I was falling, falling and screaming, screaming and falling. I was dying again.

Adira found herself crying quietly, for once her awakening not precipitated by raised scales and wild Flares. She'd grown sleepy waiting for Aja, until finally in desperation, she'd shifted to Xaran form. The change left her dangerously vulnerable while she slept, but she'd feared what her waking might do if she suffered a nightmare in dragon form.

This dream had been deeply troubling, and she feared her subconscious was warning her of what she already knew, deep in her heart. A queen's mating flight was always productive, and though she and Aja were two different species, from different worlds, the shift must have allowed enough of their physiology to match to produce offspring. What form that offspring would take was another matter entirely. Newly hatched dragons were so violent, they were kept contained for decades before their elders could trust them to control their instincts. Live births of queens were even more violent, as it should be expected, given a female's more dominant nature. A female offspring would be aggressive, eager even, to kill whatever was within range. Aja would make an easy target for a young queen unless she could manage to birth the child alone.

It was an unpleasant choice – to leave Aja when the time came and give birth in isolation, with no certainty of the outcome, or stay with him and risk his death by the teeth of his own child. Would she be forced to kill a daughter, or die herself? Could their offspring's species be decided by their mother's form? Adira wondered if she could control the child's outcome by remaining human for the rest of the pregnancy. Although such a choice was incredibly risky for her, if it guaranteed a human child, it was worth it. If Adira gave birth in dragon form to male offspring, Aja would never live long enough to actually meet his children, but if she gave birth to a live female, he would certainly not live beyond the first few moments of her existence.

And what of Aja? Would he be happy to learn of the pregnancy? Would he hate their child if it was born a dragon, or worse, use it to bridge the gap between species, bringing the dragons to their knees? How could she live with that?

Adira covered her eyes with her hands, wracked with quiet sobs. She cried herself out, nestled among the dying grasses she'd gathered for a small bed of sorts. The Empress Adira, resorting to grass mattresses, she thought to herself, brushing bits of grass spikelets from her hair that dissolved like ash, spreading seeds floating through the air.

She recalled now the intense moodiness that had preceded both of her clutches, how poor Mar had suffered terribly from her fits and rages. She had no reason to expect anything different in Xaran form, in fact recalled now that many of the Xaran servants with child had spoken of terrible cravings for strange foods, of sudden fits of tears that ended as quickly and inexplicably as they began, of smells once enjoyed, now not to be tolerated. And morning sickness! Adira's eyes widened. At least as a dragon she had never been subjected to such an indignity.

As though the very thought was the trigger, Adira felt her stomach lurch. It was a horrid feeling, one she'd not suffered since before her conversion, in that other life, as Jenna. Even then, she only vaguely recalled that she had suffered the morning sickness once before. The sick roiling in her belly rose and rose, until she staggered to her feet and rushed away from her bed, becoming violently ill not six steps away. The illness lasted for several minutes, forcing her through shuddering dry heaves, a misery that left her gut aching. Shivering with revulsion, she made her way to the river to rinse her mouth. As she crouched by the bank, she became aware of two things.

The first thing she noticed was the streak of vibrant color separating the horizon from the night sky; Pil's first foray into the sky. The second thing she noticed - she was not alone. She almost leaped to her feet with a glad cry for Aja's return, but recognition froze her in her hiding spot. For beyond the dried river reeds, she heard not one, but at least three distinct voices.

"The general won't be pleased with our failure," said Sad Voice.

"But he'll understand, won't he?" asked Young Voice.

Sad voice offered a comforting platitude involving Pil and Hadra, and life after Halon. Then Young Voice said something that caught her attention.

"What about the Choosing Assassin?" He said her mate's name with a tone of awe, and Adira began to guess at how powerful and how important Aja really was to the rebellion. "He's going to be pretty angry when he learns of the general's plan."

Young Voice sounded more worried about Aja's reaction to the plan than their failure to execute it, and Adira leaned forward to catch Smooth Voice's response.

"Aja serves the rebellion, as do we all."

She frowned at the devout fervor she detected from Smooth Voice. That sounded like the marketplace refugees who had nearly stoned her just a few short weeks ago. The world was full of fanatics these days, she mused.

"What do we do next?" Young Voice asked.

Sad Voice replied, "We head back to headquarters. Aja will be Swimming this vein soon enough. We should try to beat him back so we're there when he gives his report."

Adira's eyes narrowed. This sounded to her like an ambush, though it could be innocent enough.

Smooth Voice was moving away, and she tipped forward even further, fingers sinking in the thick mud by the riverbank with a disgusting squelch. She froze, afraid they'd heard, but the sound, though loud to her ears, was too far for them to detect.

Smooth Voice continued without interruption. "From what we've heard, he's too involved in that Xaran girl he's found to even realize we were there. If he'd been at his post instead of off with her somewhere," he leered, "he'd have sensed us tonight when we entered the Empress' chambers."

Adira's chest expanded on a breath of fury. The general had ordered her execution, even as he'd sent Aja to assassinate Sik. The resulting chaos of two assassinations would send the world tipping into outright war. *Fool!* She thought. *Dead fool*, she thought a moment later, and though she was fangless, her smile lacked none of its former sharpness.

The would-be assassins lingered, and she glanced at the sky with new worry. Aja should be back at any moment, and she feared what might happen if they met up while he was unprepared, ignorant of their duplicity. A chilling thought struck. Was he unaware? She reassured herself of his ignorance the next moment – he would not have flown with her to the edge of Sik's borders if he'd been duplicitous with their plans, he would have argued to keep her in her chambers, ready for the deadly blow, to be delivered in her sleep, much as Aja attempted now with Sik. Even as she tried to reassure herself, she couldn't help but consider an even simpler plan. How easy it had been to lure her here, leaving her in Xaran form, vulnerable to a simple blade. The weapon need not even be Chrym. The only thing that kept her from rushing her would-be assassins was the simple fact that they seemed utterly unaware of her presence. That alone might prove Aja's innocence, and she couldn't bring herself to prove otherwise.

The voices finally left, and she returned to her grass bed, torturing herself with various scenarios that proved Aja's innocence or betrayal. She waited, uncertain what to do next. A minute passed, then two. She waited while the sky rapidly brightened, Hadra making her appearance on the horizon as predictably as Pil. Her mate should have been back by now. As the sky continued to brighten, Adira became aware of a great agitation to the south. Sik's death had been discovered. She watched the colony's furious activity, ever-widening circles of dragon rage, and realized it was only a matter of time before they turned that agitation and aggression outward.

Aja's family had died in a dragon attack, perhaps caused by her own antagonizing behavior toward Sik, and the violence about to erupt would pale in comparison to Sik's rages. Ten thousand or more mature dragons were circling in confusion and growing rage – no Xaran caught out in the open would survive. She knew what Aja would want, how desperate he would be to save as many of his people as possible, but even she could not fly quickly enough to save the Xarans from what was coming.

The dragons broke suddenly, heading in a northerly direction, which would eventually bring them to her territory, perhaps from suspicion, or perhaps in response to her pheromones, not yet fading in spite of the bond she had formed. The dragons were moving swiftly, though not as swiftly as she had feared, and she realized they were stooping on every village along the way. They were queenless now, and if Aja had succeeded in his plan, this was simply the normal wild behavior that took place before a new queen claimed the colony after the *darkening* claimed their leader. If he had failed to make her death appear natural, what she was witnessing now was pure vengeance, but either way it wouldn't end until they exhausted their rage or were forcibly stopped.

There was a third possibility, and it was ultimately why she had agreed to fly Aja south. A dragon queen had died. A colony was in chaos, easy to claim. She'd done it before, and had increased her territory and her ranks with each rival's death. Though she had not killed Sik herself, the other queen's sudden death would have triggered a massive shift in their physiology and the pheromones that formed the colony's bond. They would serve the first queen to signal her intent to rule. Adira was right here, she could easily avert all of the carnage these creatures would wreak.

She thought of Aja, and their unborn child, her fears of how her dragon nature might affect the child's outcome, and then she shifted. Let the other queens assume Adira had finally tired of Sik's advances and killed her. In a way, it was true, and far less dangerous than the truth. She launched skyward, a blazing comet in the sky, signaling the dragons, *Come to me, I am your queen.*

Like a thousand swarming bees, they rose, forming a great dark cloud streaking across the sky. Higher and higher she rose, releasing as many pheromones as possible, and another thought occurred. Could she kill two birds with one stone? There was only one way to find out.

When at last Adira came to ground, even she was exhausted. Dragons scattered around the defeated queen's court in varying degrees of consciousness. First General Oryd arrived sooner than she might have expected – there was no way to disguise a mating flight, no matter where it occurred on the planet. With his own queen dangerously absent and such a great disturbance to the south, the clever dragon had quickly reached the conclusion she'd hoped for.

When he came upon her, she was barely upright, though she forced herself to seem confident, unconcerned by his rage. Worry for Aja was uppermost in her mind – she had not yet ascertained the circumstances of Sik's death and whether her assassin had escaped.

"Where is he?" Oryd hissed, Flaring so violently that he struck sparks off the stones he touched. "Your mate?"

"You do not ask instead if I have bonded?" she asked with dangerous softness.

He flinched as she suggested the worst possible outcome for him. A missed mating flight and a mate-bonded queen - there would be no other opportunity for him.

"Have you?" he demanded, and she forgave him his impudence in light of the terrible falsehood she had perpetrated.

"No bond, and no mate."

It happened from time to time, that a queen Flared too strongly even for another dragon to withstand. Sik had been known for such behavior, which usually made the privilege of siring her offspring the last privilege a dragon in her colony could expect.

Oryd's Lacings were wild, and despite her own worries, she felt an unwelcome sympathy. A mate-bond was not under her control, and she was certainly not going to risk Aja by admitting the truth. The best she could do for her First General, whom she had come to like despite herself, was to let him down gently, allowing him the hope that there might yet be a mating flight, at least until she found a way to reveal the truth. A tiny, cowardly voice in the back of her mind suggested that perhaps there would be no need. Unlike her, Aja was not of a particularly long-lived species – it was reasonable to expect they would both be gone from this world long before another mating flight could be anticipated. Oryd would be free then, to find a new queen, hopefully one without an existing mate-bond, since that seemed to be his greatest desire.

Her First General looked wildly about, seeing only thousands of dragons, most too exhausted to do more than open great yellow eyes and hiss at the newcomer. Adira knew that it would appear exactly as she intended, the finale of a mating flight.

"No mate-bond," he repeated flatly, and she inclined her head, secretly relieved at how well he was taking the news.

"Then let us hope for many hatchlings to replace our losses in the coming war." He launched skyward without bidding her goodbye, and she stared after him, barely repressing an agitated hiss of her own.

His parting jibe touched on her own concern – it had been tens of thousands of years since she'd last killed a queen, but she remembered well the upheaval that ensued. With the death of Padra, she had become a full-fledged empress, and the other queens had feared she would not stop there. It had taken a great deal of diplomacy, something dragons were not greatly known for, to appease their fears. Even though Sik had clearly been the aggressor in their relationship, the others would not take kindly to the news of her death, suspicious or otherwise, since it coincided with Adira's subsequent claim of even more territory.

Adira could easily defeat each of the remaining queens singly, but if they joined together, an unheard of act, they could well overthrow her. Such a pact was unlikely, but then so was a mate-bond between a dragon and a Xaran, a Chrym Swimmer, a queen's assassination by Chrym, or a shape-shifting empress. There had been a lot of unlikely events in recent months, and Adira was no longer quite so sanguine about her predictable world.

At last she found the strength to drag herself to the dead queen's chambers. She was not surprised to find Sik's Weaving rooms empty, even less surprised to come across the queen's remains, untouched, unmourned by her thousands of Xaran slaves. Her rooms were still warm, though the gold had cooled, leaving Sik's massive, heavily scaled body partially submerged, and a random memory from an earlier life surface. She seemed for all the world like a frozen wooly mammoth, caught in one moment between life and death, frozen for all time, and Adira was equal parts relieved to see no signs of violence and disappointed that her death appeared so peaceful.

She found the thought of freeing Sik from her golden tomb distasteful – it would be a task for her newly acquired dragons to perform. Though she had no intention of ever using her rival's chamber, it would not do to leave her rotting carcass here.

A quick glance had shown no sign of Aja, and though she knew now that he could move through Chrym itself, she had no way of knowing whether he remained in the vicinity unless he chose to show himself.

"Aja!" she hissed, feeling the fool, but there was no response. She had to believe that he had escaped, perhaps was even now waiting for her by the river. She had no way of leaving while the colony was in upheaval, no way to send him a message. She wished now that she had thought to leave a warning – if he was not aware of the general's plans for her, he might very well proceed to the rebel camp and be taken unaware. She was certain now that he would never betray her, but if the rebel general ordered a second assassination by his master spy, would Aja think to dissemble, to maintain his good standing long enough to escape?

She hoped so, for if one thing had come of this night's work, it was a very healthy respect for what a Chrym wielding assassin could do. She could melt Chrym, but it required awareness and significant effort. It was clear that the opportunity would not be afforded her if the rebels sent another to finish the task.

She understood Aja's growing fear over her refusal to accept the general's offer. He had recognized a simple truth that her supreme confidence, her utter arrogance had blinded her to – the general would not allow a threat to the rebellion to live. General Tal was far more dangerous than she had given him credit for, and Aja had known it. Her heart ached as she thought of him, searching by the river bank, waiting for her, but having underestimated how quickly her mating pheromones had faded over the past several days, she had to remain here to cement her bond with her new dragons, and ensure they entered her ranks with a minimum of fuss. She had no concerns over First General Oryd's ability to maintain his place within the colony – his fury alone would carry him through the coming days and weeks, but he might well find some promising officers among Sik's court.

CHAPTER 26

Aja emerged at last by the river bed, exhausted beyond belief. He found himself grateful that he'd thought to mark the spot with a small Chrym nodule. Not only did it ensure a private place to emerge, but the pureness of the substance gave him the last little boost he needed to finish the grueling Swim successfully.

Closing his eyes, he felt the suns' rays slowing warm him. *Am I dying*, he wondered, as he shuddered convulsively from the chill that gripped his body. If he survived this, he would never complain of Adira's heat again. As if the thought summoned her, he felt a shadow cross his face.

"Adira, my love," he thought he said, but the words slurred together, and he slipped into unconsciousness to the sound of feminine laughter.

It was hours later before he awakened, finding himself in the dark interior of a strange home. Domestic sounds filtered through the room, gradually distinguishing themselves into separate, recognizable noises; a woman humming, a child singing, stoneware dishes coming together with a heavy clink.

He opened his eyes slightly, attempting to observe his surroundings without raising the alarm. He was in a small open room, with many windows and doors. Heavily filtered sunlight passed through patio blinds and he watched a small child run circles around the house, visible by the top of his head, then full body flashing into view, past the doorway, top of his head, top of his head, another doorway. Around and around the boy went. Each time he made a full circuit he called a number, the slender woman at the stove singing a child's counting song to help him keep track. The scene was so reminiscent of his childhood that he felt a lump form in his throat along with the sting of unbidden tears.

When he was certain that he was alone with the woman and child he attempted to rise, only to find himself shockingly weak. On his third try, he managed to raise himself to a sitting position, listing dangerously to the left until he was able to swing his legs to the floor and lean back against the wall. The cot he occupied had been shoved into a corner of the room, presumably so that he could be kept under a watchful eye while not impeding the family's movements through their small home.

"Oh, you're up!" Open curiosity lit a somewhat homely face, but the subsequent smile that crossed her lips and brightened her eyes erased his first impression. "Sel was starting to think you'd never wake." "Your son?" Aja asked, surprised by the rough croak that emerged from his throat and the rasping pain the words caused.

"Here." She offered him a cheerfully painted ceramic cup, filled with tepid water, but at least it was clean. "Husband." She answered his question briefly, then elaborated, perhaps feeling her short answer had been unfriendly. "He's out in the fields, gathering grain."

Her little boy had come in, and pressed against his mother's legs, face hiding in her skirts. "This is Vedranae, Ved for short." She introduced her young son with a mother's obvious pride. "I'm Anit."

He drank thirstily, growing painfully aware of his full bladder. One need at a time, he told himself, sucking the water down until there was nothing left. As he lowered the cup, she correctly interpreted his look and matter-of-factly pointed him to their facilities several hundred feet away, a simple structure with handles built into the walls on two sides as a means of moving the outhouse to a new location when the existing pit needed to be covered.

To his chagrin, he discovered that he was unable to walk the distance on his own, and in the end, was forced to lean heavily on his savior's arm while her young son watched with bright, curious eyes.

"What's your name?"

Ved had moved beyond the shyness that gripped most young children in the face of the unknown, reaching up for Aja's hand as Anit placed his other arm over her shoulder to steady him for the long walk back.

"I'm Aja." His voice was still rough, and he coughed, wincing as his lip split open.

"Did you see her?" the boy asked excitedly. "Is that why you're hurt?"

Aja looked in question to Anit, who glanced nervously at the skies.

"We should get inside quickly now."

"My wife, Jenna," he said, taking a chance that Adira might have introduced herself as such if she had encountered any of the villagers. "Is she near?"

Anit looked away at his question and his heart sank. "You were alone when we found you, just hours after the Golden Empress flew to face Sik."

Adira had flown to Sik's colony without waiting for him? Had she doubted his success and chosen to face Sik in the hope of saving him, or had she flown to control a queenless colony? Unable to ask the questions he truly wanted to, he asked instead, "How long ago was that?"

"The morning we found you. Just after Hadra rose, Sel noticed a giant dark cloud in the sky. But it wasn't a cloud, it was the largest dragon swarm we've ever seen. They circled for several minutes, then broke and began attacking the nearest villages."

Remembered terror shone briefly in her eyes.

"We were headed for shelter when a brilliant golden streak shot up into the sky as though Halon had been reborn. It was the Empress Adira, and for a moment I thought she intended to devour Pil and Hadra as well, but then I realized she had simply opened her wings to catch the suns' light, seeming for all the world to be calling the dragons. And to her they flew, heading up, up, until we could no longer see them."

Aja's mind was working furiously. He had expected the dragons to be in an uproar, but had underestimated their rage and confusion over the loss of the queen. A wild attack on the countryside had not been part of the rebellion's plans.

"Whether she meant to or not, the Empress saved us. We'd heard she was nearing a mating flight, and perhaps Sik's latest aggression set her over the edge. Word we've had from other villages is that she and Sik met in battle just before dawn, and Sik fell, defeated. Adira has flown, though no mate-bond has come of it. She resides now in Sik's court, at least until she recovers."

A mating flight? How was that possible? Adira had sworn they were bonded, but perhaps a bond between a dragon and Xaran was not the fixed, life-long bond that formed between dragons. Perhaps Sik's death and the subsequent swarm had triggered such a strong biological response that Adira had been compelled to fly. If that were the case, would she return, or was she lost to him? He felt as though he should know if the bond had been severed, but would he? He only knew he ached without Adira, but perhaps he would have felt this way over her absence regardless of a bond, heartsore and unsure of where this latest news left them.

Anit seemed bitterly satisfied over Sik's defeat until she caught Aja's eyes. At his expression, she hesitated, then helped him back to the cot before turning briefly away. He heard her instructing Ved to run to the river for more water, and to the field to bring his father in for dinner, giving him time to come to terms with his loss. When she returned, she held a single sandal in her hands, an expression of deep sympathy in her eyes.

"This was all we found out there with you. This, and your pack." She indicated a small shadow under the cot and he reached for it, surprised to find it intact.

"You didn't open it?"

"Wasn't ours," she answered with the plain honesty and simple dignity of good people.

Aja nodded. "I'm sorry, not everyone is," he paused, "generous, these days."

"You mean the church people, I expect."

Again he was startled by her plain speech. She caught his look and shrugged.

"There's not much love for them here."

She told him the whole story then, of how his village had been rebuilt, the Church placing specific families here with no explanation. At least, not until they'd come to know each other, to form a true community. It was then that each family discovered they all had one thing in common. A strong Gift had manifested in their family line within the past two or three generations. The Church was openly breeding Gifted Xarans.

"In a few years, our oldest will go to the Choosing," she said flatly, rubbing the scar on her forearm as she looked at Aja's tattoo.

Aja frowned. "I thought the Choosing Ceremonies had ended," he said cautiously.

"Oh the big ones, for sure," she replied bitterly. "Now they come around randomly, more often to villages like ours where they expect to find the Gift, but they make their way to every town eventually."

This was not good news, and he wondered why Davi's boys were unaware of what was happening. The church was definitely utilizing new tactics, and whoever was behind it was smart, very smart. He wished he'd had the time and energy to meet with Garn and Dita immediately after Sik's assassination. Finding this new threat would have to be a priority after he found Adira and gave his report to the general, assuming he still had a place with the rebellion after coming clean about his bond with the Empress.

"I just don't understand why the rebels would kill the priests and then leave our Gifted young where they could be picked off later," Anit burst out.

"Rebels?" Aja echoed, shocked to hear them publicly named.

"Oh, Sel insists there's no rebellion, that the priests killed each other off in a failed power play." She huffed impatiently.

At his questioning look, Anit elaborated. "Well Imperion Cayl is still in authority, even after all the killings, so the coup must have failed. Or," she added with the tone of one who had argued the point many times with lesser minds, "it was the rebellion, and they just haven't had a chance to finish cutting off the serpent's head."

Aja had often wondered himself why the order had never been given to take the Imperion. In the early days, as he was building his reputation and rising through the general's ranks, he'd not had the authority and respect he commanded now. By the time he'd risen high enough in the general's army to have a voice, Tal's advisors had argued that their goal had been achieved, the Choosing Ceremonies had been ended, or at least significantly disrupted, and the assassination of the current Imperion would only lead to a new high priest who might choose to reinstate the mass ceremonies. General Tal had agreed, and as far as Aja knew, Imperion Cayl had remained fairly secluded, keeping a low profile, seeking to retain the Church's influence through less ostentatious means. It appeared now that he had only been biding his time, building new webs of power and deceit.

"What would you have the rebellion do, assuming they exist," he asked, curious to hear from an outside point of view.

"For starters, I wouldn't just leave Gifted lying about, waiting for the Church to scoop them up. If the Gifted have value to the Church and the dragons, surely they have value to the rebellion, if only to keep them out of their hands. And I'd finish the job with Imperion Cayl," she added emphatically.

Anit had a good point. Aja's mind was racing. Why had no one thought of it sooner, he wondered. The possibilities were staggering. If the rebellion could reach villages like this one before the Church, they could grow the ranks of their Gifted at an unprecedented rate.

What then, he asked himself, following the line of thought Anit had introduced. Will we institute our own Choosing Ceremony? He shied from the thought, uncomfortable with the very idea, though in all likelihood the villagers would be thrilled to have their child go to the rebellion instead of the Church. Not unlike the Xarans who saw service to Adira as an honor, rather than slavery, his inner voice whispered. It was a day for uncomfortable realizations.

Then there was yet another unpleasant reality. The rebellion gained numbers through two means – survivors, and the families that inevitably formed from those survivors. It was what made their number of Gifted so low, but it also meant that the rebellion was not responsible for separating families. If they came to villages to test for Gifted, there was no way the rebellion could take an entire family for one youngster. First of all, they didn't have the resources to feed such a massive influx of people, secondly, remaining hidden from the dragons and the Church would become exponentially more difficult, not to mention the dangerous journey to their hidden city. More people would know their location, creating greater danger of discovery through espionage.

The alternative was even less pleasant. Instead of growing their ranks via orphans and childless parents, the rebellion would be forced to separate children from still living family members, who would spend their lives serving the cause, all the while not knowing if their parents and siblings were safe. Visitation would be severely limited if not outright denied for all the reasons that bringing entire families were unwise. Gifted born within the rebellion had access to their families on a regular basis. It would not be so for Gifted brought in from the outside.

"You would part willingly with a Gifted child," he asked doubtfully.

"If it meant keeping them safe from the Church," Anit shrugged in acceptance. "I'd rather my child with the people doing something about the Church, than with the Church, or worse, enslaved to some queen who's as like to kill them as not."

It was clear Anit saw the rebellion as the lesser of two evils, but he wondered how she would feel about it if she knew the dangers Gifted rebels were placed in, all the greater for the levels of their Gift. And how would the rebellion deal with Gifted who chose not to be separated, Aja wondered. Would the general order their removal by force, deeming the addition of much-needed resources a necessity? How far would General Tal go to gain a few more Gifted Swimmers? It could mean the difference in winning their secret war against the dragons and the Church, so why had the rebellion not taken advantage of the opportunity created by the Choosing assassinations?

It was a curious puzzle, and Aja thought that perhaps his own uneasiness as he considered the possibilities of Anit's suggestion might best answer their peculiar blindness. The Choosing Ceremony was an abomination to the Xaran rebels, who found it barbaric to be forcibly separated from their families and thrown into slavery until their Gift was burnt out, or bred to produce more Gifted for the Church and their masters. To do the same in the name of freedom had simply never occurred to them.

"You risk much, speaking of a supposed rebellion, arguing sedition to a stranger."

Anit gave him a level stare. "I know who you are."

His face was carefully blank as he responded. "Who do you think I am?"

Another level stare.

"All right then, I'll spell it out for you. There's no question you're Gifted."

He opened his mouth to protest, but she cut him off with a raised hand.

"It's no use denying it. When we found you by the river, you were face down in the dirt. I rolled you over, and you were covered in Chrym. It melted from your skin before my very eyes, back into the soil, but Chrym doesn't do that unless you've got the Gift, and a powerful one at that."

She was counting off fingers as she spoke. Finger number two joined the first.

"You carry the scar of Choosing under that armband of yours, and that just shouldn't be possible. My guess is that the rebellion has found a way to get past the Choosing undetected, maybe to get folks into the Church."

Anit couldn't know that the rebellion had already considered the possibility, but Chrym responded to the Gift in unpredictable ways, and they couldn't be assured that a Gifted spy wouldn't be outed by a sharp-eyed Imprana, the entry level priests who moved up the church ranks through constant politics and intrigues, often using each other as pawns in their efforts to gain higher rank and privilege. Given that concern and the fact that Gifted spies had less value within the Church since the disruption of the great Choosing Ceremonies, it made little sense to spend their limited resources in that direction. A well-trained, un-Gifted spy was better placed in the Church, with a Swimming partner outside Church politics, but placed close enough to meet regularly and relay valuable information quickly.

After the Choosing assassinations, Imperion Cayl had relocated to Sik's temple, renaming it the Great Church. Wary of new developments, Aja had placed several un-Gifted spies, and a pair of Swimmers, Davi's boys, to bring them news of the Church's movements more swiftly. The Church had been deceptively quiet, and eventually Aja had needed Garn and Dita in other places. It appeared as though he should have kept them at their posts in Sik, where Imperion Cayl's plans had taken shape so subtly that the rebellion had been unaware of new moves to provide the Church with Gifted slaves and to sow dissent in Adira's relatively religion-free territory. They'd underestimated the Imperion, much as Cayl had underestimated the rebellion several years earlier.

Sel and Ved's arrival spared Aja from having to confirm or deny Anit's accusation, and Sel readily accepted his explanation of having been caught in the open during the escalation of hostilities between Adira and Sik. Sympathies were expressed for the loss of his wife, presumed dead in the chaos of the dragon queens' battle, followed by Adira's mating flight.

They spoke of commonplace things over the evening meal, and Aja pronounced himself fit enough to travel in the morning. Which direction he would head was still undecided, north to the rebels and General Tal, or south to Sik's court, and Adira.

CHAPTER 27

"By Pil's morning light, you're in a bad mood!"

Aja looked up, irritation creasing his face. "Then why come over to subject yourself to it?"

He threw his arms wide to indicate the vast, unoccupied space all around him.

Davi scowled back as he settled onto the stone retaining wall, inches from his friend's hostile form.

"It wasn't personal, you know it wasn't."

Aja had heard it so many times he could nearly repeat Davi's apology word for word. Predictably, his friend continued.

"General Tal had to investigate the rumors, had to prove you were above reproach."

Aja hunched his near shoulder and flicked the small stone he'd warmed in the palm of his hand, striking a nearby weed, neatly beheading the cheerful purple bloom. Davi whistled, a low sound of admiration.

"Who was that meant for?"

Aja remained silent. Go ahead and wonder, he thought. Maybe it was meant for all of them, himself included for being such a naïve fool.

"If he hadn't investigated, it would have spawned rumors of favoritism, or worse, incompetency."

Davi had picked the one-sided argument up where he'd left off. The worst of it was, they were right, Aja was no longer theirs. Just hours before arriving at the rebel city, he'd been entwined within Adira's arms, relieved beyond words to have confirmed their bond, furious to learn of the General's orders, and questioning whether peace between the Xarans and dragons was even possible.

Thank the stars Adira was able to warn him of their plot. Without that advance knowledge, he would have entered camp, pleading her case, trying to gain more time. Given the rumors swirling about his loyalties, it would have been the worst thing he could do. Instead, he'd been able to feign shock and fury over being denied the opportunity to kill two queens in a single night, thus firmly cementing his status as a legend. Though there were still doubters, he was fairly certain he'd regained General Tal's trust.

"Instead he missed a golden opportunity. A simple rumor, from a single source, cost him the chance to take out the two most powerful queens on the planet." Aja spoke at last, using Davi's desire to make amends as a weapon, a tool to gain information.

"That's just it," Davi said earnestly, relieved that Aja was at last engaging in conversation. "It wasn't a simple rumor, and it wasn't from just one source."

Aja looked up, allowing disbelief and scorn to color his voice. "I would have heard if there were rumors circling the camp."

"True," Davi agreed. "But we started to hear things after you left."

"From Phyx?" Aja guessed.

Davi's lips twitched. The Swimmer in question was new to the rebellion, too old to have escaped the Choosing, but unmarked all the same. Aja had expressed his suspicions to Davi and the general, but they had been unwilling to entertain the possibility that Phyx was not what he seemed. General Tal deemed Phyx as too obvious for a Church spy. Davi had agreed, arguing that Phyx was far too outspoken about the rebellion's failings. No Church spy would have joined the rebellion and immediately made such waves – a spy would have remained as innocuous as possible. Aja had argued that it was the perfect cover, but they would not be dissuaded, believing it was more likely that Phyx's origins were as he claimed. Born to a pair of Adira's Gifted Weavers and stolen away as a young man, he'd been enslaved by the Church and gifted to a western queen, where he'd suffered for years. Upon discovering the true extent of his Gift, he had promptly fled to the east, searching for and eventually finding the rebel stronghold.

"Phyx doesn't deny that he heard a few things about you during his travels, but there was nothing to his reports that indicated disloyalty."

Aja waited in silence for several moments before exploding with, "Then why is General Tal so willing to believe my supposed treachery?"

It was Davi's turn to scowl at the ground.

"Sefti," he finally said.

Aja's eyebrows rose. "Sefti?" he repeated incredulously.

"The boy has an over-fondness for fruit and may or may not have remained in the market a few times after you thought he left." Davi scrunched his face apologetically. "He heard a few things about Adira's new pet," Aja scowled at the term, "and then he heard a few things more."

"Then he may have made the mistake of talking about those marketplace rumors when he returned to the city. Word got back to General Tal, who demanded a full report."

Davi grew silent then, and Aja sensed he wouldn't like what came next.

"We'd already realized that Sik was using our Gifts up so rapidly we wouldn't have enough strength if it came down to a battle, and the general was... worried about how things were progressing with Adira."

With his precious Choosing Assassin, Aja silently interjected.

"He pulled us from Sik's court two weeks before the assassination, to get us rested, then sent me to Adira's court."

Aja froze. "No. I would have seen you."

Davi smiled. "Perhaps. If you hadn't been so enamored of a certain Xaran girl."

Aja was suddenly furious with himself. Careless in his newfound love, he'd risked Adira's life by acting the lovesick boy.

"Don't feel so badly," Davi tried to make light of it. "I was glad to see you finally in love."

He shrugged. "But it was that very thing that caused the General to truly doubt you. He worried that if you'd fallen for one of Adira's trusted servants, you might balk at killing her empress. General Tal weighed all the evidence, then paired me with Phyx to take out Adira after you were given the order to take out Sik."

Aja clenched his fists against the fury those words caused. Great Pil and Hadra, if he'd rejected Adira's demand to fly him to Sik's territory, he would have returned to find her dead. His stomach turned at the thought of discovering Adira, lying in a cooling bed of gold, a tiny scarlet trickle slowing drying under one closed eyelid, the only trace of the Chrym weapon that had stilled her ancient heart. Would they have even bothered to wipe away the evidence, or would they have left it for him to take care of, as punishment for having fallen in love and out of General Tal's favor?

Davi mistook his silence and slapped his shoulder. "Cheer up, Aja. You may yet get your chance at her, and in the chaos that follows, you may still win the girl."

"You're going after the empress again," Aja stated, a new coldness winding its way through his heart like stones shifting, making way for a heavier burden.

"You are," Davi corrected cheerfully. "The general wants to see you." He hopped up and sauntered loosely across the shaded courtyard, blissfully unaware of the razor-thin blade Aja carefully returned to its hiding place.

CHAPTER 28

Adira felt revulsion churn in her gut and struggled silently with the most unlikely urge to vomit. In all her thousands of years, she'd never experienced anything like it, was in fact quite certain that dragons simply did not vomit. She reminded herself sternly of that fact in the hopes that it would help her gain the upper hand against her unruly stomach.

Impara Rikor watched the Empress closely, keeping his expression carefully charming, with just a hint of hero worship. It wouldn't do for the golden bitch to sense his hatred. In a single night, Empress Adira had undone years of hard work. All his carefully laid plans for the aging and maddened Sik were destroyed, but he still had hopes that something might be gained from this debacle. Unlike her predecessor, Adira was hard to read, appearing at the moment to be either extremely bored, or on the verge of eating someone. Rikor supposed it was possible for an extremely bored dragon to eat someone and congratulated himself on having the foresight to be near, but not too near the golden dragon when he and his brothers had entered her court. Impara Ukon was growing animated, and Rikor shifted slightly to the left, putting a little more space between himself and his brother. The fool was going to get himself eaten, and Rikor had no intention of being caught in the crossfire.

"You must take action," Ukon was gesturing wildly, spraying spittle in his fervor.

Rikor shifted left again. One simply did not give orders to a dragon, especially a queen who had just killed and mated. Adira's eyes shone a bit brighter, and she yawned widely. Ukon stammered to a halt, briefly silenced by the gaping maw that blazed out at them.

"Pil and Hadra preserve us," whispered one of the lesser Imperial who had accompanied them to Adira's court. Unfortunately Ukon's sense of self-preservation disappeared as soon as Adira's delicately scaled lips closed on that terrifying view.

"Sik knew, she understood what was at stake!" He looked wildly around for support, and Rikor carefully avoided eye contact. His fellow Impara had no sense of diplomacy, displayed no tact in their first meeting with the Empress. Given his current behavior, Rikor was mildly astonished that the man had risen to such an exalted rank. Perhaps Sik's madness was catching. It was the only explanation for such foolishness, for it was as clear to the lowest novice that Adira was as unlike Sik as the day to the night sky. Their differences were not solely restrained to their appearance, though they were strikingly different in that regard as well. Where Sik had been massive, heavy scaled and heavy bodied, mad eyes blazing as brilliantly as her crimson Laces, Adira was almost dainty in appearance. It was not just her diminutive size or the paleness of her scales that caused this perception. She was truly lighter in mass than any dragon Rikor had ever seen. Even the youngsters emerging from the hatching grounds were larger, though truth be told, Rikor had only ever seen Sik's offspring. Unlike those heavy, ungainly beasts, the empress was long-bodied and slender, like a river reed, grown overnight in the rainy season. Unlike the river reed, the fierce intelligence in those large golden eyes warned she would not be so easy to bend.

Abruptly rising to her feet, the empress towered over them, tail lashing the air as she extended her wings, stretching like a great cat. Ukon stopped in mid-sentence, mouth gaping like a village idiot. Rikor thought there need only be an errant fly to complete the picture, but Ukon regained his composure and his voice in the next moment.

"Please," he insisted, moderating his tone only slightly. "The Church seeks only to keep you safe. Sik believed, Sik listened, and still she is dead."

At that, the empress lost all patience.

"Yes," she hissed, shocking them all with the speed at which she moved, one moment halfway across the room, the next moment looming over Ukon with one great unblinking eye staring at him from just inches away. The Impara blanched at her proximity, fixed in place by that glowing golden eye, nearly as large as his head.

"Ssssik believed," she continued, drawing out the slight sibilance in her former rival's name to make her anger clear. "And what did that get her? Dead, but not at the hands of these fictitious rebels of yours." Her scales rose into delicate spikes, but Rikor wasn't fooled by their dainty appearance. He would bet Pil and Hadra's next rising that each scale was sharp enough to shred any substance on the planet, save Chrym.

"You encouraged her madness, her aggression, her foolishness."

The last word was practically spat at Ukon as the Empress at last raised her great head. "Your Church is filthy, an abomination."

Rikor heard the rustling of thousands of agitated wings and smiled inwardly. The Empress might have weakened the Church in her territory, but Sik had allowed them a great deal of influence, which they had extended, not just over Xarans, but the dragons as well. It had been a careful strategy, employed over decades by the brilliant Imperion Cayl, whose vision was beyond compare. He had set out to influence a queen, and against all odds had succeeded. It was infuriating that the *darkening* had killed her at such a pivotal time, but as Imperion Cayl suggested, perhaps not all was lost.

Thanks to Sik's observance of Church law, the dragons of her court had begun to accept many of the Church's dictates and beliefs as their own. Adira's disparagement of their religion would weaken the fragile new bond between colony and queen, which could create an opening for another queen to steal newly enthralled dragons.

"You will not speak to me of your wishes. You will not dare to make demands of me. If the people have needs, you will see to them in my name. That is the extent of your power." She rose up higher, higher, and cast a burning look down on them. Rikor stiffened as she made eye contact.

"You will tell my people that Sik is dead, by my tooth and claw." He bowed deeply, thoughts racing as Adira claimed a victory she hadn't won, carefully showing appropriate respect while Ukon babbled apologies, realizing at last the extent of his errors. When he rose from his supplication, Rikor found her golden gaze still upon him. "This one," her gaze flicked to Impara Ukon and back to him, "is no longer welcome in my presence."

Rikor bowed again. "I understand, Magnificent One. If I may," he hesitated, waiting for her to invite his conversation. It was a risk, for she was truly at the end of her patience, but he had gained her attention and it wouldn't do to report back to Imperion Cayl that he had failed to take advantage.

She finally nodded, and he continued carefully. "The Church has some residual grain from this quarter's tithe that might help to feed your citizens. I humbly petition that our great empress allow us to open our coffers to feed those in need."

It was a subtle suggestion that she held power over the Church, that she determined whether the people went hungry or had food, and he wondered whether she would recognize the implications, the position he had placed her in. If she agreed, the people would be fed at her command. When the Church closed its doors, their coffers supposedly empty, it would be by her orders as well. When she nodded regally, he barely hid his smile of triumph. The game had begun.

After they had backed the requisite number of steps from Empress Adira's presence and turned to leave, Ukon muttered, "This fool will not last half as long as Sik."

Rikor barely had time to register the words before a blast of heat struck him, followed by an ominous snap, though in truth, the snap was not nearly so ominous as the understated thump that followed. It was about time Ukon paid the price for his stupidity, he thought dispassionately, even as he struggled with the outrage and terror that warred within him. He had been less than two feet from the other Impara when the Empress struck, his back turned, a hair's breadth from death. He felt his skin burn and knew blisters would soon follow.

Rikor forced a calm he didn't feel and lowered himself into a deep bow as he backed further away. One very large golden claw had stabbed through the stone floor just inches from his own feet. Whatever bond he felt they had formed, it was clear the empress did not share. From the corner of his eye, he observed as that taloned foot claimed the remainder of his fallen brother's body.

"I've already lasted longer than Sik," the empress ground out as he finally moved beyond range of her furnace-like heat. The resulting blast of additional heat from her open mouth sent one of the younger Imprana shrieking down the corridor. He would never advance beyond his current rank if he couldn't control his fear, Rikor thought contemptuously. It was a point of pride that he was able to briefly meet the Golden Empress' eye as he rose from his bow.

"Indeed, Great One." There was no tremor in voice or hand to betray his nerves. Great Pil and Hadra, this queen was fast – fast and unpredictable. He observed the dragons on her periphery, watched how they followed their new queen's movements, completely absorbed and enraptured by her sudden violence. She exhibited all the signs of a successful mating flight and they were enthralled anew, her earlier sacrilege towards the Church forgotten. Rikor felt a bitter surge rise in the back of his throat. This queen *was* their religion, and in one swift act, she had reclaimed any steps he might have taken to discredit her in their eyes. Adira was beyond dangerous. Rikor felt it in the burning of his skin and the itch down his spine as she cocked her head and gazed after the fleeing Imprana, looking for all the world like a cat about to pounce.

Those golden eyes turned to Rikor next. Rikor forced his rigid muscles to bend, another deep bow, several more steps back. It would not do to show haste, nor could he afford to appear insolent in his retreat. There would be no further bold eye contact with the empress after such a challenge to the Church's authority; any direct challenge would come from another front. Rikor consoled himself with that thought and steeled himself to turn his back once again on the great golden form before him.

He was far enough from her heat to feel perspiration form on his brow and dampen his short hair. Her proximity had actually done him one small favor, burning off any moisture before his body's nervous response could betray him further. Stiff muscles nearly locked his joints into place, and it took all his will to straighten and turn. The first step away was an agony of suspense. The soft scrape as Adira finished the rest of her impromptu meal made the hairs on the back of his neck rise, and he nearly broke when a second Imprana fled. He gritted his teeth to prevent the chattering that threatened and forced a second step, then a third. By the time he reached the entrance of Adira's court, his jaws ached and he was soaked in sweat. The remaining Imprana were in no better shape.

One of the youngest among them looked at the others, face white, lips trembling.

"There was no blood."

His voice was a razor-edge from shock.

"She bit him in half right in front of us. She *ate* him! How could there be no blood?"

"Shut up, you idiot," another Imprana answered. "There wasn't any blood because she cauterized the," he faltered slightly over the words. "When she bit down, she cauterized-"

"But she ate him! Can she do that?"

"Idiot!" the other man repeated.

Rikor let out a sharp whistle, calling them to order.

"You've seen what this queen is capable of." He stared at each of them in turn. "What she thinks of the Church."

They all nodded solemnly.

"Go after your fellow Imprana and return them to the temple. I'll report to Imperion Cayl."

As they turned to leave, a sudden smile crossed his face. "Oh, and feel free to... instruct them on the proper conduct of clergy in the presence of a queen."

One of the young faces staring back at him took on a new, sharp focus at the thought of disciplining his fellow priests, and Rikor knew he had found a kindred spirit. It would do well to discover that one's name and follow his career lest he find himself an unknowing victim one day, he mused as the Imprana sped off in different directions.

Sending them after their lost brothers gave him the opportunity to give a direct report without other faces and names to catch the

Imperion's attention. It was a tactic that had served him well over the past decade and had propelled him beyond the rank of Imprana and Imperal at an unprecedented rate. He was one of the youngest Impara in the history of the Church, and he had every intention of becoming Imperion one day. Such ambition required an uncommon focus, and Rikor allowed himself few pleasures in life. Perhaps this new Imprana, with his eagerness to punish the transgressions of his brothers, would allow him an outlet for his own desires. He smiled and cast off the last tightness that gripped his shoulders. When he finally turned to the great temple, his stride was loose and easy. He had a course of action to follow, and if it was not the one he'd first intended upon arrival at Adira's court, it would have much the same result.

CHAPTER 29

Adira was unable to shake the anxiety that wormed its way through her mind. The waking hours were difficult, but at night, her memories rose to haunt her, terrible specters that taunted her with love lost, dead children with wide staring eyes, and dreams of falling, always dreams of falling. Falling and dying. Worse still were her fears of what effect her dragon nature might have on her unborn child. A daughter, she was more and more certain, though she had only two prior experiences to go by in her current incarnation. Still, there were the dreams, ever-present, always showing a girl-child, the strange nausea which persisted day and night, though she never succumbed, and the terrible cravings. It had become dangerous for Xarans to be in her presence, and just days after felling that noxious priest she had banned all servants from her quarters, the temptation to repeat herself too compelling for her own peace of mind. Apparently Xaran flesh was what she craved, and it would distress Aja if she killed his people, my people, she corrected herself.

"I believe the other queens may attempt to rise against you."

First General Oryd had returned less than twenty-four hours after his furious flight, compelled to her service by pheromones and his own strong sense of loyalty. Adira found that she relied upon him more and more. He was the one thing she could count on as her world shifted and her perceptions betrayed her. Without Aja by her side, she felt the strain of the mate-bond and struggled to maintain her focus for any length of time. The more immediate physical changes as her body underwent the metamorphosis of childbearing were a strong counterpoint to the ache of his absence. At times she felt as though the tide of misery and uncertainty might drown her. Oryd was the pillar she clung to when all seemed lost.

"You may be right." She found herself uncaring, wondering where Aja was at that moment. Did he think of her, ache for her as she longed for him?

Oryd's teeth snapped impatiently, his Lacing strong with irritation. Adira's golden gaze rose to meet his narrowed eyes. She sighed and his posture changed from stiff anger to solicitation in a heartbeat.

"The pregnancy wears on you already."

She understood his concern. Her exhaustion was yet another indicator that she carried a girl child. In spite of the fact that a queen might lay a thousand or more eggs when the result of a mating flight was male offspring, the live birth of a single female was far more difficult, and the pregnancy itself was an exhausting process, as though even in utero, the young queen challenged her mother for sovereignty. She feared giving birth in dragon form, sensed the savagery of her nature already taking form in the child within her, though her fear was more for the child and for Aja than herself.

The source of Oryd's concern was far different. Though she tormented and challenged him, her First General would not welcome her death, would never seek it, either through overt action or dereliction of duty. As such, a female offspring would be deeply concerning to him.

"The queens," she said, seeking distraction. "How many do you think will challenge?"

"It's not how many," Oryd responded, surprising her. "It's whether they will form an alliance and challenge together."

Adira felt shock ripple through her, and realized a moment later that her Lacing had betrayed her. Another side effect of the pregnancy, her absent mate, or both, she had far less control of her body than she should, especially if she needed to prepare for battle.

Oryd courteously ignored her alarm signals, though several nearby dragons hissed and mantled their wings in alarm. These were unsettled times, and a new queen suffering a moody pregnancy did not help matters.

"You believe they would ally against me?"

She felt disconnected from the words – an alliance of queens had seemed an impossibility just weeks earlier, even if news of a human rebellion surfaced. Oryd Laced, a mixture of discomfort and agitation and she fixed him with a stern look.

"Whether I like the answer or not, I need to hear it." Her tone was firm, more like the empress of old, and she watched the steadying effect it had on him.

"There are rumors," Oryd began. "Barely overheard whispers among the servants."

Adira's eyes began to glow, the lids dropping to slits in the dragon equivalent of a scowl.

"Why must we trust to overheard whispers? Are none of my own people here yet?"

Adira frequently used her most trusted servants to obtain information that was otherwise unavailable to her. Some of the families in her inner circle had served her for a hundred generations or more, and she trusted them implicitly. They would not be swayed by Church rhetoric or the fearful babbling of Sik's oppressed people.

Oryd shrugged. "The road is long, and the dry season is upon us."

"Then fly them here."

She immediately regretted her sharp tone, but Oryd took no offense, long used to her short temper.

"Of course." He nodded deferentially, the perfect response to soothe her nerves.

"The rumors," she prodded.

A barely imperceptible pattern began to emerge on the First General's body. It took a moment to register – alarm.

"The High Priest was less than pleased by your treatment of his Impara."

She snorted.

"I'm sure he deserved his fate," Oryd continued in a conciliatory manner.

Another snort.

"But it was hardly diplomatic."

"I assure you, it was entirely necessary."

Oryd nodded in concession, and Adira felt an alarming sense of hilarity roll over her. This was not good. Unpredictable nausea, cravings and mood swings, along with a human rebellion, all while dragon war loomed on the horizon. The timing of this pregnancy could not be worse.

"Be that as it may, it seems the Church feels obligated to impose penalties."

"Penalties?"

Adira felt her scales rise up, an intense Flare causing even Oryd to flinch away. She controlled herself with effort – it would not do to immolate her First General.

"They dare assume they have the position, the authority, to levee penalties against me?"

She winced at the volume of her tone and made an effort to modulate her voice as she continued.

"What kind of penalties do they think they can effect against me?"

"For starters, they've forbidden any Church service to take place within your territories."

It was a clever tactic. Adira's long-held territories would suffer little if at all, having remained virtually free of the Church's poison save for small pockets of the population, but here in Sik's newly liberated territory, the Church held sway with a power she suspected was born mostly of fear. Fear of Sik, and of the Church itself. It would take years, perhaps generations for Adira to undo this damage, but the Church could do much to interfere with her progress. It had never been her intent to remove the Church abruptly, but rather to slowly wean their influence from her new subjects, easing them away from their sickly dependence and the cruel demands of their religion.

"What else?"

"It's difficult to prove without our own people in place, but they seem to be circulating rumors that you are to blame for the current shortage of food."

Adira hissed in fury. She had been appalled to discover the condition of most of the Xarans living in Sik's territory while the Church demanded tithes far above what most families could comfortably afford, many of them going hungry for much of the year to avoid the penalties the Imperion imposed for failure to pay.

"I'm the one who opened the Church's coffers in the first place," she exclaimed.

Oryd shrugged, a shifting of massive shoulders and wing tissue.

"When they stopped feeding the poor, they claimed their coffers were empty, having been drained by your insatiable appetite."

"Now I wish I'd eaten more than one of those foul priests," Adira muttered.

She found Oryd's surprised chuckle oddly endearing, particularly as he tried to cover it by clearing his throat moments later.

"Next time I'll save you one," she continued, still in the grip of good humor.

He reared up and looked askance at her, unsure of her mood or perhaps her sincerity.

"I am perfectly capable of catching my own meals, Glorious One. And personally, I prefer far less bitter fare," he added with aplomb.

She barely contained the laughter that threatened to emerge. After the past decade of tension leading up to her mating flight, she was actually having fun with First General Oryd. She would have loved to further engage in their teasing banter, but the Church clearly had an agenda that needed to be addressed.

"Do you feel they have the influence to broker an alliance?"

Oryd knew immediately what she meant.

"Yes, my Empress, I fear they do."

She was silent for a moment.

"Is there any indication which queens they target?"

The names Oryd rattled off had her scales rising again. Alarm – Oryd had a very good reason to broadcast that particular pattern, for he had named two ancient queens, old but skilled in battle, and three young queens, foolish in their youth, but strong and willful. The Church had been smart to go after these five. The two mate-bonded queens had too much to lose by engaging in battle. Their mates would never let them fly alone, and regardless of any alliance the Imperion might broker, a bonded male was too tempting a target to dangle in front of another queen.

That left five queens engaged in talks with the Church. Two alone would have given her a worthy battle. If all five joined together, victory was far from certain for either side. She bared her teeth. Forewarned was forearmed. She might not control the number of her enemies, but she would control the when and where of their engagement, she vowed to herself. They would not find her so easy to end as they hoped. She had a reason to survive, her ennui of millennia dissolving in a heartbeat as the mate-bond was formed. She wished briefly that Aja were there with her, then discarded the notion for the foolishness it was. His presence would not aid the situation and would likely cause more harm than good. He was safer in the rebel camp, where another faction plotted to end her. The irony of that fact did not escape her.

CHAPTER 30

Several thousand miles to the west, Rikor bowed before yet another queen. Klis was the youngest of the queens, and more easily swayed by her fear of Adira. Scales risen to sharp, fearsome spikes, Klis whipped her tail in a frenzy, golden eyes blazing. Rikor backed discretely away, taking care to keep a good distance between himself and that tail. Klis had a reputation for being careless with her servants, and between her mouth and tail, it was far more likely the latter would end him.

"She dares! She actually dares!"

Klis was working herself up, nearly going airborne with each step. It was oddly like watching a young child play hop-skip, and Rikor lowered his eyes to shield any amusement that might betray him. These ridiculous creatures thought themselves so high and mighty, yet at the moment, Klis could not be more comical and contemptuous to his eyes.

"It would seem so, most beautiful one."

He smiled inwardly as the young dragon queen mantled her wings proudly in response to his praise. Klis was well known for her vanity, and until his first audience with Adira, Rikor might well have considered her to be the most lovely of the dragon queens, aesthetically speaking of course. Heavy bodied and possessed of the obsidian scales that marked all queens save Adira, Klis had the palest and broadest red Lacing of any queen, a hot rich pink that covered most of her body, with the narrowest of black bands intersecting in a delicate pattern. Those wide pink stripes were glowing so brightly at the moment, she could have illuminated the chamber without benefit of torches, and Rikor had to force his mind to work past the dizzying swirl of shadow and light she created with her frenetic movements. He swallowed against the nausea that threatened and forced himself to remember the task at hand.

"If one recalls her history, it was only the intercession of Sik, Cala and your mother that prevented her from taking all the dragon territories for herself."

It was a stretch, at best, to say that any queen, together or singly, had stopped Adira. By all accounts, Adira had stopped killing queens when there were none left who cared to challenge her. That truth would not serve the Church, and Rikor doubted that Klis cared enough to study the histories for herself. By placing her mother in such exalted company as Sik and Cala, the oldest dragon queen left on the planet, Rikor had virtually guaranteed that the vain young queen would not challenge his version of their history.

"She mussst be ssstopped."

It was a measure of Klis' upset that her sibilance had become so pronounced.

"If I may?" Rikor allowed the question to float between them, a tenuous tether that served to draw the young queen back to him, and focused her attention on the problem at hand. She gave a nod that might have seemed regal if he hadn't just observed her in a full-blown temper tantrum.

"Cala and Bithra are ready to rise against Adira, this time not just to contain her aggression, but to end her entirely."

Klis' golden eyes widened and her mouth opened on a wordless hiss of surprise. He barely controlled his flinch as that great, glowing maw bathed his face with a furnace blast of fetid heat.

"Your pardon, glorious one," he said, his tone both pained and admiring. It had the desired effect as Klis shut her mouth with a loud snap.

"The remaining great ones band together?" It was a quiet query, more an internal dialogue, he thought.

The young queen's vanity was the key to solidifying a dragon alliance. The two older queens had been easy to convince for they remembered Adira's past aggression, and lived daily with the fear that one day she might come for them. They resented that fear, and hated Adira for making them live with it, millennia after millennia. It had been easy to facilitate an alliance between those two, but Imperion Cayl was certain it would take more than two queens to end the Golden Empress, and after seeing her in action, Impara Rikor was inclined to agree. These large, savage beasts were clumsy in comparison to the empress, who would fly circles around her opponents. One or even two against her might merely serve to annoy, or worse, amuse her. Imperion Cayl needed a significant force, one focused by the experience of an ancient such as Cala or Bithra. The Imperion required the inclusion of at least three other queens to be assured of victory. Rana had joined, as had Qora. If Rikor could convince Klis, they would have their five queens. Five against one; the Imperion was certain the Golden Empress would not prevail.

"They would do well to have your support in such an endeavor, most beautiful one."

He hated the cloying tone he was forced to affect and wondered if she could sense the insincerity that lay just below the surface of his properly subservient expression, but Klis was no Adira, and merely preened at his observation.

"Yes, they are powerful, but those two are so ancient they've nearly forgotten how to take the sky."

"Indeed. I observed your glorious flight as we made our way to your shining city, and wondered at your grace."

Rikor managed the lie smoothly, nearly two decades of deception and power plays within the Church serving him well in his role as ambassador to the dragon queens. Klis seemed heavy in the sky and slow in her turns, straining for height as though her wings might fail at any moment. Rikor wondered suddenly if even five dragon queens would be enough to take the empress down if they didn't have an additional advantage. The Church had been steadily hoarding some of the best Weavers for centuries, and their captive breeding program had produced truly stellar results, among them, a handful of the highest Gift.

If the alliance failed to destroy her, Adira would predictably return to Sik's court, where she continued to cement her bond with her new colony. It would be a small matter to position a battery of archers with Chrym Weavers to ambush her before she could return. If she survived the battle itself, she would not be without injuries, and the Weavers would be able to direct the arrows' flight to those injuries, making it look as though she had succumbed to blows suffered during the battle, thus preserving the Church's innocence. He pleasured himself with the thought of Adira's death, and almost hoped she would survive the battle so the Church could end her instead. Rikor thought for perhaps the thousandth time how much better life might have been for him had he been born with the Gift. He ached for the pleasure of delivering the killing blow, but convincing Klis to join the battle would have to do for now.

"If Your Greatness would join with Cala and Bithra, we believe Rana and Qora might also be swayed." Rikor sneered inwardly as Klis continued to bow with pride. Let her think they had come to her first after the great queens if it got them what they wanted. "They fear your power already, and wish to prove themselves worthy of your admiration."

Klis snorted. "I have doubts they would prove effective in the battle. Frankly, I'm astonished that either of them prevailed against their mothers."

Rikor hid a smile, bowing low in agreement. It was a shame that more dragon battles didn't end in the death of both queens, but he supposed it was too much to hope for. The thought triggered another, and he made a note to suggest to Imperion Cayl that depending on the outcome of the battle they engineered, the Church might use their archers and cut the number of queens even further. The older queens were less manageable, and would eventually be killed, so why wait if the opportunity presented itself? Young queens like Klis on the other hand, were an essential evil. Klis and Qora, and even Rana, in spite of being a millennium or two old, were nearly childlike, easily swayed by avarice and vanity. They would be easy targets, a necessary figurehead for the Church, but who had decreed they need more than one queen? The thought deserved consideration, but Rikor could not let himself become distracted in Klis' presence.

"Still, they might be useful, as nothing more than fodder if need be." Klis continued, oblivious to his end game.

"A brilliant strategy, my queen," he enthused. Little did she know how closely her thoughts mirrored his at that moment, the stupid beast. His back ached from all the bowing, and he was going to have to flog a dozen servants tonight to ease the sting of his fawning behavior, but it was worth it all to watch Klis succumb to his manipulation.

"Cala and Bithra have proposed a meeting on your southernmost border." The disturbing dragon version of a smile crossed Klis' face, revealing razor-sharp teeth backlit by the fiery internal furnace that always burned within every living dragon. Her pink Lacing added a subtle tint, which gave those very large teeth the appearance of having torn into something large and recently living. Rikor suppressed a shudder. He would be relieved beyond words to finish his negotiations with Klis.

"It seems I've already made a name for myself if they seek to meet on my borders."

She favored him with another unpleasant smile, accompanied by a sly look. "But one can never have too much respect, eh Impara Rikor?"

Her familiarity was offensive to him, even as he prided himself on so quickly establishing himself as a confidant of sorts. It had taken much careful manipulation to convince both older queens that Klis' southern border was their choice of meeting spots.

Imperion Cayl himself had chosen the site for several reasons.

Firstly, it was the furthest point from Adira's territory, and least likely to result in discovery. Secondly, he had rightly deduced that Klis would take the most convincing of the younger queens, and meeting on her own border would appeal to her vanity. The other advantage to their current location was that they were far closer to Klis' southern border than Cala's main temple. Imperion Cayl had removed his presence shortly after Adira took up residence in Sik's palace, a subtle protest of her treatment of the Church designed to create tension in her newly acquired territory. He currently resided in Bithra's great temple where the Church also held tremendous influence, though not as much as they'd enjoyed in Sik. Bithra was pleased to host the Imperion, unaware that she was just a stepping stone to his ultimate goal – a stronghold in Klis.

This foolish queen had no idea how valuable her territory truly was. The depth of the Chrym veins running through her province made Mining difficult, but it also made Swimming nearly impossible, as there were very few points where the veins were shallow enough for a Swimmer to surface and rest, which made it easy to restrict unauthorized travel. The surface terrain of Klis was even less hospital; jagged rocks split the earth as far as the eye could see, forcing travelers to stick to several main roads which were carefully maintained by Klis' subjects to facilitate the passage of mined Chrym back to the palace. Rikor's master would be pleased to have all of his careful planning rewarded when Klis finally committed to meet with the other queens.

Klis enjoyed enthusiastic praise, and it was some time before he was able to bow himself from her presence, silently hoping all the while that she did not survive the coming battle. If it would guarantee that he never had to sing the praises of her ghastly, bloated self again, he would gladly join the line of penitents for a long session of flogging.

Instead, he thought it high time he join the priests delivering the flogging. It had been so long since he'd performed that particular duty, he feared the others might believe he was going soft, which simply wouldn't do. In truth he refrained from flogging the penitents too often because he enjoyed it so very much. At times it felt like a need to hurt someone else, and that was uncomfortably close to weakness. The Church was a dangerous place to show vulnerability, even for a duty as respected as flogging. Best to show restraint, to treat this pleasure as the responsibility others perceived it to be.

There was always Loshi, his personal attendant. Rikor allowed himself a tiny smile. Poor, sweet little Loshi. The delicate little Weaver had come into his possession just a few years ago during a tedious Choosing Ceremony, held in secret and in fear, thanks to the Choosing Assassin. What a treasure he'd found that day in Loshi and her twin brother. Zetequilon performed admirably to keep his sister safe, but little did he know their darkest secrets. Separated from her brother, in fear for his life, she had become the private outlet for all Rikor's darker needs. It had taken less than a year to bend her so perfectly to his will that it would never even cross her mind to seek safe haven. Rikor's thoughts calmed as his plan settled into place. First the flogging, then Loshi, and if there were any true gods in this world, he would be there to see the great empress brought down, would see the light leave her eyes, forever dimmed with the knowledge that the Church - no, that *he*, Rikor, had ended her.

CHAPTER 31

"We're waiting, and that's the end of it."

General Tal stared down the men under his command as Aja clenched his jaw against the words he wanted to say. The separation from Adira had weighed on him over the past two weeks, and he was wound tight as a garrote.

Still furious over the general's deception, he had pushed hard over the past several days to be sent back to Adira. The push had been necessary – there were those who felt Davi and Phyx might be better suited to assassinate the newly flown empress, and many who still questioned his loyalty. That was the brilliance of rumor campaigns, especially ones that touched on most deeply held fears. If the Choosing Assassin's loyalties were in question, the rebellion might well be in danger of falling apart. He felt eyes on him everywhere he went these days, and recognized that one misstep could mean death.

He stayed close to the node and watched Davi and Phyx with apparent unconcern. They were the only two who might be sent in his stead. He could not afford to lose them, could not stray from the node, which was his only escape route, his only way back to Adira. The node became his chain and anchor, the immovable object he circled, day and night. It seemed logical, for as the only way in or out of the city and unable to Leap as Aja could, the other two Swimmers would need to be in direct contact with the node in order to leave.

Or so he assumed. Phyx was still a dangerous unknown, his full abilities untested as far as Aja was concerned. It was easy enough to feign a weakness of Gift that did not exist, and all too possible the other man could Leap to Chrym from a distance. He only hoped he would sense the Leap through his proximity to the node. It would be better by far to simply eliminate the threat the other man posed, but here in the city, any death would put the entire army on high alert, and with his current questionable standing, he would be at the top of the list.

It was better to wait, tortured by all the possibilities he might fail to account for. Wait, and be ready. Ready for a call to action, whether it was he who was called or another. Either way, he planned to be the first to reach Adira.

Severn broke the stalemate. "Our informants tell us it seems likely the empress carries a female."

Aja paled. If their child was female and contained all the power and violence of Oryxa's child, Adira was in danger on all fronts. General Tal had other concerns. "Another cursed queen! What if the empress forms her own cabal? Pil and Hadra preserve us then!"

For whatever reason, a queen who ruled more than one territory occasionally ceded land to a newly born daughter rather than driving her away. The general had to be worried that Adira would produce another of her kind and create a dynasty on Ryxa. She certainly had enough territory to share, assuming their daughter was interested in brokering a peace with her mother.

Aja found it disconcerting to think of a dragon, any dragon as his child. Would she recognize him as her father? Would it matter? If she was born with a lust for violence and turned on Adira, would he – could he – step in to stop her? Would Adira forgive him? Could he forgive himself?

"Perhaps we consider another offer of alliance with the empress." The suggestion came from Davi and Aja was grateful for it though he was careful to show no sign. All eyes swung to the aging Swimmer, then to Aja, who kept his expression blank and avoided his friend's gaze. It wouldn't do to show how desperate he was for General Tal to keep the possibility of an alliance on the table.

"We've heard that the Church is stirring unrest among the other queens," Davi continued. Aja caught a flicker of uncertainty in the older man's eyes as he failed to give his friend any cues. Heads nodded, murmurs rose throughout the room.

"But if we have a strong alliance with a queen like Adira, one who may someday recognize us as equals, or at least free, we have only one battle to fight."

Aja felt hope rise. Davi had practically handed him another way out. Not daring to speak for fear he would sway the general's advisors the wrong way, he silently willed his old friend to continue his line of thought.

"She's in more danger than ever. Though the mating flight did not result in a bond, she's weakened by a female offspring. She has several thousand new dragons that require constant attention throughout her pregnancy to reinforce her control."

Strictly speaking, that last was no longer entirely true. A colony that had been taken over by a new queen often suffered massive casualties as the pheromone bond shifted, but Aja knew from recent conversations with Adira that most of the disappearances his ancestors had assumed were desertions were actually deaths as the males battled for supremacy in the new order. He also knew that the adjustment period was a lot shorter than their intelligence had previously suggested and within a day or two at most, the colony would be completely under the new queen's control. By now Adira's bond with Sik's colony was permanent, with or without a mating flight. It was highly unlikely, if not outright impossible, that any male within her new territory would leave at this point unless they happened to be her own offspring, lured from their mother by Sik's pheromones millennia ago. Aja didn't bother to correct Davi's misconception – it worked in his favor and would raise bothersome questions as to how he knew such details of colony bonding.

"The Church aligns the remaining unbonded queens against her. If we can break that alliance, or use it to form our own, we strike a blow at the Church that may take them decades to recover from, and at the same time, take a huge step towards independence."

Davi's enthusiasm was catching, and several other men seemed in agreement.

"I still say we let this proposed battle take place. No need to show our hand, and Imperion Cayl will take care of at least one queen, more if we're lucky. There's time to deal with the Imperion later."

Severn was firm in his suggested course of action. As usual, he supported the option that required the least risk and offered the least reward. One of the other advisors said as much and the room erupted into argument again. The general was forced to evict them all, his choice to be made in private. Aja stalked away from the war room, fearing that choice would remain as it had always been, with the death of his beloved. Either way, he had placed himself in the best possible position for any foreseeable outcome.

"Aja!" It was Davi, gesturing for him to wait up.

As Davi came even with him, he draped an arm around his shoulders. "What do you think my young friend? Have we given the general enough to think about?"

"I think he's going to have one hell of a headache." A deeper voice came from the shadows just ahead. Aja felt Davi's muscles tense in surprise, but he had seen Phyx step into the darkened doorway moments earlier to wait for them. The other Swimmer was far too versed in shadows for his taste.

"I don't disagree with you," the other man continued, "but I also see Severn's point. The coming battle could eliminate far more than one over-reaching queen, and while the Church is focused on their power play, we focus on taking out their key players. Both the Church and the dragons are weakened."

"Weakened." Aja felt compelled to point out. "And focused entirely on us, and perhaps desperate enough to consider the kind of alliance we're trying to build for ourselves."

Phyx tipped his head in acknowledgment. "That's always a danger. But we could also use that as an opportunity to broker peace with one of the bonded females. Perhaps we've gone about this all wrong. Rather than target the empress because of a bond that may or may not happen, perhaps we should approach a queen with more to lose."

Aja could see the direction Phyx was heading. A queen with a bond might be more amenable to an alliance, particularly if the rebels proved how vulnerable her mate truly was.

"You suggest a dangerous game," he warned.

The other Swimmer smiled. He was difficult to read in the best of times, and the darkened hallway gave Aja no further clues. "To what other purpose will you put all these Weavers the rebellion seems so intent on gathering? The armory has run out of room."

Phyx adopted a nasal tone to mock advisor Severn, whose influence had kept so many of their precious Gifted close, out of harm's way, their talents wasted shaping weapons that the rebellion couldn't, or wouldn't use. "We need to protect the blood, the legacy of our people."

Phyx snorted and shook his head in disgust. "If that man had his way, we'd all be put to stud, nothing more than breeding livestock."

Aja couldn't help but agree, and wondered if Davi felt the same way. Though the choice of marriage and spouse had been his, there was no doubt that many women with the Gift had been dangled before him. His friend's thoughtful words answered the question.

"If the general ever agreed to such an effort, we'd be no better than the Church."

"True enough." Phyx slapped Aja's shoulder and it took an effort of will not to stiffen in response. "Alas, such philosophical debates must wait for another time. I'm off to bed."

He backpedaled away from them. "Can't be too rested when the call comes." The taunt echoed down the hallway and Aja had to work to keep himself loose under Davi's arm. His friend's next comment made it clear he hadn't been entirely successful.

"Ah, don't worry. If the general decides to go with the assassination attempt, you're first up. Phyx is just messing with you."

Aja grinned and slapped Davi's shoulder. "You're right. But the man does have a point. A good night's sleep will do us all a world of good."

The two parted company, though Aja wasn't sure how much sleep was in his future.

CHAPTER 32

Rikor watched the sky, anticipation curling in his gut. High above, far out of view, three queens circled. Two others, heavy and massive, cut through the sky above him and moved north. He regretted that he would not be there to see them engage the empress, but if Pil and Hadra were with him, the battle might rage to the south before she was brought down. Imperion Cayl had chosen not to send any of his highest ranking priests to the north. His reasons were many; their involvement couldn't be too obvious in the event of failure, coupled with the all too real danger of becoming casualties if the battle raged too close kept him close to Bithra's great temple. Imperion Cayl was also a master of opportunity, and Rikor admired the man's sense of showmanship. When Adira was defeated, Cayl was prepared to saturate her court with Impara, ostensibly there to offer food and shelter, though it would come at the cost of servitude to the Church. Adira's people had wealth that would be theirs. More importantly, they had a preponderance of Gifted men and women within their community, and Imperion Cayl had a use for all that power.

No matter how things turned out today, the game was afoot, the challenge issued. Adira would have no choice but to answer. The Imperion hoped she would expect Cala and Bithra to challenge her and would join the battle with no thought as to what might lie above. It had taken every ounce of persuasion his master possessed to convince the five queens of his battle strategy. Who was he, a mere Xaran after all, to offer tactics on aerial assaults? In the end, they had agreed to a mock battle, enacted by their own dragons, one of whom was told only that he flew to meet an opponent. They tested the outcome several times, each with an unsuspecting combatant, and every time, the dragons diving from above made victory a certainty. Then had come arguments over who would challenge directly, and who would dive. The younger queens had all wanted to meet the empress in that glorious first clash, and Rikor had personally been inclined to allow Klis that 'honor,' being rather certain that the initial engagement carried the most danger to the challengers, but Imperion Cayl had been resolute. Cala and Bithra would carry the fight to Adira. They were most likely to challenge, would be expected. That left the greatest chance of surprise for the remaining three to strike from above.

"Master?" Loshi bit her lower lip as Rikor glared down at her.

Pointing off in the distance, she brought his attention skyward once again. "What is that?"

He squinted, straining to expand his sight. A sudden exclamation caused his little pet to flinch in alarm. Rikor could not believe his luck. It appeared as though Adira was coming to them.

"What is it?"

Imperion Cayl was old, his eyes not suited to distance.

"It appears as though the golden empress flies to meet her challengers, master."

Rikor's triumphant smile was dimmed by the frown that furrowed the Imperion's brow.

"What troubles you, sir?"

The older man raised a hand to his brow, shielding his cloudy eyes from the suns.

"Does she know our plan and seek to overset us?" The old man murmured to himself, a scowl darkening his face. "Could she know?"

Rikor felt a tingle of fear. The Imperion had placed a great deal of faith in his young Impara. If their plan failed, he had much to lose. Confidence he did not feel colored his voice as he responded.

"She's been too preoccupied with her mating flight and cementing her place within Sik's colony to notice us," he sneered. "We are beneath her, an abomination."

It was not an exact quote, but close enough to suit him.

"Don't mistake preoccupation with stupidity, my young brother. She flies early in the day, and she flies far. She flies through another's territory without protection because she has no need. She has not lived this long through stupidity. If she is without fear, she has good reason to be."

Rikor swallowed. "She won't prevail, master."

"We'd best hope not. The last time we Xarans rose against her, we lost a sun. This time we may not be so lucky."

"That's just a legend," Rikor protested.

"No boy, it's truth, handed down from one Imperion to the next. It's why I had hoped to keep the Church's involvement from her knowledge."

Rikor stared in growing horror as the golden empress drew closer. He had privately mocked the true believers for years, far too cynical to fall for such obvious propaganda. The Xaran people had suffered after the last rebellion, it was true. He had always accepted that a third sun once faithfully rose on their horizon, dutifully following in his God-parents' path, but never once had he believed one creature capable of ending Halon's passage. She had simply taken advantage of the catastrophic event and forever tied her glory to the death of the child sun, much as she had claimed victory over Sik. He set his jaw. None of it mattered now. The plan was in motion and they would prevail because they must. As the golden empress herself had proven, gods died. It was Adira's turn.

CHAPTER 33

Adira pushed herself forward as she spotted the two massive queens laboring toward her. She had flown this route every morning for the past four days, ever since their spies confirmed that the Church had indeed brought the remaining five un-bonded queens together in an alliance against her. She smiled grimly against the whistle of wind, a sound she likened to a scream of protest as she cut through the sky. Thinking back to that first morning, she remembered Oryd's furious protest.

"You cannot do this!"

"I can't?" she'd returned mildly.

"You mustn't!" He'd moderated his tone slightly.

"And if I don't fly out to meet them? If I let them choose the place and time, what then?" She asked the question gently, indicating with a nod of her great head the Xarans who had already suffered so much under Sik's rule, those pitiable and pathetic creatures who were just starting to hope for a better life under Adira.

Oryd followed her gaze and sighed. "Your foolish heart will betray you to your death."

"Perhaps. Perhaps not. I know only that I will not allow anyone to dictate my actions."

"True always to yourself. It's one of the things I most admire about you, my Empress." His tone suggested that it might well be the one thing he most hated as well.

"I think there are other things you've always admired about me," she teased, hoping to lighten his mood.

He looked away, wings furled so tightly against his body they barely showed against the faint light that heralded Pil's arrival on the horizon. In all their years together, she'd never seen her First General so

224

distressed. His usual rages abandoned, he seemed to have given up all hope, descending into a rare quiet she found somewhat unnerving.

"They are five strong, Adira." It was a measure of his concern that he dropped all honorifics and used her given name.

"I can count."

Silence was her only answer. It seemed he was going to make her do all the work in this conversation.

"I choose the time. I choose the place. I choose height, velocity, temperature." She Flared, an incredible concentration of heat that was nowhere near her full potential. "I have the heat of a small sun within me," she reminded him. "I know their plan, thanks to you."

A small tremor passed over his frame, a pale blue luminescence followed, like the wake of a ship passing through still waters.

"You shouldn't fly. You're tired. Stay close to home, see if this dies down."

His tone was almost pleading now. "They have much to lose. Perhaps they won't act against you in spite of the Church's urging."

She smiled. "They'll fly, Oryd. We both know they will. They've been waiting millennia for this moment. My only choice is to take the battle to them."

Pil crested the horizon at that moment and a strange trick of the light caught Oryd's eye, creating the appearance of an empty window pane, the iris obscured by the angle at which he held his head. Then he shifted, glancing down, eyes bright and golden once again.

"Fly early, greet them with Hadra on the horizon." It was a sound tactic, and she was glad to have her First General back.

"Yes," she agreed. "Pil will be at an angle, and to the left as I fly south. If I time it right, Hadra will crest the horizon just after I engage the first two, blinding the other three as they stoop for the kill, or forcing them to wait until the advantage has passed."

A wild Lacing of blue accompanied those words – he was distressed by her casual acceptance of possible death. It was no surprise, really. His sole purpose since the moment he joined her colony had been to serve and protect his queen. That biological imperative would not abate merely because she chose a reckless course of action. There was only one drive stronger than the need to protect his queen. No dragon could rise against a queen, even to protect his own. The only exceptions were a mate-bonded pair, and in spite of all his hopes and plans, they had never forged that connection.

Even so, she suspected he longed to fly with her, guarding her flank as she went into battle. It was not unheard of, for a queen to bring many of her best soldiers into battle. They would circle the raging queens, calling encouragement and warning. Physically interfering was beyond them, but their presence could often bolster a failing queen. She had seen it happen when Sik challenged her ancient mother and nearly lost her own life in the process.

It was part of the reason Oryd was so despondent as she prepared for her first flight. Forbidden to join her, he was consigned to waiting; waiting for her return, or another to take her place. She nearly pitied him enough to change her mind, but would not bring him into battle, could not bear the idea that he might see her fall, that within moments of her death another queen might claim him. And he would serve, without question, without hesitation. Such was the power of the pheromone bond between queen and colony. It was better that he wait to learn her fate, and his, than to see it happen.

And so it was that Adira flew alone, before dawn every morning for the past handful of days. The highest, fastest thermals carried her, but dissatisfied with their speed, she put all her strength into broad forward wing strokes. Aja would not have survived such travel, but she was made for it, in fact reveled in it as she passed first her own southern border, then another. No queens rose to meet her on the first morning, or the next, and she wondered if Oryd was right after all. Perhaps her sisters were not brave enough to meet her in open challenge as the Church had hoped.

But now here she was, on the fifth day, so high in the sky that her would-be attackers had been unable to spot the tiny speck of gold amongst the stars they climbed toward. *Good,* she thought. *Let them climb. I know where they are now.*

She dropped rapidly through the clouds, forced to overcome a moment of vertigo as a thin cloud wrapped around her face before tearing away. For a moment she was Jenna again, falling to her death. She banked her wings and slowed her descent. A sharp head shake and she was Adira once more, powerful and in control of her destiny. She dropped lower, until she was even with the two queens who had now spotted her, and were swiftly approaching from the south. Too swiftly, she realized, if she wished to take advantage of Hadra's rise. Though her light would strike them sooner than the dark shape of the Xarans her sharp eyes had discerned at ground level, Hadra was still too low on the horizon. It appeared that the priests intended to watch the spectacle they had created from a safe distance. She took satisfaction from the knowledge that they would soon learn there was no such thing as safety during dragon battle, even for observers on the ground.

Adira veered off course, a lateral flight toward the rising sun that forced the queens high above to strain, laboring wings and lungs to catch her. She allowed herself another smile. She knew the thermals well, knew that they fought cross currents that lived to catch unwary wingtips, tired limbs that strayed from a body tuck. They would be buffeted by the change of course, far worse than if they had flown directly against the thermal. These were young queens, born and raised on Ryxa. They had never known the cold, brutal travel between stars, knew only the comfort of rich air in their lungs. Adira doubted they were prepared for the strain they now fought through in order to maintain their position above her. On the other hand, dragon instinct was a powerful force, and one that she could not discredit. It had kept a tiny, newly formed dragon alive so many years ago she could not remember the time of her birth. Instinct might yet counter stupidity, and she would do well not to forget that.

Closer now to Hadra, she judged the time was right to close on Cala and Bithra. She shifted her wings with a snap that reverberated through her entire body, and wheeled neatly about in mid-air. High above, her peripheral vision caught movement as the more cumbersome queens overshot their target. Adira smiled as her maneuver highlighted another advantage these young, barely tested queens could not anticipate. They did not face their mothers, ancient and earth-bound, ready for eternal rest, but rather a creature born of death itself. Adira was meant for the sky, and she ruled this domain as no other. A scream of challenge ripped from her throat and triggered another moment of vertigo along with the memory of another scream, this one filled with terror. Her momentary distraction enraged her. She could not afford to lose her focus. Two queens were challenge enough. She needed all her wits and every advantage at her disposal to emerge the victor over five.

Adira closed her eyes for a moment, blocking out everything, willfully calling up memories of her early days on the planet, searching for the memory of laying weak and helpless on the planet's surface, the instinct pushing her to live. Yes, there it was. She pulled those memories and the need to survive forward, allowing it to fill her heart and mind.

Eyes open, she immediately caught sight of the queens above her, black scales glinting distantly in Hadra's first glowing rays of light. They had moved into position as she closed on the two queens before her. At the last moment, she twisted away from a direct clash and slipped up and over Bithra. It was not an unexpected move and the other's tail rose to greet her. Bithra struck only air however, as Adira gracefully slide-slipped the maneuver, dropping down on her far side, using the queen's massive body as a shield against Cala even as she raked sharp claws down Bithra's shoulder and into her side, nearly tearing one wing completely away. The wounds were deep, and Bithra's shriek of pain and rage were just as satisfying to her soul.

"You think to challenge me? I'll rot in the fires of the Great Sun before I let you take what's mine."

She was unaware she'd spoken aloud until Cala answered. "You've taken what wasn't yours to begin with. Now pay the price!"

The other queen had sacrificed the advantage of height in a clever rolling dive that brought her under the injured Bithra, placing her in a perfect position to disembowel the golden empress. Adira's speed and flexibility served her well – she pulled her body up and away from Cala's reaching claws even as her own extended. Talons clashed, came away empty, but Bithra was bleeding heavily and losing altitude, and Cala had lost all advantage by dropping beneath her. The massive queen now labored to stay aloft and protect her back from Adira's sharp talons, incapable of the acrobatics her opponent possessed.

As hoped, Hadra's sudden appearance on the horizon had forced the young queens above to delay their dive, but if she hadn't already been aware of their position, they would have taken her by surprise and ended the battle right then. Instead, she tucked and rolled at the last moment, allowing the four queens to come together in a massive tangle of bodies, the laboring Cala taking the brunt of the blow.

Adira heard a snap as the ancient queen broke, back or neck, it didn't matter. She was done, falling like a stone, dropping past Bithra, who struggled to slow her own descent. Two were down, or close enough to be inconsequential. She felt a brief spurt of satisfaction as she realized the battle had carried them over the priests far below. Let them scatter as her opponents fell, showering them with blood and the scales of defeat.

Her bloodlust boiling, she fell upon the nearest of the remaining queens, but to her surprise, Rana was far more maneuverable than she had seemed. The young queen flipped backward, and Adira overshot her target, feeling claws rake deeply even as she extended her own wings to brake her forward progress. Her deceleration eased the sting, and Rana's strike ended as Adira flipped over, nearly head over tail, and then again, a lithe twist of her long body allowing her to take the younger queen by the throat. Before she could finish Rana off, she felt the impact of another body, claws digging into powerful shoulder muscles. Instinct brought her wings in close against her body, protecting the only thing keeping her aloft, even as her sudden dead weight forced the others to strain in an instinctive response to their uncontrolled drop. The queen above her released in a panic, unable to take advantage of her position long enough to take Adira at the base of her skull, a preferred killing tactic. She grimly held on to Rana – she needed to end this quickly now. A swift shake, a shower of blood, and the younger queen went limp. She slipped from Adira's mouth and dropped away, racing Bithra back to earth.

That left Qora and Klis still in this battle, and Adira was no longer at full strength. Blood struck her face, the only warning before Klis dropped again. She performed a somersault in mid-air and used the momentum to swing her tail in a great arc that caught one of her remaining opponents with a glancing blow. Wing tissue, if she was not mistaken, but not enough to ground either of them.

They had lost too much altitude, and now Adira realized the second part of their plan. Too late to avoid it, she had flown into the range of the archers stationed below the battle. She had time only to pray that the Church hadn't dared use Weavers to improve their accuracy, then the arrows loosed. She had Flared during the battle, but not enough to melt Chrym, and several of the arrowheads struck her, tearing deep. Fortunately the metal stayed in place once the force of the arrows was expended – all the proof she needed that no Weavers had joined the battle yet. Her shriek of pain was primal, answered by Qora and Klis, who sensed their advantage and closed in for the kill. She felt teeth and talons pierce battle-hardened scales to tear into her flesh, their weight bearing them all down.

The battle had raged close enough to the planet's surface that they were prepared to touch ground, to finish her on the earth, brought low in every sense of the word. Her teeth connected with flesh again, and she felt satisfaction at the shriek of pain that followed, but was herself silent now, fighting tooth and nail for survival. The instinct was raging, and she saw the archers reload. They wouldn't care if they hit one or all of them, and she struggled against the mass of the other two queens, managing at the last moment to put Klis directly in their line of sight as the ground rose up to meet her.

The impact stunned all three dragons, claws and teeth loosening their grip as they slowly regained their bearings. Adira heard a wheezing gasp, felt the dry hot air of Klis' exhalation against her face. The young queen had been pierced by so many arrows she resembled a pin cushion. At least one had punctured a lung, and Klis struggled to draw air. Unlike a Xaran, the wound was not necessarily fatal, and Adira gathered herself to finish Klis before she regained her own strength. It was still two against one, and she felt Qora begin to twitch as she came to her senses.

On the ground, Adira had a distinct disadvantage. Her diminutive stature gave her two opponents much greater reach, and she could not afford to let them regroup enough to coordinate a second attack. She lunged forward to take Klis by the throat, but missed as a powerful blow caught the back of her head. Qora had managed her own strike just moments before Adira could finish the other queen. Adira heaved violently, feeling Qora's teeth lose their purchase and slip along the horns that reinforced her skull. She snapped her head to the side, completing the defensive maneuver that prevented the other queen from sinking those fangs into the base of her skull and severing her spine. One horn broke as Qora finally lost her grip and Adira shook her off completely while Klis struggled to her feet. She could feel Chrym grating against bone, tearing deeper into muscle as she crouched low to the ground between the two queens, and could only hope Klis felt the pain more deeply than she.

The archers had reloaded and the only thing keeping her alive was the bulk of the two youngsters who had just realized that all they needed to do was step aside and let the Church finish her off. "Ssssstupid hatchlingssss," she hissed as they tried to maneuver her into the archers' range. "Do you think they'll let you live after what they've done today?"

"Do you think *we* care as long as you're one of the dead?" Qora hissed back, beyond reason.

"Then welcome to Halon," Adira replied and called up the full force of her Flare, just in time to greet the deadly arrows that whistled through the air at the grounded queens.

Klis and Qora thrashed and shrieked as they were blasted from both sides. Her Flare had not melted the Chrym that landed farthest from her immediate vicinity, which meant that several barbs remained to stab painfully into the others' exposed hindquarters. In spite of the archers reloading yet again, the two young queens scrambled backward, awkward in their haste to escape her blazing heat.

Adira lunged forward, landing between them as she brought her internal temperature even higher, as hot as she had ever burned. The archer nearest to her caught fire, his clothes smoldering, then lighting in slow motion. Klis and Qora screamed in tandem with the archer, a strange harmonic forming as they began to sizzle and smoke too.

"Still don't care who lives or dies today?" she taunted, but Qora was beyond answering, beyond words now as the golden empress expressed her contempt. Adira expanded her scales, losing precious blood as the wounds created by the Chrym arrows gaped wide. It was a necessary act, for the metal had indeed melted, but trapped within her, the bubbling liquid was an agony she could no longer deny. Blood and liquid metal exited the wounds and she shuddered with relief as the last of the foreign substance left her body.

The remaining archers had begun to fall back, but Adira's blood was up. Leaving her defeated opponents behind, she surged forward, or would have, if her legs hadn't given out. The suns were shielded behind clouds, but that wasn't right. It was a bright sunny day in the middle of the dry season. The fields were burning, the Xarans fleeing as the slowest among them caught fire and fell. Why was it so dark then?

With the last of her strength, she threw herself skyward, instinct screaming at her to flee. It was unheard of for a queen to abandon the battleground without finishing her opponents, but in her weakened state, she was no match for another attack from the Church's soldiers. Klis and Qora would think twice about challenging her again, assuming they survived in the aftermath. The Church could well take advantage of their current state, though they had always preferred an indirect path to power. Too many unprecedented changes had occurred within the past year for Adira to guess with any certainty what Imperion Cayl planned. With unfettered access to the most Gifted Xarans, she had been forced at last to acknowledge that the Church might well have the power to end the dragons' reign.

But instinct was now telling her to rise, high beyond the limited sight of the earthbound creatures below, and she did, body laboring to remain airborne, muscles screaming at the climb. She was unaware that she screamed aloud with the effort, but those remaining below would carry that sound into their nightmares for years to come. She reached a thermal at last but kept winging upward, afraid they could still track her movements. Up she climbed, searching for and finding the super thermals that circled the planet in untiring streams. It was easier to let the current carry her where it pleased. In her current state, she would end up where she needed to be much sooner if she actually circled the planet in the opposite direction instead of flying against the thermal to reach her destination. She was nearly half a planet away by now. Six of one, a half dozen of the other. The strange thought drifted through her mind and she caught herself before her failing body dropped from the thermal. Teeth gritting against the effort, she kept her wings open, cupped to catch the thermals that were no longer her friend. In her exhausted state, they threatened now to tear her apart, to throw her from the sky she had so recently claimed as her domain. But Adira's will was strong, and she bowed to no one.

She kept herself aloft with the promise that the Church would suffer for their transgressions. There was not enough Chrym in the world to stop her, and if she had to set the entire planet on fire, she would end them. Her rage and hate kept her going, but it also kept the pain of her wounds at bay. Slowly but surely, she felt that pain more and more, and a new fear wormed its way into her heart. What of the child?

In the heat of battle, there had been no time to give consideration to the baby she carried, but as she struggled to stay alert, she could no longer ignore her fears. Had the bloodlust, the deaths of at least two queens soaked into her child's genetic makeup? Would she come into this world filled with violence and rage? Adira's options had dwindled and she had only one choice left if she wished to save their child.

Eventually she spotted her destination; the rocks that marked the entrance to the buried city nearly indistinguishable at this height, even to her eyes. It had not seemed possible, but dropping from the thermal was more painful than struggling to remain within the current. As she broke through the edge of the stream, she caught a wingtip and spun wildly, dropping in an uncontrolled descent. Such was her exhaustion that she nearly allowed the fall to continue, but instinct screamed, and she pulled on reserves of strength and will she hadn't known existed. At last she leveled her flight into a rapid but more controlled drop. Her breathing was harsh and heavy, a desperate pant as she closed the distance between herself and safety.

CHAPTER 34

Half a planet away, Rikor watched as the Imperion's frail body was placed on a healer's bed. Caught up in the panic that ensued during Cala's fall, the high priest and his closest advisors had all suffered injuries of varying degrees. Rikor cradled his arm against his chest and cultivated a look of concern. It wouldn't do to move too quickly, but if the Imperion did not recover, he had work to do, alliances to shore up, markers to be called in, and blackmail to enact. He could not afford to wait for another Imperion to age and die in the natural order of things. If a new leader was to be named, he intended it to be him.

His master's eyes fluttered open, and he weakly gestured him near.

"Rikor." It was a hoarse gasp, rough and dry.

"Yes, master." He moved closer, ignoring the pain in his arm, the ribs he was certain were fractured. If he ever found the horse that had trampled him, he would make sure the servants ate well that night, after the beast had suffered an appropriate amount of time, of course.

"The queens." The Imperion coughed and gestured impatiently at a healer, who lifted his head and carefully offered a few sips of water.

"The surviving queens." His voice was stronger. "They saw our use of Chrym."

Felt was more like it, Rikor thought, and dark pleasure welled up at the memory. He wished he could go back in time, hear their screams again and again, but the Imperion had a point to make, and Rikor raced ahead of him.

"Shall we end them or let nature take its course?"

He was fairly sure that at least four queens remained where they had fallen. Cala and Rana were indisputably dead, Klis and Qora badly injured and unmoving. His last glimpse of them had revealed still, smoking lumps surrounded by ash. If they were alive, he doubted they would last the night.

"You underestimate the rejuvenating power of a dragon."

Rikor kept anger from his expression through long practice. In recent weeks the Imperion had taken to publicly criticizing him, downplaying his knowledge of dragons and their own history. Perhaps he would know more if the Imperion didn't guard his library so jealously. He held back the words he wished to say and asked instead, "You believe them capable of healing from such terrible burns?"

"Dragons were born of fire. If they don't die outright, we must assume they will recover, given enough time."

Rikor pursed his lips. That was unfortunate, unless... he could only hope that the Imperion would issue a death sentence. Perhaps he could nudge his master towards a favorable decision.

"They won't rest easy, knowing that we were in possession of Chrym, and used it against a queen, even if it was in their defense." That was an understatement.

The old man coughed, his answer too garbled to understand. He gestured to the healers, who lifted him up and placed several pillows behind his back so that he could recline in a more upright position. As soon as his breathing eased, he ordered the healers away so they could converse with greater privacy. Damn his luck, Rikor thought. Imperion Cayl already appeared more alert and in control. It seemed as though he might recover after all.

"No, they won't forgive our interference, or our criminal possession of Chrym," he said, returning to their conversation. "Cala and Rana were the first to fall. What of Bithra?"

"She came to ground quite some distance from our observation point," Rikor reported. "Before the battle dropped within range, I saw several of her dragons arrive and aid her from the ground."

"So she abandoned the battle before we took action," the Imperion mused. "We can use that."

Rikor and the other Impara who had not been completely immobilized by their injuries ranged in a semi-circle around their leader, waiting for orders.

"I had rather we controlled one of the younger queens, but Bithra is far more likely to survive the battle."

Rikor controlled a frown, seeing the direction his master's thought traveled.

"Qora merely requires the right persuasion, master. She is far more malleable than the others."

He made the suggestion with seeming indifference though he was certain by the Imperion's stare that he had not fooled the older man.

"No. She saw us use Chrym against not one, but three queens. She cannot live to spread that tale."

One of the other Impara frowned.

"Master, wouldn't it be better to have a queen such as Qora under our control? Her fear after witnessing a Church-ordered execution of another queen would virtually guarantee her submission."

Chel echoed Rikor's own thoughts. Why guide from the shadows when they had the opportunity to take outright rule of their planet through might?

The Imperion smiled. "Hmmm. An interesting notion. I wonder that I had not thought of it before."

Quick as a striking snake, his hand lashed out, catching Chel's robes to drag him forward. The startled Impara moved with his master's hand, bringing him within range of the spittle which sprayed from the Imperion's lips with the force of his next words.

"If we leave a queen alive, one who knows our true strength, how long do you think she'll tolerate our presence in her court? How long before she chances outright rebellion? Perhaps we would prevail, perhaps not, but either way, we would be in open war against the dragons."

He shoved Chel away and stared at the other men.

"What happens if we kill every queen on the planet?"

They stared back, realization dawning. Unlike a mate-bond, the colony bond did not result in death when a queen died. It merely freed the colony to find a new queen, and if they didn't find a new queen, they would wreak havoc.

"You fools saw how Sik's colony behaved before Adira claimed them. Do you think we have enough Weavers in the world to fight that battle?"

Rikor felt sickness churn in his gut. The Imperion's scenario did not even take into account the potentially hundreds or thousands of queens that had left the planet, searching for new worlds. From time to time, they would return, some with hundreds of thousands of dragons in their colonies. Without a queen to oppose them, the Church would be forever in a state of battle, against both the dragons and the rebellion.

Chel dared to argue. "But if we control Qora –"

The Imperion cut him off with a slash of his hand.

"Enough about Qora. In spite of their intelligence, these beasts are just that, beasts. Worse, they will never bow to a yoke of any kind. My decision is made. Destroy Qora and Klis while we have the opportunity. Set our spies to search out Adira. We have Weavers in every Adiran court. I want her dead. In the meantime, we'll make what we can of

Bithra."

Impara Ynez nodded sharply and turned away. He directed all of the Church's highest level Weavers, and as such, would be the one to send a Swimmer to alert their people in Adira's territories. Of the remaining Impara, that left Rikor as most senior. He kept his eyes downcast, not wishing to offend and lessen his chances of being present for Klis' death. The silence drew out. The Imperion was taunting him. At last the order came.

"Impara Rikor."

He snapped to attention.

"You will take our least cowardly archers back to the field of battle," he sneered. "If both queens live, and have not been joined by their colony, you will exterminate them, removing any trace of Chrym in the process."

Rikor bowed and turned away.

"Rikor." His master called his attention back. "Speed is of the essence. If our involvement becomes known among their colonies, I'll take it out of your hide."

He paled and bowed deeply. The Imperion did not jest about punishments. The floggings he'd inflicted as a younger man were legendary, and the sentences now carried out on his behalf often required more than one man to finish.

"Yes, master," Rikor replied with the respect Imperion Cayl was owed and hurried away to complete his task.

Regardless of his wish to see Klis dead, they needed to remove all trace of their involvement in the battle if they could. The two younger queens had not brought any of their colony with them into battle, a mistake that would in all likelihood prove fatal. He had hoped to use the execution of Klis to bring Qora to heel, but Rikor was certain they could still end this day with at least one queen firmly under their control.

Once away from the Imperion, it took longer than Rikor cared to gather sufficient archers. He would have preferred to use just one Weaver, imagined the look of horror on Klis' face as the Weaver drove a tiny sliver into Qora, all the while knowing that she was next, but the Imperion had been clear. Oh well, he would just have to hope Klis had recovered enough to open her eyes and see death staring her in the face. He intended to be front and center, the last thing reflected in those vapid eyes before they dimmed forever.

CHAPTER 35

Another week of waiting had worn Aja's nerves as thin as the garrote wire hidden in a seam of his sleeve, but at least he could take a certain grim satisfaction that it had done Phyx no favors either. The other Swimmer spent the time waiting, always within a certain radius of the Chrym node, ostensibly to stay up to date on what was happening as the dragons battled and how the Church responded, but Aja knew he wanted to be able to Swim for Adira's court at a moment's notice.

Phyx made no bones about his desire to replace Aja within the rebel camp, and the assassination of the Golden Empress would go a long way in that regard, given Aja's current status. Still under suspicion of treason, he had picked up a few tails of his own, which made tracking Phyx's movements problematic. Still, he managed to escape their surveillance periodically to make his own preparations; he had trained them after all, and knew every trick better than most.

The only thing that still held him in the camp after the general's betrayal was his uncertainty over Adira's fate. News had come quickly of the battle and her injuries, and everyone assumed she had returned to her new colony. But there had been no sightings of his lover since she left the battlefield, and he feared the worst, though he thought he would surely know if she had died.

"Phyx!" The general's aide called the other Swimmer, who straightened abruptly from the light doze he'd fallen into. Aja kept to the shadows as he moved closer to overhear their conversation.

"Any news?"

"Still no word on Adira's location, but Bithra is moving quickly to consolidate her own power base. Since Adira didn't claim their colonies, she jumped at the chance to expand her territory, just as we suspected."

"And what about Imperion Cayl," Phyx asked. Aja's nerves tingled at the way the other Swimmer spoke the high priest's name. There was something hidden there, a darkness that hinted at a rage beyond any hatred Aja had ever harbored, even for Sik. Phyx might have his own agenda, but he was no friend of the Church, of that Aja was abruptly certain.

"He's moved his residence to Klis' court now that Bithra's claimed her colony. She's settled there as well."

Aja smiled grimly. Klis had ruled a large rocky province, harsher than most. Its only advantages were the rich Chrym veins that ran deep below the surface, where only the most Gifted Miners could reach. Most queens had no interest in resources so difficult to gather, and Klis had little worries that any queen would challenge her to gain her lands. She'd been a fool to engage with Adira at the Church's urging, and it had cost her her life.

"That was smart. There's plenty of Chrym, but it's too deep to safely Swim, at least not for any length of time. They've insulated themselves against a Gifted attack, and coming from over land is pretty much impossible. In the meantime, they could build narrow channels to send their own spies out into the world, and it could take years for us to find a way in."

Phyx echoed Aja's thoughts with eerie precision, and his estimation of the other man's intelligence rose another notch. He was going to have to kill Phyx before he left, or Adira would never be safe again.

"It may be even worse than you think," Kaperamatu responded. "New information suggests that Adira didn't finish Klis or Qora before leaving the field."

Aja's heart sank as he digested Kaperamatu's words. The only reason Adira would have left an enemy still standing was if she was too injured to finish them off. It was becoming imperative that he find her.

Kaperamatu answered the question Phyx's furrowed eyebrows asked. "We now have reason to believe the Church used their Weavers to kill them once they were incapacitated."

"Holy suns!" Aja could see Phyx considering the ramifications of this new information. "Imperion Cayl is finally making his big move. Bithra's a surprise though – I was sure he'd choose a mate-bonded queen. Easier to control with a mate to protect," he finished cynically.

The rebellion had considered holding a queen's mate for ransom in exchange for protection, but quickly realized there were far too many variables to consider in such a long-term captive scenario. A mate-bonded dragon pair was virtually immortal, with endless time and patience. Eventually they would find a way to escape human control, and their vengeance would be swift and indiscrimanatory. Aja was surprised Phyx didn't agree with the general's conclusion, but then the general tended to be more straightforward in his solutions, whereas Phyx came at every problem sideways. His unpredictable nature was just one of the many things that made him so dangerous. Lost in his thoughts, he suddenly realized that Phyx had left the corridor and was nowhere in sight.

"Damn him to Pil's mid-day light," he muttered before calling to Kaperamatu.

"Matu!" The younger man turned with a ready smile that changed quickly to a guarded expression as he recognized Aja. In spite of his efforts, he had clearly not undone the damage caused by Sefti's reports and the subsequent rumors that still circulated through the rebellion.

"Any news?" he asked, as though he'd not overheard a word of the younger man's previous conversation with Phyx.

"No news of Adira, but Qora and Klis didn't survive their injuries. The Imperion makes camp with Bithra in Klis' court, but we're not clear yet on how strong their alliance is and what our next move will be." Short and to the point, Matu made it clear he was conversing with Aja out of necessity rather than choice.

"Is General Tal free?" Aja asked. The general had made himself unavailable to him for some time, and he wondered if the toxic rumors had made Tal fear for his life in the Choosing Assassin's presence.

"I'm afraid not," Matu replied, his gaze shifting uncomfortably under Aja's direct stare. Aja kept his bitter humor in check and inclined his head in response.

"Perhaps I should send Phyx to Klis for information," Aja suggested. He outranked Phyx for now, and it was well within his rights to order an information gathering mission for the general.

Alarm flashed briefly across Matu's face. "No, I believe the general has requested all Swimmers to remain at the base camp for the time being."

"Oh?" Aja arched an eyebrow before allowing a slight scowl to crease his forehead. "As the ranking Swimmer, shouldn't I have been informed of this decision? What if I had ordered everyone out this morning?"

"It was a recent decision," Matu hastily assured him.

"Yes, I'm sure it was." Aja's smile was less than comforting. "Please be sure to let me know as soon as any new decisions are made. I'm sure I won't be hard to find."

The less than veiled reference to the surveillance the general had ordered caused the corner of Matu's eye to twitch. "Yes, yes," he agreed hurriedly. "You'll be the first to know when we decide to take action."

Would that be before or after Phyx's blade slid between his ribs, Aja wondered, and resolved to take action before the situation reached that point.

CHAPTER 36

Rikor watched from a safe distance as the archers took aim on the still smoldering forms of Klis and Qora. He regretted that he couldn't be closer, but the dragons were still more than capable of a deadly Flare, and he was far too close to victory to risk it all for the pleasure of a more personal kill. With the Weavers present, there was no need for accuracy, but he enjoyed the ceremony of it too much to hurry things along.

Klis stirred and uttered a piteous moan, one empty eye socket turned towards the sound of human voices. Adira's final Flare had burned the young queen's face so badly there were areas of exposed bone, but to his shock, Rikor could already see several places where tissue had begun to regenerate.

"Who's there?" Klis demanded, scales hardening in a rush as she belatedly sensed danger. The hiss of pain that escaped was uncontrollable as she turned to look with her good eye.

"No!" she shrieked as she watched twenty archers level Chrym-tipped arrows at her prone form. Rikor smiled as she scrabbled painfully away. This was nearly as good as he had hoped.

"Klis!" he called playfully. "Where are you going?"

His laughter mocked her as she pressed against Qora's immovable bulk, too weak to climb over the other queen's body.

"No," she moaned more quietly, good eye tilted to the sky, no doubt hoping to spot her colony, flying to her rescue.

They would arrive soon, but far too late to help her. Reminded of the urgency, Rikor ended her torment long before she deserved, and uttered a short command. The song of the arrows brought a smile to his face, and the sounds Klis made as the Chrym penetrated her scales and the Weavers forced the metal to burrow through flesh and bone made him ache with pleasure.

By comparison, Qora's death was bitterly unsatisfying. Klis' death had failed to rouse her companion, and she died without a sound. Furious with disappointment, he ordered a scale removed from each dragon as a memento, and consoled himself over Qora's easy death by watching the unlucky archer struggle to remove the deadly spikes without injuring himself in the process. They were on their way back to the Imperion when Zetequilon found him.

"Master Rikor!" Even before he caught sight of his young slave, the panic in his voice warned Rikor that bad news was on the horizon.

"Leave us," he ordered the archers, aware of their curious gaze as his young servant stood anxiously before him, breathless and trembling with fear.

"Zetequilon," he greeted the younger man with an oily smile. "I hope for Loshi's sake you've accomplished the task I set for you."

Loshi's twin blanched and threw himself at Rikor's feet.

"I tried, I swear on Pil and Hadra, I tried!" he babbled, hands gripping Rikor's sandals too tightly for comfort.

Rikor danced back, kicking the young man in the head. "What do you mean, you tried?" he asked ominously.

"She didn't return to Sik's court," the younger man wept through his hands. "I Swam all the way to her court just to make sure she wasn't there, and she wasn't. I don't know where she is, but I swear to you, she didn't come within range of your archers."

Zetequilon's eyes rolled back in his head and he collapsed. Rikor grimaced in disgust and kicked at his thin body through his robes. Perfect! The fool had burned himself out and would be of no use to him for days to come, which was truly a pity, given his trusted position within the rebel's camp. It was more important than ever that they know General Tal's plans, and with Rikor's best spy no longer at Aja's side, they would be in the dark at the worst possible time. Not only did they not know how Tal planned to respond to their latest move, but they could not confirm Adira's death or even her location. The Imperion would not be pleased.

CHAPTER 37

When Adira finally landed, she expected to fall into darkness immediately, but the blessing of unconsciousness was not hers. She lay for some time, feeling the welcome warmth of Pil and Hadra, a palpable caress to her dragon senses. She soaked in the suns' energy, tiny zinging signals working their way through torn and swollen tissues, slowly leaving repaired cells behind. The healing would take a long time, but it didn't matter; she was going nowhere. Too exhausted even to shift, she remained as she had landed, obscured from view by the circle of stone she'd searched for and found. She had no pursuers left who would seek her from above, save perhaps Oryd and his soldiers, and they would not think to search northeast of Adira's home city when the battle had taken place far to the south of Sik's province, on the other side of the planet, so she was safe to rest here until sleep claimed her at last.

The chill of night woke her, and she moaned as stiffened muscles shifted and gathered for the first time in hours. The sound was loud, the resulting silence oppressive. Every insect and small predator within earshot froze as she moved for the first time in hours. Afraid to give herself time to think, she pulled her remaining energy into the shift. The shift to human form was exhausting, but would also serve to speed the healing process. She expected that with wounds this severe, she would require further healing time, but hoped that the worst of her injuries would at least close. Rana's claws had cut deeply, leaving wide furrows that continued to weep sluggishly, the thin crust broken by her new movement. Open wounds were dangerous, and it was a testament to how severely the other queen had injured her that they had not closed yet.

The pain of the shift caught her by surprise. Although moving from one form to another was never pleasant, this was a new level of pain, as though she were caught in a sandstorm with every nerve ending exposed to the stinging, scouring grains as they scraped her raw. She solidified at last, nearly weeping with effort and pain, a pain which now centered in her womb. She sank to the ground, cradling her stomach. Had she lost the baby?

A tiny flutter answered her. They were both safe for now, but she had to keep moving. There were pouches of Chrym paste and clean water stored in the municipal building below her, and she needed that food now more than ever. Determined not to fail, she forced herself upright and took her first faltering step forward. Being in human form while weak and injured was not as bad as she had feared, which was a good thing, a very good thing indeed, considering the decision she had reached during the painful journey here. Come what may, she would not take dragon form again until this pregnancy had run its course.

CHAPTER 38

Oryd snapped his wings out to catch the leading edge of a super thermal, ignoring the twinge of overworked muscles as he focused his gaze on the planet below. Adira might be tiny, but those golden scales were a beacon to his sight. He would find her, no matter how long it took.

He cursed the delay that had kept him from her side, but with impeccable timing, Sik's First General Telek had challenged him on the very same morning Adira met the other queens' challenge. He still struggled to understand the outcome of that life and death struggle, even as he searched for his empress in the aftermath of her own battle. As his eyes scanned every rock and crevice for movement, he allowed himself to recall that morning.

"Oryd!" The bass challenge was issued from Sik's training grounds, and from the reaction of the males around him, Oryd knew without question he was being summoned by Telek, Sik's former First General. He allowed a broad smile to lift his lips, disguising his very real concern over what was to come. Since reaching sexual maturity, Oryd had never been defeated, not in training or in true battle, but Telek was a class of dragon outside his experience. He would never show it to these other dragons, but for the first time, Oryd feared he was outmatched.

Having learned from a master, he sauntered to the training grounds, Lacing anticipation with a hint of amusement. The other dragons made way, forming a circle around the bloodstained sands beyond the queen's palace grounds. No human structures marred the planet's surface here; the Xarans weren't foolish enough to build anywhere near this place. When he arrived, Oryd was shocked to find bleached dragon bones mixed with the dark sand, though he carefully hid his disgust from the males who surrounded him. Very few of his own colony were present, but even among those he might call family, he had few friends. They would be all too pleased to see him fall, he thought. Or perhaps not, given the brutal nature of the dragon he now faced.

A First General who allowed those who fell on the training ground to rot into the earth was not a dragon who tolerated weakness. Oryd couldn't imagine the level of contempt such an act required. Even the males he had most hated had received better treatment after their deaths, and he felt a welcome rage build in his heart over the discourtesy Telek showed the fallen.

The object of his anger was a massive dark green male who bowed his chest and glared at him from across the sands. By the length and thickness of his horns, Telek was truly ancient. Oryd took his measure without revealing his own reservations. Telek was powerful and clever, and from what Oryd had learned, the old First General had served at least three queens before Sik. That made him possibly the oldest dragon on the planet. Males were far less prone to the *darkening* than females, but even so, such age was unusual, given their tendency to violence towards one another. Telek was formidable indeed to have survived so long. None of his thoughts showed as Oryd slowly mantled his wings and bowed his own chest at his challenger.

"I challenge you for the rank of First General to Empress Adira," Telek formally announced, and Oryd saw that he was pleased his opponent had noted the bones of the fallen. Perhaps he had not controlled his Lacing as well as he thought.

"I accept your challenge," he replied, sounding for all the world as though he'd just been invited to fly a regular border patrol, though his eyes narrowed slightly as he continued his inspection of the older dragon, searching for any weakness in his opponent. They were well matched in size, he noted with satisfaction, and if Telek had thousands of millennia of experience on him, Oryd had a few millennia of his own, watching the best aerial fighter he'd ever known in daily practice. He knew tricks this ancient one couldn't dream of. The thought gave him a much-needed boost as Telek launched skyward a split second before his own claws left the ground.

The next few minutes were spent in eerie silence as each dragon strained for a height advantage. At last it was clear that neither would outpace the other, and Telek struck first. Even though he'd been expecting it, Oryd was stunned by the power of Telek's blow. It took every ounce of will to fling his wings wide as Telek closed on him, risking a disastrous injury as he halted his forward momentum to allow Telek to overshoot his target, but Telek was faster than he'd imagined, and scored first blood, long yellowed teeth scoring Oryd's throat as he shot past in a blur of green.

The power of those jaws nearly ended the battle right then and there, but Oryd Flared quickly to cauterize the wound and tucked into a corkscrew dive. The older dragon immediately followed as he'd expected, and once again Oryd changed his trajectory, bones screaming with the strain as he nearly doubled back on himself to score a vicious blow along Telek's exposed abdomen. Telek roared, the first sound either male had made since going airborne, and from the planet below, a faint roar echoed as a thousand dragons responded.

"They sound hopeful," Oryd taunted as they closed on each other again.

"They know better," Telek panted, and then they were locked together, wings tucked to protect the membranes that kept them aloft as teeth and claws searched for weak areas. Scales and blood swirled around them, caught in the turbulence of their struggle as each particle drifted gently toward the planet's surface. Oryd and Telek dropped quickly from the sky, their combined mass accelerating their velocity, and they broke apart at the last moment to rise laboriously upward again.

Both had suffered serious injuries, but Oryd could see that Telek suffered a slight tear to his right wing membrane, just below the shoulder joint. He Flared to cauterize his own wounds and dug deep for the strength to finish this battle. This time his climb was faster than Telek, and he dove first. Telek attempted to repeat the switchback the younger dragon had just used so effectively, but Oryd struck before the ancient First General completed the maneuver and scored a solid strike on the green dragon, eliciting a second roar of pain.

They repeated the rise and fall two more times before both dragons reached the peak of their climb and closed again. Oryd's lungs were burning, and even with repeated Flares he'd lost too much blood. Telek was in no better shape, but Oryd feared his greater experience in battle would soon begin to tell. His youth was no match for the patience this old dragon displayed, and he was one mistake away from death.

Telek read defeat in his opponent's eyes, and when they closed for the last time, his right wing faltered slightly, causing him to slip sideways, giving Oryd an opening. The blue dragon's head snaked forward, teeth finding and tearing at the ancient general's throat. Telek's claws dug briefly at his body then loosened as his wings lost their strength. Oryd roared in victory as Telek's body plummeted to the planet below.

He relived the battle now as he skimmed the planet's atmosphere. What had seemed a miraculous victory at the time now felt hollow as he recalled the relief in Telek's eyes when he dropped from Oryd's claws.

Had Telek's slip been deliberate? Why would he have given Oryd the victory? He found no easy answers as he soared in ever-widening circles, seeking his queen.

CHAPTER 39

The thunder of wings filled the air as Bithra's latest conquests rose in unison beneath her. She smiled at the sound and forced herself to ignore the twinge of discomfort as newly healed wing membranes protested the strain of flight. It had been a week since the battle, with no sightings of Adira. As far as Bithra was concerned, that made her the victor. As soon as her wing had healed enough, she'd taken steps to expand her territory. Tyleas, her First General, tucked under her wingtip to observe the flight patterns of her new males. How a colony flew together could tell a dragon a lot, not just about the strengths and weaknesses of a particular dragon, but also the strength of their leadership. If she knew Tyleas, he was carefully gauging the new competition, in particular, Klis' First General, Zedron.

"Our advance scouting party has reported that Zim flew to claim Cala yesterday morning," Tyleas reported casually.

Bithra Flared with rage, but the blue dragon didn't flinch. Just moments earlier she'd been reveling in the knowledge that she would soon rule more than half the planet. How dare Zim claim what was hers? But she knew exactly why Zim dared; although mate-bonded, the other queen was renowned for her vicious nature and used her bloodthirsty nature to firmly hold her territory. Since her return to the planet countless years earlier, she had killed her own mother to claim her territory, and had gone on to murder two newborn daughters, preferring to take no chances that they would follow in her footsteps. Bithra bitterly accepted the loss of a premium territory, knowing she didn't dare challenge Zim even in the best of health.

"Anything else you'd care to share?"

Tyleas' subtle Lacing informed her of more bad news.

"Ceyliru as well?" Bithra shrieked with fury, barely noticing as her newly bonded dragons answered. She would have to move swiftly if she hoped to gain even half of what she'd thought to claim. To her knowledge, no queen had ever claimed more than one colony in a day. She would be the first, she resolved, and promptly wheeled toward Rana's territory as Klis' newly bonded males mirrored her movements. At least Klis and Rana shared a border, both with each other and her own territory.

It was at Imperion Cayl's urging that she had flown to claim Klis first, a decision she now regretted. Cala and Qora were at the far edges of her newly expanded empire, and the remaining two queens had been quick to take advantage of that weakness. If she had flown just a day sooner, and claimed the farthest region she might only have lost the one territory. But no, she consoled herself, the injuries she had suffered in battle would never have tolerated such a flight. Indeed, she already struggled to remain aloft, and forced herself to move higher, seeking a super thermal to assist her travels.

She hissed at the strain of entering the fast moving current, but was instantly relieved as she spread her wings and allowed the steady stream of air to carry her with minimal effort to Rana and a new colony in need of a queen. She could only hope Zim and Ceyliru were busy forming a proper bond with their new males, and glanced uneasily at the blue and green dragons slipping into the thermal behind her. This could end very badly, she thought. Tyleas Laced the same concern, but she was set on her course despite her own misgivings.

Even though Klis was the smallest province, it still took hours of coasting on the super thermal to reach Qora, and Bithra used every moment to her advantage, secreting massive amounts of pheromones which flooded the newly bonded dragons gliding in her wake with a powerful chemical signal; *follow, serve, protect, obey* ... worship. By the time Rana's palace was in sight, she was pleased to see the glaze in their eyes as they submitted to the power of her claim. It was none too soon as the dragons below took note of her presence in the sky and bellowed a challenge. Bithra smiled and painfully tucked her wings to dive.

CHAPTER 40

Aja pivoted and fell backward in a controlled roll that brought him to his feet beyond Phyx's range. The other Swimmer grinned and spread his hands wide as though the blade aimed at Aja's kidney had been in jest.

"Worth a shot, eh?"

He smiled tightly in response and drew his own blade. The two men had been playing a deadly game of cat and mouse for weeks, and he was glad it was finally over, though a small part of his heart ached. Win or lose, the rebel camp was truly lost to him now, along with the people who had formed a new family of sorts for a young orphan so many years ago.

"I've been watching you for a while now," Phyx taunted, and Aja bit back a retort as the older man flipped his dagger from hand to hand, feinting a forward thrust to gauge his opponent's responses. They were in a deserted part of the camp, where few people might wander by. Aja had taken a chance late in the day to slip away to replenish a few special supplies he would need when they discovered Adira's location. Earlier in the week, he'd begun to lace the camp's water supply with tiny doses of pesa root. Years ago, he'd discovered that the root, when dried and steeped, lost none of its potency, yet was nearly flavorless. In such a small amount, the pesa wouldn't have an obvious effect, but over time it would weaken the other Swimmers' Gifts, giving Aja a much-needed advantage if he were going to reach Adira ahead of a would-be assassin.

Phyx must have followed him and waited for him to return from the desert. Once again, Aja found himself reluctantly admiring the man. There were very few people in this world who were capable of surprising the Choosing Assassin.

"You're pretty good, but I think I'm better." The humor slipped from Phyx's eyes, and Aja allowed his mind to empty of everything except the man in front of him and the need to stay alive.

The men were well matched in height, though Phyx was slightly heavier in build with longer arms. Aja had watched the other man skirmish with their soldiers and knew he was fast, but he was also overconfident. They circled each other warily, blades glinting in the waning light, eyes straining to catch every movement in the shadows.

Aja palmed a flat stone from a hidden sleeve pocket and flicked it in the dust at Phyx's feet a split second before he charged. It was a tactic he'd picked up years earlier, and as expected Phyx reacted to the motion on instinct, making his response to the actual threat too slow to completely block the thrust. First blood went to Aja, and the other man's face darkened with a flush of anger.

They continued to circle, and Aja resisted the urge to roll his shoulders and loosen the muscles in his neck. He caught the slight tension in the other man's next step and anticipated the strike, twisting and stepping in at the last moment to catch Phyx as he fully extended. Aja's blade swept up, and if the blow had landed, he would have severed the tendons in Phyx's dominant arm, but the other man was surprisingly flexible and nearly dislocated his shoulder as he whirled out of range.

"Ah, ah, ah," he taunted, tsk'ing Aja before settling back into a crouch, blade extended. But the play was over, and Aja could see determination settle over Phyx's face like a mask.

Several more strikes were made before one of them made a dangerous mistake. The two men closed on their final encounter, with a flurry of blows too fast to follow in the darkening evening. They fought now by instinct and feel, and Aja felt the kiss and burn of Phyx's blade slide along the base of his neck. He let his opposite leg buckle, pulling him down and away before the blade could cut deeply, and Phyx caught his near ankle with a powerful kick that sent the Choosing Assassin to the ground. The move left both men disarmed, but the older Swimmer took advantage, ruthlessly catching Aja in a choke hold that he was unable to break, in spite of several vicious body blows.

"I'm going to kill you, and then I'm going to kill Adira, and after that, no one will remember your name," Phyx gloated as Aja's struggles weakened.

The words gave Aja a surge of strength and he heaved against the other man's hold.

"I won't let you kill her," he vowed, as stars exploded within his darkening sight. His next words were a desperate bluff. "I'll Dive and kill us both first if I have to."

The other man's hands loosened in surprise, and Aja was finally able to break free and scramble forward. He spun to face Phyx and gasped for air.

"I was right," the other Swimmer said. "You've switched your loyalties to her." In the near complete darkness, it was impossible to read his expression, but Aja sensed, more than saw, the shadow of his hand reaching for his dagger.

"At least I still believe in something," he responded bitterly, and Leaped, reaching hard for the vein that ran so deeply through this section of the camp that most were unaware of its presence, grateful now that he'd been paranoid enough to plan every escape route over a vein.

"Gods damn it!" Phyx cursed as the younger man dissolved in front of him. He sensed the vein, but his connection was weak, like a man who's had too much to drink, and abruptly he realized he'd been drugged. He could easily have made the Leap and pursued Aja further, but the Choosing Assassin had been a step ahead all along. Phyx stared at the ground a moment longer, then straightened and turned to the man he'd sensed hours earlier, hiding in the shadows, watching him watch Aja.

"You can come out now," he called, unsurprised when a sparking flint lit a small torch, and Davi's troubled face flickered into view. The aging Swimmer sheathed his dagger, and although Phyx wondered exactly who he'd come to aid, those thoughts didn't show on his face as he cleaned his own blade and tucked it back in his forearm sheath.

"I don't believe it," Davi said, clearly shocked that his young mentor was guilty after all.

Phyx shrugged his broad shoulders and brushed the other man aside. He didn't have time for hand holding. He still had a mission to complete, and what he'd learned here tonight might change everything.

CHAPTER 41

Aja Swam northwest, toward the city ruins Adira had shown him just a few months earlier. It was dangerously close to her palace, but he'd spent weeks piecing everything together, and it was the only place that made sense. Where else would his injured mate hide if not right under everyone's nose? He knew her well enough by now to realize that even at the worst of times, she had a certain disregard for danger, almost contempt for her enemies, though she'd not thank him to point that out. He was certain Adira was there, waiting for him to join her. He had no doubt now that she'd survived the battle, but worried over the severity of her injuries since she hadn't returned to her colony. What would he find, he wondered, and pushed himself harder than ever before.

Those worries kept him from dwelling on the general's betrayal, and it was still a few hours before morning when he Surfaced through the abandoned city's node. Although he couldn't sense her within range of the node, he was not surprised to find a torch burning in the node chamber. Relief nearly brought him to his knees. Her condition couldn't be too bad if she was able to shift and make her way to the node room, let alone keep a torch burning here for weeks in hopes of his arrival.

Assured now that she was relatively safe, he took the time to see to his own needs. Chrym paste, stored on a shelf by the door, helped with the muscle fatigue and steadied the tremor in his hands as he examined his wounds. One advantage to Swimming was that it had kept him from bleeding out until he could reach safety. The cut near the base of his throat was scabbed an angry red, and parts of the freshly closed cut broke open as he applied a healing ointment. The normally stoic Choosing Assassin hissed as the medicine hit the wound, and placed his hand on the wall to steady himself.

The movement brought his attention to the more serious injury – a deep laceration across his ribs from a blow that would have disemboweled a less gifted fighter. Phyx was better than good, Aja admitted to himself as he eased his ruined shirt over his head and knelt to examine the injury. Long and deep, the cut continued to ooze as he wiped the worst of the blood away and applied ointment and a powder, meant to seal the wound more quickly. He finished bandaging the injury with practiced hands and when he stood again, he noticed that Adira had placed a supply of fresh water in the node chamber as well. He used some of that precious fluid to wash the worst of the battle from his body; he didn't want to greet her covered in filth. The rest he drank greedily before setting off in search of his beloved.

He found her fast asleep in the library, much as he expected. Smaller than its counterpart in the rebel camp, this room was only three stories high, but its size wasn't what made it so attractive to Adira. High above the floor, several deep cracks ran parallel along the vaulted ceiling. Aja had managed a dangerous climb on one of their earlier visits to assess the stability of the structure and declared himself reasonably satisfied. Those openings allowed light to pass into the room below, but also carried heat and occasional rains from the planet's surface, making it the only room in the subterranean city with any semblance of fresh air. Unfortunately, the very things that made the space so appealing to the empress had also ruined the room's original purpose. All but a few glass-encased volumes had long since crumbled to dust under such hostile conditions. It had become Adira's favorite room during their visits, but to Aja, the space was filled with ghosts created by thousands of stories which would never be read.

"Adira," he whispered, keeping out of range in case she woke violently.

She stirred and frowned in her sleep before curling more tightly into the fetal position she favored in human form. Aja felt a flood of tenderness as he looked down at this deceptively delicate woman. He ignored the pain in his ribs to squat next to her, surprised to find himself enjoying this quiet moment before their reunion.

"Adira," he whispered again, and suddenly impatient he threw caution to the wind, reaching out to tuck a stray strand of hair behind her ear. He touched her more firmly when she still failed to respond, resting a hand on her damp chestnut hair to feel the heat of her skull underneath. Was she warmer than usual? She had no visible injuries, but could there be something else wrong, something that had forced her into hiding? Movement caught his eye, and he glanced down to see her beautiful golden eyes open, watching him worry over her.

She reached out to smooth the frown lines from his forehead, moved beyond words by the tenderness he revealed to her in this quiet moment together. She was overwhelmed by the love she felt for this man, and didn't try to hide it as she smiled up at him.

"I've missed you," she said simply and sat up to be folded into his arms. When the intensity of their reunion finally passed, they fell asleep with limbs entwined and hands clasped, feeling at peace for the first time in days.

A few hours later, Aja awakened as the first hint of light filtered through the ceiling and lay quietly watching Pil's golden fingers slip and slide across the floor until they caught the red and gold of Adira's hair in a fiery nimbus of light. Her eyes opened the moment the sunlight reached her skin, as though she felt it like a physical touch, and perhaps that was true. Her gaze went immediately to his face, and she smiled to catch him staring.

"Don't be embarrassed," she said as he made to rise. "I love that you can be yourself with me."

He relaxed into her arms again. "I'm always myself."

"No, you're always who you need to be. For the rebellion, for the Church, but never for yourself. With me, you don't have to hide this side of yourself, the person you might have been before Sik, before the rebellion."

She was right, he realized. He'd spent a lifetime filling any role the rebellion required because it enabled him to be something other than an orphan. Adira had given him a new role, and he relished the idea of being her partner and lover, whatever the future held. Reminded of the future, he abruptly recalled his concerns about her health.

"What about you, love," he asked tenderly, stroking her face. "It killed me to stay with the rebels, but until I knew where you were, I couldn't come to you." His words brought alarm to her eyes, and his heart pulsed heavily. Something was definitely wrong.

"Does the rebellion know where I am," she asked anxiously, sitting up and glancing around the library, as though searching for hidden assassins.

"No," he assured her. "Why are you so concerned? There's plenty of room in here to shift, and even in human form, between the two of us we could easily fend off anything General Tal can send at us."

He caught her flinch as he suggested taking dragon form, and instincts built by years of spy work told him something was very wrong.

"You can't shift," he said flatly, careful to keep the alarm he felt from his tone.

She shrugged and scowled at the rows of disintegrated books. "I could if I had to," she insisted.

"But…" he pressed her to elaborate.

"But I'm afraid for our baby."

Aja blinked and froze like a lizard in the shadow of a koteeri. He'd heard plenty of rumors that her mating flight had been successful, but he'd discarded them as just that, rumors, refusing to accept she might have flown in truth. Now it appeared the rumors were true, just not in the way the Church or rebels believed.

"Well?" she prompted, and he was reminded that for all her warmth the night before, she was not entirely human, and might have certain expectations of her lover which he couldn't begin to guess. He could only respond as the man he was.

Aja scooted across the floor to wrap his arms around her, his hands finding and spanning her abdomen. He pressed his face against her sweet smelling neck and nuzzled the skin gently, letting her feel the smile that formed on his lips.

"A baby," he repeated, and opened his legs to wrap around her. She leaned into him, softened by his response, though no less worried.

"I can't shift," she warned as his hands continued to wander.

"Mmmhmm," he murmured, his attention on other things. She shivered and pressed against him harder, inviting further liberties.

"We're trapped here, possibly until the baby's born." The last word was a gasp as she arched against his hands.

"What a pity," Aja replied. "I'm not sure what we'll do to fill the time." His lips stopped any further protests; they would worry about the future later. This moment was for celebrating.

CHAPTER 42

"Tek," Loshi called softly, dangling a cluster of grapes within her twin's reach. "Please wake up." She glanced nervously at her master, who lounged casually on a bed of cushions across the room. Impara Rikor grew impatient with her brother's illness, and it was just a matter of time before he took matters into his own hands. She knew from experience that his methods for reviving someone suffering from burnout would be far from pleasant.

"Please," she whispered frantically, and was finally rewarded by a fluttering of lashes and a faint groan. "Tek!"

Rikor rose from the bed and stalked across the room to stand at her back, one knee digging painfully into her shoulder blade as he brought his hand down to pull her against him. His presence never failed to cause a flood of self-loathing over the feelings he stirred in her; love and lust, fear and hate, all tangled together, as twisted as the man who owned her. He squeezed her shoulder and she barely restrained a whimper as Zetequilon's eyes finally opened. She saw the ghost of a smile cross his lips before he recognized the pain she tried to hide and looked up to find its cause.

"Master Rikor," he rasped.

"Are you sure?" Rikor responded pleasantly, and the tone was all too familiar. Loshi sat frozen as she watched him toy with her brother. "What a poor master I must be."

"I'm sorry, master?" Tek sat up carefully. Rikor was in a dangerous mood, and one wrong step would end bloody for himself, Loshi, or both of them.

"You said that already!" Rikor lashed out, striking Tek on a cheek still bruised from days earlier. Loshi trembled and looked down at her clasped hands. "But what kind of master can't get his servants to follow the simplest orders?"

Tek swallowed and looked at the floor. It was covered with a rich red velvety fabric, a change from his master's previous quarters. His sister was dressed in a simple skirt and blouse as always, her dark wavy hair hanging loose as Rikor preferred. The poor quality of her garb was just another reminder of her status, Tek thought bitterly. If only Aja had trusted him with more information, given him more responsibility, he might have earned a better life for Loshi. But he'd chosen badly, for Aja was not the man he'd been taught to hate. Rather than taking the poor simple Sefti he'd been offered and using him up, he'd instead chosen to shield the new recruit from the darker aspects of war. As soon as Tek realized his mistake, he'd done everything he could to change Aja's mind, but the best he'd managed was to become an occasional courier. In spite of Aja's tenderness towards his carefully crafted persona, or perhaps because of it, Sefti had been surprisingly effective under his master's direction, but failure wasn't tolerated.

Tek kept silent now, knowing from past experience that any excuse would only make his punishment worse. When Rikor left Loshi's side to pace, the twins exchanged a hopeful glance. Pacing was usually a sign that their master was deep in thought, planning moves and countermoves. If he had a use for Tek, perhaps their punishment wouldn't be so severe.

"Our spies in Adira have nothing, and the rebels are on lockdown so I can't get information in or out." Rikor's eyes blazed with frustration. Tek absorbed the news with a sinking feeling. Rikor had other spies in the rebel camp. He should have realized, he supposed, but in spite of a careful breeding program, Swimmers were such a rarity for the Church these days that he hadn't expected Rikor to have access to more than himself.

"You're going to return to the Choosing Assassin," Rikor sneered the name, his inexplicable hatred for Aja as predictable as ever, "and you're going to bring me every bit of information he has."

Tek slid from the bench to kneel on the floor, leaning forward until his head touched the carpet. "Thank you, master."

The whistle of the leather whip was his only response, and Tek clenched his fists and closed his eyes until it was over. Loshi broke before he did, and Rikor grabbed his sister from her place on the floor as she broke the silence with a plea for mercy, dragging her from the room to exact a different kind of punishment. Tek remained on the floor and allowed a bitter tear to leak from his good eye. They would never escape this man.

CHAPTER 43

Rikor was hard pressed to keep the glee from his face as the rest of the Impara gathered in Imperion Cayl's quarters. Former Imperion Cayl, he amended, as he stared dispassionately at the withered and empty husk of his mentor. Alive, Cayl had possessed a commanding presence, but in death, his body was shockingly frail, diminished more greatly than he could have imagined by the loss of the great man's intellect and passion. Rikor might once have looked up to the man, but in recent years Cayl had failed to grasp his vision of the future and had become an obstacle to be removed. The younger man had been steadily poisoning the high priest for months, waiting for the day when his aging body could no longer fight the drug's damaging effects.

Rikor was certain that with Cayl removed, it was a matter of days before he claimed the mantle of Imperion. He stared down the other Impara, silently reminding them all of each and every dark secret he had learned, information that would ruin any who voted against him. Nearly two decades of hard work were coming to fruition, and in spite of his best efforts, he felt a smile play at the corner of his mouth.

Earlier in the day, he had not been in such a good mood. Much of his morning had been wasted as he watched Loshi tend to her unconscious brother, rushing to gather a fruit platter to tempt him into waking as though he was royalty and Rikor didn't even exist. Anger coiled darkly in his heart as he watched Loshi brush a gentle sisterly kiss across Zetequilon's lips. It brought to mind another, less platonic kiss, and Rikor was suddenly in another place and time, crouched in the dry heat of the afternoon sun along a riverbed, watching the girl of his dreams make advances towards another.

Fury welled up as she brazenly undressed and joined a young Aja in the river. Their kiss was brief and almost chaste, but he couldn't forgive Tam her interest in another. When the chance came, he'd made sure her father learned of her transgressions and only wished he could have watched her beating. It must have been severe, for it was days before she left the cottage again, and when she went about her chores, her movements were careful and slow. She still had no interest in Rikor, but at least she no longer watched Aja with lovesick eyes.

Rikor recalled the day of the burning, when he'd cornered Tam alone by the river and professed his love for her. He still flushed with shame to recall how she'd laughed and brushed past him. He barely remembered grabbing the rock and striking her, though his dreams were filled with the feel of flesh, warm and yielding beneath him as he spent his rage on her unconscious form. He remembered her eyes opening as he finished, the shock and horror, followed swiftly by rage.

He had tried every threat he knew to keep her silent, and in the end, the only thing that saved him was Sik. When Tam escaped him and fled for the village, Rikor stayed near the river, considering his options and wondering how bad his punishment would be. He was not yet of marrying age, so binding Tam in marriage would not satisfy the price for such a violation. He came up with one wild scenario after the next, playing every excuse through his mind again and again. Could he convince them she was lying? No, he recalled the blood and semen on her thighs – it was clear the girl had been raped. Could he convince them someone else had lain in wait? Maybe Aja?

He was busy considering the possibilities when Sik dropped from the sky and the screaming began. Rikor hid in the river, doubled over in agony as the water temperature rose to a nearly unbearable point. It was almost enough to drive him from the river, and only the feel of the hot air sucking the oxygen from his lungs as he surfaced to breathe kept him where he was. When the flames finally went out, Rikor stumbled back to the village, searching for Tam, but there was nothing left but ash. When the Church found him, he was weeping before the ruins of her cottage. The Imprana sent to collect survivors assumed he mourned the loss of his family, and he never disabused them of the notion.

The shuffle of feet brought Rikor back to the present, and another opportunity to be seized. He caught Impara Ebi's attention and motioned for her to call their brothers and sisters back.

"Imperion Cayl was murdered," he announced. "Imperion Cayl was murdered by none other than Aja, the Choosing Assassin."

Ebi frowned slightly, but Rikor was gathering momentum.

"Imperion Cayl was murdered by the Choosing Assassin, and the Church must answer his crime. We must strike back!"

The other Impara began to nod, faces settling into matching expressions of self-righteous anger and resolve.

"With Imperion Cayl gone, they'll assume we're weak. We must move quickly to elect a new high priest, one with a plan for victory." Rikor looked each Impara in the eyes, confident in his ability to win them over. He'd just killed the Imperion after all, and managed to blame another for his death. Nothing was beyond him now.

CHAPTER 44

Phyx surfaced just outside Adira's city and lay quietly, recovering his strength. The rebel Swimmer had spent the past several days traveling every major Chrym vein on the planet in search of Aja and Adira. There had been no sightings anywhere, and with no other leads to follow, he returned to her court where the rebels had placed several spies, hoping to spot the traitor and follow him back to Adira.

When he entered the great marketplace outside the palace, he spotted young Sefti making a purchase of dried figs. Making his way over to the youngster, he leaned casually against a nearby wagon and waited to catch the young man's attention. Sefti turned from the merchant and visibly started as he recognized his fellow Swimmer. Phyx wondered at how anxious the other man appeared, but put it down to nerves – Sefti was young and still unschooled in matters of espionage. Aja had been his mentor, and no doubt the young man was conflicted about his duty, divided by loyalty to a man who had been a legend, and a cause that meant everything to his people. He'd have to live with his choice, however he decided, just as Phyx had so long ago.

"Any news?" The youngster asked, his voice betraying his anxiety. Another time it might have seemed endearing, but for some reason it bothered Phyx that Sefti had failed to toughen up under Aja's tutelage. It seemed incongruous that the great Choosing Assassin would have kept such a bumbling youth in any confidence, and Phyx resolved to take a closer look at Sefti once things had settled down. Something didn't sit right with him, and he wasn't one to leave puzzles unsolved.

"No," he replied, and unlike Sefti, his voice and mannerism gave no indication of his thoughts. "The traitor has gone to ground, and I can only assume he knew where to find the empress all along."

"How do you know?"

"I've circled Ryxa, visited every major Chrym node we know of, and no one's spotted him. Aja's good, but he's not that good. I know I injured him the night he escaped. Someone would have noticed an injured man, and someone would definitely have noticed anyone asking after Adira."

Sefti nodded, a flash of admiration appearing briefly on his face before he selected a fig and popped the entire fruit in his mouth. "Makes sense," he mumbled around the sweet treat.

"Will you kill him?" The sorrowful question took Phyx by surprise.

"What do you think we're here for?" he asked.

The younger man flushed and dropped his gaze. "Maybe we could talk him out of it, get him to come home." There was a certain wistfulness to his tone as he spoke of home, and Phyx almost softened. By Pil and Hadra's light, Sefti seemed less a young man at this moment, and more a child. He suddenly saw what had drawn Aja to the younger man, remembering he had lost a younger brother to Sik. Would this new knowledge be useful, he wondered. Could he use Sefti to draw Aja out? He discarded the thought for now, certain General Tal wouldn't condone what he had in mind, especially for a Gifted soldier.

Of course, there were plenty of things Tal didn't know about, like the detour Phyx had taken earlier in the week to Bithra's new court, where Imperion Cayl had moved the high temple. His face remained carefully blank as he relived the satisfying moment of Cayl's death, the old priest's mouth gaping as the tiny Chrym needle pierced his heart. Phyx knew another high priest would be named soon enough, but the Church's distraction caused by the brief vacuum of power was essential if he was to succeed. It was unfortunate that Aja was proving so hard to locate – they were running out of time.

CHAPTER 45

"So it's confirmed then." Rikor stared into space as Tek greedily consumed several sweet candies from the tray in front of him, carefully keeping his master in sight. "Aja has betrayed the rebellion."

His smile made Tek's blood run cold. "There's nowhere left for him to hide. Well, almost nowhere," he amended. He turned cold eyes on Tek. "You're sure Tal hasn't found him yet?"

"Yes, master," Tek confirmed quickly. "They circle the globe, searching day and night, but have found no trace."

"We'll bring him out of hiding," his master assured him with a tight smile that chilled his blood.

Rikor left the chamber in a swirl of bright, unrelenting red, and Tek thought bitterly that the colors of the Imperion uniform suited him perfectly. Red for blood, red for danger; he'd met no man more dangerous than Rikor, save perhaps one, and that man was now hunted by the entire planet.

He remembered the first time he'd met Aja. The older man was already a legend, but true to his character, he still performed regular orphan roundups like all the men and women under his command. Searching for survivors in burned villages was emotionally taxing, and he wouldn't give orders he wasn't willing to carry out from time to time himself. Of course Tek hadn't known that at the time, he only knew what his master had told him.

Hiding in the ruins of a newly destroyed village, Tek had prepared himself for the role he must play, cursing the fates that had given him to a cruel master, only to exchange him for a master who was likely far worse. Rikor had told him what kind of man Aja was, and if a man as terrible as Rikor feared the Choosing Assassin, Tek had no illusions regarding his fate. If he failed to convince Aja of his loyalty, he would die, either at his master's hands or by the Choosing Assassin's weapon of choice, a razor-thin stiletto of Chrym. And so Sefti was born, a young man who had lost everything but the desire for vengeance. Gifted, but not too Gifted, lest he risk burnout, soft as clay, ready to be shaped however the Choosing Assassin wished.

Based on what he knew of Aja, the persona he created seemed perfect, but he'd made a critical error in trusting Rikor's judgment of the man. Within days of meeting him, Tek realized he'd made Sefti too soft, too tender to suit the other man's purposes, and found that Aja treated him like a younger brother, rather than a young soldier. Other than Loshi, no one else in this miserable world had ever protected him, and Tek had come to like and admire the man as much as Sefti ever could have.

Now he waited in Rikor's chambers, expecting new orders that might bring Aja's death, and he burned with shame and rage at his betrayal of the one man he might have called friend. If not for Loshi, he would have followed Aja anywhere, a truth he feared Rikor suspected, for the priest had kept his twin from visiting with him this time. Tek sank to his heels in front of the modest altar in the corner of the room and prayed.

Several floors above his little pet, Rikor set his plan in motion. It was time to draw Aja out of hiding, and Bithra was eager to expand her territory and claim a new title, that of Empress. A queen required regular contact with her colony to maintain her bond, which meant Adira's colony was vulnerable to another queen's influence in her prolonged absence. If the gods smiled upon him, perhaps one day Adira would know who had destroyed her empire. He wondered if she would have respected him more all those months ago if she'd known what he was capable of, and admitted she probably would have eaten him on the spot.

"Any news from Impara Ebi?" he asked a lowly Imprana, who started and shook his head in response.

The delay chafed, but Impara Ebi was the perfect choice to manipulate Bithra into taking action, nearly as sly and quick-witted as Rikor himself. It was a pity she had no interest in men; Rikor might have enjoyed an occasional romp with his fellow priest, though he preferred his women with fewer curves. Pleasantly distracted by thoughts of Ebi and Loshi, Imperion Rikor settled back on his throne and waited for confirmation that his plan was in motion, sipping occasionally from the flask he kept within his robes and ignoring the ornate cup that sat openly on a tray by his elbow. He would not be so easy to dispose of as his predecessor.

CHAPTER 46

"I have to do something!"

Aja watched Adira pace from one end of the ruined library and back to him, literally glowing with frustration. Her agitation was so strong he could almost feel the waves of energy pulsing from her to crash against him, against the walls, against everything holding her bound to this place. She resents me, he thought.

"Do you regret us? Do you regret our child, and the mate-bond?" he asked aloud.

She whirled toward him, and for a moment, he thought she would say the words that would break him, but she softened and swept toward him, stroking his face with soft hands as she murmured assurances.

"How could I?"

He closed his eyes on the surge of relief that left him nearly breathless. Her next words were not so endearing.

"The timing could have been better, to be sure, and it would obviously make things so much easier if you were a dragon. What are the odds, that having survived an eternity of loneliness I should find my bond mate and lose my empire because of it? The irony is not lost on me, that having found the one thing which makes an immortal life worth living, I lose everything I spent that lifetime earning. If only we could fight them!" she burst out, pressing her forehead against his.

Aja kept his eyes closed and focused on the touch of her fingers to ease the sting of those words, still stroking his face, whisper-light as they traced the faint lines that burst like a sunbeam from the corners of his eyes, firmer as she found the tension at his temples and began a soothing massage. He wanted to tell her his heart ached over what he had cost her, but he would never give her up.

"It's just that so many of my people will suffer under Bithra," she said quietly, "and there's nothing I can do to save them."

He pictured her as the Empress, comforting a little orphan, human and Giftless, and abruptly knew what needed to be done. It would be difficult, perhaps impossible, but Aja resolved to free as many of Adira's servants as possible.

He opened his eyes and smiled down at her. His mate would need to be distracted if he were going to slip away undetected. Aja's hands reached for the ties of her dress, and she stepped out of the pool of fabric and into his arms, as warm and willing as ever. The gentle swell of their child pressed between them, and he was careful not show any misgivings over the rapid pace of her pregnancy as he told her how much he loved her, using words and touch to speak a language meant only for her.

She fell deeply asleep soon after their loving, and he worried anew over how easily she tired, though he would not admit his concerns to her. It might be foolish and superstitious, but he was afraid that if he poisoned her with his fears, he would weaken her further and lose her to the child they had created. Adira needed to be strong – more importantly, she needed to *believe* she was strong if she was going to survive. She also needed hope, which he meant to give her now.

He rose from their nest of clothing, careful not to disturb her sleep, and made his way to the node room. There was no true vein to Swim from here, just a smattering of Chrym which formed tiny pools, like stepping stones that led the way back to Adira's court. Leaping from one pool to another was exhausting, but it allowed him to reach Adira's palace without being spotted. Once inside the palace, he knew immediately that Adira had been right to fear for her people. Bithra had not been kind to the humans who served her enemy when she claimed the palace. Weavers who had once taken pride in their service, who had walked with vigor and purpose through the halls of the palace were grey and worn. The non-Gifted servants scurried from one point to another, like mice hiding from a hungry koteeri.

Aja's jaw clenched and he fantasized about driving a Chrym stake through Bithra's heart, but that would solve nothing, and he knew it. Abandoning the servants in the palace for now, he made his way through the tomblike corridors to the small community beyond the palace grounds where the families of the Gifted lived. It was here that he would make his offer, and rescue as many as he could, if they were willing to be saved. He slipped into the first house on his list and waited patiently in the main room for his target to return, moving swiftly to silence her cry of alarm.

"Aja!" she exclaimed quietly once he released her, eyes darting anxiously. "What are you doing here? You're putting my family in danger. We could all be killed just for talking to you, or I could choose to turn you in for a reward that would feed an entire village for generations. The Church is generous when there's an Imperion-slayer on the loose."

"Imperion Cayl is dead?" Aja asked, and he saw a lessening in Dede's tension at his obvious surprise.

"I can't tell if you're that good, or if you really weren't involved."

"I thought you knew me better than that, Dede," he reproached, and her eyes narrowed.

"I did too, Choosing Assassin." She threw the title at him, a marked reminder of the deception he'd played in Adira's court. "Is our queen dead? Answer wisely, Aja, or I'll do more than turn you in," she palmed the handle of the wicked blade resting against her hip, and Aja hoped it wouldn't come to that.

"Empress Adira is alive, but recovering from terrible injuries," he mixed truth and lies, not daring to share how vulnerable Adira was, even with someone so clearly loyal. "I found her after the battle and have been nursing her to health since then."

Dede quickly muffled her cry of relief, glancing toward the front of the house before pulling him into the small kitchen off the living area.

"I told Mika she was still alive. What can we do to help?" She spoke urgently, and Aja knew he had passed the first hurdle.

"The Empress is worried about you, about all of you. I've come back to help you and the others escape, Dede."

She blinked once and he could see thoughts shifting behind those dark eyes as she considered the simple sentence and all its potential ramifications. This was why he'd gone to Dede first. It seemed a great irony to call someone so brilliant un-Gifted, but value came in many forms to those capable of recognizing it, and he would need her help in order to have even a chance at success.

"Did you betray our Empress to her enemies?" she asked.

"I love her," he responded, and she nodded as though unsurprised.

"Love doesn't preclude betrayal. Sometimes I think it's what makes betrayal possible."

"I didn't betray her. I serve her still."

"She sent you to save us?" For the first time, Aja saw a flicker of hope in Dede's eyes.

"She suffers, knowing you suffer." He answered truthfully, and Dede finally relaxed her guard to truly welcome him into her home.

"Our shifts have nearly doubled since Bithra claimed Adira. You'll have a long wait before Mika comes home."

Aja winced to have his suspicions confirmed. Weaving was

exhausting work, more difficult even than Swimming in some respects. Swimming required power, but little finesse. It was more like instinct than effort to move through the Chrym. Creating a massive piece of jewelry to the specifications of a demanding dragon on the other hand, required tremendous concentration. Double shifts would quickly lead to exhaustion, mistakes, and more punishment.

"I'll be back," he promised Dede, deciding his time was better spent making other arrangements. He gave her a final instruction as he borrowed some items to create a simple but effective disguise. "Bring the ones you trust here when your husband returns and I'll explain what I can."

He trusted her judgment, but more importantly, Adira's servants trusted her implicitly. If he had Dede on his side, they would listen, and hopefully follow him to safety. But if he were to have any chance of leading them undetected out of the city, he would need help from another quarter.

Aja returned to Dede's house near midnight, having completed the necessary arrangements to spirit several families from the palace to safety. He was dismayed to find far more people waiting for him than he had anticipated. Dede read the look in his eyes and sent her husband for tea while she pulled Aja aside for a private conference.

"How many can we take?" she asked somberly.

"Maybe half the families here," he answered.

She pursed her lips while she considered the problem. "Do we all have to go at the same time?" she asked.

Aja cocked his head slightly. "What are you thinking?"

"Bithra's guards don't watch us closely, and the new Imperion hasn't arrived yet." She allowed herself a grim smile as she continued. "I hear the roads from Klis aren't all that hospitable."

Aja exhaled in humorless agreement.

"If we start with the littles and some of the spouses, the court won't notice a few less mouths to feed. Then tomorrow we take the Gifted who want to come."

Under normal circumstances Aja would never have risked it, but based on the number of people who risked their lives tonight just to be here, just to have a chance at escape, they had passed the point of caring. Dede's expression assured him she understood the seriousness of what she suggested.

"Can everyone here make sure their shift ends at the same time tomorrow night?" Aja asked the group.

"If we can't, don't wait for us," replied a slender, jet-skinned woman and he searched for her name. Nyeeri, he recalled. A gifted

Weaver, and one of Adira's favorites before his arrival, he was somewhat surprised to see her among the deserters.

"I've got two girls, both showing strong signs of the Gift," she correctly interpreted his look. "If you think I want them worked to death under Bithra or some rutting priest, you are sadly mistaken."

Aja nodded. "I understand."

"I doubt it, but I'm glad for your help, all the same." From the dark look in her eyes, Aja suspected she'd had some experience with the Church already.

"Let's get to it," Dede interrupted briskly. "We've got a lot of littles, and only a little time left before Pil blesses us with his presence. What do you need us to do, Weaver Aja?"

In the end, the plan was painfully simple. Children old enough to walk went two at a time with an un-Gifted adult, who each carried a sack of grain across their back. In reality they carried two sacks – an inner sack which hid a child too small to walk, insulated by a thin layer of grain in the outer sack. Aja insisted the infants be lightly drugged to prevent any crying, which triggered fierce resistance, but Dede overcame the parents' objections by drugging her own child and handing her to Aja.

"Keep her safe," she demanded.

"You're going with her," her husband objected. Dede smiled and shook her head, and that was the end of the argument.

By first light, the entire first group was gone from the city, and the Gifted were back to work in the palace. Aja had taken them as far as the marketplace, where he left them with directions on how to meet their next guide. He couldn't promise safety, but he could at least give them a chance at freedom.

He spent the daylight hours resting in Dede's home, dozing in a light sleep which was interrupted toward dusk by a furious pounding on the door.

"Open up, mistress Dede!"

Dede cast a frantic glance at Aja, but he had already disappeared from sight. She wasted another moment searching fruitlessly for his location, then cracked the door open to peek out. Her gaze caught an almond-skinned woman whose uniform indicated she was in charge of the guards forming a semi-circle around her front door. Dede felt a heavy drumbeat of terror jump to life in her chest. Had they been found out?

The guard's next words drove all thought from her mind save one. "There's been an accident, mistress Dede. Your husband is dead."

She stepped from the house with a wordless cry of grief and was seized by rough hands.

"No!" she screamed as torches found the dry thatch of the roof, but the soldiers showed no mercy and pulled her away to watch as her home burned to the ground with Aja inside.

Dede's trembling legs could barely hold her when she was finally led away. She bit her lip and remained silent as they brought her to the Trying Grounds, where the worst criminals were sentenced and executed. She heard the captain declare her crimes, but the woman's voice came from far away. Her gaze was fixed on the pile of bodies just beyond the spot where she'd been ordered to stand, and Dede suddenly became aware of a horse standing nearby, its labored breathing explosive in the silence. It was a moment before she realized it was her own sobbing breath she'd mistaken for another's. She closed her mouth and tried to calm herself, though she couldn't tear her eyes away from the faces that stared back at her. Every family member of every Gifted slave who had agreed to leave with Aja seemed to be in that pile of flesh, from grands and spouses – even the littles had been killed. Some of them looked as though they were merely sleeping, but others still held an expression of terror that made her flinch away until a particular pair of eyes caught her gaze. She couldn't say how or why it happened, but as she stared at the now empty eyes of her best friend Zala's youngest, a girl of just twelve, she felt fear slip away.

Thank the gods she'd ordered her oldest to go last night, she thought. Her son had fought bitterly to stay, but she and Mika were resolute. All of their children were safely away, even those who thought they were ready to die as men. Dede smiled and swung defiantly to face her accusers moments before the arrows loosed and her world went dark.

Years of training kept Aja quiet as he watched Dede stagger and fall. He could do nothing for her now, but there was still hope for her husband and the rest of the Gifted servants who had chosen to flee. Although their families were expendable, considered no more than a convenient lesson for those who thought to disobey, Xarans born with the Gift were too valuable to Church and dragons alike to be executed for an escape attempt. Aja had no doubt he would find Mika and the others under heavy guard, in one of the most secure areas of the palace. Fortunately for them, he was intimately familiar with the space he suspected they would be held, having spent many hours slipping unnoticed through Adira's home when he first arrived, mapping his escape route, and then back up plans to back up plans.

CHAPTER 47

When Aja made his presence known to them, the Gifted slaves were in a heavily guarded area of the palace, but the soldiers were clearly expecting little to no trouble after the brutal display Bithra had ordered on the Trying Grounds two days earlier. He had already taken out two sentries who blocked their path to freedom when he came across a third. Aja smiled grimly at the young guard slumped against a stone wall, his breath almost heavy enough to be a snore. Anyone caught sleeping on guard duty in the rebel camp could expect to receive a severe beating, but this young man would not be so lucky. The Choosing Assassin slipped a blade between his ribs, expertly piercing his heart and leaving him propped against the wall, still "sleeping" at his post. With luck, he would go unnoticed for the next half hour or so.

"Aja!" The other prisoners quickly hushed Dede's husband as he slipped into view, but after a brief scuffle, Mika reached a hand through the bar to grasp at Aja's arm. "My wife, have you seen Dede?"

Aja stilled in his efforts to break the lock and looked Mika in the eye.

"No. No, no, no," the other man moaned softly. "We should have gone together. We all should have just gone that first night."

"There's no point in regrets," Aja responded, hardening himself against the guilt he carried. He'd had his own doubts about their plan, but allowed his sense of urgency for Adira outweigh those fears. Now others had paid the price for his mistake, and they had paid dearly.

"Anyone who still wants to come needs to be ready to follow me without question." He looked them all in the eye, reading fear and grief, but no hesitation until he came to Nyeeri.

She shook her head and backed away from the torchlight as he looked at her, the motion barely visible in the darkness at the back of the cell.

"I don't deserve to be saved," she said, so quietly he had to strain to catch the words. "It's my fault they're dead."

Aja froze, then worked harder to break the lock as Mika swung towards the other Weaver.

"What do you mean, it's your fault? Nyeeri? What did you do?" Mika's voice rose in a howl of fury as he reached for her, but Nyeeri didn't raise a hand to defend herself. The others grabbed him and pulled him away from her, and Aja heard the heavy sound of flesh striking flesh before Mika sank to the ground. Everyone froze for a long moment as they listened for an alarm in the aftermath of the grieving man's outburst. Several seconds passed before a loud exhale released them from the tension that held them in place. Aja finished with the lock, and hastily motioned the captives back when they would have pressed the door open.

"Just a minute," he said as he poured oil over the metal hinges and rubbed hard to make sure the surface was fully coated. Cell doors weren't made to open silently for good reason. Finally satisfied, he stepped back and gestured to the others.

"All right, let's go. Follow me and stay low."

Two men lifted Mika's limp body from the floor and stepped from the cell, but Nyeeri remained in the corner, face turned away.

"Nyeeri," hissed one of the other Weavers.

"No," came the low reply. "It's my fault they found out. If only I could have kept my mouth shut when that sun-damned Impara came for me."

She shook her head, and in the dim light Aja could just make out her expression, a mix of pain and self-loathing.

"I should have just taken what he did to me, but I had to have the last word, had to leave him knowing he'd never touch me or my girls again."

She dropped her head to her hands and stood weeping silently. Aja stepped across the threshold, ignoring his jangling nerves as he stepped willingly into a prison cell to comfort her.

"Nyeeri, we're not leaving without you." He looked back at the others as he said the words, silently compelling them to agree. A few Weavers shuffled their feet before one spoke up.

"I don't know what you've been through, but I know what you're going through now, and I know you never meant for this to happen. I'm not sure I can ever forgive you, but I know Dede would want me to try."

Mika reached his hand through the door, and Nyeeri stumbled forward into his arms with a choked cry. From a distance, Aja heard the sound of booted steps – it was just before dawn, and the guard was changing.

"We're leaving. Now!" He moved swiftly and silently from the cell and led the freed captives through the path he'd made, ignoring stifled sounds of shock as they discovered the young guard's body. The trauma to the other guards was less visible, or perhaps they were already becoming used to the sight of death, for they were silent as they continued on. Once they reached the hidden tunnel that led under the palace to the marketplace, Aja relaxed a bit. The worst of their journey would come tomorrow night when the palace was on full alert and he had to sneak more than a dozen exhausted Weavers through the deserted marketplace and into the desert beyond the city, but for now they could rest easy, or at least as easy as grieving hearts would allow.

Even though Aja saw no evidence that the tunnel had been discovered in his absence, he set the Weavers to stand watch in pairs and slept lightly, waking as each shift passed until night fell again. Nyeeri, he noted, had not strayed from Mika's side and watched the older man constantly, as though she feared he might change his mind at any moment and condemn her for her actions.

"It's time," Aja said, and the Weavers gathered behind him at the tunnel's exit for their final instructions. "We're going to cross in groups of twos and threes," he explained. "Once we clear the tunnel, every group needs to pick a different route. We meet up again at the far side of the marketplace, under the ancient stone." He referred to a giant slab of marble that had long ago been carved and placed on massive stone columns to serve as the formal entrance to the city. Time had worn the stone supports away, and the entrance had fallen into disuse centuries ago. Aja had cleared a path through the rubble months earlier and camouflaged it well to serve as a possible escape route if his negotiations with Adira went poorly. This would be their path to the desert and the stone outcropping where they would meet their guide for the next leg of their journey, though he didn't share that information just yet.

"If you're spotted, try to get away, but if you can't lose them, don't lead them to everyone else. If you're caught, make some noise so we know not to wait. We won't expect you to hold out for long."

The Weavers nodded, their grim expressions acknowledging the consequences of failure. No one had any illusions about the treatment they would receive if they were caught. Aja pressed the lever that opened the secret door and slipped out with Mika and Nyeeri following right behind. A few footsteps beyond the door, he caught the sound of the next set of Weavers and felt a moment of relief that they were following his instructions.

They were about a third of the way across the marketplace when the alarm was raised. Torches flared bright in their path and Aja doubled back with a curse, leading Mika and Nyeeri through a twisted labyrinth of covered carts to avoid their pursuers. He ducked into a narrow alleyway that led to the fountain where he'd once sat with Adira and pressed against the wall next to the two Weavers as their pursuers ran past. It wouldn't take the guards long to realize they'd lost them and double back, and Aja set off again as soon as it was safe, aware that the older man struggled to catch his breath at their faster pace.

He was worried about Mika, but couldn't let that decide their path through the marketplace. The first turns he took seemed random, but as their new direction emerged he thought he heard a faint groan from the Weaver.

"Sorry, Mika," he whispered as they took brief refuge under a cart. "Are you going to be able to make it?"

The older man panted as he leaned against the spokes of one of the wheels. "Go on without me," he gasped. "I won't slow you down anymore. You're too important." Mika grabbed his hand as he spoke. "Dede realized it before any of the rest of us. If anyone can save our Empress, it's you. Nyeeri, you keep him safe," he said before throwing himself from under the cart and rushing away. Nyeeri choked back a protest as footsteps rushed by, clearly in pursuit.

"Take him alive," a woman's voice called, and Aja pulled Nyeeri in the opposite direction, moving quickly now that Mika was gone.

"He made a choice, will you honor it?" he asked as they reached the stone meeting place and a small group of Weavers rose to greet him.

"I'll do my best," Nyeeri answered, and followed him into the desert.

CHAPTER 48

It was early morning before Aja turned his path to the ruined city where Adira waited. Deeply exhausted and unspeakably angered by the senseless violence he'd witnessed, he was anxious to find peace and solace in his lover's arms. Though they had all knowingly accepted the risk, he felt the weight of too many lost lives; Dede and Mika, Citay, and Vilet to name a few.

After two nights of tense cat and mouse hiding to get the remaining captives out of the city, and he'd left the survivors on the south side of the capitol with instructions to find their next guide. He couldn't take them to the rebels himself, not with a death sentence on his head, but Tal would never punish these innocents for Aja's crime, nor would he force the Gifted into service if they chose a quiet life. In spite of their differences, he had no doubt these refugees would be safe with his former friend, and might even serve to blunt Tal's anger.

Perhaps it was his exhaustion, or maybe just eagerness to be reunited with Adira that made him careless as he Dove into the first Chrym puddle that would lead him home, but Aja failed to notice the man who had quietly observed his movements over the past few days, the man who now followed him into the Chrym, grimly determined not to lose his quarry this time. Unaware of the danger that trailed him, Aja moved quickly through the subterranean ruins to the library.

"Adira," he called as he entered the room, already feeling a lightening of the terrible pressure that built every time they were separated. He threw his arms wide to catch her rushing form against him, but her expression warned him just in time to throw his arms up in self-defense instead.

"You! Miserable! Bastard!" she yelled, punctuating each word with a blow. "You left me! You left me here, waiting for days!"

She was weeping now, tears of fury and of fear, and Aja realized that for perhaps the first time in her life, Adira had been forced to struggle against the futility of waiting for a loved one who faced danger on her behalf. Adira the Empress had never waited for anyone to fight her battles, and to be fair, Adira the human hadn't asked this of him either, he'd done it as much for himself as for her, though knowing that wouldn't have helped her through the past several days.

He noticed the letter he'd written in explanation on the floor next to their mattress, crumpled and torn and pieced back together and winced. *It's a good thing she can't kill me*, he thought as she landed a particularly well-placed blow. Adira was shockingly strong, even in human form.

"Adira," he protested, still shielding his face and body as her furious greeting slowed. "Please, my love. All my efforts to return to you in one piece will be for nothing if you keep this up."

She sputtered with fury and spun away, nearly crackling with rage. "Well?"

He thought better of the sharp response that sprang to his tongue and walked across the room to their modest bed. Sinking down onto the thin mattress, he shared his news with his mate, both the good and the bad. Partway through the retelling, she relented enough to join him on the bed, though she stared ahead at the doorway as he recounted his rescue attempt. After days apart, he could barely take his eyes off of his lover and knew the moment she began to soften towards him. It came as a surprise then, when she stiffened and pulled away from his touch, her golden eyes still staring at the open door. Hurt washed over him at her rejection and was quickly replaced with shock as a familiar voice drawled, "Perhaps I should have waited a bit longer."

Aja was off the floor and halfway across the library before the words fully registered, blade out and murder in his eyes. Phyx stepped into the room to give himself more room to maneuver but kept his dagger sheathed. A lot depended on these next few moments, and how he handled himself now meant the difference between life and death for his people. Aja and Adira had to agree to his proposal, but first he had to survive long enough to get them to listen. He danced back from Aja's first attack, and then the second, aware that Adira slowly circled, waiting for an opening. They moved in perfect synchronicity, and Phyx knew he had only moments to make his pitch.

On Aja's next offensive, Phyx stepped unexpectedly into the blade's path, gritting his teeth as the metal sliced through skin and muscle, before catching against his rib cage. Though painful, the wound wasn't life-threatening, and more importantly, Aja was temporarily unarmed.

That moment would be brief, for he was well aware that Aja had at least a dozen weapons concealed on his person at all times. Quick as thought, Phyx unsheathed his own blade and whirled to present it, hilt first to the woman who now stood directly in front of him.

Her eyes blazing, Adira snatched the dagger from his hands and raised it to plunge into his heart. He saw her falter, and a thin flash of light caught his eye before the garrote slipped around his throat and tightened. He buckled as Aja's knee found his back, driving him forward and down to give the other man more leverage, but he kept his hands down and maintained eye contact with Adira, commanding her attention.

"Aja," she called her human lover, then again more urgently.

Phyx coughed, then gagged as the pressure on his windpipe eased. Aja kept the garrote around his neck, but obliged the empress and allowed Phyx to breathe again.

CHAPTER 49

"How can there be a hidden colony?" Adira asked again.

Phyx recognized a rhetorical question when he heard one, and waited patiently for her to accept what he'd told her. He felt drugged by the power he sensed in her presence, even dimmed as it was in human form. Her newly formed mate-bond was clear to anyone who knew how to recognize it, and he was glad he hadn't killed the Choosing Assassin when he'd had the chance, though he had the good sense to keep that thought to himself. The golden dragon paced before him while he remained seated, cross-legged in the middle of the room, hands on his knees and unarmed in an attempt to show good faith. It was unnerving to be in the presence of such power cloaked in human form, but he kept that thought hidden as well.

Aja on the other hand, made no attempt to hide his thoughts from his expression. Phyx was well aware the other man wanted him dead, plain and simple, but Adira's curiousity had won out for now. Aja had good reason to want him dead – his non-threatening posture was entirely misleading as the other man well knew. Phyx had only to think it, and any Chrym within range would respond. Perhaps Aja could stop him from killing Adira, perhaps not. It wasn't a chance Aja was willing to take, but Adira's wishes took precedence for now.

"Tell me again," she commanded, and Phyx complied.

It was an impossible tale of a dragon created, not born, a pale fragile creature too weak to survive, let alone flourish. But flourish Oryxa did, and by the time she arrived on the planet now called Ryxa, she was a deity among dragons. But deities were lonely creatures, and one day she met a Weaver who touched her soul as no dragon ever had. She gave up her immortality to take human shape and claim the human as her lover, but when her throne was threatened, she took to the skies again and defeated her enemies. The price for victory was terrible, and Oryxa was forced to remain a dragon until she produced a clutch of a thousand eggs. The offspring she and her mate produced were violent, even for dragonkind, and wild of heart. One by one, they left the planet, seeking new worlds and a queen to call their own. At last Oryxa was free to return to her love, but over the years he aged, while she did not, and she grieved that their time would soon come to an end.

The ancients believed in a sentient power that ran through the planet like life's blood and could grant a wish to any being worthy enough, and Oryxa became fixated on the idea that she might make her lover immortal. After the birth of their only daughter, Oryxa made the pilgrimage to the Chrym source, and there she built a great temple. She spent weeks and months in meditation and prayer, but her wish was never granted, and her mate died of old age. Mad with grief, she took dragon form one last time and Flared as hot as the great sun god Pil, intending to destroy the ancient power that had denied her, but as the metal melted around her, she sank deeply into the vein and was consumed by her own fury.

"No, it can't be," Adira interrupted Phyx as she paced the length of the room, nerves humming with agitation. "How would such a pure Chrym source go undetected?" she challenged.

"The dead zone," Phyx replied simply.

Aja snorted. "The dead zone has been explored time and again. It's called the dead zone because there's nothing there."

"You only *think* there's nothing there." Phyx couldn't keep his pride entirely hidden, and Aja scowled in response.

"It's not possible," Adira repeated, but both men could see the hope she worked so hard to hide.

"I'll explain everything, but only once we're safely there." That was the deal, take it or leave it. The mate-bonded pair stared at each other as they weighed their fears and desires and against the unlikely hope Phyx offered.

They could have no way of knowing how desperate the situation was for Phyx's colony, for he kept his thoughts carefully hidden as he watched Aja. He had little concerns over what Adira would choose. She was clearly desperate for eternal love and would take any chance, however slim, that Aja might be spared the fate all humans eventually suffered. Aja was the one who might need more persuasion, but it was a delicate balance between pushing too hard and letting them reach for what was offered. It was because he watched the other man so carefully that Phyx saw the moment his worry for Adira's safety won out.

Perhaps the Chrym source existed, perhaps it was all a lie, but they couldn't stay here forever, and if Oryxa's descendants still lived in the hidden city, they might be able to help when the time came for their child to be born. It was the only hope Aja allowed himself as Adira turned to Phyx and said, "When do we leave?"

CHAPTER 50

In the desert south of the once-Adiran capitol, Tek watched the families Aja had risked his life to save as they gathered their few belongings and struggled to their feet. Exhausted by days of hiding and cold nights of painfully slow travel, sometimes crawling across terrifyingly open terrain, they were all the worse for wear.

Tek followed the Chrym vein that traveled deep beneath the ground to the southern border where the rebel camp waited. He knew the more Gifted among them could sense vein, that he should leave them to make their own way and return to his master, who would welcome news of so many new slaves within his grasp, but he couldn't make himself do it.

"Are we almost there, Sefti," asked the little girl snuggled in his arms, and he smiled tenderly as he pushed her hair from her face.

"Not yet, Derina." For some reason this little orphaned girl reminded him strongly of Loshi, and he pictured her in his master's service, growing up and one day taking his sister's place in Rikor's bed. His mind shied from the image of her innocence destroyed by the Imperion, and he knew he couldn't betray her, not even for Loshi. Especially for Loshi, who had once been this little girl, trusting the wrong man to keep them safe. For once he would choose someone over himself and his twin, and though he knew it would cost him his life, he was finally at peace with his decision.

A shadow passed over one of Ryxa's many moons, and Tek realized they weren't alone in the desert. A sharp warning froze everyone in place and they waited while the danger high above them studied the desert floor and moved on. Tek sensed the node in the distance, and let it pull him forward. He would get these people to safety and finally be worthy of Aja's respect.

EPILOGUE

High above the planet's surface, Oryd soared, unceasing in his efforts. Weeks earlier he had seen Bithra's arrival – watched with hate and longing in his heart as his colony rose to answer her call. What would it be like, he wondered, to belong to one of the great red and black queens of Ryxa? A queen who rose more frequently than Adira, who offered a greater chance at a mate-bond? Perhaps Bithra didn't share the empress' repulsive interest in their human slaves. Perhaps she wouldn't inspire such fits of rage in him. Perhaps those rages were so great because Adira inspired another feeling, a feeling he couldn't bear to name in her absence.

It was because of that feeling that he chose to fly higher, using a super thermal to escape the pheromones that would enslave him to Bithra. It was that unnamed emotion that enabled him to turn his back on a potential mate-bond and accept his self-imposed exile, simply to continue his search for a queen who might never accept him as her mate. He knew of no other dragon in the history of his kind who had chosen such a fate, but then he pictured Telek, Sik's ancient First General, and thought perhaps there was more than one way to escape an unwanted claiming. Who could say for sure if Telek had wished to die at his teeth? The only thing he knew for certain anymore was that he could never give up on Adira. She was out there somewhere, and he would find her, no matter how long it took.

CHURCH HIERARCHY

Imperion – highest rank within the Church, held by a single priest until death

Impara – second highest rank within the Church, held by 6-12 priests in every province, depending on population

Imperal – third highest rank

Imprana – lowest rank, held by novitiates and true believers who have the most direct contact with the general population